An Irresistible Force

"But artists made this cathedral," Ariel continued. "They had the intensity, the passion to make their wanting real. Scientists don't have that."

He took a step toward her. His blue eyes were burning; his mouth was a tight line. At first she thought she had made him angry. But he didn't argue or rail at her. Instead he was looking at her as he had last night.

"You're wrong," he said. "A man who spends endless hours alone in a laboratory, repeating an experiment again and again, has as much passion as a stone carver. The desire for knowledge burns in the veins just as intensely as the desire to create. It *is* a desire to create."

Ariel stared at him. He looked as surprised as she was by his words.

"If you think that because a man is a scientist, he does not want . . ."

His fists had clenched. Ariel held her breath.

"You're wrong," he said again.

His gaze transfixed her. Ariel had to struggle to produce a response, even though she wanted more than anything to speak. "Does he want only science?" she murmured at last.

"Only . . . ?"

Did he also want love, with the same sort of ferocity?

BANTAM BOOKS BY JANE ASHFORD

THE BARGAIN
THE MARRIAGE WAGER

The Bargain

JANE ASHFORD

Bantam Books
New York   Toronto   London   Sydney   Auckland

THE BARGAIN

A Bantam Fanfare Book / October 1997

ISBN 0-553-57578-3

Published simultaneously in the United States and Canada

Bantam Books are published by Bantam Books, a division of Bantam
Doubleday Dell Publishing Group, Inc. Its trademark, consisting of the
words "Bantam Books" and the portrayal of a rooster, is Registered in
U.S. Patent and Trademark Office and in other countries. Marca Regis-
trada. Bantam Books, 1540 Broadway, New York, New York 10036.

PRINTED IN THE UNITED STATES OF AMERICA

OPM   10 9 8 7 6 5 4 3 2 1

The Bargain

Chapter One

——— ✦ ———

Lord Alan Gresham was icily, intolerably, dangerously bored. As he looked out over the animated, exceedingly fashionable crowd that filled the large reception room, his blue eyes glittered from under hooded lids. His mouth was a thin line. Revelers who glanced his way, curious about his very plain evening dress and solitary state, looked quickly away when he met their eyes. The women tended to draw their gauzy wraps closer despite the enervating warmth of the room, and the men stiffened. Whispers began to circulate, inquiring as to who he was and what the deuce he was doing in Carlton House at the prince regent's fete.

A damned good question, Alan thought, well aware that he was the object of their attention. He was here against his will, and his better judgment. He was wasting his time, which he hated, and he was being kept from truly important work by a royal whim. He couldn't imagine a situation more likely to rouse his temper and exhaust his small stock of patience.

Alan watched a padded and beribboned fop sidle up to

the duke of Langford and murmur a query. The duke did not look pleased, but he answered. The reaction was only too predictable—surprise, feigned incomprehension, and then delight in having a tidbit to circulate among the gossips. Alan ignored the spreading whispers and continued to watch the duke, a tall, spare, handsome man of sixty or so. This was all his fault. Alan wouldn't be trapped here now, on this ridiculous quest, if it weren't for the duke. He clamped his jaw hard, then deliberately relaxed it. He wasn't being quite fair, he admitted to himself. The duke, his father, was no more able to refuse a direct command from the sovereign than he himself was. Prinny's whims and superstitions had brought him here, and until he satisfied the prince, he could not return to his own life. Let's get it over with, then, thought Alan. The waiting was about to drive him mad.

"Well, I hope my eyes are not like limpid forest pools," declared a very clear, musical female voice behind him. "Aren't forest pools full of small slimy creatures and dead leaves?"

Somewhat startled, Alan turned to find the source of this forthrightness. He discovered a girl of perhaps twenty with lustrous, silky brown hair and a turned-up nose. She didn't have the look of the *haut ton,* with which Alan was only too tiresomely familiar. Her gown was too simple, her hair not fashionably cropped. She looked, in fact, like someone who should not, under any circumstances, have been brought to Carlton House and the possible notice of the prince regent.

Or of the dissolute-looking fellow who was bending over her now, Alan noted. He had the bloodshot eyes and pouchy skin of a man who had spent years drinking too much and sleeping too little. The set of his thin lips and the lines in his face spoke of cruelty. Alan started to go to the rescue. Then he remembered where he was. Innocent young ladies were not left alone in Carlton House, at the mercy of the prince's exceedingly untrustworthy set of friends and hangers-on. Their families saw to that. Most likely this girl was a high flyer whose youthful looks were very good for business. No doubt she knew what she was doing. He started to turn away.

"No, I do not wish to stroll with you in the garden," the girl said. "I have told you so a dozen times. I don't wish to be rude, but please go away."

The man grasped her arm, his fingers visibly digging into her flesh. He tried to pull her along with him through the crowd.

"I'll scream," said the girl, rather calmly. "I can scream very loudly. My singing teacher said I have an extraordinary set of lungs. Though an unreliable grasp of pitch," she added with regretful honesty.

Her companion ignored this threat until the girl actually opened her mouth and drew in a deep preparatory breath. Then, with a look around at the crowd and a muttered oath, he dropped her arm. "Witch," he said.

" 'Double, double toil and trouble,' " she replied pertly.

The man frowned.

" 'Fire, burn; and, cauldron, bubble,' " she added.

His frown became a scowl.

"Something of toad, eye of newt . . . oh, I forget the rest." She sounded merely irritated at her lapse of memory.

The man backed away a few steps.

"There's blood in it somewhere," she told herself. She made an exasperated sound. "I used to know the whole thing by heart."

Her would-be ravisher took to his heels. The girl shook out her skirts and tossed her head in satisfaction.

His interest definitely caught, Alan examined this unusual creature more closely. She was small—the top of her head did not quite reach his shoulder—but the curves of her form were not at all childlike. The bodice of her pale green gown was admirably filled and it draped a lovely line of waist and hip. Her skin glowed like ripe peaches against her glossy brown hair. He couldn't see whether her eyes had any resemblance to forest pools, but her lips were mesmerizing—very full and beautifully shaped. The word "luscious" occurred to him, and he immediately rejected it as nonsense. What the devil was he doing, he wondered? He wasn't a man to be beguiled by physical charms, or to waste his time on such maunderings. Still, he was having trouble tearing his eyes away from her when it was brought home to him that she had noticed him.

"No, I do not wish to go with you into another room," she declared, meeting his gaze squarely. "Or into the garden, or out to your carriage. I do not require an escort home. Nor do I need someone to tell me how to go on or to 'protect' me." She stared steadily up at him, not looking at all embarrassed.

Her eyes were rather like forest pools, Alan thought; dead leaves aside. They were a sparkling mixture of brown and green that put one in mind of the deep woods. "What are you doing here?" he couldn't resist asking her.

"That is none of your affair. What are *you* doing here?"

Briefly, Alan wondered what she would think if he told her. He would enjoy hearing her response, he realized. But of course he couldn't reveal his supposed "mission."

A collective gasp passed over the crowd, moving along the room like wind across a field of grain. Alan turned quickly. This was what he had been waiting for through the interminable hours and days. There! He started toward the sweeping staircase that adorned the far end of the long room, pushing past knots of guests transfixed by the figure that stood in the shadows atop it.

On the large landing at the head of the stairs the candles had gone out—or been blown out, Alan amended. In the resulting pool of darkness, floating above the sea of

light in the room, was a figure out of some sensational
tale. It was a woman, her skin bone-white, her hair a deep
chestnut. She wore an antique gown of yellow brocade,
the neckline square cut, the bodice tight above a long full
skirt. Alan knew, because he had been told, that this was
invariably her dress when she appeared, and that it was
the costume she had worn onstage to play Lady Macbeth.

Sound reverberated through the room—the clanking
of chains—as Alan pushed past the guests, who remained
riveted by the vision before them. The figure seemed to
hover a foot or so above the floor. The space between the
hem of its gown and the stair landing was a dark vacancy.
Its eyes were open, glassy and fixed, effectively dead-
looking. Its hands and arms were stained with gore.

A bloodcurdling scream echoed down the stairs. Then
a wavering, curiously guttural voice pronounced the
word "justice" very slowly, three times. The figure's
mouth had not moved during any of this, Alan noted.

He had nearly reached the foot of the stairs when a
female guest just in front of him threw up her arms and
crumpled to the floor in a faint. Alan had to swerve and
slow to keep from stepping on her, and as he did so,
something struck him from behind, upsetting his balance
and nearly knocking him down. "What the devil?" he
said, catching himself and moving on even as he cast a
glance over his shoulder. To his astonishment, he found
that the girl he had encountered a moment ago was right
on his heels. He didn't have time to wonder what she
thought she was doing. "Stay out of my way," he commanded, and lunged for the stairs.

There was another terrible shriek, but even as Alan
pounded up the long curving stairway, the apparition at
the top vanished into darkness. Cursing, he kept going.
He didn't believe for one moment that the ghost of a
recently dead actress was haunting Carlton House, whatever the prince might say. It was some sort of hoax. And
he had to uncover it, and the reasons behind it, before he

would be allowed to leave and take up his own pursuits once more.

He reached the broad landing—now empty. The corridor leading off it was also completely dark, all the candle sconces extinguished. He paused a moment to listen for footsteps, and once again was jostled from behind. He turned to find the same girl had followed him up the staircase. "What the hell do you think you're doing?" he demanded.

"I must speak to her," insisted the girl breathlessly. "I must find her. Which way?" She gazed left, then right, along the lightless hallway.

Alan was never sure afterward whether there had actually been a sound. But the girl exclaimed, pointed, and darted off to the left. After an instant's hesitation, he went after her.

The light from downstairs barely penetrated into this upper corridor, and the little there was cast disorienting shadows along the floor and walls. Alan could just see the girl blundering along ahead of him toward a half-open door, which seemed to still be swinging.

The girl reached the door, pulled it open, and went through. Alan, directly behind her by this time, followed at top speed. Then, in one confusing instant, he careened into her with stunning force, the door slammed shut, and there was the unmistakable click of a key turning in a lock outside. A spurt of eerie laughter was capped by total, black silence.

A moment ticked by. Though he was jammed into a tiny space, Alan managed to reach behind his back and grip the doorknob. As he had expected, it did not turn.

He heard a muffled sound, between a sob and a sigh. "She didn't wait for me," murmured the girl, so softly he barely heard.

"You mean the so-called ghost?" he replied sharply. "Why should it?"

"You frightened her off," she accused. "She would have stayed for *me*."

"If you hadn't gotten in my way, I would have caught it," he retorted. "What is your connection with this affair?"

There was a silence.

"Could you move, please?" the girl asked. "You're crushing me."

"I am directly against the door," he answered. "There is no room to move. I insist upon knowing—"

"We're in some sort of cupboard, then. I'm mashed into a corner. Can't you open the door?"

"It's locked," Alan replied, with what he thought was admirable restraint.

"Locked? It can't be."

"I assure you that it is."

"If this is some sort of trick to get me alone . . ." began the girl suspiciously.

"Believe me, I have no such desire."

"You mean, the ghost locked us in?" she said incredulously.

"Someone pretending to be a ghost appears to have done so," he amended. "To prevent discovery of the hoax."

There was another silence. Alan cursed the darkness, wanting very much to see his companion's face.

"You don't think it's really Bess Harding's ghost?" she asked finally.

"There are no ghosts," Alan pronounced with utter certainty. "That is a ridiculous superstition, rejected by all sensible people."

"Sensible," she echoed very quietly. "I suppose you're right." She sighed.

For some reason, that tiny movement made him acutely aware of the fact that their bodies were pressed together along their entire lengths. He could feel the soft curve of her breasts at his ribs, and her hip cradled by his thigh. He moved slightly, trying to disengage, but this only intensified the sensations. She had a heady, flowery scent, too, he realized. It was intoxicating in these confined quarters. "We should make some sound, so that the prince's servants can release us," he said tightly. Following his own advice, he kicked backward with one foot and produced a satisfying thud on the door panels.

"Won't they be afraid to come up here?" the girl asked.

"For a while. But eventually someone will investigate. My father most certainly will."

"Is your father here?" she asked, sounding oddly wistful. "Of course he will come for you then."

"Who are you?" Alan said, personal curiosity as strong as his investigative instincts.

"Who are *you*?" she retorted, with the same spirit she had shown downstairs.

"Alan Gresham," he answered.

"One of the prince's friends." Her tone made it clear that she didn't think much of the Carlton House set.

He found he didn't want her to draw this conclusion. "No," he said. "The prince summoned me here to . . ." Alan hesitated. The prince had made it clear that he didn't want his uneasiness about the ghost mentioned.

"To rid him of the ghost," the girl concluded, taking the matter out of his hands. "Just like him. Let someone else clean up the mess. Make no effort to really settle the matter."

"You are acquainted with the prince?"

"My mother was."

"Indeed." From her tone, and the prince's notorious romantic history, Alan concluded that the connection had been intimate.

"My mother, the ghost," she added bitterly.

"Bess Harding was your . . . ?"

"Yes," was the bald reply.

Matters became clearer to Alan. "So you came here tonight—"

"I had to see her!" the girl exclaimed. "She can't be just . . . gone. I came as fast as I could from school, but by the time I reached London, everything was over. They'd buried her and . . ." Her voice caught, and there was a pause. "I heard about this . . . haunting. So I came." She sounded defiant now. "I know it isn't the thing, but no one asked me for an invitation, and I was sure she would appear tonight, so I—"

"Why?" interrupted Alan sharply. "Why tonight?"

"I was told it is the largest, most important party the prince has given in weeks," she answered. "Mama wouldn't miss something like that."

"But, Miss Harding—"

"Ariel," she cut in. "You may as well know my name is Ariel Harding. She named me from *The Tempest*." When he said nothing, she added, "Shakespeare, you know."

"I believe I've heard of it," he responded dryly.

"Umm. Well, I knew she wouldn't be able to resist such an occasion. So I came." There was a pause, then she moved slightly. "You don't think it's really my mother?" she asked again.

It was a moment before Alan could reply. Her small movement against him had sent a jolt through his entire body. This was entirely unacceptable, he told himself. He was a man of science. He was not subject to random physical attractions. "I do not," he said, more harshly than he might have under other circumstances.

"But who can it be then?" she wondered, brushing against him once again.

"Someone who expects to gain from the situation," he answered curtly. "We really must get out of here." He began to kick the door again, much more forcefully this time.

"Gain, how?"

"Possibly a political opponent of the prince who wishes to discredit him," said Alan through gritted teeth. "Perhaps someone looking for personal revenge." He kicked again, hard. "Halloo," he called. "Is anyone there?"

He was rewarded by the sound of cautious footsteps in the corridor outside. "Hello?" said a tentative voice.

"It's Alan Gresham," he replied loudly. "I'm locked in this cupboard. Open the door!"

The footsteps advanced a bit farther. "How do I know it's Lord Alan?" the voice inquired. "You might be a demon from the depths trying to deceive me."

"If I were, I should burst through this door and drag you down to hell," roared Alan. "Now, let us out!"

But the footsteps were already pounding away.

"Well, you might have known that would frighten him," Ariel Harding said. "When someone is coming after a ghost, you do not threaten to drag him down to—"

"Be quiet." The feel of her against him was becoming intense. He refused to give in to it. It was irrational; it was meaningless; it was the consequence of simple physical reflex and extremely awkward circumstances.

"Are you really a lord?" asked Ariel. "What sort of lord?"

"A courtesy lord," he replied in clipped accents. "I am the sixth son of the duke of Langford, and thus am technically Lord Alan."

"Sixth?" murmured Ariel. "Good heavens. Do you have sisters as well?"

"I do not. And I don't see what that has to do with—"

"Alan?" put in a voice from outside.

"Father," he replied with great relief. "Can you get someone to unlock this door?"

"Unfortunately not," was the reply. "There seems to be a problem about the key."

"The numskulls have lost it," declared another voice.

"But don't worry, I have them fetching an ax. We'll have you out of there in no time."

"Your Majesty! This is a cupboard. My back is right up against the door."

"Useless blunderers," said the prince. "Someone will be sacked over this."

"Your Majesty!" called Alan again.

"I heard you," answered his father. "Don't worry."

"This is like one of the French farces my mother used to act in," commented Ariel.

"I'm glad you are amused," replied Alan tightly.

"Oh, it's not very amusing to be *in* it. It's much more fun to watch."

"Undoubtedly." Alan was listening to the confused noises outside. It sounded as if an entire army was gathering to effect their rescue. It was going to be damned embarrassing to emerge from a cupboard with an unknown young woman.

"Why did the prince choose you?" asked Ariel.

"What?"

"Why did he choose you to unmask the ghost? Because you are the son of a duke? That doesn't seem like a very good reason."

"He didn't have a very good reason," muttered Alan, remembering the conversation he had had with the prince five days ago.

He had been summoned to London without warning, ordered to wait upon the regent at Carlton House. And wait he had, thought Alan bitterly. Prinny kept him kicking up his heels in a gaudy parlor for two hours before a liveried footman appeared and indicated that he should follow. Alan had to slow his athletic stride to keep from bumping into the man as they traversed the corridors and antechambers of the huge house, passing knots of curious courtiers and numbers of busy servants. Alan found the place like a giant anthill, teeming with creatures who had certain specified functions and did not seem to see any farther than three inches before their eyes.

Finally, they had passed through a pair of carved and gilded double doors and into a large reception parlor that at first seemed to him crowded with people. At one end stood a loose group of ten or fifteen men dressed in the height of fashion and talking desultorily with one another. A servant with a tray wound among them offering wine. In the center of the chamber was a small circle of what appeared to be government officials. Most of them carried sheaves of papers, and all of them looked impatient. At the far end was a huge desk with a few armchairs scattered around it. Two young men sat at the corners of the desk bent over pen and paper, busily recording the pronouncements of the man occupying the main chair, and the center of attention.

Alan's eyes followed all the others toward George Augustus Frederick, prince regent of England and Ireland due to his father the king's distressing illness, and found little trace of the handsome, laughing youth of an early portrait he had once seen. The prince was fat. His high starched neckcloth hid several extra chins. His extremely fashionable clothes couldn't disguise his girth. He didn't look very happy either, Alan thought. Of course, with workmen smashing power looms around the country and people marching in the streets of London to express their disgust of the ruler's treatment of his wife, he had little to be happy about.

Receiving a signal, Alan walked down the long room and made his bow before the controversial man who ruled his country.

"Langford's youngest, eh?" the prince said.

"Yes, Your Majesty."

The prince waved a pudgy, beringed hand. "No need to be formal. Your father's a friend of mine, you know."

"Yes, sir," replied Alan.

"That's why I sent for you. Sit down, sit down."

A servant appeared at his elbow with a tray, and Alan accepted a glass of wine that he did not want.

"Never see you about London," the prince commented, sipping his own wine with obvious relish.

"No, sir. I visit very rarely."

"Not like your brothers, eh?"

"No, sir." When his host seemed to be waiting for more, Alan added, "As a sixth son, I have felt able to go my own way."

"Sixth." The prince shook his head, then eyed his visitor with surprising shrewdness. "Up at Oxford, are you? Studying new inventions and the like?"

"I am a man of science, sir, a fellow of Balliol College."

"Right, right." The prince rubbed his hands together. "Just what I need. I take it you haven't heard about my little . . . problem?"

Alan had heard of a variety of problems, from the vilifications of the Whigs to scandals involving various women to rumors of unattractive physical ailments.

"The ghost," prompted the prince.

Alan simply stared at him.

"Glad to see the story hasn't spread outside London," was the response to his bewildered look. "It's embarrassing. A dashed nuisance, too."

"Did you say ghost, sir?" Alan asked.

"Bess Harding," came the morose reply. "The actress?" Seeing Alan's blank look, he added, "She was one of the great ladies of the stage. Gorgeous creature. Why, ten years ago, we . . ." He cleared his throat. "Never mind that. The thing is, Bess, er, died three weeks ago, and now she's haunting Carlton House!"

"Haunting," Alan repeated carefully.

"It's outrageous," complained the prince. "We were good friends. No reason for this at all." He looked at Alan as if for confirmation, and Alan found himself too bemused even to nod. "Makes it look as if I had something to do with her death, don't you see?" the prince elaborated.

When Alan remained uncomprehending, the regent added, "She killed herself." His voice and look grew briefly solemn. "Terrible thing. Took a razor to her wrists. I've never been more shocked. But it had nothing to do with me."

Alan watched as an almost wistful expression passed over the prince's pudgy features, as if he might have liked knowing that a gorgeous actress had ended her existence for his sake.

"We've been nothin' but friends for years," the ruler conceded. He straightened his shoulders. "And I can't afford another . . . that is, any scandal just now. We've got to get rid of the thing."

"We, sir?" Alan asked, his heart sinking.

"I'll be of whatever help I can," the prince answered stoutly.

"You are asking me to—"

"Man of science," interrupted the monarch. "Just the ticket. I won't have some interfering priest in here with bells and books and mumbo jumbo. This ain't a theater, by God, it's my home. That's why you're the perfect man for the job."

"Sir, I don't think—"

"You'll know how to go on at Carlton House, fit right in," the prince continued, ignoring Alan's growing desperation. "I won't have a pack of commoners wandering about the place, sticking their noses into things they won't understand."

"But, sir, I—"

"She keeps appearing at evening parties," the prince told him in a deeply aggrieved tone. "Don't see how she could do this to me."

"Sir, surely you don't believe that this is actually, er, the dead woman."

thing about it, perhaps we should concentrate our energies on getting out of this damnable cupboard!"

She made a sputtering sound. He felt her stand up straighter along every inch of his body, which was again washed by a wave of heat.

"No wonder it is so crowded in here," Ariel said. "Your giant intellect must take up more than half the space all by itself."

Was this chit of a girl laughing at him, Alan wondered incredulously?

There was a sharp sound at his back, as some sort of tool was inserted between the door and jamb. A splintering noise from near the keyhole heralded a crack of light that wavered, and then quickly expanded as the lock was broken and the door pried open, finally flying back to crash against the corridor wall.

Alan felt an odd moment of regret as he took a step back and turned toward their rescuers. Ariel Harding had roused his always active curiosity, he realized. He would be rather sorry to see the last of her.

As he'd feared, the hall was full of people. Around his father and the prince stood a crowd of servants and guests all peering avidly in his direction and trying to discover what was going on.

"All right?" murmured the duke.

Alan nodded, taking another step and thus revealing Ariel to the onlookers.

"Hallo?" said the prince. "What's this, then?" He moved closer, holding up a beribboned quizzing glass for a better look and casting an experienced eye over Ariel's rounded figure. He appeared to find much to admire, taking his time to savor the glowing skin of her neck and shoulders and the voluptuous shape of her lips. "Thought you were chasin' the ghost," he admonished Alan without shifting his gaze. "Not that anyone wouldn't rather be shut in a cupboard with this—"

"We were both chasing it," broke in Ariel. "And *I*, at

least, intend to find out the truth about Bess Harding's death."

"Eh?" sputtered the prince, looking uneasily aware of the crowd around him. "Truth? Everyone knows the truth. Fit of despair. Took her own life. Always a moody creature, was Bess. Terrible thing. But nothing to do with—"

"She had to have some reason," interrupted Ariel again. "Why is she coming here? I want to know—"

"Perhaps we should adjourn to some other room," said Alan in a loud voice. "I'm sure the others would like to get back to the entertainment." He ignored the many interested expressions that contradicted this assertion, and gave the prince a significant look.

"Yes, indeed," replied Alan's father. He fixed one of the senior servants with a commanding gaze. "Escort everyone downstairs."

There were some protests, but in a few minutes the hall was clear of everyone but the prince, the duke, and Alan and Ariel. "What's going on here?" blustered the prince. "Who is this girl? What's she doin' in my house? Never seen her before in my life. Don't believe I invited her, by Jove." He gave a very creditable impression of outraged virtue.

"I am—" began Ariel.

"Assisting me in the investigation," interjected Alan smoothly.

The other two men looked at him.

"I am not—" attempted Ariel.

"She possesses certain key facts that will help discredit this hoax," Alan said.

His father frowned, looking deeply puzzled.

"Facts, is it?" said the prince. His sharp look faded as he examined Ariel yet again. A gleam came into his eyes and he chuckled. "I've known a few ladies who possessed some fascinatin' 'facts.' Taught me a good deal, they did." He started to turn away. "Do as you like, my boy, but don't be diverted from your task, eh? Come along, Langford, I want a drink."

The duke followed him down the corridor, in which the sconces had been relit. But he cast several curious looks over his shoulder as he went.

"Why did you say that?" exploded Ariel when they had gone.

"What?" answered Alan.

"That I am assisting you."

"You might have knowledge that could be useful," he replied. "If you do not blurt it out before a crowd, that is."

She drew in an angry breath. "I am not in the habit of—"

"As you nearly did just now," he continued. "You were about to tell them all that you are Bess Harding's daughter, weren't you?"

Ariel stood very straight. "I am not ashamed of being her daughter," she declared. "She was a great actress."

"No doubt. But that is no reason to broadcast information when you do not know who is listening."

"Who . . . ?"

"Our so-called ghost may have been standing right here, enjoying her triumph. She had ample time to change her dress and return."

"She . . ." Ariel put a hand to her lovely lips. "If it's not Bess . . ." She faltered. "It has to be a woman, doesn't it?"

"It certainly was a woman who appeared here tonight."

"Yes," she whispered. "But who would . . . ?"

"Precisely."

He straightened his coat and pushed the now-ruined cupboard door closed. "Let us go somewhere private, and you can tell me everything you know about this matter."

She stiffened. "Why should I?"

Alan looked surprised. "So that I can resolve the situation and be done with it."

"The ghost, you mean?"

"Exactly."

"What about my mother?" she demanded.

Trying to temper his impatience with sympathy, Alan looked down at her. "I am very sorry about your mother. The prince was right, it was a terrible thing."

"He wasn't right, because he knows nothing about it and hasn't bothered to find out."

"Perhaps so, but—"

"I must speak to the ghost," she went on, "and ask her what she knows. I *will* discover why my mother is dead!" She glared up at him, defiance and something more poignant in her hazel eyes.

"Don't get hysterical," he said uneasily.

"I am not hysterical. I'm never hysterical. I am simply utterly determined."

"You are being unreasonable," accused Alan. "I know that as a woman, you are prone to illogic, but you must see that—"

"I won't tell you anything, or help you in any way with the ghost, unless you agree to do the same for me as I search for the truth," she said.

"Don't be ridiculous. You are a woman. You have no notion how to conduct an investigation, even if you were capable of sustained—"

"I know who my mother's friends were," she offered. "I have her things. And her servants will talk to me, and no one else. They are very loyal." Her voice broke a little on the last word.

"Some of that information might be useful," he conceded.

"Well, then . . ."

"And it might not," he added. "This haunting may have nothing to do with your mother, if it is simply someone trying to discredit the prince."

"But you should eliminate the possibility that it is related to her death," Ariel said.

He was surprised. "That would be a logical course of action," he admitted.

"No one else is better placed to help you do that," she pointed out.

"That may be so, but—"

"So, we are agreed?" She held out her hand as if to shake his and seal the bargain.

Alan gazed at her small white hand. His eyes ran up the slim arm attached to it and met the deep hazel eyes fixed on his. This was most likely a complete waste of time, he thought. She was a woman, and thus a creature of instinct and whim rather than rational thought. She could not have anything valuable to offer that he would not discover himself. However, there was something about her . . . He suppressed this irrelevancy. A scientist considered all alternatives, he told himself, no matter how remote they might be. "Very well," he said. He took her hand firmly and shook it.

Chapter Two

———— ❖ ————

There, that looks all right, doesn't it?" said Ariel, pushing the silver tray an inch to the left on the small side table. The crystal decanter and glasses had been polished to a high sheen, and the lemon wafers on the enamel plate had been purchased from the confectioner that very morning. "It's the sort of thing Miss Ames used to serve important visitors at school," Ariel added. "I imagine it will do for a lord, don't you?"

She turned to look at the only other creature in the room, a huge cat with blue-gray fur the color of smoke and preternaturally glowing golden eyes.

"I got fish heads for you, so you needn't worry," she told the animal.

As if he understood, the cat rose and stretched, first digging his claws into the carpet and extending his whole spine in a concave arc, then pushing out his hind legs one at a time. He started toward the door. Ariel followed.

"It's Lord Alan Gresham coming to call," she informed the cat. "He's going to help me find out about Bess's death."

Downstairs in the kitchen, she unwrapped the fish heads and set them on the floor for the cat, who began to eat at once. His sonorous purr echoed through the room, and Ariel bent to run a hand over his extraordinarily thick, smooth coat. "What would I do without you?" she murmured.

She had returned from school to find an empty house. Her mother's servants had scattered after the suicide, she discovered; no one knew where they had gone. The magistrate in charge of looking into the death had seemed interested only in dismissing it from his mind. After he had had the contents of her mother's wine cellar conveyed to his own house, Ariel thought bitterly. When she had gone to ask for his help, he had been thoroughly foxed at eleven in the morning. Her mother's solicitor had been no more encouraging. He had suggested that she think of the future rather than the past, and had given her the one piece of good news she had received in London. Her mother had left her enough money to live on, if she was careful.

"How did she manage it?" Ariel asked the cat. "She always spent every penny she had. I remember the bill collectors pounding on the door, and Bess sending a footman running out the back way to borrow the money to pay them."

She rose and went back up to the parlor to await Lord Alan. But as soon as she sat down, the silence of the place dropped over her like a heavy blanket. It was a little unnerving, staying here by herself. She had never lived alone. And these were certainly not the best circumstances for trying it out. Memories of her mother became uncomfortably vivid in the dense quiet. When she had heard of the haunting at Carlton House, she had almost . . .

Ariel shook her head sharply. She would hire new servants, she thought. She was not entirely sure how one went about this, but it could not be too difficult. And

more important, she would find the truth. That would
put everything to rest. She had an ally now; she was no
longer totally alone. She was managing perfectly well.

Hoofbeats sounded in the street. Ariel listened, but
they clattered on by. A board creaked upstairs. Of
course, Bess would not at all approve of her agreement
with Lord Alan, Ariel thought, or of his visit here today.
Though men were a great part of Bess Harding's life, she
had not trusted any of them, particularly not where Ariel
was concerned.

Ariel clenched her fists. Just when she'd been insisting
upon coming home from school permanently, her mother
had ended her life in that horrifyingly bloody way.
Whenever she allowed herself to think of it, she was overwhelmed by grief and incomprehension and anger. How
could Bess have done it? How could she have left her in
this awful way? And even more critically—why? Ariel
caught her lower lip between her teeth. That question lay
behind her every thought now, and everything she did.
Why had Bess done it? Ariel was obsessed with finding
an answer. She had to find it, she thought, if she was ever
to have peace again.

Something touched her ankle. Ariel started, then saw
that the cat had rejoined her. He sat at her feet, staring
up. When she met his steady golden gaze, he blinked
once, then began to groom his thick fur.

Ariel watched his quick efficient movements. The cat
had appeared on her second day alone in the house. She
still didn't know whether he actually belonged here, but
he looked nothing like the half-starved street cats one saw
in the city. He had some secret entry of his own; he
appeared and disappeared at will, vanishing like the
smoke he resembled. She'd named him Prospero, because
he was majestic and magical, and because it reminded her
of her own eccentric naming.

"Were you here when she did it?" Ariel asked him.
"Did she speak to you as I do?"

Prospero's tongue rasped between the toes of his front paw. Fastidiously, he bit at one curved claw.

"If only you could tell me," said Ariel. Her breath caught on a sob, and she repressed it almost savagely. She had decided on the long, long journey back to London that she was not going to give in to grief. She meant to act, and to find comfort in discovering the truth. "With Lord Alan's help, I'll be able to do it," she told herself. "Bess always said that to accomplish anything you must have powerful friends."

She looked up to find the cat staring fixedly at her. "Lord Alan and I have a business arrangement," she told the animal. "We are to exchange information, and absolutely nothing more."

It seemed that Prospero's golden eyes narrowed.

"It's true," insisted Ariel. "He is a man of science."

Delicately, dispassionately, Prospero yawned, showing a ribbed pink mouth and a flash of small white fangs.

When the knocker sounded against the wood of the front door a little later, Ariel had to answer it herself. As soon as she opened the door, her eyes were drawn upward. She had forgotten how large he was, she thought, standing back to let Lord Alan Gresham enter. His coat and breeches were of plain dark cloth and his shirtfront unadorned, and his height and broad shoulders seemed to fill the entryway. Or perhaps it was his air of assurance and command, she thought. Were the sons of dukes born with it? A shaft of sunlight from outside drew red-gold glints from his deep auburn hair, which curled a little despite being cropped close to his head. His blue eyes held an intensity and intelligence such as Ariel had never seen before, and there was steely determination in the set of his square jaw. Momentarily, something seemed to flutter deep inside Ariel. She had never been alone with a man in her life. First her mother, then her schoolmistresses, had seen to that. She was very glad it was a warm day and he had no cloak for her to take. She had a dreadful suspicion that her hands might be shaking. Stuff and nonsense, she told herself severely, and raised her chin.

"This is an old house," he commented, looking at the paneling and the intricate carving of the stair banister. "Seventeenth century, isn't it?"

Ariel nodded. The house, which was the only home she had ever known, was tall and narrow, with a twisting staircase up through the four floors and rooms paneled with polished walnut and oak. The windows were small and mullioned; some of the floors slanted a bit alarmingly; and the ceiling was somewhat low, she noticed for the first time, as Lord Alan ducked his head under a huge beam.

"My mother loved it," she said. "I used to think that she would have been more at home in the court of Charles the Second. She seemed like someone from another century."

He looked slightly surprised. But he said only, "My family's home in Kent is from the same era."

Ariel glanced at him suspiciously. Was he patronizing her? she wondered. The country seat of the duke of Langford must be a huge mansion, hardly to be compared with her modest house. Perhaps he was mocking her instead. Ariel's jaw set. She was quite accustomed to snubs. She had endured years of them at her fashionable school once the other girls had discovered her parentage. Though the headmistress had been scrupulously fair, she could not prevent the girls from venting their spite in private. But they had not found her easy to despise, Ariel thought defiantly, and neither would this nobleman.

She examined him for the signs she knew so well—the subtle sneer, the haughtily raised brow, the malicious spark in the eye. But his expression was unreadable as he deftly avoided hitting his head on the low beam and started upstairs. In the upper parlor, she offered him Madeira from the tray she had set out earlier, and he accepted a small glass.

"This was Bess Harding's house?" Lord Alan commented then.

Ariel nodded. "She left it to me."

"It occurred to me that it might be helpful to question her servants. They may have heard something that will offer a clue to this haunting."

"Yes," said Ariel. She very much wanted to speak to her mother's servants herself. She had been chagrined, and a bit hurt, to find them all gone.

"Well?"

She looked up to find that Lord Alan had raised one auburn brow.

"Perhaps you could summon them?" he added.

"Oh. The thing is . . . they've disappeared."

"Disappeared?"

"Well, gone away, I mean. I suppose it did not occur to them that I would be coming home, and they thought they needed new positions." She could hear the resentment in her own voice, and she fell silent. She had been away for years, she reminded herself.

"I don't understand." He seemed to listen for the first time to the deep silence surrounding them. "Who is here with you?"

Warnings her mother had given her echoed in Ariel's mind. "I'll be hiring servants," she said firmly. "But if you could find the old staff, I'm sure it would be very useful to—"

"You are alone in this house?" He said it as if the idea were incomprehensible.

When it finally sank in that there was no one else here, what would he do, Ariel wondered? She had to trust him. There was no one else to help her. It was impossible to meet at Carlton House or a public place. She could only hope it hadn't been a mistake to ask him to call.

A flash of memory from ten years past came vividly

back to her, summoned by the intensity of Lord Alan's gaze. She and her mother had been sitting at their dining table in a pool of candlelight. Supper was long over, but Bess stayed at the table, and so Ariel stayed with her. Her mother was silent, distant and cold, drinking brandy. Something had happened. Ariel didn't know exactly what. At the theater, after the play, there had been some incident—something that had punctured the buoyancy of a good performance. Bess wouldn't tell her about it, but it had brought on one of the black moods that descended on her mother from time to time and plunged the entire household into gloom.

"Stop staring," Bess said sharply. Her hands swooped down on the decanter and she poured a tiny bit of brandy in a small glass. "Here," she said, sliding it across to Ariel. "Try it."

Doubtful, Ariel took the glass, raised it to her lips, and cautiously touched the tip of her tongue to the amber liquid. It burned and tasted horrible. Wrinkling her nose, she put it down.

Her mother laughed, and as usual, Ariel gauged the quality of the sound as a connoisseur might have judged the vintage she'd just been offered. There was as yet no edge of hysteria, no threat of a night when Bess would have to be soothed till dawn.

"You're ten years old," Bess said then, as if the fact had just occurred to her. "It's not long before you're a woman."

Ariel simply looked at her, knowing better than to reply to this tone.

"You'd best face the truth of it now," her mother added. "Men will want you, and if you let them, they'll take everything you are and expect gratitude for their theft. They'll talk of devotion, but what they mean is bondage."

Ariel shivered. Her mother had made the word sound like the knell of doom.

"Men don't see us, really," Bess went on, almost as if she were talking to herself. "They see a story that satisfies their secret desires, an image that rouses their lusts. So you tempt them, echo their dreams, and when they fall at your feet, you take what you want."

She sounded like one of the plays she acted in, Ariel thought. Except that love so often conquered in those. "What about love?" she asked in a small voice.

Bess glared at her. "Love? Is that what you think you want?" She bared her teeth. "Believe me, its price is too high." She reached across the corner of the polished table, grasped Ariel's wrist, and squeezed it hard. "There's only one sure course in this life, and that's to rely on yourself. Most people don't give a brass farthing for you. And the ones who do will want to 'help' you as they see fit, not give you what you want. Only you can get that. You understand?"

Ariel gazed up at her. She'd seen this mood before. It was as if a cold fire had ignited in Bess, so that she blazed with ice and spoke like an oracle. It frightened Ariel, not because of anything her mother might do, but because of the otherworldly crackle of her personality.

"You don't understand," Bess accused. Letting go of Ariel's wrist, she stood, resting her palms on the table and looming over her. She had always loomed, Ariel thought now. She still did.

"Miss Harding?" said a deep voice.

She started, and found that Lord Alan was looking at her with what seemed to be a mixture of uneasiness and concern.

"Are you all right?"

She had to appear calm and composed and logical, Ariel thought. She had to keep this situation under control. Love was the last thing to be thinking of; she couldn't imagine why it had entered her mind. "We should search for the servants," she began.

"Some member of your family must be summoned," he interrupted. "You cannot stay here alone."

Ariel sat straighter in her chair, relieved at this response to her solitude.

"We must send word at once," he added.

He said it so easily, as if it were so simple and obvious that an idiot would have thought of it. He was so very large, and secure, and confident in his position and wealth of family connections. "I will be perfectly all right," she said. "I will hire servants."

"You need someone other than servants," he declared. "In these circumstances . . ." He looked around the room as if he now found the place uncanny. "I would be happy to send for anyone you name," he finished.

"I have no family," she informed him stiffly.

He looked as if he found the idea incredible. "There must be someone."

"There isn't," she told him, in a tone that she hoped would close the subject.

"That's impossible."

He sounded maddeningly certain. "Do you claim to know more about my family than I do?" she demanded. "Bess had no family, and I had only . . . Bess." Her voice wavered on the last word, and Ariel bit her lip to stop its trembling. This was intolerable, she thought. He had no right to look at her that way, with some sort of irritated kindness.

"Your father?" he suggested.

Ariel's fingers curled into fists in her lap. This conversation was going exactly where she did not wish it to go. "He is . . . not available," she said.

Lord Alan's face grew hard. "He could be made to be."

"No, he couldn't," she answered curtly. She wasn't going to tell him about the many, many times she had asked Bess about her father. Or about the stories Bess had made up, changing them each time, so that it became a kind of game between them, though terribly serious to Ariel. She wasn't going to mention the agate ring, the only thing in the house that she knew had come from her unknown parent, and which she had been frantically searching for since her return. She refused to expose herself to this aristocrat and risk the kind of ridicule and contempt she had learned to endure at school.

"He might be important to the investigation," Lord Alan urged.

If he was, she couldn't do anything about it, Ariel thought, since she had no clue to his identity. She caught her breath on a sob, and immediately suppressed it.

A silence fell. Ariel waited for Lord Alan to probe further, to force her to admit that she was the bastard child of a common actress, and then to reject any further contact with her. Let him, she thought. She had hoped for help, but she would go on without it if necessary. She was accustomed to isolation, and to relying on her own resources.

"Aunts and uncles?" he said finally, sounding not at all censorious. "Cousins? There has to be someone."

Ariel shook her head.

"Are you sure? We could consult records, ask neighbors. Where did your mother come from?"

He seemed genuinely engaged with the subject. There was none of the mock solicitude and sly entrapment she had endured over the last ten years. "Nowhere," Ariel blurted out. "She came from nowhere."

Lord Alan raised his auburn brows in inquiry.

Something in his eyes, or the silent house, or the situation made Ariel, uncharacteristically, rush on. "Once when I was small, we were driving somewhere. There was a fire up ahead, and we had to stop. Bess pointed to it and told me to look. I remember she said, 'What a spectacle.' "

The picture was sharp in her mind. She had had to struggle to her knees on the seat of the coach and hang on tight to the strap to see out. The fire was being swept by high winds along an ancient row of tall wooden houses, many of them caulked with pitch so that they went up like torches, with a burst and a roar. Rainbows of sparks crackled over the street and a great pall of red smoke billowed into the heavens. Even far from the flames, ash fell, and the smell of charred wood caught at Ariel's throat. Dazzled and terrified, she had listened to the fire breathing like a gigantic animal.

"It took a while to turn the carriage, because the street was so crowded," she said breathlessly. "Bess was laughing and saying the fire was glorious. And then when we finally were moving again, all of a sudden she pounded on the roof and told John to stop the coach. She made me get up again and look out." The pall of smoke had made it seem like dusk, she remembered. "There were people walking along the street, carrying whatever they'd managed to save from the fire. But Bess was pointing at an alleyway beyond them."

Ariel glanced quickly at her companion, then away. "It was narrow and twisting and muddy. The houses leaned, and their doors were all cracked and broken. There were piles of garbage rotting, and some kind of disgusting liquid running along the center of the lane."

Ariel stared at the wall and recited from memory. "My mother said: 'I came from a place like that. When I was younger than you, I lived in just such a street. I fought dogs for scraps. I stole from the dead. Plenty of people died on that street.' " She let out her breath. "She shook me a little, then she said, 'I want you to remember that. Will you remember?' "

Lord Alan made a quick gesture, but said nothing.

"I couldn't forget," Ariel finished with a shiver. "How could I? It was the only thing she ever told me about her past." She looked down at her hands clenched on her lap. "She didn't leave anything either. How will I ever find out her secrets?"

The last came out on a desperate, rising note, and Ariel at once bit it back. Why had she told him this? Hadn't she learned years ago that anything she confided would be giggled over in corners and used to humiliate? She had resolved never to tell anyone about herself again. And yet after two days' acquaintance she had taken that terrible risk with this duke's son. Her mind was becoming unhinged with grief, Ariel concluded. She had to get hold of herself—now. She had to change the subject. But looking up and meeting Lord Alan's acute blue eyes, she could think of nothing to say.

The girl looked positively frightened, Alan was thinking. He could see no reason for it, but the shadows in her eyes and the tension of her body were unmistakable. She was trying to hide the trembling of her hands. Clearly, the death of her mother had deeply affected her. But why fear? No doubt she was afraid of being alone, he decided. She was young and female, and thus constitutionally unable to appreciate the pleasures of solitary work and thought. It must be rather odd to have no family at all. "I have always been surrounded by dozens of relatives," he said almost meditatively.

Ariel stared as if he had said something completely unexpected.

"A burdensome number," he added.

"Burdensome?" She looked even more astonished.

That was better than frightened, he thought. "Yes. It often takes a good deal of ingenuity to keep clear of them."

She shook her head, as if a bit dazed. "Clear? You want to avoid seeing your family?"

"Some disreputable third cousin or eccentric great-aunt is always popping up and creating a nuisance," he told her, relieved to see that she seemed to have recovered her composure.

"Nuisance?" she echoed.

"They want to borrow money, or be squired about

London, or stay at the house for months at a time to save themselves a few guineas when they haven't the least need to do so."

She smiled slightly, and Alan felt a surge of gratification all out of proportion with the occasion. "My Great-uncle Oliver amassed one of the largest fortunes in England by the simple expedient of never going home," he added. "Indeed, he didn't have a home. He saved the expense by visiting his relatives, in turn, through the year. You could judge the season by it. If Uncle Oliver was visiting, it must be April."

She laughed, and Alan felt his heart lift in the most incomprehensible way. "They can't all be like that," she protested.

"Not all," he conceded.

"You told me you have brothers?"

"Brothers," he echoed feelingly. "You can't imagine what it's like having five older brothers."

"No," replied Ariel softly. "I don't suppose I can."

"Everything has been done before you get to it. Everyone you meet has opinions about you—and not always favorable ones. You are born part of a mob, and you have to fight to become yourself."

"You do?"

Alan looked up and found that she was gazing at him very steadily. Why had he said that, he wondered? It had nothing to do with the matter at hand. He had come here for information, and so far he had gotten none at all. "I'm happy to visit the family at holidays and do my duty on great occasions," he said, closing the subject. "But I need the rest of my time for my work."

"Your work with light?"

"Yes." He was amazed that she'd remembered.

"How can you study light?" she asked. She gestured at the shaft of sunlight flooding through the window. "It's just . . . there." She moved her hand in and out of the glow, briefly illuminating its delicate shape.

She really was like a creature of light herself, Alan thought. He had seldom seen such coloring. The rich brown of her hair, the greens and browns of her eyes, the peach tones of her skin emphasized by the golden sun—they all seemed to fit with the subtly rounded figure, those full lips that made a man . . .

"Like air," she added.

"What?"

"Light is like air—all around but insubstantial. How can you study it? You can't put it in a jar and . . . and pour chemicals over it."

"No. But you can bend it and refract it through prisms and . . . other things." She couldn't really understand this, he thought, though she looked genuinely interested.

"Prisms," she repeated. "And mirrors. People use mirrors to send signals because they reflect light. I've read about that."

"They do," he replied, more and more surprised. She actually seemed able to hold on to an abstract idea for more than an instant. That was most unusual.

Ariel moved uneasily under his gaze, seeming suddenly self-conscious. "We are supposed to be discussing our investigation," she said.

They were, thought Alan, and he did not precisely understand how they had gotten so far off the subject. He did not even recognize his twinge of regret as he took a slip of paper from his waistcoat pocket and unfolded it. "I have laid out an investigative plan following last night's incident. After you have given me all the information you possess, I will proceed to—"

"We must find the servants," interrupted Ariel. "Mama's dresser, Clarisse, was a very . . . resourceful person."

Alan looked at her.

"And John the coachman was a man of . . . varied experience."

She had been about to say something else, Alan noted,

wondering what. The things he had learned about Bess Harding so far made him suspect it was unflattering.

"The whole staff was well acquainted with the prince's servants, and Carlton House," she explained. "It would be quite simple for them to get in. I wonder if they have something to do with the haunting."

"It isn't the work of servants. How would they have the time, or the funds necessary?"

"Oh. I suppose you're right. But we must speak to them!"

Her impassioned tone unsettled him a bit. She seemed to take everything with such emotion. "They'll be searched for," he said. "The prince has put a number of men at my disposal. But what I most want is to speak to the actors who performed with Bess Harding. And they seem reluctant to meet me."

"They would be eager to help Bess's daughter."

"Would they?"

"Yes."

She looked as if she hoped she was right, Alan thought.

"We could go to the theater tonight," she said, clasping her hands together. "Actors are usually in good spirits after a performance." She looked suddenly delighted. "We might even attend the play. It has been so long since I was in a proper theater."

"I don't see the need for that." Alan found playacting a waste of time.

"It would be fun," declared Ariel.

He frowned.

"And . . . and more to the point, you could get a look at everyone before you meet them. Form a . . . an opinion of their characters, so you could better judge whether they are hoaxing the prince."

Alan hesitated. The vast silence of the house descended

again. A shadow moved in the corner of his eye, but when he turned, there was nothing there. She obviously dearly wanted to go. He supposed it couldn't do any harm. "Very well," he said slowly. "I'll procure a box."

Though she looked exultant, Ariel made no reply.

Chapter Three

———— ✤ ————

Ariel opened the door of the big wooden wardrobe standing in the corner of her bedchamber and looked at the dresses that hung there. They were all made of pale pastel fabrics; they all had moderate, tasteful ruffles or ribbon trim; they were modest, unobtrusive, and extremely suitable. Every item of clothing she possessed had been approved by the headmistress of the school where she'd lived for so long. In fact, every single thing about her had been evaluated and reshaped by Miss Ames.

It hadn't been long after that night at the dining table, when Bess had repudiated love, that she told Ariel she was being sent off to school. When Ariel had protested, saying she wanted to stay home with Bess and the theater, her mother had cut her off ruthlessly.

"Is it your ambition to grow into a young woman and be auctioned to the highest bidder?" she nearly growled. "That's what they'll expect of me, I suppose."

At the time, Ariel didn't understand what she meant,

but she knew that angry gleam in her mother's eyes, and she kept quiet.

Bess let her fist fall on the dressing table, rattling all the vials and bottles sitting there. "Not while I'm living," she cried.

And so she'd been sent away, Ariel thought—all the way to the other end of Britain, in fact. She had been exiled from the thrilling world of the theater and from her mother's vivid, complicated presence. She'd been forced to become somebody else, at least on the surface.

How she had hated Miss Ames when she'd first arrived at school as a resentful, rebellious ten-year-old, she remembered. The place was the antithesis of her life up to then. Instead of the color and noise and bustle of the London streets, it had offered cool gray mists and moors, endless quiet, and what had seemed to Ariel an unhealthy obsession with neatness and order. Accustomed to flamboyance and the broadly expressed emotions of actors, she came up against an ideal of restraint, a whole system of conduct based on the unspoken. The only way she'd survived those first weeks was to think of it as a performance, to assume the role of the gentlewoman. But what was role and what was real by this time? she wondered as she continued to stare at her row of pale insipid gowns.

Closing the wardrobe door with a snap, she turned and left her bedchamber, walking up the winding stairs to the top floor of the house, where she had to duck her head to pass through the low doorway of a large peaked storeroom. Tonight, she was going once more to the theater, which she had missed so much, and for so long. She was returning to the world of her childhood. She was *not* going to do so as a dowdy schoolgirl! People—especially men—were easily impressed by one's appearance. She had a sudden vision of Lord Alan Gresham, his cool gaze shaken by surprise, his stern jaw dropping in admiration. It was an amazingly gratifying picture. She wanted to dazzle him, she realized. Just as she wanted to show him how very useful she could be, and how knowledgeable she was about certain things, at least. Like the magistrate and the solicitor, he seemed to find her negligible, and a hot determination was growing in her to prove how wrong they all were. Nodding, she turned to the long wall of the storeroom that was crammed with wardrobes set side by side.

Bess Harding had adored beautiful clothes—beautiful new clothes. Scarcely a week had passed when she did not order a costume from her genius of a dressmaker. Some of them she never even wore. Some she gave away to her friends. Most made a brief appearance at plays and parties and then ended up here for a time, until the space was exhausted and a great sorting and discarding occurred. A smile touched Ariel's full lips. Her mother had had the most magnificently dressed maidservants in the city. And she was pretty sure Jack the coachman had lined his pockets by selling the garments that were rejected. Miss Ames would have been shocked to her civilized core by the extravagance and waste of it.

Ariel hadn't had time to come up here before, but now was obviously the moment. With a kind of triumph, Ariel flung open the door of the first wardrobe and began to examine the contents.

Two hours later, she stood again in her own room, before the open wardrobe doors, examining herself in the long mirror mounted on one of them. The pale gowns were gone from the hooks, replaced by a rainbow of color. And the young woman who stared back from the depths of the mirror was transformed as well. Her narrow dress was of emerald satin, drawing glints of green from her hazel eyes. The high waist and low neck emphasized the curve of her bosom, and the short puffed sleeves showed off her arms. The gown was a little long, for she was shorter than her mother had been, but not enough to matter if she managed the skirts properly. An emerald pendant dangled from a golden chain at her neck, and she had found a spangled green scarf for a wrap.

She looked like a different creature altogether, Ariel thought with great satisfaction. "I'm not a debutante," she told Prospero, who sat in the corner like a statue of a cat. "And I never will be. Why shouldn't I wear what I like?"

Prospero gave a long, slow blink.

"There is nothing wrong with trying for an effect," Ariel responded. "My mother used to say that good clothes give one an air of authority."

The cat rose and walked around her in a circle before drifting out of the room.

"I will not be treated like a child," Ariel called after him, "so I should not dress like one."

Predictably, there was no reply.

When Lord Alan Gresham arrived to fetch her, he wore evening dress. And he looked quite handsome in it, Ariel thought. But it was the flicker of surprise and admiration in his blue eyes that she really savored. There was something deeply gratifying about the way he offered his arm and continued to gaze down at her as he escorted her to the carriage waiting outside. A current of excitement rippled through her as he sat down beside her and the carriage started off on the short journey to the theater. It was as if something long buried was coming to life again, like a flame stirring out of banked coals.

"What is the play tonight?" she asked.

"Something called *The Pirate's Revenge*," Lord Alan replied dubiously.

Not one she knew, Ariel thought, with a mixture of anticipation and disappointment. "A melodrama," she replied. "I'm sure there'll be sword work."

He looked slightly startled.

"And a ship. I wonder if they'll use . . . but I mustn't spoil it for you." She smiled at her companion, who was gazing at her as if she had said something curious. "You'll enjoy it," she added encouragingly.

"Unlikely. I have no time for playacting. There are far too many intriguing problems in reality to be diverted by fictions."

"You can learn a great deal from plays," Ariel told him.

His expression showed that he disagreed, though he said nothing. She started to argue, then decided to bide her time.

When they entered the theater and made their way to the box Lord Alan had reserved, Ariel was nearly overwhelmed by the sights and sounds and smells of the place. She had not forgotten any of it, she realized. It was all there, only temporarily obscured by years of rules and conformity.

"There are peepholes in the curtain," she said as she sat down. "You can't see them, but some of the actors are most likely observing us right now, checking whether the house is filled. My mother used to let me look when I was so small I had to stand on a chair to see out."

Every detail of that first time came flooding back to her. "You can see through here," Bess said, lifting her up. Ariel put her eye to the tiny hole and gazed out into the noisy theater.

It was nearly full that day; there was a new play, and the king and queen were expected. The sight of the audience took Ariel's breath away. The glitter of innumerable candles illuminated the wealthier patrons in the tiers of boxes at the sides. Their clothes were strewn with gilt thread and jewels. In the galleries along the back sat scores of lesser members of the audience. Even from behind the curtain, Ariel smelled the heavy mixture of melting wax, a hundred perfumes, and unwashed bodies. The noise was terrific. In the pit, which occupied the floor of the theater, extravagantly dressed gallants strolled and flirted outrageously with any lady who caught their eye. A little intimidated by it all, Ariel drew back to make sure that her mother still stood beside her. She was there, gazing through another peephole.

Reassured, Ariel let her gaze rove over the theater itself, with its carved and gilded walls and ceiling. Garlands, cupids, and great symbolic figures of comedy and tragedy graced them, a riot of shape and color that was almost dizzying.

"It was like magic," Ariel murmured. In this building, she had been repeatedly enthralled by tales of ghosts and heroes, princesses from far isles, witty ladies of fashion, and villains deep dyed in evil.

"I beg your pardon?" said Lord Alan, leaning closer.

"My mother used to tell me things about people in the audience," she replied. "She knew everyone." Best not to say the sorts of things she had told, Ariel thought, remembering.

"Ah, the new Countess of Mallon," Bess pointed out one night. "See, third box in the second tier." Ariel looked and discovered a young woman, a girl really, very finely dressed in white with silver lace. "The great romance of last year." Her mother laughed. "The lovely innocent and the rake. People said it was like a storybook. He full of protestations of reform, swearing he'd never met her like. She prettily doubting, and then convinced. Her parents forbidding and then giving in. And now we find her at the play alone, and her new husband squiring his latest mistress."

"Where is he?" Ariel asked. She couldn't follow all of her mother's sarcastic narratives, but she relished them nonetheless, not for the content, but rather because she knew Bess talked this way to no one else.

"Just across. Both wearing black. And so dies a love match."

"Who are all those people in the first tier?" Ariel asked.

Her mother looked. "The Sandersons. All eight of them hugger-mugger in one box, as usual." Bess laughed without humor. "Take note, my dear. The rich are wondrously tight-fisted. They'll squeeze a penny till it shrieks. That's why they're rich. You'd think one of the wealthiest men in England could take a second box, would you not?"

"Who are the children?" A richly dressed boy and girl in the box had first attracted her attention. She had little contact with those her own age.

Her mother laughed again. "Children? That pair celebrated their betrothal not a sennight since."

Ariel looked again. She couldn't believe the girl was much older than ten. The boy might be twelve. "Betrothal?" she repeated.

"An old-fashioned family," replied Bess. "Child marriage isn't common now, but old Sanderson had a very important reason for it."

"What?"

"Money. Those two are cousins, and heirs to vast chunks of England on both sides. It all flows together on their marriage, and Sanderson is making very sure that it does, before they are old enough to make any false steps."

Ariel gazed at them. "Do they want to marry?"

"The gossips say that they hate each other most cordially. Ah, there's the duchess and her footman. I've been longing to see him."

"Why?" Her mother never showed much interest in other people's servants.

"Indeed, most handsome," Bess murmured, her eye to the peephole. "And from what they say, a man of *large*—" She broke off and straightened. "Never mind. You should go to your place now."

Something that she wasn't supposed to hear, Ariel concluded. The theater always teemed with gossip. Like her own home, it was a place of mysteries and secrets.

"I had a hidden seat in the prompt box," she said softly now. "I was there nearly every day. I learned some of my mother's parts by heart." She could almost see her, Ariel thought—confident, resplendent before the painted scenery, speaking in perfect rounded phrases. Ariel was always amazed at the contrast between her mother in life and the gallery of characters she portrayed. Rather than the mother she knew—carelessly improvident, ruled by flashes of mood, doting on and then quarreling with an endless succession of servants—in the theater she saw women with purpose as well as fire, strength along with style. Sometimes, guiltily, she found herself wishing for a mother like one of these imaginary characters.

The musicians began to play. "Oh, it's starting," exclaimed Ariel, and leaned forward to watch the curtain rise.

Ignoring the first speeches spoken by the actors, Alan watched her taking it all in. His gaze ran over the taut line of her throat, the glow of her skin where it curved into the bodice of her gown. What had become of the pert schoolgirl he had met at Carlton House, he wondered? There was little trace of her tonight, in this sleek, glittering creature in emerald-green, with her hair piled high and jewels shining at her throat. Had he made a mistake? Was she, in fact, the high flyer he had at first taken her for? And if so, what was she after?

He had no large fortune to tempt such a woman. The life he had chosen allowed him to live very comfortably on the income that came to him from two small estates, but it would not stretch to the kind of gifts and luxuries a fashionable mistress expected, to the kind of emerald pendant this one wore, for example.

No, she couldn't be after money. But what then? This talk of investigation and discovering the truth was nonsense, of course. Women hadn't the tenacity or sense of purpose for such a thing. What did she want?

Alan's insatiable curiosity, either an admirable trait or a besetting sin, depending on who one asked, was becoming thoroughly roused. He was certainly not ignorant of women. His family had made sure that he met a large number of lovely, eligible females of the *haut ton*, hoping that one of them would convince him to abandon his eccentric plan of staying on at the university. And he had not denied himself other sorts of female company when desire drew him to some willing woman who understood that such diversions meant nothing.

But Ariel Harding was not like the women he'd met before, either during the two London seasons forced on him by his mother or the sporadic connections he had formed for himself. She had so far displayed no tendency to flirt or fawn. She had not pouted or preened or cried. What was her game?

In response to some interplay on the stage, Ariel laughed aloud, then turned to look at him and share the joke. Her smile lit her face. Light from the many candles danced in the hazel depths of her eyes. She looked open and honest—and thoroughly delightful. He could detect no scheming shadows in that gaze. An unfamiliar tremor of sensation moved in Alan's chest—as if something had come loose from its moorings for a moment.

He shook his head, shook it off. The prince regent's rich, heavy cuisine did not agree with him, he thought, nor did all these nights in hot, overcrowded rooms where the air was tainted with smoke and perfumes and inane conversation. He needed to get back to his quiet, ordered laboratory, to the company of rational men. If he could only get this ridiculous business of the ghost settled, all would return to normal. He turned toward the stage, his jaw set. When would the damned play be over? He was sick to death of waiting. He wanted to get something done.

The antics of the actors continued, oblivious to Lord Alan Gresham's impatience. Numb with boredom, he made a halfhearted effort to comprehend the story. It seemed to involve a pair of witless young lovers, separated for reasons that he had missed at the beginning of the play. These insurmountable obstacles had, inexplicably, forced the hero to become a pirate in the West Indies. Did anyone in the audience actually believe that a young nobleman could, upon arrival in the islands, immediately gain command of a pirate vessel, Alan wondered? And did they imagine that his crew of bloodthirsty blackguards would tolerate endless maundering laments for his lost Lucinda? The idiot would have been robbed, gutted, and thrown overboard on the first night. And Alan would have very much enjoyed seeing such a scene enacted.

As for Lucinda, her scenes revealed her as precisely the sort of simpering, sniveling female he most despised. Indeed, she epitomized all the weaknesses of the feminine character. She was a slave to emotion, incapable of clear thinking and prey to moods that led her to take actions he found insane. When she determined to disguise herself as a cabin boy and join her hero on his ship, Alan gave up listening. It was beyond absurd. These idiot playgoers would swallow anything. Did they imagine a gently reared young woman would not be immediately found out on a pirate ship? Was it credible that her supposed true love would not recognize her instantly? And did any of these people have the least inkling about the unhappy fate of cabin boys in such company?

When the curtain fell for the interval, Alan was ready to suggest that they leave, returning to question the cast another time. But one look at Ariel's glowing face told him that this plan would not be well received. "Shall I order some refreshment?" he asked resignedly.

"Yes, please," responded Ariel. "Wasn't it cunning, the way they made the waves move around the ship? I haven't seen that before. And did you notice how quickly the backdrops were changed from the London drawing room to the street in the Indies? They must have some new method for hanging them. The ship was rather well done, too, although I think it's the one they have always used for *The Tempest.*"

Alan gazed at her, surprised. He had expected some feminine rhapsodies about the romance of the story and the handsome hero.

"Charles Padgett and Mr. Balfour were there," Ariel continued. "I almost didn't recognize Maria Edgecombe under all the paint and false hair. She was the fortune-teller." She turned her animated gaze on Lord Alan. "Do you think we could have lemonade? I'm not very partial to wine."

He gave the order. Then, watching her looking around the audience, he was moved by curiosity to ask, "What did you think of the story?"

Ariel shrugged. "Passable."

"You did not find it unbelievable?"

"The actress playing Lucinda is not particularly convincing," she conceded.

"But the events, the whole idea. It is quite impossible." He was actually rather interested in her answer, Alan realized.

"It's a story," said Ariel, looking at him as if he had said something odd.

He was about to reply when there was a knock at the door of their box and it opened to reveal two tall, good-looking young men dressed in the height of fashion. "Alan, you sly dog," said one of them. "First we hear you're living at Carlton House, and now we find you've acquired a *chère amie.*"

"Might want to have a haircut though," commented the other, looking him up and down. "Your rig-out is tolerable, but the hair, old son." He shook his impeccably groomed head.

"Do go away," responded Alan.

"Here now! Is that any way to greet your brothers?" said the one who had spoken first.

"Your *older* brothers," added the other. "Show a bit of respect, eh?" He waggled his fingers at Alan in good-natured mockery. "Going to introduce us? Don't worry, we won't try to cut you out. It's past time you set up a—"

"Miss Harding, these are two of my brothers," interrupted Alan. "Lord Sebastian Gresham and Lord Robert Gresham. Pay no attention to them."

"Hold on," objected Sebastian.

"Miss Ariel Harding," Alan finished with a significant glance at his brothers.

"Harding?" said Sebastian. "As in . . . ?"

Ariel was examining their visitors with great interest. They were clearly cut from the same mold as Lord Alan—tall, handsome, broad-shouldered men with auburn hair and blue eyes. Robert was slighter, with a narrower face and paler coloring; his hair was almost red. Sebastian, the largest of the three, had the upright bearing and luxuriant side whiskers that marked him at once as a cavalryman; he looked like a lazy, good-natured lion. But although both the newcomers were far better dressed than Lord Alan and obviously very much at their ease, neither of them possessed his air of calm command, his look of razor-sharp intelligence, or his imperturbability. "Do I call them Lord Robert and Lord Sebastian?" she asked. "Are they younger sons, too?"

Robert goggled at her.

"They are," confirmed Alan, one corner of his lips turning up.

"Some connection of Bess Harding?" asked Lord Sebastian, who was not one to give up on an idea once he had grasped it.

Ariel raised her chin. "I am Bess Harding's daughter," she answered proudly.

"Miss Harding is assisting me in my investigation for the prince," Alan added. "My *confidential* investigation."

Sebastian waved this aside. "Father told us to keep mum about the matter."

"Didn't know Bess Harding had a daughter," Robert said, seeming unable to tear his eyes from Ariel.

"I have been away from London, at Ames's Academy for Young Ladies, for several years," she replied with dignity.

Lord Alan's brothers looked at each other, then at Alan.

"You have mistaken the situation," he told them.

"What situation would that be?" asked Ariel sweetly.

"Oh, come," responded Lord Robert. "Daughter of an actress, that sort of thing."

"What sort of thing?" repeated Ariel in bell-like tones. She fixed Robert with a steady gaze and added, "Precisely?"

Robert coughed. "Er . . ." He glanced at Lord Alan for help, and received a bland stare in return.

"Well?" demanded Ariel.

Robert shifted from one foot to the other. Sebastian grinned, then took a step backward when she looked at him.

"I believe my brothers are surprised to find a female involved in my investigation," suggested Lord Alan.

Ariel turned to him. "Do you?"

"That's it," agreed Sebastian quickly. "Surprised. Why, Alan's always saying that females don't have two thoughts to . . . er . . . that is . . ."

"This is deuced odd," commented Lord Robert. "But then, I should have expected it. Your whole life is deuced odd."

"That depends upon your point of view," said Alan. He raised his head at the sound of a chime. "The play is about to start again. Don't let us keep you from your seats."

"I don't understand you," complained his brother Sebastian.

Alan smiled at him with real warmth. "I know," he said.

Chapter Four

I would like to discuss what you and your brothers were talking about," said Ariel at the end of the play as they waited for the audience to clear out.

"It's of absolutely no consequence," Alan replied.

"I disagree. They thought I was your mistress. Why can't you just say so?"

He threw her a startled look.

"I don't see how we will work together if you persist in treating me like a fool," she continued. "It wastes time. And of course, it is quite annoying, not to mention insulting."

Most uncharacteristically, Alan found himself speechless. "I thought to spare you embarrassment," he answered finally.

"Really?" She raised her eyebrows. "It would have been far less embarrassing if you had simply stated that I was not, instead of circling the subject as if there might be some doubt."

Alan had no answer to this. She was right, of course, but he had never encountered a woman who claimed to share his preference for forthright statements rather than polite evasions.

"We had better settle this matter right at the beginning," Ariel added.

"What 'matter'?"

Ariel took a bit of time to rearrange her diaphanous wrap around her shoulders. "We have made an agreement to aid each other in our investigations. It does not include anything more."

Alan raised one auburn brow. "More?" He was well aware of what she meant, but for some reason he wanted to hear her say it.

She looked directly at him. "I know that men are ruled by their passions," she stated. "You cannot help it, I suppose."

"Indeed?" Oddly piqued, Alan added, "And how did you come by this comprehensive knowledge?"

"My mother was . . . thoroughly conversant with the subject," replied Ariel stiffly.

"Was she?"

His companion's back grew even straighter. "She thought it best to warn me, so that I would not . . . would not be . . . ensnared by a fantasy of love. Or . . . or anything of that nature," she added hurriedly.

"Did she? Well, I am in total agreement with her," commented Alan.

Ariel blinked at him.

"The concept of love is simply a pretty story that people concoct to disguise self-interest and the basic need to perpetuate the race," he added. "It does not, in fact, exist."

He seemed to have her full attention now, he was happy to see.

"And I can assure you that *my* passions are wholly under the governance of my intellect, which is man's particular gift, after all. I have told you—I am a man of science."

"Well," replied Ariel, "I just wanted it to be clear that there will be nothing of that sort between us."

"Commendable. I prefer to be clear."

"And if you should find yourself swayed by the influence of—"

"You need not be concerned about such a contingency. I am swayed by logic, by facts, by concrete evidence—and by nothing else."

She did not look entirely pleased by this assurance, but she nodded. "So we are agreed then. We have a . . . a business arrangement, and nothing more."

"Absolutely."

"Good." She rose, head held high, the skirts of her emerald silk gown rustling around her. "Let us go to the office first." She walked down the steps ahead of him. "I wonder if it's all still the same?" he heard her add in a wistful tone.

Reaching the bottom of the stairs, they walked past the stage and down a long uncarpeted corridor. The wooden walls were unadorned. It was rather dusty. It was a complete contrast to the lavishness of the painted scenery, Alan thought, and even to the backstage areas he had visited once or twice when he was living in London.

Ariel stopped before a half-open door near the end of the hall. "Mr. Balfour?" she said, pushing it farther open. "It's Ariel Harding."

Alan caught up with her in time to see the surprise on the face of the slender man who sat at a shabby desk inside the small cluttered room, the evening's receipts spread out before him.

"Ariel?" he said, as if he couldn't believe it. He rose and held out a hand. "You've grown up. Has it really been that long?"

"I'm afraid it has. This is Lord Alan Gresham."

Watching the man closely, Alan thought he recognized

the name. But the only sign was a flicker in his pale blue eyes, and he couldn't tell what thoughts lay behind it. He examined Balfour, realizing that he was older than he first appeared. The stage makeup he still wore covered lines in his face. And his blond hair was liberally streaked with gray, less noticeable against its paleness. He was a small man, but lithe and wiry; probably much stronger than he looked, Alan concluded.

"Lord Alan is helping me look into my mother's death," Ariel was continuing.

A shadow passed across Balfour's narrow, mobile face.

"He's working for the regent as well," said Ariel.

Implying, Alan thought wryly, that he was working firstly for her.

"Of course you've heard about this haunting at Carlton House."

Balfour nodded, with another flicker in those unrevealing eyes. Alan understood suddenly how difficult it was going to be questioning actors, who were accustomed to counterfeiting feelings of all kinds.

"Mr. Cyrus Balfour is the manager of the theater," said Ariel, turning to Alan. "He is an actor as well, but he oversees everything." She smiled at the smaller man. "My mother used to say that he does all the worrying, so the rest of the cast doesn't have to."

Balfour's face grew shadowed again. "We all miss her like the very devil." He paused. "It was so sudden, so . . . horrible."

"I know." Ariel's smile had faded, and she looked fierce. "I want to talk to you and the others about what happened that night. I *must* discover why she—"

"None of us was there," Balfour protested.

"And about this supposed haunting," Alan put in firmly.

Ariel waved her hand as if this was obviously secondary. "People must know things," she urged. "Someone must have noticed—"

"There was nothing to notice," Balfour interrupted. "Bess was the same as ever." He shook his head. "Chance, fate, an overwhelming despair; I suppose it could happen to any of us at any moment."

Alan eyed him, not sure if this was genuine emotion or acting.

"Well, if it happened to me, I hope someone would try to *do* something about it," declared Ariel. "You will help me, won't you?"

"I don't want it all brought up again," Balfour replied. "Everyone's been nervous as a sack of cats. They're just beginning to calm down."

Alan was about to argue with the man when he realized that Ariel was looking at Balfour with wide, injured eyes, as if she could not believe that he would refuse her this simple request.

The manager shifted uneasily. "You know how it is in a theater. Actors are . . . volatile. The least thing oversets them."

Ariel continued to gaze at him like a startled deer.

"And then the play doesn't go, and the audience stays away . . ." He glanced at her, then looked quickly away and sighed. "Oh, very well. Ask your questions. I suppose the harm has already been done."

Ariel smiled sweetly, and Alan felt a twinge of sympathy for Mr. Balfour. "I knew I could count on you," she said. "Bess always said you were steady as a rock."

He grimaced. "When she was happy with me, she did. But if she didn't get a role she wanted, or if one of the young ones upstaged her . . ." He shrugged expressively.

"Were you in her black books when she died?" asked Alan.

Mr. Balfour turned to look at him. "Just what do you mean by that?" he demanded.

Alan met his irate gaze without wavering. "It would be useful to know if she had quarreled with anyone. Particularly the man in charge of the theater where she performed."

"Are you suggesting—"

"Bess and Mr. Balfour were friends for years and years," explained Ariel, throwing Lord Alan a reproachful look.

Balfour took a deep breath; his fists were clenched.

"I am merely seeking information," replied Alan blandly.

For a moment the tension in the small chamber rose, then the anger seemed to drain out of the manager suddenly; he sat down and hunched over the desk. "No one could draw the audiences like Bess," he said heavily. "See this?" He gestured at the coins and crumpled bills strewn before him. "It would have been twice as much with Bess onstage tonight." Forgetting his makeup, he rubbed a hand over his face, smearing it slightly. When he saw the paint on his palm, he swore. "We were friends, but I had more reasons than that to keep Bess happy."

"Had my mother quarreled with anyone?" said Ariel quietly after a moment.

Balfour sighed. "You know how she was, Ariel. She and Maria were forever sniping at one another. She raked one of the young girls over the coals a month or so ago, and then gave her a silk gown a few days after. There was nothing unusual that I saw."

Ariel nodded somewhat sadly.

"What about outside the theater?" asked Alan. "Had she any . . . that is, were there any particular 'friends' who . . . ?"

"Who was her latest conquest?" put in Ariel without embarrassment, earning a surprised glance from Alan.

"The earl of Dunbrae," answered Balfour matter-of-factly, "gave her a ruby the size of a quail's egg."

Ariel's eyes had narrowed. "I didn't find it in the house. I suppose one of the servants may have . . ." She trailed off.

"She might have hidden it," suggested the theater manager. "Wasn't something you'd just leave lying about, believe me."

Ariel nodded. "Bess and the earl were . . . ?"

"He seemed mad about her—as they all were. And she was leading him a merry dance."

Ariel nodded again, as if this were what she had expected to hear.

Alan remained silent, having been suddenly struck by the notion that he would no doubt be expected to approach the earl, an irascible man thirty years his senior, and attempt to interview him about the death of his mistress. He was having no difficulty, unfortunately, picturing the scene.

"We'll talk to the others," Ariel was saying. "If you should remember anything else . . ."

Balfour shook his head. "Nothing to remember," he replied. When she started to speak again, he waved a hand. "I'll try, I'll try."

"Thank you." She smiled at him, and the manager gave her a wry look in return.

They returned to the dusty corridor and followed it until it took a sharp turn into another, which clearly stretched across the back of the entire building. A series of doors opened off it, and a number of voices could be heard. "You should let me talk to the actors," said Ariel.

"I beg your pardon?"

"You're likely to upset them," she explained. "You did Cyrus, and actors will require an even more delicate touch."

"I am capable of questioning all sorts of people," declared Alan. "My ability to get to the heart of a matter and elicit the facts has been much admired."

"But we want much more than the facts."

"More? There is nothing 'more.'"

"Of course there is. Just let me take the lead," said Ariel.

"And ask nothing about the events at Carlton House, as you did with Balfour?" He shook his head. "I think not. That is why I am here, and I shall certainly question everyone about it."

"It is only because of me that you have the opportunity," she answered. "And I think you might be a little more—"

A head appeared at one of the open doorways along the corridor. "Hullo?"

"Mr. Padgett," said Ariel, sweeping forward to greet the man. "It's Ariel Harding."

The head cocked, then the rest of the figure appeared—a tall, muscular fellow, Alan observed, with a magnificent profile and a leonine mane of pure white hair. His face was handsomely craggy and showed few signs of age, though he must be past fifty.

"Little Ariel?" boomed the newcomer. His voice was deep and resonant, clearly trained to reach the farthest balconies. "My brave and tricksy spirit?" he continued. " 'Thou shalt have the air at freedom.' "

Ariel stood straighter and clasped her hands in front of her like a child making a recitation. " 'Full fathom five thy father lies,' " she intoned. " 'Of his bones are coral made/Those are pearls that were his eyes/Nothing of him that doth fade/But doth suffer a sea-change/Into something rich and strange.' "

"You haven't forgotten! Good, good." The older man turned to Alan as if they had been acquainted for years. "I taught her the whole part of Ariel when she was eight years old. I thought it might go over well—a child as the magician's helper, you know. We were going to suspend her from a cord and let her fly across the stage. Even had the wings made."

"*How* I wanted to do it!" declared Ariel.

"Pluck up the backbone, you were," agreed Padgett. "But Bess didn't like the idea, so it came to nothing in the end." He looked very solemn suddenly. "My condolences, my dear. Awful thing."

"Yes." Ariel paused and swallowed. "This is Lord Alan Gresham," she said then. "He is helping me look into Bess's death. Lord Alan, this is Mr. Charles Padgett. But you will have heard of him, of course."

Padgett preened a bit.

Refusing to be pushed, Alan said, "Will I?"

The older man drew himself up into a magnificent huff.

"We came to talk to you about Bess," Ariel added quickly.

Neatly implying, Alan noticed, that they were consulting him first and foremost, without of course saying so.

Padgett appeared to consider remaining offended, then gave it up for a more congenial role. "Come into my poor premises, and I will do what I can," he replied, gesturing them grandly into the room behind him.

It was a tiny, wildly cluttered chamber, the walls bulging with costumes hung on hooks, the floor crowded by an overstuffed armchair and a mirrored dressing table on which pots and vials and tubes vied for space with scraps of false hair, bits of putty, and a vast litter of personal objects. The disarray, and the closeness of the atmosphere, made Alan take a step back. When Ariel sat down in the armchair, he indicated with a gesture that he would stand. Padgett spread his hands, then took the stool before the vanity. There was barely an inch between his knees and Ariel's, Alan saw. How did the man bear such disorder?

"A sad, sad thing," Padgett intoned. "Poor lovely Bess. We shall not see her like again." He put a hand over his heart and bowed his head.

After a moment, Ariel said, "Did you notice any difference in her? Had anything happened to make her . . . despondent?"

The older man shook his head slowly. "Our lives outside the theater were quite separate, of course. But she seemed the same as ever. There may have been a bit of wrangling now and then." He made an eloquent gesture. "But that is the nature of our profession." He looked at Lord Alan. "We pour out our souls, you know, on the stage. It taxes the nerves, and makes it difficult to tolerate the . . . quirks and foibles of others."

"How difficult?" inquired Alan.

Padgett smiled at him in a kindly way. "We murder one another only on the stage, my dear sir. Naturally, we have our jealousies and romantic mishaps and irritations." He put his hand over his heart again. "We are but human, after all. However, our work gives us a splendid outlet for our humors."

"Not always, apparently," Alan pointed out.

There was a horrified silence.

"There has to be a *reason* she did it," Ariel burst out.

Padgett looked grave. "Dear child, I don't think you will find it here. Bess was admired by most everyone, and even those who had . . . less cordial feelings knew she filled the seats." He looked suddenly shrewd. "Actors don't risk their livelihood."

This was the most honest thing he had said so far, Alan thought.

Ariel was looking at the small patch of floor under her feet. "There must have been some sign," she insisted.

"Bess was simply Bess," Padgett said. "Well, except . . ."

Ariel's head came up. "What?"

The actor shrugged. "This can't have anything to do with her death. It is too long ago."

"Please tell me."

"A year or so ago," he began, then paused. "No, I suppose it's more like two years; I noticed that Bess seemed . . . distracted—as if she had something important on her mind. Our work here at the theater had always been her life, you know. She thought of little else."

He frowned. "It's hard to explain, really. It was an impression, a vague feeling. Before that time, one could feel Bess present in every fiber. Afterward, she wasn't entirely here any longer. She still performed brilliantly, of course. Yet something was missing." He waved a hand in the air. "Perhaps you noticed it yourself, Ariel."

"I saw her only for short visits," she answered quietly. "She had Miss Ames arrange special instruction or expeditions for most of my long holidays. I didn't really have the chance to notice."

Watching her, Alan saw a flicker of hurt in the depths of her hazel eyes.

"Probably, it was nothing," said Padgett cheeringly. "People do change, after all. And I may have been mistaken."

In silent agreement, Alan shifted slightly in the doorway. "Tell me," he said. "If you wished to make it appear—onstage—that an actor was floating above the ground, could it be done?"

The older man swiveled around to look at him.

"Being behind the scenes here, I find myself becoming interested in stagecraft," Alan added.

"Ah." Padgett brightened. "You're thinking of something like the ghost in *Hamlet,* perhaps?"

"A perfect example," he agreed.

The actor was nodding. "It's very hard to place the ghost high off the stage," he declared. "If you use a platform or a harness, they're almost always visible. But you can achieve a fine effect near the ground. You shorten the costume, you see, so that it doesn't reach the floor. Then you put on dead black stockings and make sure the lighting is all upward. The feet just disappear into the shadows and voilà"—he made a dramatic gesture—"the ghost is floating." He beamed.

"Fascinating," replied Alan. "Do you know anything about this supposed haunting at Carlton House?"

Padgett looked startled. "I've heard of it," he replied cautiously.

"No more than that?"

He shook his head, his gaze seemingly riveted on Lord Alan's face.

"Such a trick with the lighting would come in very handy for creating Bess Harding's 'ghost,'" Alan pointed out.

"I haven't been near Carlton House for three months," stated Padgett. He ran a hand through his mane of white hair. "I've never been one of that set. Prinny don't like my politics."

"Can you prove that?" asked Alan.

"Are you calling me a liar, sir?" The actor stood, throwing out his massive chest. "I may not have been born to the nobility, but my word is good."

"Of course it is," soothed Ariel, also rising. "Lord Alan wasn't doubting you. He is merely looking for information."

"Well, I haven't any," answered Padgett truculently.

Ariel moved toward the door of the tiny room. "We must catch Maria before she goes. You will let me know if you remember anything further about Bess?"

The older man took a visible breath. "Anything for you, my dear child," he replied finally. His tone clearly implied that the same did not go for others who might be present.

Ariel gave him a brilliant smile. "Thank you," she said, and urged Lord Alan out into the corridor once again.

"We will never get anywhere if you continually undermine my lines of questioning," Alan protested.

"We will never get anywhere if you antagonize everyone we speak to," she retorted.

"We are not here to engage in amiable chitchat, or to hear useless reminiscences. We must get to the heart of the matter and adhere to the facts."

"But what he said about my mother being different the last two—"

"Moonshine," snapped Alan. "A waste of time."

Ariel gave him an exasperated look. She started to speak, but they had reached a closed door near the end of the hall, and instead she raised her hand and knocked on it.

"Yes?" replied a resonant female voice. The door opened to reveal a tall, statuesque woman with lustrous black hair and a striking, hawklike face. Her dark eyes showed a sharp intelligence as she looked from one to the other of them. She was dressed in street clothes, clearly ready to depart. "Yes?" she said again.

"It's Ariel Harding." She looked more hesitant than before. "How are you?"

"Ariel?" The woman looked her up and down.

"This is Lord Alan Gresham. Lord Alan, this is Maria Edgecombe, the chief actress at the theater here."

Maria gave her a piercing look. "Since your mother died," she amplified. She subjected Lord Alan to a thorough examination. "One of Langford's sons?" she asked.

Alan nodded. This was a woman who knew every man's lineage and his fortune to the penny, he thought.

"Ah." She glanced at Ariel. "You haven't wasted any time. Very sensible, of course, to find yourself a protector at once. However did you manage it? I thought you were immured at some school in the wilds of the country."

"The prince regent has asked Lord Alan to investigate the incidents at Carlton House. I met him when I went there to see . . . what was going on. He is helping me look into Bess's death."

Alan looked at Ariel with some surprise. Her tone was subdued—not deferential, but certainly cautious—quite different from the one she had used with the two actors.

"I see," Maria was saying. "Clever of you."

"Miss Harding is not—" Alan began.

"I wanted to ask you if you had noticed anything that might explain what happened to Bess," Ariel interrupted.

Maria frowned.

"I thought she might have said something, or behaved unusually."

"She was her customary scintillating self," was the acid reply.

"You and she were rivals?" asked Alan.

The actress's dark eyebrows arched as she gave him a thin smile. "Bess Harding and I set each other's backs up the moment we met—which was more years ago than I intend to admit to you. We sparred continually, but it was little more than a habit by this time."

"With her gone, your position at the theater apparently improves," Alan observed.

"My 'position' is as precarious as ever, my lord. Walk out of this room and down to the other end of the corridor, and you will find a line of lovely young women vying to take my place. Already, I'm relegated to playing the queen, the sorceress, even the fortune-teller." She gestured at the pile of false hair that lay on her neat dressing table. "Actually, Bess and I were finding that pursuit by 'time's wingèd chariot' was making us into allies. Grudging allies, I admit. But still . . ." She spread her well-cared-for hands.

"Did you see anything, or hear anything that might explain what . . . what she did?" put in Ariel.

Maria turned to her. "No. But afterward, I saw Clarisse."

"Where has she gone?" Ariel cried.

"I don't know. I gave her a bit of money."

"Who is Clarisse?" asked Alan.

"My mother's dresser and personal attendant," said Ariel.

"Ah." He paused, then added, "This business at Carlton House—can you tell me anything about that?"

Maria gave him a broad, malicious smile. "Can I? Or will I?"

"You know something."

"Know?" She shook her head. "I might have suspicions."

"Of whom?" he asked sharply.

"Whom." She let the word roll on her tongue. "I believe I will let you discover that for yourself, my lord. You seem a man of . . . parts."

"Clarisse gave you no hint of where she was going?" said Ariel.

Maria turned to look at her. The sardonic cast of her expression softened slightly. "If I were you, I would inquire among the émigrés. She would go to her own people."

Ariel nodded. "I should have thought of that. We will get in touch with them right away."

She seemed ready to set off at once, Alan noted. "I ask again," he said. "Of whom are you suspicious?"

"Save your stern looks for the youngsters," answered Maria airily. "I must go. I am expected for supper, and the gentleman must be kept waiting just the proper amount of time. And no longer." She moved toward the door.

Alan blocked it.

"What will you do, beat me?" wondered Maria mockingly. "Talk to the youngsters, I tell you."

"What youngsters? Who are you talking about?"

"The young actors," responded Ariel rather absently. "We can catch some of them in the tiring room." She also moved toward the open doorway.

Confronted by both women, Alan finally stepped aside. He could not, after all, shake the information out of Maria, he acknowledged with regret. "I'll call upon you again," he assured her.

Maria clasped both hands to her splendid bosom. "Oh,

my lord," she cooed. Then, with a laugh, she slipped past him and away.

"Irritating woman," muttered Alan.

"This way," said Ariel, starting back along the corridor the way they had come.

"Where are we going now?" he demanded.

"To talk with the younger actors. I don't know them, but my connection to Bess should be a sufficient introduction."

Still feeling disgruntled, he strode along beside her.

"You know, I have been thinking," Ariel went on.

"Commendable," he muttered under his breath.

"No matter what we do, everyone is going to assume I'm your mistress," she said.

He paused in the middle of the corridor and looked down at her.

She shrugged. "They will. It can't be helped."

"We will disabuse them of the notion," he responded.

"Mmm. Well, I was thinking," she repeated. "Since we have such a clear agreement between ourselves, and know that nothing of that sort can occur, perhaps we should just let them think so."

"I beg your pardon?"

"Then I could go about with you—to Carlton House and other places—quite freely. No one would question it or suspect our real purpose." She gazed along the empty corridor.

"Out of the question," he said.

She raised her eyes to his face. "Why?"

"You seem to be forgetting an important point."

Ariel frowned a little and continued to look inquiring.

"Your future," he explained impatiently. "Once this is over, your reputation would be ruined."

"Oh." She waved a hand. "I have no good name to preserve," she informed him. "I am Bess Harding's daughter."

Her tone seemed a mixture of resignation and pride

and a certain forlorn stoicism. Unexpectedly, Alan felt protective. "What does that signify?" he objected.

She simply looked at him.

"I don't see that it need taint your life."

Ariel's hazel eyes flared with indignation. "I didn't say tainted! I would never say that. I am simply . . . not like other people."

He started to speak.

"We are wasting time," said Ariel, starting to walk again. "My idea is a good one. We shall use it when necessary."

He came up with her in one long stride. "No," he said.

"Why must you always disagree with me?" she demanded. "I am very well able to—"

Alan caught her upper arm and spun her around to face him. She was lighter than he had allowed for, and the force of his grasp caused them to collide at the center of the hallway.

Ariel let out a startled, "Oh."

He had meant simply to correct her muddled thinking once and for all, but as in their very first encounter, her breasts pressed softly, tantalizingly, against him. Light danced in the pools of her eyes, and her extraordinary lips were slightly parted. Before he could think, Alan bent his head and took those lips for his own.

They were like rose petals, only warm and possessed of a vitality that sent a charge like electricity through his whole body. He had to put his arms around her and pull her even closer. He let his mouth move on hers. She was stiff at first, but then he felt her lips soften and yield to his. Her body loosened and gave in to his embrace. Desire seared Alan's veins like lava, compelling, primal. There was nothing in the world he wanted but her.

Then reason intervened like a sledgehammer. Shocked by his impulsive action, Alan jerked backward. Ariel looked dazed; she swayed a little on her feet, and he was forced to support her for a moment. Then he let his arm drop and stepped back. "I beg your pardon," he said.

She took a deep breath.

"I don't know what possessed me." He paused. For the appalling fact was that he didn't know. He hadn't intended to kiss her. On the contrary, he had been quite thankful when she had set firm boundaries on their relationship. The last thing he wanted was female simpering and sighing complicating his investigation.

So *why* had he kissed her, he demanded of himself? There was a rational reason for everything; there must be one for this. He looked down at her flushed face—the wide hazel eyes, the beautifully sculpted lips. Beneath her emerald-green gown, her breasts rose and fell rather rapidly.

She had a number of physical attractions, which he had noticed from the first, Alan reminded himself. And he had responded to them without conscious volition. This was not beyond the realm of reason, but it was unacceptable. It had to be stopped. Of course, it could be. Now that he was aware of the tendency, he would repress it. Iron resolve stiffened his back. "You may rest assured that such a thing will never happen again," he said. "Please accept my apologies."

"Apologies," repeated Ariel breathlessly.

"Exactly."

"I—"

"What's this, then?" put in a mocking voice from behind Ariel. "An assignation backstage? Sneakin' about, are we? Dodgin' an irate father, or a husband, perhaps? Here, all of you, come and have a look at this."

Ariel and Alan faced the end of the corridor. They watched it fill with a group of young men and women, some of them recognizable from the play they had seen.

"It's coming out of the woodwork they are," said the one who had spoken first, obviously an Irishman.

Alan saw Ariel take another deep breath.

"Perhaps we'll begin chargin' a fee for use of the premises," continued the young actor. "What about it, lads? Aren't we owed as much?"

There was general laughter and calls of agreement from the group.

Ariel cleared her throat. "I am Ariel Harding," she said when it was quieter. "Bess Harding's daughter. This is Lord Alan Gresham. We've come to talk with you about Bess's death, and also about what is going on at Carlton House. I'm sure you've heard about that."

The members of the group exchanged glances.

"I hope you will help us," she finished.

There was a brief silence. She had stated their mission much better in earlier conversations, Alan thought. She was clearly shaken by his behavioral lapse. He found this idea surprisingly unsettling.

"Help you how?" demanded one of the actresses then. "And what does it matter? No one cares about people like us."

"The prince has asked Lord Alan to help," replied Ariel. "And he has put men at his disposal."

"To rid his house of the ghost," retorted the Irishman. "That's all Prinny wants." His green eyes danced with wicked mirth. "And he may not find that so easy."

"I want to find out what happened to my mother, and why," answered Ariel. "It has nothing to do with the prince."

Members of the group looked at one another again.

"What do you want from us?" asked the Irishman.

"Anything you remember. Any hint of what Bess was thinking. The smallest thing might help, Mr. . . ."

"Heany's my name. Michael Heany."

Ariel smiled at him.

After a moment, he introduced the others. It seemed that he was their spokesman. "We all admired Bess Harding," he told Ariel. "Not that we didn't have our troubles with her now and then."

Two of the young women laughed nervously.

"But they always passed away like a summer storm," he went on. "In the end, she was a generous soul, and a great actress as well."

Ariel's eyes filmed with tears.

"We'll not be letting her memory die like a snuffed candle," Michael Heany added. "Not while there's anything we can do."

"And just what are you doing?" asked Alan.

The young actor flicked him a glance. Some of the others moved uneasily or looked at the floor. "A lord, is it?" Michael replied. "What do you care for Bess Harding? You'll just do whatever his corpulent highness asks."

"I care about the truth," snapped Alan, stung by this characterization.

The other man sneered.

"Is there anything you can tell us?" Ariel interposed. "Please."

Alan watched the group's faces soften somewhat. And after a moment, they crowded forward and began to offer Ariel opinions and impressions. Mainly useless, Alan thought as his trained mind began to catalog each remark and file it away, but he felt admiration, nonetheless, for the way she had won them over.

The silence in the carriage as they drove away from the theater was thick and awkward. Ariel sat as far from him as it was possible to be in the small space and as immovable as a pale image in the dim light. "The younger actors said a great deal, but very little of it was to the purpose," Alan attempted after a while.

Ariel made a noncommittal sound, barely audible over the clatter of the hack's wheels on the cobblestones.

"Still, it was important to interview them," he added.

Taking a deep breath, she turned toward him. "Lord Alan," she said.

He waited, and when she didn't continue, said, "Yes?"

She took another breath, clasping her hands before her. "My mother always warned me that if I were open and friendly with a man, he would take advantage of the opportunity and attempt to seduce and ruin me," she said in a rush.

Alan sat back, startled by this forthrightness.

"She said men would pay no attention even if I told them very clearly that I wanted no such thing."

He began to protest, but she cut him off.

"Apparently, she was right," Ariel concluded. "I had thought we agreed ours was not that sort of relationship."

"I apologized." He spoke a bit curtly. He was not used to being reprimanded by anyone, let alone a chit of a girl. And it galled him tremendously to be in the wrong in this matter.

"Bess said apologies and pretended remorse are just a ruse to lull one's suspicions," she added. "Because all men care about is satisfying their physical urges."

"Your mother was a veritable fount of wisdom," he muttered.

"I had thought I made it very clear from my manner that we have a purely business arrangment," Ariel went on a trifle pompously.

"Oh, yes? Such as when you suggested that you pretend to be my mistress?"

She faltered slightly, then said, "I meant only that we should use society's prejudices to further our investigation. As you knew quite well."

"*Your* investigation," he countered. "I can't see that it would be any help in mine."

"I see." She gazed out the window, away from him. "So, this is the end, then."

"What?"

"We cannot go on with this, under the circumstances."

She sounded disappointed, and a bit forlorn. For some reason, her tone stung Alan sharply. "The circumstances," he repeated, "do not warrant such a conclusion. You are putting far too much weight on a . . . a momentary aberration."

"Aberration?" she echoed.

"Yes, a unique deviation from the normal—"

"I know what the word means," she retorted. "But my mother always said that it *is* normal for—"

"Do spare me any further homilies from Bess Harding!"

There was a charged silence. Alan struggled to regain his customary measured calm, which he had somehow lost yet again in the presence of this unexpected girl.

"No doubt your mother had reasons for her opinion," he went on finally. "However, her observations apply to a limited group of men, of which I am not a member. You may be assured that the unfortunate incident of today will not recur."

"But she said—"

"I have told you, she was mistaken."

The hack pulled up before Ariel's house. She hesitated, looking at him. "You are suggesting that we continue the investigation, on the same terms as before?" she asked.

"I said I would find your mother's former servants," he reminded her. "I keep my word."

Ariel continued to gaze at him. He couldn't make out her features, but he gained the impression that she was debating with herself. "And there will be no more—"

"I have said there won't," he snapped.

The silence lengthened once again until the driver leaned down from his high seat and said, "Anything wrong, guv? This is the h'address you gave me."

Ariel opened the coach door and started to climb out. "Very well," she said, "as long as that is quite clear." She jumped down to the cobbles before Alan could move to assist her.

He leaned out the carriage door, wanting to say something further. Nothing occurred to him, however. His only thought was that the empty house looked very dark and forbidding. "Will you be all right in there?" he asked.

"Perfectly," was the wary reply. Ariel walked quickly to the front door, unlocked it, and disappeared inside. The latch clicked decisively into place behind her.

"Bad luck, guv," commented the driver.

Alan didn't bother to correct his assumption that he had been trying to seduce Ariel. He merely told the man to take him to Carlton House, then sank back against the cushions to contemplate the events of the evening and to analyze yet again his loss of control. Aberration was indeed the word for it, he thought. He had been subject to some intrusion of emotion, some flash of irrationality. And the cause was quite clear. His current mode of life, with its constant exposure to the prince regent and his deplorable set of friends, was enough to unbalance anyone. Sir Isaac Newton, Copernicus himself, would have found it impossible to think clearly in such chaos, he concluded. But now he was forewarned. He would be on his guard, and no such thing would happen again. Very pleased with this chain of reasoning, Alan relaxed. He refrained from examining the pleasure he felt in knowing that he would see Ariel Harding again soon.

Chapter Five

❖

The following morning, Ariel sat in the front parlor of a house that seemed, today, quite empty and echoing. She had risen early and sat down directly after breakfast to make a list of all the things that *must* be done. But she had gotten no further than item one before breaking off to stare into space, the pen forgotten in lax fingers.

"Do you think I am making a mistake?" she asked Prospero, who sat beside her. The cat had materialized in his mysterious fashion just as she was assembling her morning meal and urgently requested a share. He was now indulging in a postprandial wash on the sofa cushion.

"Lord Alan has assured me that nothing of that sort will happen again," Ariel told him.

Prospero raised his head and met her gaze squarely with his great golden eyes.

"Even though Bess said that is all men care about," Ariel added.

Prospero's stare was unwavering.

"Which of them do you think is right?"

Prospero blinked, then he rolled over on his back, seeming to savor the softness of the sofa cushion. He stretched, his back legs splayed into the air, his front paws reaching for the sofa's armrest, into which he sank his claws.

"You are not being very helpful," Ariel said.

He paused, looking surprised.

"Yes, I know you are only a cat," she responded. "And I imagine you take ruthless advantage of every female you encounter. I have no one to rely on but myself in this matter; I see that."

The cat flexed his claws in the armrest.

"The trouble is, I do not wish to break off contact with him." Ariel frowned. "I know that is what my mother would advise, but I need his help in my investigations." She bit her lower lip. "I shall treat him as Melisande did Franco in *The Grandee's Daughter*. He soon learned his lesson in that play," she said with satisfaction.

Prospero sat up with an agile twist and resumed grooming his blue-gray fur.

"I am quite capable of carrying it off," Ariel informed him.

He didn't even pause.

"I am," she insisted. But in the face of his seeming skepticism, she had to admit one flaw in her plan. The trouble was, she could not get the kiss out of her mind. It kept coming back to her—the feel of Lord Alan's lips upon hers, the strength of his arms around her, the deeply unsettling mixture of consternation and delicious surrender that had engulfed her. He had left her breathless and dizzy. She had not been at all repelled. On the contrary. And now she found herself wondering what it would have been like if the kiss had gone on a little longer, if it had turned into something even more . . .

Ariel shook her head. In all her lecturing, Bess had never once suggested such a reaction. She had insisted that there were only two choices with men—they were to be avoided, or they were to be used. Let them get the upper hand for an instant, and you were lost.

A tremor shook Ariel. Was she lost? Then, just as quickly, she shook it off. She had formed a mutually advantageous partnership with Lord Alan, she reminded herself. Each of them was contributing. Perhaps they were making use of each other. And when their task had been accomplished, the connection would be severed. He was a duke's son.

She was very clear on all these things, Ariel told herself as she turned back to her list. "There will be no more kisses," she told Prospero firmly. But when she looked, she found the cat was gone.

In another, far more fashionable part of London, Lord Alan Gresham was being admitted to an elegant stone town house that occupied one entire side of a broad square. Although it was much too early for a morning call, he strolled through the open door with easy confidence, justified when the dauntingly correct butler greeted him warmly by name. "We so rarely see you in London, my lord," he added.

Alan acknowledged this with a nod. "Is my mother in the drawing room?"

"In her private parlor, my lord. I believe she is writing letters."

"To James and Randolph, I suppose," he replied, referring to two of his brothers.

"No doubt, my lord," agreed the butler.

Alan climbed the stairs, turned at the landing, and continued upward. James captained a navy ship currently cruising tropical seas. Randolph was a churchman holding a living in the far north of England. His mother kept in close communication with both through the mails.

Near the end of a wide corridor, Alan knocked on a

paneled door and was bade enter. He turned the knob and stepped into the small, exquisite room where his mother spent her private hours. Striped paper of cream and deep green was accented by a touch of gilt; the draperies and carpet were the same dark green, and the chamber was made unique by a collection of odd items from around the world, gathered during various family members' travels. An arrangement of six small portraits dominated one wall—the Gresham brothers, each painted at the age of five years. Alan cast the pictures a slightly jaundiced glance as he moved forward to kiss his mother's cheek.

One look at Adele Gresham, duchess of Langford, made it immediately apparent where the red hair came from in the family. Her fashionably dressed locks were of a rich deep color between chestnut and strawberry, only very lightly touched with gray. She was a tall woman, rather angular, with arching brows and an aquiline nose. In combination with her direct, discerning gaze, these features led many to conclude that she was self-absorbed and snobbish. And her inability to tolerate fools and poseurs added to this reputation. She had grown up as a great beauty, a great heiress, and child of a great noble family. She had married suitably, dutifully, and been fortunate enough to find love in her marriage. She was a woman of immense dignity and presence, but beneath all this, she also had a great heart, and ample room in it for her most eccentric, unpersuadable son.

"So, you have come to see me at last," she said, looking him over carefully but making no comment on his plain garments. "And after only two weeks in London. Fancy that."

"We have met at a number of gatherings," was the mild reply.

"Of course. And we could have nothing to say to one another that could not be said publicly at an evening party. I suppose you want something, and that is why you have come?"

Accustomed to his mother's arch manner, Alan merely smiled. "What news from James and Randolph?" he asked.

Her expression softened. "Nothing from James in two months, except that."

Following her pointing finger, Alan observed a wooden carving in the shape of a small, squat human figure with a large head. "Something from the islands? Why do you have it facing the wall?"

His mother grimaced. "See for yourself."

Stretching out an arm, Alan turned the figure, and saw that it possessed greatly exaggerated male organs in a highly visible state. Indeed, it was difficult to observe anything else about the figure, one's attention was so immediately riveted. He began to laugh.

"Very funny," said the duchess dryly. "Unless the package happens to arrive when one has morning callers, and one opens it in front of two very stuffy women and their seventeen-year-old daughters."

"You should have known better, with a packet from James," answered Alan, still laughing.

She nodded. "So I should. It is a mistake I shall never repeat." Her lips twitched very slightly. "But who knows what effect the incident may have on those two young girls' lives?"

"For shame!" Alan said with a laugh.

"You know my views on the education of females," was the severe reply. "Keeping them in total ignorance is simply a guarantee that—"

He held up a defensive hand. "I know, I know."

"I shall never understand why the Good Lord chose not to bless me with daughters," she added.

"Too frightened of the result, I imagine," teased Alan.

The duchess gave him a mock haughty look. "What *do* you want?" she demanded.

"Some servants," he responded. "Two, I think. An older woman to do some plain cooking and a housemaid of some kind, to answer the door and that sort of thing."

"I thought you were staying at Carlton House," said his mother, surprised by the request.

"I am. They are for a . . . friend." The difficult part was coming up, thought Alan, but the knowledge that Ariel Harding was living all alone in that dark house had been preying on his mind.

The duchess was observing him speculatively. "The 'friend' whom Robert and Sebastian encountered at the playhouse?"

It had been too much to hope that she wouldn't have heard. "Robert and Sebastian have nothing to do but gossip," he complained. "If they took up some useful profession—"

"You are hard on your brothers," interrupted his mother, who watched his face carefully as she voiced this old objection.

"I have no quarrel with James and Randolph," he replied. "They are doing something with their lives. And I suppose Nathaniel has duties as the eldest which fill his days. But Sebastian wastes his time playing the rake and grooming his mustaches, and as for Robert—"

"Not everyone has your interests and ambitions," she put in. "And I am not going to forget my question in an argument we have repeated many times before. Are the servants for this girl?" She waited for the answer with a good deal of concern hidden behind an impassive expression. Adele had always felt that Alan, whose whole soul had been taken up by his work, would be in grave danger should he ever become seriously susceptible to the opposite sex.

"She is the daughter of this dead actress," said Alan stiffly. "She is not my mistress, as Robert and Sebastian undoubtedly told you. She has been of some help with my inquiries, and I am concerned about her. That is all."

"Concerned," echoed his mother.

"She is fresh from the schoolroom and alone in the world," he continued. "Her mother's staff has abandoned the house where she lives, and I don't believe she has any idea how to hire servants. You have scores of them. I'm sure you can spare two."

"I have exactly the number of servants necessary for running my household," said the duchess dryly. But she had already determined to grant his request. It would give her an opportunity to discover whether this young woman, so "alone in the world," was planning to ensnare Alan. He would not be like Sebastian, she knew, managing an affair of the heart with discretion and ending it with no great ill feeling on either side. Alan would take it all very hard. She did not intend to allow some theatrical creature to hurt him and perhaps spoil him forever for marriage and a family. "I suppose I can spare a housemaid," she added grudgingly. "I have no trained cooks at hand, but I'll find someone who knows her way about the kitchen." She already knew precisely who she would send.

"I knew I could count on you," responded Alan warmly.

"Indeed," said his mother. He could count on her to see that he didn't make a fool of himself, she thought. As he rose from his chair, she added, "Now that you have got what you wanted, you are going, I suppose?"

"I have no time to spare. I must clear up this matter at Carlton House so that I can return to my work."

This was a good sign, thought Adele. He was not so besotted that his preoccupation with his work had changed. "How is your investigation going?" she asked.

"Passably," he answered. "I expect I shall have the answer soon."

"Splendid." Possibly she was making too much of this girl, Adele thought. She would know once she had met

her. Nothing had ever diverted her maddening youngest
son from his obsession with science.

"I'll leave this matter in your hands then," he added.

The duchess nodded, pleased with the relief in his
voice. "Think no more about it."

He bent to kiss her cheek as he took his leave, happy
to dismiss one item from his mind and move on to the
next. As soon as he returned to Carlton House, he would
request reports from the men searching for Bess Harding's servants. He needed to find someone to send into
the French émigré community. And perhaps a new man
more familiar with the network of stable owners and
coachmen; he wasn't satisfied with the information from
that quarter. It wouldn't be long before he had some information for Ariel, he thought with satisfaction. He
wondered how thankful she would be. A vivid recollection of the soft surrender of her lips intruded suddenly,
and he suppressed it. There were things to be attended
to, facts to be marshaled and interpreted. "Thank you,
Mother," he said, turning toward the door.

"You're welcome," she said to his back, adding, "I
think," only after the door had closed.

Late that afternoon, just as Ariel had returned from
the market square with some bundles of provisions, she
heard a commotion in the street outside the house and
went to the kitchen window to see what it was. From this
basement vantage point, she could see only the wheels of
the carriages—there were two of them stopped in front of
the house—and the legs and feet of what seemed to be a
crowd of people. However, the wheels were painted
golden yellow, with an intricate design picked out in dark
blue, and the shoes and articles of clothing she glimpsed
were all of the finest quality. "Do you think it is some
friend of my mother's?" she asked Prospero, who had

been carefully observing the foodstuffs as she unpacked them.

An authoritative knock sounded on the front door. Ariel brushed at her skirts, regretting that she had put on one of her own dowdy dresses this morning, and hurried up the stairs. She discovered a liveried footman standing on her doorstep. He was so tall that she had to lean her head back to look at his face. "Miss Harding, if you please," he said, managing to imply disapproval of the entire neighborhood in those few simple words.

"I am Miss Harding," she replied with a touch of defiance.

The footman looked scandalized, and somewhat at a loss.

"Thank you, William," put in a cultivated female voice. The footman's broad shoulders moved aside, and Ariel found herself facing a tall, red-haired woman. "I am Adele Gresham. How do you do?"

Instinctively, Ariel dropped a small curtsy. The woman's manner reminded her all too vividly of her school's headmistress, Miss Ames. Then she registered the name. "Gresham?" she repeated.

"May we come in?"

Too surprised to do anything else, Ariel stepped back, and what seemed like a whole troop of people entered the small entryway of her house.

"A fine old place," commented the duchess, surveying the carved panels and banister. "I suppose the drawing room is on this floor, rather than upstairs?"

Ariel indicated the door on the left. Her house was indeed too old to have been designed with a large withdrawing room on an upper floor. The biggest chamber, and the one her mother had used for receiving guests, was right next to the entryway.

Adele Gresham swept into it. Ariel didn't see her give any sort of signal, but none of the others followed. Feeling a bit apprehensive, she joined the older woman.

"A pleasant room," said the duchess. She sank gracefully into one of the satin-covered armchairs that flanked the fireplace. "You haven't overwhelmed it with modern furnishings. It's best to let the old lines show, isn't it?" She nodded at the modest curtains on the small mullioned windows and the trestle table against the far wall.

"My mother chose everything," replied Ariel. She remained standing in the middle of the room.

"Ah." The girl was not precisely what she had expected, the duchess thought. Robert had described a sophisticated beauty in jewels and silk. Instead, she found a schoolgirl who looked braced for a reprimand. The discrepancy made the duchess impatient. She disliked puzzles. "I've brought you some servants," she stated. "A housemaid and a sort of cook/housekeeper."

Ariel stared at her.

"I say that because Hannah is rather more than a cook. If you have errands and that sort of thing, be sure to ask Ellen."

"Why?" blurted Ariel.

"It is just more fitting. Hannah is actually—"

"No, I mean, why have you brought me servants?"

The duchess's natural forthrightness surfaced once more. "Alan asked me to," she answered.

"Lord Alan told you . . . he asked you . . ."

"He said you had no staff for the house. He was concerned." Observing the younger woman very closely, Adele remained undecided. She was the daughter of an actress, of course, and so she might be putting on a very good semblance of surprise and innocence. But if so, it was really remarkable. "Are you going on the stage yourself?" she couldn't help asking.

"What?" Ariel struggled to get her bearings. "No. I . . . I never had any talent for acting."

"Ah. That must have disappointed your mother."

"No, she was very glad." This conversation was absurd, she thought, making another effort to take control of it. "Who . . . ?"

"Glad?" The duchess raised her arching brows even farther. "Why, glad?"

Ariel pressed her lips together, letting silence interrupt their headlong exchange. "She didn't want me associated with the theater in any way," she answered finally. "If I had had her gift, it would have been too tempting. Who are you?"

"Adele Gresham," her visitor repeated. "Alan's mother."

Ariel continued to stand in the center of the room. "And he asked you to bring me servants?"

"To find you two women to help," was the reply.

"How dare he do such a thing!" exploded Ariel. "It was none of his business."

The duchess blinked and sat back slightly.

"I am not some sort of . . . of charity case to be discussed and passed along for good works! I'm not a child or an idiot, to have arrangements made behind my back as if I was not capable of taking care of things myself."

The duchess observed her with greater interest.

"Thank you very much for coming," finished Ariel. "It was kind of you. But I shan't be needing your help. I hope you didn't take much trouble over it." She moved toward the door of the room, signaling that the visit was over.

Adele didn't move. "Do sit down," she said.

Ariel looked at her.

"You need some staff," continued the older woman. With an almost imperceptible motion of her head, she indicated the film of dust on the table and the polished wood floor.

Ariel flushed. "I shall hire some servants," she said.

"Where?"

"I . . . there are agencies." She paused. "Aren't there?"

The duchess nodded. "I must warn you, however, that the best ones may be somewhat dubious. They are not accustomed to dealing with a girl of your age."

"They will deal with me if I can pay fair wages," retorted Ariel.

"Yes. But they may try to palm off untrained or unsatisfactory servants on you. You will need to watch for that."

She considered this.

"It would be much easier simply to take Hannah and Ellen, for a while at least."

"Why should you want to help me?" Ariel demanded.

"I didn't, when I came," was the surprisingly straightforward reply. "But you aren't what I expected."

Ariel stood straighter. "Your other sons told you about me," she concluded.

"They told me something," Adele agreed.

"They don't know anything about it!"

"No?"

"Lord Alan is helping me look into my mother's death. That is all."

"Ah." The duchess's keen gaze had scarcely wavered. "Won't you sit down? It's wearisome looking up this way."

Flushing a bit again, Ariel hesitated, then went to sit opposite her visitor.

"It was terrible, what happened to your mother. Please accept my sympathy."

Confused, Ariel glanced at her, then away.

"You were away at school?"

"Yes."

"Where?"

Ariel threw her another quick glance. "Ames's Academy for Young Ladies. In the north."

"I've heard of it. Quite a distance for you to travel. I would have thought a school nearer London . . ."

"Why are you here?" But even as she asked, the answer came to Ariel. "You wanted to see what I was like. You think I am an adventuress out to trap Lord Alan."

The duchess merely raised her brows.

"Well, I'm not!"

It was the truth, Adele thought, as far as this girl could see it.

"So you can go. You don't have to worry."

She wasn't worried, or not in the way she had been. The duchess thought a moment. Perhaps she was more worried than ever.

Ariel stood again.

"Why not let Hannah and Ellen help you until you can hire your own staff?" Adele suggested. "That way, you can take as long as you like and find really good servants."

"Have you brought them here to spy on me?" asked Ariel.

The child was far too intelligent, thought the duchess. This really was an unfortunate situation.

"All right. Let them," declared Ariel defiantly. "There is nothing wrong for them to see. I'll show you. But I shall pay their wages!"

"Of course," replied Adele much more quietly.

Ariel bit her bottom lip.

"Come, I'll introduce you," added the duchess, rising.

Ariel stepped to the door of the room and opened it. In her entryway, she found two footmen, an older woman, and a dark-haired girl who was sitting on the steps of the central staircase and scratching the stomach of Prospero, who sprawled beside her in wanton feline contentment.

At her appearance, the girl jumped up, causing the cat to leap to his feet and race upstairs. The footmen stood a bit straighter. The older woman simply looked at her.

"Hannah and Ellen, come in," said the duchess's voice from behind her.

They complied, leaving the door open.

"Miss Harding, this is Hannah Enderby. She has been with me for a number of years and will make you a superior housekeeper."

Not certain what to do, Ariel nodded. Hannah didn't curtsy, for which she was rather grateful.

"This is Ellen Jones, who has been well trained as a housemaid."

The dark-haired girl did curtsy, saying, "Hello, miss," in a soft Welsh accent.

"I think you'll find them completely satisfactory," concluded the duchess.

"Yes, thank you." Hannah had a watchful air, noted Ariel. She wondered how much the duchess had told her.

"I must be going." Adele began to pull on her gloves and moved into the entryway. One of the footmen opened the front door, while the other went out to the waiting carriage.

Ariel stood looking up at the older woman. "Thank you," she said, somewhat grudgingly.

"We shall see," replied the duchess with a small smile. Giving Ariel a nod, she went out.

An awkward silence fell in the front parlor.

"Perhaps you'll show us the house, miss," Hannah suggested.

"Of course." She wasn't going to be intimidated, Ariel thought. Let her watch; there was nothing to be seen. She squared her shoulders. "We'll start in the kitchen," she said.

Chapter Six

———— ❖ ————

When Lord Alan Gresham called at Ariel's house a few days later, he was pleased to be admitted by a neat housemaid and made to wait while she inquired whether Ariel would receive him. This was better, he thought as he was ushered into the reception room. Ariel must be far more comfortable. And it would be much easier to keep their interactions commonplace and correct now that the normal amenities of existence were back in place.

Alan liked order. He appreciated routine. They gave one the space to theorize and experiment; they left the mind free to soar. Nothing was more distracting to the higher mental processes than . . . A sound from the hall broke this train of thought, and in the next moment Ariel entered the room.

She looked a bit flustered. Tendrils of her glossy brown hair had escaped a knot at the back and framed her face in wisps. Her skin glowed even more vibrantly than usual, and there was a smudge of ink on her left forefinger. She wore one of her schoolgirl dresses again, a little creased. Looking conscious of his scrutiny, she smoothed it and said, "We were inventorying the linen."

Alan felt his mood of calm satisfaction waver and shift. Like light hitting water, he mused, and refracting, diffusing from its straight, focused path. The very air in the room seemed to shimmer and settle into a new configuration. The color spectrum moved a point up the scale.

He shook his head and blinked. What was this twaddle? How had it gotten into his brain? He didn't think such things. He frowned at Ariel. She was doing it again. Somehow, her mere presence in a room could disrupt the atmosphere. Something about the nature of her personality, he supposed, and its scattered energies. Nothing was more distracting to the higher mental processes than this young woman.

"Your mother's dresser, Clarisse Duchamps, has been found," he told her a bit curtly. "She is staying with an émigré family in Kensington."

Ariel's expression sharpened and her hazel eyes lit. "We must go and see her at once," she said.

"I have made arrangements to call there later this morning."

"Did you tell her we were coming?" Dismay tinged Ariel's voice.

"She won't run away again," Alan assured her. "She has no reason to, and in any case, the house is being watched."

"You shouldn't have given her time," she said.

"Time for what?" he asked, puzzled.

"To make up something."

"Make up? What do you mean? If she tries to lie, I shall—"

Ariel brushed this aside impatiently. "She'll be sitting there concocting a marvelous story in which she is the most important character," she said. "Clarisse always wanted to be an actress herself, but she is only good offstage."

"Whatever theatrics she indulges in—"

"It just would have been better to catch her unawares," Ariel interrupted. "But it can't be helped now."

Was she actually offering to forgive him for a lapse in judgment, as her tone implied? Alan wondered. Did she still imagine that she could conduct an investigation better than he? "Miss Duchamps is not some sort of criminal that we are taking in charge," he pointed out, rather mildly.

She looked surprised.

"To give her time to order her thoughts—"

A spurt of laughter escaped Ariel.

Alan merely raised his brows and waited.

"I don't think Clarisse has ever made an attempt to order her thoughts," she told him.

"Indeed? A typical female, then."

She looked at him.

He had expected a heated reply, but none was forthcoming. Ariel Harding was not a typical female, he conceded.

"Shall we go?"

Deliberately, he slipped his pocket watch from his waistcoat pocket. He was in control of this outing. "It is approximately twenty minutes by coach, allowing for some congestion in the streets. We should leave here in fourteen minutes in order to be on time for our appointment."

Ariel raised her eyes from the watch, then bit her lower lip.

"Ample time," he finished, snapping the watch shut. "Perhaps you should tell your maid to get ready."

"For what?"

"To accompany you," he said.

"Oh." She appeared to contemplate the idea.

"The whole point of getting you servants was to—"

"Without consulting me," she broke in as if reminded of a grievance. "Giving me no warning. Simply a duchess on my doorstep all of a sudden. How would you like to be treated in such a way?"

"Duchess," he echoed.

"She wanted a look at me," accused Ariel. "To see if I am a scheming creature who intends to—" She stopped abruptly and flushed.

"My mother brought the servants herself," said Lord Alan, to confirm what she had implied. He hadn't expected this.

Ariel nodded. "Of course they are very good ones," she added stiffly. "Better than I could have hired myself, I suppose. Ellen is a most superior housemaid. But Hannah doesn't really belong in a kitchen. She is far too—"

"Hannah?" interjected Lord Alan rather loudly. He experienced a sliding sensation, as if he had stepped onto what looked like solid ground, and found loose gravel under his feet, carrying him in a direction he did not at all want to go.

Ariel gazed at him.

This was all getting much more complicated than he had expected. It was always this way with people, he thought. They couldn't be predicted; they couldn't be counted upon to remain where they were put or to act as one planned they would. He strongly preferred the reliable elements in his laboratory. If one put an experiment in train, it followed logical, observable steps. The outcome might not be precisely set, but the variables were all under one's control. Pieces of equipment did not go careening off on their own to begin some entirely different operation. Beams of light did not suddenly turn right around and dazzle one's vision. "Perhaps we should be on our way," he said, still a bit loudly, he realized.

Ariel's eyes had remained on his face. "It hasn't been fourteen minutes," she pointed out.

"Nonetheless." He rose.

"Won't we be too early?" wondered Ariel, curiosity clear in her face.

"I'll wait for you outside," he responded, starting for the door.

"Hannah," she murmured to his retreating back. "What is it about Hannah?"

Half an hour later, with Ellen occupying the forward seat of the carriage, they pulled up before a plain cottage on the edge of Kensington. It was surrounded by a white picket fence over which sprawled the branches of a climbing rose. "Clarisse is staying *here*?" wondered Ariel.

Lord Alan nodded. "The house is owned by one Armand Delon, who tutors young people in French and deportment. He lives here with his wife and three children."

Ariel shook her head.

"What?" he asked.

"I can't imagine Clarisse in such a household," she said.

"I suppose she found it a refuge."

"Umm."

They passed through the low gate and walked up to the front door, which was painted a cheerful light blue. It opened before Lord Alan could knock, revealing a slender woman of medium height with very black hair and very white skin. "Come in," she said, her voice a Gallic lilt. "How glad I am to see you."

Clarisse's brilliant black eyes remained fixed on Lord Alan, Ariel noticed. She herself might not have been there at all, not to mention Ellen. Her mother's dresser hadn't changed, she thought. Indeed, Clarisse never changed, despite the years. She had come to the Harding household more than a decade ago, and she still looked the same—lithe, vivacious, self-absorbed. She was also a genius with clothes and ornaments and hair, as her present ensemble clearly showed. And that was what had kept her with

Bess Harding through the years, despite clashes and tears and shouting and innumerable fits of pique.

"Hello, Clarisse," she said pointedly.

This forced the other woman to look at her.

"It's been a long time," she added.

"You haven't grown very tall," Clarisse replied, holding herself straighter to emphasize her own greater inches.

"No," Ariel conceded. She was about to add that Clarisse hadn't grown any more amiable, but she decided it was foolish to antagonize her just now.

Leaving Ellen on a chair in the hall, they went into a small reception room, blandly furnished except for a magnificent gilded clock on the mantel shelf, and empty. Ariel heard children's voices from the back of the house, but saw no sign of them.

"Please," said Clarisse, indicating the sofa and armchair with a sweeping gesture as she sank onto the former in a rustle of silk. Ariel had to suppress a smile at her expression when Lord Alan chose the chair, leaving her to sit beside Clarisse.

"We've come to speak to you about Bess Harding's death," said Lord Alan without preamble.

Clarisse clasped her hands at her bosom. "Ah, *quelle horreur.* I cannot bear to think of it."

He leaned forward a little. "I know it's difficult."

Ariel watched Clarisse's large, expressive eyes fill, and the tears spill exquisitely onto her cheeks. She was reining in her own questions with great difficulty. It was obviously best to let Lord Alan conduct this interview.

He was holding out a linen handkerchief. Clarisse took it and gently wiped her eyes, never taking them from his face. "*Merci,*" she said. "You are kind."

"Take all the time you need," he said.

"That terrible night." She shuddered.

"Yes?"

"All was as usual. We had no guests."

We? thought Ariel.

"It was late. I had gone up to my room. To undress for bed." Clarisse flashed Lord Alan a flirtatious glance. She somehow managed to give a vivid impression of disrobing without moving on the sofa, Ariel thought.

"Bess was in one of her moods," the woman continued. "She had locked herself in her bedchamber."

Ariel tensed and leaned forward. "Why?" she asked.

Clarisse glanced at her, then gave an eloquent shrug. "Why did she ever?" she answered, spreading her hands. "One never knew when Bess would despair, or rage . . . or laugh."

"There must have been some reason," urged Lord Alan.

Clarisse turned her full attention back to him. "She was an artist," she declared. "We artists, we are at the mercy of our feelings, because they are so strong, you see." She put her hands to her bosom once again, directing his attention to the rounded curves of her breasts above the low bodice of her gown. "It is a burden we bear." Her dark eyes were wide and glowing.

"So the household retired for the night?" asked Lord Alan. "Was there no sound, no sign?"

"None," responded Clarisse dramatically. "Only silence."

"And in the morning?"

The dresser looked a bit disappointed at the way her narrative was being received. "We rose as usual," she said. "When Bess did not come out of her room, we were very quiet, thinking she slept. But by the afternoon, we began to worry, eh? So we knocked, and when there was still no sound, John the coachman broke the door." Her hands fluttered again. "And there she was, on the floor. Ah, the blood—blood soaking her blue dress. It was the one with the embroidery."

The shock of the words pulsed along Ariel's nerves. She could see it far too vividly.

"It was so strange," Clarisse went on in a distant voice. "Everything seemed very slow. I saw the lace on her dress. I saw the little curls I had made in her hair. There were pieces of a broken brandy glass on the floor. I saw all these things." She turned and stared at them, but not as if she saw.

Ariel swallowed.

"And then my eyes fixed on the razor, half-hidden by her skirts, and all clotted . . ." Clarisse choked. Raising her head, she took a gasping breath, then pointed dramatically to a decanter and glasses sitting on a small side table. Lord Alan went to pour her a little wine. She drank it off in one gulp. "I fainted then," she told them. "When I woke, the other servants were shouting and wailing. We called for the watch, and then we packed up our things and departed. Who could stay in such a house?" She held out the glass for more wine.

Lord Alan looked at Ariel, his expression concerned. She folded her trembling hands together in her lap. "What do you remember about that day?" she asked shakily. "Something must have happened."

Lord Alan blinked, seeming surprised at her ability to question after what she had heard.

"It is all a blur," protested Clarisse.

"No, it isn't. You remembered the broken glass and the lace."

The Frenchwoman held up a protesting hand. "Do not press me."

"Clarisse, Bess is dead. I must find out why."

Lord Alan was staring as if he couldn't take his eyes off her.

"I do not know!" exclaimed the other woman. "It was horrible, what she did. Her soul will never—"

"She was often blue-deviled," insisted Ariel. "But she always recovered. What was it that made her . . . ?"

"I do not know, I tell you! My lord, don't let her bully

me." She laid a hand on Lord Alan's arm and gazed up at him imploringly.

Clarisse was recovering nicely, thought Ariel, and used the irritation she felt to deflect other emotions. "I am not bullying you," she began. "Surely you can see how important—"

"I can bear no more," declared Clarisse. She lay back on the sofa cushions, closing her eyes, one corner of her mouth jerking a bit.

Ariel sat back. The impact of the story she had heard was threatening to overwhelm her. Clarisse never noticed anything but herself anyway, she thought. It was useless trying to make her remember things about other people. Ariel listened to Lord Alan asking about the other servants and where they might be found and whether she knew anything about the haunting of Carlton House. Clarisse disavowed any knowledge, and probably she was telling the truth, Ariel thought. Her mother's dresser would have been thinking only of herself.

"Thank you for speaking with us," Lord Alan said. "You have been very helpful."

Clarisse moved her shoulders in a very French gesture. "I am looking for a new position," she told him. "I am a *merveilleuse* dresser. Ariel will tell you so."

It was the first time Clarisse had spoken her name, Ariel noticed dryly.

"I will mention it to my mother," Lord Alan promised her.

Clarisse leaned toward him. "Is there not perhaps something in *your* household?" she murmured.

He began to shake his head.

"Could we not come to some arrangement?" she went on. "I am very, very *accommodating.*"

"I fear not," he said, his face impassive.

"Ah." Clarisse sat back and shrugged. "*Eh bien.* If you would tell your mother of my situation."

"She is a duchess," put in Ariel, unable to resist.

"Vraiment?" Clarisse perked up immediately.

"I'll tell her," promised Lord Alan, rising, and obviously wondering what his mother would make of this new request.

"You will have my deepest gratitude," responded Clarisse, standing also and leaning against him for a moment as if she were too shaken to stand.

Lord Alan righted her and then looked at Ariel, who rose and found that her own legs were unsteady. Hiding this as best she could, she moved toward the front door.

"I miss her," said Clarisse suddenly. Her eyes filled again, and the tears spilled across her white cheeks.

Gulping back an answering sob, Ariel fled to the waiting carriage.

When Ellen and Lord Alan joined her, Ariel was huddling slightly in the corner of the seat and making a heroic effort not to cry. Lord Alan tapped the roof to signal the driver and then turned to her. "Are you all right?"

Ariel nodded.

"I did not realize it would be so . . ." He stopped, clearly at a loss.

"I told you Clarisse would give a performance." In an effort to control her voice, she sounded curt, she realized.

There was a silence. Ellen's eyes were huge.

Lord Alan gave the order, and they started off. The silence lengthened until it became uncomfortable, but Ariel could not manage to make innocuous conversation after what she had heard, and Lord Alan seemed disinclined to do so as well. As they clattered through the streets of Kensington and on into more fashionable precincts of London without a word, Ariel retreated into her own thoughts. What could have been different about that day, she wondered, in contrast to all the others when her mother had sunk into a black mood? What had tipped the balance too far? And if she had been at home, as she had wished to be, could she have prevented it? This was the question that plagued her in the dark hours of the night and made it so critical that she find the truth.

When they arrived at her house once more, Ellen opened the carriage door and jumped down. Ariel tried to follow, but she found that the unsteadiness of her legs had increased during the short journey. She tripped on the uneven cobblestones and nearly fell.

"Take care," said Lord Alan, stepping forward to take her arm. He supported her through the front door and into the parlor next to it. "Are you all right?" he repeated then.

"She's dead, and no one cares. No one!" Ariel had started shaking uncontrollably. Lifting her hands, she watched them shake as if they were something separate from her. She couldn't seem to get enough air. Her mind was racing, but there were no thoughts in it at all. A sound escaped her, part grief and part fear.

"Ariel."

She turned to look at him, but there was something wrong with her vision. Everything was blurred; she couldn't see his face. The sound came again, as if from some external source. She put her shaking fingers to her mouth.

And then strong, muscular arms enfolded her. Her head fitted into the hollow of his shoulder as if they had been designed for each other.

"You're freezing," he said.

Ariel burst into tears.

Alan held her, feeling the sobs shudder through her slender body and wrack her ribs, feeling the tight-strung tension that vibrated through her. His usual response to crying women was helpless distaste, and hasty retreat, but this was different. He had watched Ariel with amazement as she remained calm in an incredibly trying situation, and even managed to put logical questions to her mother's former servant. He had seen her wrestle with the feelings the dresser's story must have roused, and triumph. He had been astonished by her strength of will and her control. So he did not begrudge her a reaction now. "It's all right," he said after a while, and immediately knew the stock phrase to be foolish and inadequate.

"I keep seeing it," she choked out. "The . . . the blood."

His grip tightened, and along with it something tightened inside.

"She didn't deserve this," Ariel cried. She straightened within his embrace, her eyes still shimmering with tears, burning with the unfairness of it.

Meeting that impassioned gaze, Alan at last understood how important Ariel's search for information was to her. All the things he had learned about her and observed about her came together in a moment of insight— the kind of moment he waited for and prayed for in his work—that brought everything clear. In her life she had been continually shut out, he thought—not told, sent away, ostracized. Bess Harding's cruel suicide had only been the worst and most final example of the sort of pain she had endured over and over. It was no wonder she wanted an explanation.

"I must know what happened," added Ariel fiercely. She gripped his lapels. "You have to help me."

How well he knew that driving need for knowledge, a need that could override almost anything else. It made a kinship between them that he had never found with a woman before, never dreamed of finding. Alan was suddenly gripped by a paroxysm of sympathy and protectiveness and admiration. "I will," he said.

Something in his tone seemed to surprise her. She looked as if she hadn't really expected him to agree, or if she had, not in such a positive, final way. "You promise?" she said, wanting further confirmation.

"My word on it," he replied.

Ariel stared at him, examining his face, looking into his eyes. Alan was suddenly reminded of a fox kit he and

Robert had once found in a thicket near their house in the country. It had been abandoned, its mother no doubt killed. It had been thin and weak and desperately in need of their help. But when they had offered some bits of food, the kit had remained wild and wary, unable to believe in succor.

Ariel gave him a tremulous smile. A last tear spilled onto her cheek and ran down it like a streak of light. "Thank you," she said shakily.

The words seemed to reverberate in his chest, setting up an echo all out of proportion with their meaning. Alan couldn't tear his gaze from her face. Abruptly, he became aware that he still held her close. Her back was lithe and supple under his hands. Her full lips were parted and the curve of her breasts, disappearing into the bodice of her gown, was exquisite.

Ariel shifted against him, and he had to catch his breath.

This was no good, he thought. This was no part of their connection. She had said so most explicitly. He had agreed. She didn't want it. She had turned to him for help and comfort.

With a Herculean effort, he set her away from him, then moved back a step himself. It was one of the most difficult things he had ever done.

Ariel looked bewildered, then flushed bright crimson and took a backward step as well.

He couldn't stay here, Alan thought. If he remained in her presence any longer, he was going to lose his battle and go beyond a mere kiss. "I must go," he said, and turned away before she could answer. Outside, he dismissed the carriage, needing the exertion of a brisk walk. As he strode away he wondered, Where the devil was science when he needed it?

Chapter Seven

"So, you see," Ariel told Prospero the following day, "my cool, dignified manner was quite successful in keeping Lord Alan at a distance."

The cat yawned, his white fangs glinting in the morning sunshine that slanted through Ariel's bedchamber window. She was sitting at the small writing desk in the corner of the room. Before her lay some papers that her mother's solicitor had sent for her to read, but she had not been able to keep her attention on them.

"Even when my composure, uh, slipped," she continued, "he did not take advantage."

Prospero applied his pink tongue to his front paw and then used the latter to groom one of his ears.

"He behaved like a true gentleman," Ariel said. "He didn't even *try* to kiss me again." She frowned. "My mother always said that there was no such thing as a true gentleman."

Had he not wanted to kiss her again? she wondered. Perhaps he had not found it agreeable? And yet it had seemed to her quite . . . Ariel cut short this line of thought. Lord Alan Gresham didn't wish to kiss her, and she didn't wish him to do so. This was splendid. They were in complete agreement. She crossed her arms on her chest, and then closed her fists. They would work together, and there would be no awkward complications along the way. This was precisely what she wanted.

Ariel lowered her arms and addressed her attention to the legal papers once again. But she had gone no further than the second "herewith" before her mind wandered again. Why shouldn't he wish to kiss her? Bess had always claimed that she was designed by nature to attract such attentions—unwelcome attentions, she added hurriedly.

He had seemed to enjoy it that first time, she thought, propping her elbow on the desk and putting her chin in her hand. She remembered the way his lips had moved on hers, gently and fiercely at the same time. She wouldn't have thought it was possible to be both. And he had held her so tight, as if he would never let go. The feel of him along the length of her body had been strange and thrilling; his was so tensely muscular and . . .

Ariel started. It was almost as if she heard her mother's voice—inside her head—snapping at her for daydreaming. Her cheeks reddened slightly. What had she been thinking of? If Bess were here, she'd be livid.

But she wasn't, Ariel thought, and never would be again. It was still hard to believe that such a strong presence had vanished forever from the world. "Why?" she said aloud. "Why?"

"Did you speak, miss?"

Ariel started violently and whirled around to find Ellen the housemaid standing in the doorway holding a pile of clean laundry. "I thought I heard you speak," she added apologetically.

"Uh, I was just talking to the cat," Ariel replied, but when she indicated the place where he'd been sitting, there was nothing there.

Ellen grinned. "He's a sly one. One minute he's under your feet staring at your meal as if it's his by right, and the next he's clean gone and you can't find him for anything."

Ariel smiled.

"What is it you call him, miss?"

"Prospero."

"Yes, but what does it mean?"

"It's from a play," Ariel told her. "Prospero was a great magician. He could call up storms and spirits."

Ellen's dark eyes grew round.

"I thought he had a bit of magic about him," Ariel added, "the way he appears and disappears."

"But you don't think he's a spirit, miss?"

"No. He is a cat."

After a moment, Ellen nodded. "My mother always says cats are mysterious creatures. But useful for the mice."

Ariel nodded as well. And then a thought occurred to her, and she decided to take advantage of this opportunity. "You've been a great help here, Ellen," she began.

"Thank you, miss."

"Did you work for the Gresham family a long time before you came here?"

"Nigh a year."

"Ah. And what about Hannah?"

"Oh, she's been with them forever, miss. She was . . ." The girl hesitated, then said, "Years and years. I'd best be getting back downstairs, miss, or she'll be wondering what's become of me."

She had been about to say something else, Ariel thought when she was gone. But she had stopped herself, and so Hannah remained an enigma. She was determined to find out more about this superior member of her staff whose mere name made Lord Alan uneasy. She decided to go down to the kitchen, where she rarely ventured since Hannah arrived, and talk with her.

Pausing at the top of the back stairs, Ariel was surprised to hear a male voice floating up from the lower regions. She hesitated, then moved quietly down the steps toward the sound.

"No, Hannah," the man was saying. "I've no plan to get my own digs. M'mother keeps an excellent table, so why go to the trouble?"

She had heard this voice somewhere, Ariel thought, taking another step.

"She and my father are busy with their own engagements," he continued. "I'm as free as I would be in rooms, with nothing at all to do, and I can spend my allowance on my own entertainment."

There was a murmur of a reply.

"Don't preach now, Hannah," was the response. "I have a cartload of brothers who take life seriously. Well, except Sebastian. So there's no need for me to do so."

It was Lord Robert Gresham, Ariel realized. What was he doing in her kitchen chatting with her cook?

"James is defending the empire. Randolph is doing good works. Nathaniel is upholding the family name. Alan is . . . er, delving into scientific mysteries. Sebastian . . ." He laughed. "Well, Sebastian is cutting a wide swath among the ladies. So, you see, there's no call for me to do anything at all."

Once again, Ariel could not hear the reply.

"Marry!" exclaimed Lord Robert indignantly. "I should say not. Nathaniel is getting himself leg shackled. He has to; he's the heir. Let that be enough for you!"

Ariel had reached the final step. Now, she could hear Hannah's much quieter voice. "All of you will marry eventually," said the older woman.

"The others may do as they please," replied Lord Robert. "I've no intention of contemplating matrimony for years and years. When I'm forty or so, and have dwindled into a deadly dull country squire, well, then I suppose I'll find some girl and do the deed. Might as well be married; I'll be as good as dead."

"You'll meet some nice young lady and change your mind," said Hannah's voice placidly.

Lord Robert made a rude sound.

Ariel started to push open the kitchen door, hesitated, then, with a small grimace, bent to peer through a crack in the paneling. She could see Hannah sitting in the corner of the room, knitting. Lord Robert was at the kitchen table, a mug before him. In his elegant coat and pantaloons, he looked completely out of place in this prosaic room. Ariel straightened and put her hand to the door again.

"How's the spying getting on?" Lord Robert asked. Ariel's hand dropped to her side.

"I don't know what you mean," answered Hannah.

"Oh, come. Mother sent you over here to get the lay of the land, find out about this Harding chit. What have you discovered?"

"I'm here to cook and oversee the household," corrected Hannah.

Lord Robert hooted. "You, a cook? You never would cook anything at Langford House. Used to order the kitchen staff about pretty smartly, if I remember. And I do."

Ariel abandoned her scruples about eavesdropping. This was just what she had wanted to find out.

"You and Mother must have concocted this scheme together," he continued. "Why else would our old nanny turn up in a place like this? Come, what have you found out?"

"You behave yourself," said Hannah mildly.

"Is she really not Alan's mistress? He's always been an odd duck, but this tops it off. What the deuce is he playing at?"

"Perhaps you should tend to your own business and leave others to theirs," was the reply.

"But, Hannah," said Lord Robert cajolingly, "I have no business. That's just the point. I keep myself entirely free to serve others."

Hannah snorted.

Ariel had heard enough. She pushed the door open and walked through. "Hannah, I just wondered . . ." she said, then stopped and gazed at Lord Robert with a pretense of surprise.

He jumped to his feet. "Oh, er . . ."

"Lord Robert stopped by to pay me a visit," said Hannah calmly. "We are old friends. I have known him since he was a boy."

"Oh." Ariel put all the amazement she could manage into the word.

"Right," he said. "Family retainer, that sort of thing. Just wanted to see . . . to see . . . that everything was all right."

"To make sure I wasn't working her to death?" Ariel couldn't resist saying.

"Eh? No, no. No question of anything like that. Didn't mean to imply . . ."

"Was there something, miss?" put in Hannah, rescuing him.

"I wondered if we might have roast chicken for dinner tomorrow?" replied Ariel.

Hannah met her eyes, and Ariel saw that the older woman was well aware that this was an excuse, and fairly certain that Ariel had been listening for some time. "Of course, miss," she answered. "I'll get a nice fowl at the market in the morning."

Ariel couldn't read her look. She didn't seem angry, or particularly surprised. It was impossible to penetrate the older woman's calm reserve. But she didn't sense hostility either. "Thank you," she said, and turned to leave.

"Got to be going myself," announced Lord Robert. "Just stopped by, you know, on my way to . . . er . . ."

Ariel glanced back over her shoulder. "You are welcome in my kitchen anytime you like, Lord Robert," she told him. She thought she glimpsed a twinkle in Hannah's eyes in response to her sweet smile.

Lord Alan Gresham gazed at the overly animated crowd who filled the prince regent's largest reception room to bursting. They were rather like a flock of marauding crows, he thought, all landed in a field of ripe corn and calling raucously to one another while they gobbled as fast as they could. Only the crows were more intelligent, he added sourly. They were after sustenance, not gossip.

"It's very noisy," commented Ariel Harding, who stood close beside him with one small white hand on his arm.

Alan looked down at her. He was still not quite certain how it had come about that he was here, in evening dress, escorting her to a Carlton House reception. He knew that when this evening party had been mentioned, he had determined that it wasn't wise for Ariel to attend. She didn't belong in a place like Carlton House. Its atmosphere encouraged just the sort of behavior he vowed to avoid, and her presence would definitely disrupt the calm, reasoned progress of his investigation. But then Ariel had been certain that the ghost would make an appearance tonight, and so eager to see it again . . . After that Alan's recollection was uncharacteristically muddled. And here they were, side by side, and the object of a host of curious eyes.

Ariel was certainly worth looking at, Alan admitted to himself. She was ravishing in a cloud of sea-green, her skin and lips glowing against the pale fabric, the sparkle of her gaze almost effervescent. His arm felt hot where she held it, and he couldn't keep his mind from drifting to those moments when he had held her in his arms. Did she have any idea how difficult she was making his life? he wondered.

"Ah, there you are," said a plummy voice behind them. "At your post, eh? Good, good."

Alan turned reluctantly to face the prince, who was moving through the room surrounded by his usual retinue. "Not alone though," the regent added. "That gel from the cupboard, ain't it?" He examined Ariel with an expert's eye, his gaze lingering in strategic areas. "Never forget a . . . face," he added with an aristocratic leer.

Ariel dropped a tiny curtsy, at the same time lacing her other hand around Alan's arm and clinging to him. Alan gritted his teeth.

"Enjoyin' yourself?" the prince asked her in a suggestive voice.

"Oh, yes, Your Majesty," replied Ariel in breathy tones that made Alan look down at her, startled. She tightened her hold on his arm. Her glossy brown curls brushed his shoulder; her breast pressed softly against his elbow.

"Alan takin' good care of you, is he?" said the monarch. He waggled his eyebrows at Alan.

"Very good care," she answered, in a way that confirmed every innuendo.

"Ah." The prince regent's pudgy features creased in a smile. "You let me know if he doesn't, and I'll . . . see to it myself."

Ariel gave him a coy look. A sound of exasperation escaped Alan.

"Now, now," responded the regent, "I'm not poaching, m'boy, just commending your taste." With a waggle of his fat fingers, he passed on to speak to another of his guests.

"Why did you do that?" demanded Alan in a fierce whisper.

"What?" said Ariel in her normal voice. She had released her clinging grip and was standing beside him as if nothing had happened.

"You know very well. You gave him the clear impression that—"

She looked up at him, her hazel eyes limpid and innocent. The heat of the room had lent a further glow to her cheeks, and her full lips were damnably inviting. What if she really were his mistress? Alan thought, as the prince, and probably everyone else in the room, now believed. Desire flared in him as he imagined what the night could bring under those circumstances. Those lips—all of her— would belong to him. He would watch that sea-green gown slip off her shoulders and fall to the floor. He would feel her silken skin under his fingers. He would not have to resist the impulse to . . .

Ariel blinked, and her lips parted slightly.

Wrenching his thoughts from these channels, Alan returned to reality, becoming aware of sidelong glances and knowing smiles from those surrounding him. That had torn it, he thought. Anyone who had missed the byplay with the prince had now been treated to the sight of him practically devouring her with his eyes. There would be no denying the rumors. Silently, he cursed the whole lot of them.

Ariel cleared her throat. "I believe that is the earl of Dunbrae," she said.

He waited for the inevitable.

"I asked someone to describe him, and I think that must be he."

Following her glance, he surveyed a large man with graying black hair and a disgruntled expression. It was Dunbrae, of course; his luck was running that way.

"Yes?" asked Ariel.

Heavily, he nodded.

She looked gratified. "How fortunate. I understand he rarely comes to Carlton House." She started forward.

"You're going to approach him?"

"Of course. It is a perfect opportunity."

"Here?" he demanded. "With all these people looking on?" It wasn't enough that she intended to question her mother's former lover, he thought. She must do it in sight of all the gossips in London.

"They won't know what we say," she countered blithely, moving off before he could stop her and forcing him to follow.

"I'm Ariel Harding," she was saying to the older man when he caught up. "Bess's daughter."

The earl's craggy face grew sterner.

"I wanted to speak to you about her," she added.

Dunbrae glowered at Alan as if to say, "Can't you control this chit?"

Alan raised a hand to do something, then let it drop. No, he couldn't, he thought. That was the trouble in a nutshell.

"I was away when she . . . died," continued Ariel. "And I still can hardly believe she's really gone."

A flicker of feeling passed over the earl's features.

"I think about her so much. If only I knew why . . ." She faltered briefly. "I hoped you might be able to tell me," she finished.

A muscle jerked in Dunbrae's cheek. "I was out of town," he said, his Scots accent evident. "I had to be in the north for a month. When I came back, they told me she was dead."

Ariel's face fell. "So you weren't there."

"I would ha' been, if I'd had any warning at all," he said loudly. "If she'd told me . . ." He bit off his words and gathered air with his fist. "I know na' more than you," he added quietly. The muscle in his cheek jumped again; pain was evident in his blue eyes.

They stood in silence for a few moments.

"I heard she comes here," the earl added heavily then. "Have you seen her?"

Ariel nodded. "Once. I tried to reach her, but—"

"Bess Harding does *not* come here," Alan couldn't help saying. "Her supposed ghost is a hoax."

The other two looked at him.

"Which will be exposed and discredited quite soon," he added.

Ariel bent her head. The earl sighed. "Aye," he said. "I know it. I should na' have come." He stared around the room with clear contempt, then made another sharp gesture. "I'll be going." He gave Ariel a piercing look and a nod, before turning away.

"Didn't she confide in anyone?" murmured Ariel. "Was it always secrets?"

Alan moved so that he shielded her from most of the prying eyes. The stark grief in her face was not for public consumption. It tore at him and made it imperative that he do something. But what?

Alan had spent a good deal of his life avoiding entanglements with other people. They were annoyingly unpredictable, and more important, they interfered with his work, which had always been his first consideration. Now, he wanted to intervene, but he didn't know exactly what to do. He had no experience of such situations. Sebastian would know, he thought, and then was surprised. The idea that Sebastian had anything to teach him was a new one.

Alan looked over his shoulder. It seemed as if a thousand people were staring, waiting for him to make a move. He needed to get Ariel away from that malicious scrutiny, to divert her. What *would* Sebastian do? "Would you like to dance?" he said.

Ariel blinked.

She might well be surprised, he thought savagely. It was a ridiculous idea. This was what came of trying to emulate Sebastian.

"Do you know how to dance?" she responded.

She never said what he expected, Alan thought. "Of course."

"Really? It doesn't seem like something you would . . ."

For some reason, her startled reaction stung him. "I have danced at any number of balls," he informed her, "and at Almack's and at country house parties."

"Have you?" She sounded wistful now. "I had lessons, at school, but I have never actually *danced*—officially, I mean." She looked toward the next room, where a group of musicians was playing for the dancers.

The starkness was gone from her expression, and the uncertain eagerness that had replaced it was irresistible. "Then it is high time," said Alan, and offered his arm.

A waltz was just beginning, and Alan swung Ariel out into the circling dancers. The speed and sureness of the movement made her breath catch. One of his hands had captured hers; the other was warm on her ribs. Her eyes were just inches from his broad shoulder, where her own fingers had somehow come to rest. For a moment it seemed that she had forgotten everything she knew about dancing. She would trip over her skirts, she thought, tread on his foot, cause them both to fall in a heap on the parquet floor. But then the strength of his arm guiding her and the rhythm of the music caught her up, and she found herself matching his movements as if they had done this a hundred times, swaying with him in the cadence of the dance.

The feeling was intoxicating—like flying. The glinting colors of the dancers' clothes and jewels blurred into the flicker of candlelight as they moved among them. The sweet strains of the violin filled her ears. She could feel the very threads of his coat under her fingertips, and she was exquisitely sensitive to every small signal of his body. He swung her in a turn, their bodies close, and her breath came faster.

He danced extremely well, she realized with some surprise. He moved to the music as if he were part of it, displaying a natural grace that she hadn't noticed before.

And he seemed to be having a fine time. She never would have predicted that. When he spun her at the end of the room and swung her back up it, they drew a number of admiring glances. Delighted by it all, Ariel smiled.

Lord Alan smiled back at her, his handsome face relaxing, his blue eyes sparkling with what certainly appeared to be pure enjoyment.

Ariel couldn't tear her eyes away from his face. He looked so different. It was as if a curtain had parted to let light flood out. "You like to dance," she said a bit breathlessly.

He merely continued to smile down at her.

"Wh-where did you learn to dance so well?" she asked, flustered by his warm, steady gaze.

His arm tightened about her waist, and they whirled together to the right. "My mother saw to it that we all learned," he answered. "She considers it one of the indispensable social skills."

"Really? What . . . what are the others?"

"An easy manner, an ability to converse, a consciousness of others' feelings, and a knack of gracefully balancing a cup and saucer on one's knee," he replied promptly.

She looked at him from under her lashes, uncertain whether it was all a joke. "Knee?" she repeated.

His smile widened slightly. "For morning calls and tea parties," he informed her. "One is always being required to manage a cup. Robert used to sit in the drawing room and practice. With the Sèvres."

She laughed at the image this evoked. "And you? I didn't think you cared very much for social graces."

"I don't."

He pulled her a little closer again and guided them in a rapid turn. Ariel felt the muscles of his upper arm flex as they moved. It was exceedingly unsettling to be so close to him, and so very conscious of his strong, dominating physical presence. She had to cling to his shoulder briefly to keep her balance. "But you like to dance," she repeated a bit desperately.

"Music is very mathematical," he replied. "It has an order and a clarity that is quite beautiful. It has nothing to do with social graces."

"So you are . . . responding to the music? When you dance?" she wondered.

"How could one do anything else?"

The musicians ended with a flourish, and the dancers slowed to a stop. In the brief moment while he still held her, Ariel gazed into Lord Alan's eyes. So often, he spoke as if what he said was obvious, and common. But this wasn't. A great many people had no response at all to music, she thought. He could have observed any number of them at her school, singing off-key or drawing tortured sounds from the pianoforte. His deep instinctive response was something special.

It was also unexpected, Ariel thought. There was more to him than she had realized. Or perhaps she simply hadn't understood what he meant by "man of science."

The warmth of his hand left her side; his fingers slipped from hers. Ariel let her own arm drop with some reluctance. All she wanted just now was to dance with him again, and explore this new facet of him further.

They stood near a row of tall windows that marched along one side of the room and overlooked a garden illuminated at intervals by torches. The windows were open to the balmy spring air, though they had little effect on the stifling atmosphere.

Alan savored one stray puff of air, drawing it into his lungs. Dancing always stimulated him, but dancing with Ariel had been an unprecedented experience. Usually, he was most keenly aware of the notes being played, the harmonies and rhythms, the admirable way the piece fitted together. This time, he had been wildly distracted by the feel of her supple body between his hands, and the way it seemed to respond automatically to any small movement he made. The duet they had created together had conjured visions of Ariel with her shining brown hair tumbling around her shoulders, and her skin glowing with something other than the exertions of the dance.

He had to stop this, Alan thought. He was here to end the "haunting," and he musn't be distracted.

He took another breath. The wind was rising outside, he noticed. Branches swayed and a bush bent halfway to the ground. Or was that the wind? Had he glimpsed a shadowy figure moving in the garden? All senses suddenly alert, he began to thread his way through the crowd toward the windows.

"Where are you . . . ?" began Ariel, then fell silent. Casting a glance over his shoulder, Alan saw that she was following him with an intent expression.

They had nearly reached the windows when light flared in the garden. Someone had opened a dark lantern, Alan thought, or perhaps more than one. And the beams were directed full on the figure framed by an arching trellis—the "ghost" of Bess Harding. It looked the same as before—the old-fashioned gown, the bone-white face, the splatters of supposed blood, the illusion of floating above the ground. But this time the figure threw back its head and held out its arms as if beseeching the crowd. Several female guests shrieked.

"Get out of my way," said Alan, pushing past a cluster of transfixed partygoers. "Pardon me. Let me pass." He twisted and shoved until he made it to the nearest open window. Without pausing he threw a leg over the low sill and ducked under the sash, straightening again in the flowerbed just outside.

The light on the ghost vanished. This time, Alan was certain he heard the squeak of dark lanterns. His first impulse was to race to the spot where the figure had appeared, but then he stopped to think. The woman, whoever she was, would be expecting that, and she would have moved. It would be wiser to listen for the sounds of flight and follow.

He was straining his ears when Ariel tumbled out of the window behind him in a rustle of silk. "Where is she?" she cried, stumbling slightly on the hem of her gown, then hurrying across the flowerbed toward the site of the latest haunting.

Alan looked to the right, where he expected to find one of the men he had stationed at the doors of the building. The fellow was there. Alan summoned him with a gesture and gave the order to search the garden. But he knew it was too late. The hoaxers had found a way in, and they were certainly departing through it right now. All he had managed was to keep them out of the house.

"There's nothing here," she said when he joined her under the trellis.

"Naturally," he replied.

"She might have dropped something, or—"

"These people are far too clever for that."

"People?"

"I heard dark lanterns. The woman has confederates."

"At least we found out something then."

"We also could have heard which way they went if you had not set up an infernal racket."

"You were just standing there! If you had told me you were listening—"

She was interrupted by a rapidly increasing volume of curses and sputters of outrage from the garden path. "Damn Bess," said the prince regent, appearing at full trot from behind a screen of trees. "How dare she do this to me? Half the town is laughing up its sleeve, and the other half is making me out as some kind of demon worshiper. Where the devil . . . ?" He glimpsed Alan, and changed course to stand before him. "There you are. Haven't you caught her?"

"No, sir," Alan replied tightly.

"Well, why not? By God, this can't go on. It's . . . it's damned disrespectful."

"We will increase the watch. No one will get in again."

"Ghost doesn't have to get in, does she?" retorted the prince, his chubby face petulant.

"There is no longer any question of the supernatural," Alan said. "The woman had very real confederates using dark lanterns."

In the torchlight, the monarch's pudgy features were suddenly shrewd. "Did she now?"

"Yes, sir."

"That puts a different complexion on things."

Alan refrained from pointing out that there had never been a ghost.

"It's someone tryin' to embarrass me, then," the prince concluded.

"Most likely, sir." Alan also refrained from mentioning that he had told him this from the beginning.

"We can do something about that!" He rubbed his fat hands together.

A spark of hope ignited in Alan. "Perhaps, then, you no longer need my help, sir? Others might be better able . . ."

"What? No, no, you've done a fine job. Carry on to the end, eh? See the thing through." The prince cocked his head and held up an admonishing finger. "Might get on faster if you cut out the dalliance," he finished, leaving Alan gasping at the unfairness of the accusation and the irony of its source.

By the time he had recovered, the prince was gone. The wind whispered in the branches. Footsteps and scraps of conversation could be heard from the edges of the garden, where the men were still searching. The buzz of noise inside Carlton House had resumed.

"I'm very sorry I kept you from hearing them escape," said Ariel quietly.

Turning, he gazed down at her.

"I should have realized that was the thing to do," she added. "I will remember next time."

A female admitting she was wrong, Alan thought with amazement, actually acknowledging she had lost an argument. She seemed to mean it, too.

"You know," Ariel added diffidently, "if it is a matter of dark lanterns . . ."

"Yes?" he prompted, curious to know what she would say next.

"Well . . . my mother's former coachman. John."

He waited.

"He . . . I believe he had a good deal of experience with dark lanterns."

"What sort of experience?"

She shifted from one foot to the other. "Well, I . . . I think perhaps he was a highwayman before he came to live with us."

"What?"

"I *think* he may have stopped my mother's coach and tried to rob her."

Alan gazed at her, finding nothing whatsoever to say.

"And failed," added Ariel hurriedly.

"And so she naturally hired him as a coachman."

She grimaced. "I don't know what happened. She would have started talking to him, of course. She wouldn't have been able to resist."

"Resist!"

"To find out about him," Ariel explained, "to discover what it was like, being a highwayman. She did that with everyone. For her work, you see."

He shook his head. He did not begin to see.

"She collected incidents and emotions," explained Ariel, "and then she used them when she acted. She would have been thinking of plays with highwaymen in them, and how she might use John's experiences for her own part, and so she would have asked him questions, and . . ." Ariel shrugged. "One thing would have led to another. John is . . . he isn't a criminal, really. He is only a little . . ."

Alan waited.

"Lazy," concluded Ariel finally.

"Lazy?"

"He doesn't like to work hard. I think he was quite happy overseeing my mother's stable and selling the occasional . . ." She stopped, and he wondered what other sort of mischief she had decided not to reveal. "He is not a bad man," she finished.

"Just a highway robber."

"This was years ago," she protested. "And anyway . . . I'm not *sure*, you see. I'm not talking about facts—just a combination of hints and interpretations. But I did wonder . . . when you said dark lanterns . . ."

"Indeed," he replied grimly. "I believe we will redouble our efforts to find John the coachman."

"He won't talk to anyone but me," she told him.

"We shall see about that."

"Really. If he discovers that you know where he is, he'll run."

"He won't be given an opportunity to do so."

She put a hand on his arm. "Please. I have to see him. If Bess was in any kind of trouble, she would have asked for his help."

In the face of her pleading gaze, he couldn't refuse.

Chapter Eight

———— ✜ ————

With this spur to their efforts, it took the prince's men only two days to track down the coachman. "But he is staying in a very unsavory part of town," Alan told Ariel when she pressed him for news. "Not a place you could go."

"Yes, I can."

"You have no notion of the kind of place we are talking of," he replied.

"Oh? I am not some sheltered daughter of the *haut ton*, you know. I won't be overset by some dirt."

"Or by footpads and bully boys?" he inquired dryly.

"I assume we will be taking some of the prince's men with us," she responded. "Surely they can keep us safe."

Alan examined her delicate features and slender frame. Who would have thought to find such courage, and such obstinacy, in this guise? "Is there anything that would stop you?" he wondered aloud.

Her hazel eyes glinted. "A stout rope, I suppose. Or perhaps chains?"

Startled, he laughed aloud. Then he found himself gazing at her. She met his eyes briefly, then looked away. It was fortunate that they were in agreement on the nature of their connection, he told himself, even as another, less rational part of him suffered sharp disappointment. "Very well," he conceded. "I will see what I can arrange."

Ariel looked triumphant. "Thank you. You really have been so helpful."

"Always glad to be of service," he replied ruefully, but Ariel didn't seem to hear.

Two nights later, they drove through twisting streets made dim by the overhanging upper stories of sagging houses. The coach wheels splashed through refuse, and at one point Alan glimpsed the body of a dead dog lying in the stream of liquid slops in the center of the lane. He glanced quickly at Ariel, but if she had seen, she gave no sign. The houses grew meaner and smaller, the people they passed either sullenly glaring or furtive. Alan made no comment. He had already voiced all his objections, most particularly to their making this visit at night, but they had been overridden by the man who had tracked down the coachman, who regretfully told him that he could only be sure of laying his hands on the fellow in the evening.

Following this man's directions, they pulled up at the mouth of a narrow alley, hardly more than a cobbled path between two ramshackle buildings. "This way," mumbled their guide, not looking happy. "We'll come in the back and surprise him. He won't have no chance to do a bunk on us."

Alan climbed down from the carriage and looked around. "This is impossible," he began.

"Keep your voice down, my lord," said their guide, alarmed.

"It is merely filthy," declared Ariel, stepping to the

broken pavement. "And we have Tom and Fred with us as well as Roger."

She had remembered their names after only one mention, thought Alan, watching her pick up her skirts and move away from the coach. And she wasn't showing the least sign of fear. He looked at each of the men in turn. They nodded and fingered their cudgels. Alan gripped the pistol in his pocket, drawing it out, then gave the signal to proceed.

They made their way slowly down the alley. About halfway, Alan realized that what he had thought was a pile of garbage was in fact a ragged man, rolled into a ball with his head on his knees. He surged forward as Ariel hesitated, then bent over the unfortunate fellow and reached out as if to touch his shoulder.

"Nothin' you can do," Roger told her.

To Alan's profound relief, she accepted this, stepping around the huddled figure with obvious reluctance. He made no sound, no move to show he even saw them.

"In here." Their guide pushed open a crooked door and motioned them forward. They crossed grimy floorboards and went through to a larger room. It was very dark, with only one candle guttering in the far corner. The air was fetid and dead. When Alan's eyes adjusted, he realized that there were people there, four or five lying on the floor or slumped against the walls. He increased the pace, grimacing as he passed a woman who sat as if broken, her legs splayed wide, her arms limp at her sides. She was dirty. Her dress was torn, and her black hair hung in lank strings. Her eyes were closed, and she was snoring slightly.

"Who are these—" began Ariel.

"Hush," commanded Roger. "We're nearly there."

He strode silently across the filthy room and opened a door on the far side. Stronger light streamed in; it came from a hallway, Alan saw as he joined the man. There was noise, too, the sounds of men talking and clinking glasses.

"Tom and me will fetch him," whispered Roger when they had gathered in the hall. "If we all go into the ale-house, there'll be a riot."

Alan nodded.

"Don't frighten him," said Ariel.

Roger looked almost comically nonplussed.

"Don't do him any damage," put in Alan.

"Aye," answered Roger.

In a few minutes, he and Tom returned with a struggling figure locked between them.

"John," cried Ariel. "Let him go."

Making sure his pistol was clearly visible, Alan nodded his agreement. The two stepped back slightly, leaving their captive free but in easy reach.

"What the bloody hell . . . ?" he said.

Ariel stepped forward; Alan at once blocked her way. "He won't hurt me," she said.

"He won't have any opportunity to do so."

John glared around at all of them. His clothes were rumpled and looked as if they could use a wash. His dark hair lacked its customary dapperness. His eyes were bloodshot and pouched, as if he'd been drinking more than was good for him.

"John, it's Ariel."

His gaze swiveled to her face.

"Ariel Harding," she added. "Bess's daughter."

His eyes narrowed. He seemed to struggle to focus on her in the dim light. Then he frowned. "Ariel? You're . . . older."

She smiled. "I've been away at school for a long time. But I haven't forgotten how you taught me to ride, and hold the ribbons on the coach box as well."

John's expression shifted from bewilderment to comprehension and back again. "What the dev . . . deuce are you doing here?" he demanded. He looked around, more alert now. "Who are these people? You shouldn't have come to a place like this. 'Tisn't proper."

"I had to speak to you," she said.

"To me?" His eyes dropped. "Why would you be wanting to speak to me?"

"I am determined to find out why Bess died," she told him.

"Shh." John threw a glance over his shoulder, then peered down the other end of the hallway. "Don't mention that here."

"Why?" asked Alan sharply.

"Because they don't like that kind of talk," John snapped. "You'll get us all thrown out in the street, and I can't afford that." He looked at Ariel. "Who's he?"

"This is Lord Alan Gresham. He is helping me to find—" She broke off as John held up a warning hand.

"Lord, is it? Why not be satisfied with what you've got, my girl, and let the past lie?"

"He is *only* helping me," said Ariel. "And I must hear your story of what happened that night. Please, John."

"I wasn't there," he replied quickly.

"You weren't at the house?" Disappointment made Ariel's voice sharp.

The man moved uneasily, eyes on the floor.

"Roger, perhaps you should go and ask some of John's friends in the taproom if they know anything about this matter," suggested Alan.

"No!" was the alarmed response. "Stay out of that, then."

"If you tell us what you know," Alan agreed.

"I know damn little," he growled in response.

"Why won't you help me?" cried Ariel. "I thought we were old friends."

John looked hunted, then he grimaced. "Come on."

Turning, he led them up a set of grimy stairs at the end of the hall, and along another corridor to a small room that held a rickety table and some stools. Leaving one of their men to watch the stairs and lower floor, Alan stepped inside. After carefully shutting the door, John turned to face Ariel. "I liked your mother," he said. "You know I did. And you, too. But I can't afford to get involved in any investigations—with magistrates and Bow Street crawling about and sticking their noses where they've got no business being."

"They wouldn't lift a finger," said Ariel. "I am doing this on my own."

John gave Lord Alan a sidelong glance.

"I have no connection with the magistrates," he conceded.

"So what are you doing here, if you're not . . . ?" This time, the sidelong glance was at Ariel.

"He was summoned by the prince regent to rid Carlton House of Bess's ghost," Ariel explained before Alan could stop her.

For the first time, John smiled. "Ah." His smile broadened. "Bess would have loved that. When the tongues began to wag about Prinny's ghost, I thought mebbe it was her. Just the sort of thing she'd *want* to do."

"Please tell me what happened that night, John," said Ariel quietly.

He sighed, looking suddenly older and tireder and gentler. "What good will it do anybody?" he asked. But he seemed to be speaking mostly to himself. He went over to the table, gesturing to the stools as he sat on one of them. Ariel obediently took another; the other men remained standing.

"I wasn't in the house," John began. "I'd gone out to the stable to check on one of the horses. Then I stayed out for a smoke, as Bess wouldn't have tobacco in her house." He smiled very slightly. "You remember how she used to rail about the 'filthy habit,' Ariel."

"Yes."

He nodded. "And she was in the mood to rail that night. So, I leaned against the stable gate and looked at the stars for a good while. By the time I came in, everyone was abed. There wasn't any sign of trouble. Then in the morning . . ." He shifted a bit on the stool. "We thought she was sleeping. But finally Clarisse knocked, and when we couldn't rouse her, I broke the door." He let out a breath and put a hand to his forehead. "She was there on the floor. Lord, I'll never forget the sight."

There was a short silence.

John looked up. "You should talk to Clarisse."

"We have," Alan informed him.

"Is there anything unusual you remember about that day?" asked Ariel, leaning forward on the stool and causing it to rock a little under her. "Anything at all?"

John frowned at his shoes, then shook his head.

"Bess hadn't come to you about any trouble?" wondered Ariel.

"If she had, I would have helped her! I would have done something."

"I know." Ariel nodded.

"Are you doing something now?" said Alan, ignoring the emotion that charged the atmosphere.

"What?"

"Being out of employment must leave you short of funds," Alan continued, approaching the question from another direction.

"I'm all right," replied John, though his appearance belied his words.

"Perhaps you've thought of a way to make a bit from Bess Harding's death?"

The former coachman clenched his fists and started to stand, but the other men came forward and he sank back onto the stool again. "What the devil do you mean by that?" he asked.

"It hasn't occurred to you that the regent would pay well to have this 'haunting' stopped?"

John stared at him for a long moment, then started to laugh. "He would, wouldn't he? Curse me if I don't wish

I'd thought of it. Prinny deserves the scare, and he spends more than I'd need on one of his perishing dinners."

"A man of your . . . experience would have no trouble arranging the incidents," Alan added.

The other shot Ariel a look, growing serious again. "Maybe. And maybe not," he responded. "But the fact is, I didn't."

"You know nothing about it?" Alan probed.

"Not a thing, your lordship."

Their gazes locked, and the tension in the room escalated to a trembling point before breaking and receding again. Alan sighed. The fellow seemed to be telling the truth. It was another dead end.

Silence fell over the shabby room again. They could hear the noise of conversation below.

"Do you need help, John?" Ariel said then. "I am living in the house. Would you like to return to your old position?"

Alan started to protest.

But the former coachman was shaking his head. "I believe I'll stay where I am for now. A friend of mine may have a job for me down Sussex way, and I'm thinking it's time for me to leave the city. Get a good safe berth before I'm too old to find one."

"You'll let Miss Harding know where you are going," stated Alan.

John looked at him. "I reckon you'll find out, whether I do or don't," he answered.

Alan simply held his gaze.

After a moment John sighed. "I'll send word along," he said.

"Is there anything else you can tell us?" Alan asked.

"Why did she do it, John?" said Ariel. "What happened?" She wrapped her arms tightly around her ribs.

He shook his head. "I've wracked my brain, and I still can't figure it. There was nothing out of the ordinary. She did go on one of her visits, but she'd been doing that for nigh on two years."

"Two years?" said Ariel, remembering that Charles Padgett had mentioned a similar period of time. "What do you mean? What visits?"

"It's nothing to do with this," was the reply.

"We'll judge that," Alan informed him.

John shrugged. "Now and then, she went off on her own," he said. "Didn't want to be driven. Didn't want to be asked where she was going." He grimaced. "Tore a wide strip off me when I did ask." He shook his head again. "Bess always loved her secrets."

"So you don't know where?" Disappointment tinged Ariel's voice.

John rubbed his palms together. "I tried following her once, and I'd swear she was heading for some back slum. But I never found out because she caught me and gave me to understand that I'd be out on my ear if I didn't keep my nose out of her affairs." He grimaced again. "Bess could be very persuasive."

"Where could she have been going?" wondered Ariel. She hesitated, then added, "She told me once that she grew up in a back slum."

"Did she now?" said John. After a moment's consideration of this, he shrugged. "I kept strictly out of it after that. You didn't cross Bess."

This seemed irrelevant to Alan, and he didn't think there was any more to be discovered here. "Shall we go?" he asked Ariel.

She looked reluctant, then stood. "I suppose . . . yes, of course." She straightened. "Good-bye, John."

"You watch yourself, miss."

"I can't let her go like that," Ariel told him. Her jaw hardened, and the look of resolve returned to her beautiful face. "I won't."

Unexpectedly, John smiled. "You always were a stubborn one. Remember that white pony?"

"Cloud!" A smile lightened Ariel's expression, too. "I haven't thought of her in years. Such a poorly named horse."

"Mean little beast," agreed John. He glanced at the others. "Kept wanting to bite, or kick, or shake her out of the saddle. But she just kept coming back, with her teeth gritted and a look on her face that said she'd win or die trying."

"And I did win," said Ariel.

"She took to you finally, didn't she?" recalled John. "I thought we'd have to put her down."

"I never give up," declared Ariel fiercely.

"This ain't a pony." John moved toward the door. "If you wouldn't mind, I'll just slip back on my own."

"You'll wait until we're gone," said Alan sharply.

John held up his hands, conceding the point. Alan put a hand on Ariel's arm to urge her out of the room. "See that all's well," he told Roger.

The stairs remained clear. "Let's go," Alan commanded, and the party began to retrace the path they had taken earlier.

The slumped figures in the outer room hadn't moved. They were sunk in some kind of stuporous oblivion, Alan concluded. Perhaps this alehouse doubled as an opium den.

They left the foul place and picked their way back to the coach, where the driver was looking rather nervous. Alan helped Ariel inside as the others swung up onto the back. Ariel had just settled herself in the seat when there was a flurry of pounding footsteps and a shout from one of their guards. Alan lurched into the coach shouting, "Move!" Ariel was thrown hard against the cushions as the carriage careened away down the dirty street with the horses of their escort pounding along on both sides.

"Is anyone following?" Alan called.

"No one in sight," came the reply from outside.

"Bloody hell," said Alan, venting his feelings.

They continued to travel at a dangerous speed until they reached a more populated area, with lighted shops and people still walking along the pavements. When the driver had let the horses drop into a walk, Alan finally relaxed a bit, letting out a breath and allowing his back to touch the carriage seat. "Right," he said, as if answering some unspoken question.

"What was it?" wondered Ariel quietly.

"A gang of footpads. Five at least, with cudgels and knives."

"They meant to rob us?"

"As I warned you might happen." Alan took a deep breath. He had not wanted to take Ariel to such a neighborhood, and he had been absolutely right. If she had only listened to him, she would not have had to endure this scare.

"Where do you think my mother was going on those visits?" she said.

He turned to stare at her.

"Do you think we could discover it if we . . . ?" Noticing his incredulous gaze, she broke off. "What?" she said.

"Have you lost your wits entirely?" he interrupted.

"What do you mean?"

"We were very nearly robbed just now, and most likely beaten, or worse."

"But we escaped," she pointed out.

"Yes, but . . . you . . . you ought to be hysterical."

"Is that what you would like? I thought you despised hysterical females."

"I do. But—"

"And in any case, the danger is past. So there is no need to be alarmed," she added kindly.

Alan found himself speechless. The more he saw of Ariel Harding, the more amazing she became. She was like no female he had ever imagined. One corner of his mouth quirked upward. No doubt she would inform him that his conclusion was a failure of imagination rather than a fact based on solid observations.

"Perhaps we could question some of the hack drivers near the house," Ariel suggested, returning to the earlier subject. "Do you think they might remember where they took Bess?"

"No."

Ariel sighed. "I suppose not. But I should so like to know . . ." She brightened. "She might have dropped hints to some of her friends. She loved being mysterious. I'll find a way to ask them at the prince's masquerade."

Alan nearly groaned. Here was yet another sore point with the prince. He had urged the regent in the strongest possible terms not to hold a huge masked ball that he had planned. Predictably, the prince had refused point-blank to cancel an affair that would offer the haunters a thousand opportunities. "You are not going to the masquerade," he said. "I will be too busy to escort you."

"But I must."

They had pulled up before her house, and in the light of the lantern that hung beside the door, he could see the obstinate defiance in her face. He grasped her arm so that she couldn't get down. "We will not continue to make a spectacle of ourselves at Carlton House," he insisted.

"Spectacle?" she repeated. She jerked away from him and opened the coach door, ready to step down. "Is that what we are?"

"With the way that you have been behaving there—yes!"

"If you are afraid I will wreck your reputation, I am sure I can find another escort," Ariel jeered.

With a muttered curse, he grabbed Ariel by the waist and swept her back into her seat, slamming the carriage door shut with the other hand. "Tell me what you intend to do," he demanded.

"Why should I?" She struggled to free herself, but his grip was unbreakable.

Alan couldn't remember when he had been so angry. Among his brothers, he was known as the even-tempered one, the one who ended disputes rather than starting them. His colleagues at Oxford knew him to be a supremely rational debater, a man who reasoned rather than attacked. And yet here he was, longing to force Ariel to obey him by sheer brute strength. "What are you going to do?" he demanded again.

"I don't see any reason to tell you," she replied.

Retaining his grip on her, Alan took a deep breath in an effort to calm himself. There was only one way he could have any control over what she might do, he concluded finally. "I'll take you," he muttered.

She turned to look at him, her surprise and dawning hope evident in the lantern light.

"And you will swear to continue to communicate your ideas to me before taking any action," he added.

"Could you let go of me now?" was the reply.

Abruptly he released her. All London assumed she was his mistress. Though she didn't realize it, she had been labeled. Without his protection now, she would be fair game for any man. "If I escort you, will you give your word to go there with no one but me?" he said.

"Yes," she said.

"*Do* you give your word?" he added. His anger was dissipating, and being replaced with a kind of reckless elation that he had never experienced before.

"I promise," Ariel assured him.

Surprising himself as well as Ariel, Alan began to laugh. "You would do quite well as a blackmailer," he said after a while.

Her eyes gleamed in the lantern light. "Perhaps I'll consider it when I'm older," she replied.

Chapter Nine

I t was very likely that Bess had had costumes made for masquerades, Ariel thought as she made her way up to the attic two days later. She had loved them. And just because Lord Alan was being stuffy about wearing fancy dress didn't mean she had to be. She intended to enjoy the occasion to the fullest. Who knew when she would get to attend another?

"Ooh, miss," breathed Ellen the housemaid, who accompanied her to the attic for the first time. "Look at all these dresses!"

"Would you like one?" answered Ariel somewhat absently. She was concentrating on the search for the costumes.

"Me, miss?" The girl seemed flabbergasted. "Hannah wouldn't allow it."

This caught Ariel's attention. "Why would she care?" she wondered.

Ellen had moved to one of the wardrobes and was stroking a silk gown. "She'd say they weren't for the likes of me," she answered, her voice distant, as if she had drifted off to some other realm.

Ariel hesitated. Ellen wouldn't have any place to wear one of her mother's dresses. But what harm could there be in simply owning one? "We'll ask Hannah," she decided. It would give her a chance to learn more about her possible adversary, she thought. She hadn't yet been able to make out Hannah's true opinion of her.

"Do you think we should, miss?" Ellen was clearly doubtful, but her fingers continued to stroke the luxurious cloth of their own volition.

"Why not? Come, we'll do it now."

They found Hannah in the kitchen, as usual. She was sprinkling some green herb into a large pot on the cookstove, and she looked up in surprise when Ariel marched in with Ellen at her heels.

"Hannah, my mother left a great number of gowns in the house here. She had a penchant for new clothes. I would like to give Ellen a silk dress. Have you any objection?"

The older woman looked from Ariel to Ellen's hopeful face. Ariel realized she was a little nervous. There was something formidable about Hannah, even though she was the quietest, most unobtrusive person.

The pause lengthened. Ellen shuffled her feet on the brick floor but didn't speak.

"Let's have a look," Hannah said at last.

They climbed back up the stairs together, Hannah beginning to puff a bit by the third floor. She stopped to catch her breath at the top, and then followed them into the attic storage room. "Merciful heavens," she exclaimed at the rows of crammed wardrobes. "No wonder you've been keeping this room locked up."

Of course she had noticed that, Ariel thought.

Hannah walked down the row, shaking her head as if she couldn't believe her eyes. "What a waste," she murmured at the end.

"Isn't it?" agreed Ariel. "I would like the gowns to be enjoyed, instead of just hanging here getting dusty."

Hannah gave her a look that said she saw right through this altruism.

"I could just keep it in my room," ventured Ellen. "To look at, like. And mebbe when I went home at Christmastime, I could—"

"Having a silk gown wouldn't let you out of any of your work," admonished Hannah.

"No, ma'am. Of course not," replied Ellen, sounding shocked at the idea.

Hannah smiled slightly. "I don't see any harm in it," she said.

Ellen gasped with pleasure and turned to stare at the dress she had been touching earlier.

"Any one you want, Ellen," said Ariel.

Smiling beatifically, the girl went to take down the dress—a stunning peach silk that was perfect for her dark coloring.

"Would . . . would you like something as well, Hannah?" Ariel ventured.

The older woman snorted. "It'd take two of them to fit round me."

Should she offer her two? wondered Ariel.

"However . . ."

Ariel waited.

"I have two nieces, down in Devonshire, who'd probably faint dead away to get a gown such as that." She was looking at Ellen, who was holding the silk gown up against her and smoothing its folds.

"Let us send them some," urged Ariel, delighted and relieved.

"I don't know what their mother would say to me," answered the older woman. "Look at that neckline. It's near down to your . . ." She sniffed.

Ellen started and flushed deep red. "I'm going to put in a kerchief," she mumbled.

"There are morning dresses that are not cut so low," Ariel responded hurriedly. "I'll show you." She moved toward another wardrobe, and was gratified when Hannah slowly followed her. "Tell me about your nieces," she added. "Are they dark-haired or blond? Here, look at this." She pulled out a sprigged muslin gown with a deep ruffle at the hem and long narrow sleeves, also ruffled at the cuff. The neckline was fairly decorous—astonishingly so for her mother, Ariel thought. Probably that was why the gown hung here; it didn't look as if it had ever been worn.

Hannah touched the muslin. "Fine stuff," she commented. "Alice would look right lovely in that."

"Good," declared Ariel. She thrust the dress into Hannah's arms. "Now, let us see. What is your other niece's name?"

"Lizzie," answered Hannah absently. She was looking down at the dress. "I don't know, miss."

"Oh, please. I would so like to think of them in these dresses."

Hannah looked up and met her eyes. Ariel saw traces of suspicion, and doubt, and uneasiness. She let the woman examine her as long as she wished. It felt very much like a test, but she was confident of her ability to pass it.

After what seemed like a long time, Hannah nodded. "Thank you, miss," she said. "The girls'll be that thrilled."

The three of them spent a pleasant half hour choosing another dress to send south, and then Ariel returned to her original purpose. She finally found what she was looking for in the wardrobe in the far corner. There were fewer dresses here; room had been left so that the elaborate ensembles would not be crushed. She took them out one by one and examined them. There was a lavishly ornamented gown in the style of the last century, with panniers and a skirt made of yards and yards of silk brocade.

But when she peered into the recesses of the wardrobe, she saw no sign of the hoop or crinolines necessary for wearing it, so she had to put it aside.

There was a Elizabethan-looking dress in deep blue silk shot with bronze. Its bodice came to a sharp point in the front, and a starched ruff, rather crushed, was pinned to one sleeve. Ariel smiled. Her mother had gone to some masked ball as Good Queen Bess, she thought, and it was just like her.

There was a classical sort of toga made of pale cream silk, but when Ariel handled it she could barely tell which was the neck and which the hem. She didn't trust its draped folds; it looked as if it would fall off at the slightest movement.

Finally, in the back of the wardrobe, she found just what she wanted. It was a Gypsy costume, with a snug narrow bodice and a skirt made of layers and layers of multicolored ruffles all trimmed in gilt ribbon and embellished with little gilt coins. The dress swayed and twinkled in her hands as if it had a life of its own. There was a matching scarf to tie over her hair, and in a small pocket she found hooped earrings that also tinkled with little bits of gilt. With a black mask, it would be a marvelous costume.

Ellen was equally excited as she helped her carry the dress downstairs. They were in Ariel's bedchamber agreeing on how it should be pressed when Ariel noticed something outside. Her stableyard was occupied by a gigantic chestnut, guarded by a stableboy she had never seen before. "Do you know who that is?" she asked Ellen.

"That's Billy," answered the girl, surprised.

"Billy?"

"He used to work in the stables at Langford House, but now he's . . . Oh, I expect Lord Sebastian's here to visit Hannah."

"Ah?"

"Major Lord Sebastian, I should say." The girl frowned. "I think."

"He is the one in the cavalry regiment?" asked Ariel.

"Yes, miss."

Ariel contemplated this information. "All the brothers seem very fond of Hannah," she ventured.

"She was their nurse, miss. And she still . . . helps them out, like."

"How?"

Ellen shrugged. "I don't rightly know, miss. She listens to them talk."

"Does she?"

Ariel considered resisting the temptation before her and rejected the idea with a shrug. "Would you put the dress away for me, Ellen?" she asked. "And, er, tidy up?"

"Of course, miss," said the maid, looking a bit surprised at this sudden change in direction.

Leaving her to wonder, Ariel ran lightly down the stairs, moving very softly when she reached the final steps that led into the kitchen. Voices were floating up toward her, and she paused to listen.

"The damned girl ignores me," she heard Lord Sebastian Gresham say.

Hannah made some inaudible reply.

"Well, I'm sorry, Hannah, but it drives a man to strong language," he answered. "I know I'm not repulsive to the ladies."

Ariel crept closely, but she still couldn't catch more than a murmur of sound from Hannah.

"Don't say comeuppance," objected the visitor. "Hannah, I'm serious this time. I mean to marry the gel. I swear you've never heard me say that before."

Just outside the door, Ariel heard Hannah say, "No."

"I always meant to marry an heiress," added her companion. "I was in no hurry though. There's a fresh crop of them every year. But this one is . . . something special."

"I'm sure she won't refuse you," said Hannah comfortably. Ariel was close enough now to hear the click of her knitting needles.

"That's what I'm trying to tell you," protested Lord Sebastian. "She won't so much as look at me. There's a flock of fellows around her every minute. I can scarcely snag a dance."

Ariel pushed open the kitchen door and went in, then stopped abruptly. "Oh. Hello, Lord Sebastian," she said.

He leaped to his feet, looming very large in this low-ceilinged room. He wore his uniform, and the buttons and braid glittered impressively. His magnificent whiskers curled along his cheeks, completing the picture of an extremely dashing cavalryman. "How do?" he said. "Just having a jaw with Hannah."

"How nice," said Ariel. She sat in the chair opposite him at the kitchen table and looked up with a sweet, expectant smile.

"I, er, I should be on my way," he responded.

"You cannot go yet. I see Hannah has the teapot all ready."

Looking slowly from one of them to the other, Hannah rose to pour the boiling water over the tea leaves.

Lord Sebastian shifted from one large booted foot to the other.

Hannah got out another cup and brought the tea things to the table on a tray. There were macaroons, Ariel noticed. She wondered if she would have been offered them above stairs, or if they had been procured for Lord Sebastian's enjoyment. She reached out and took two. "So, I understand you are pursuing an heiress," she said cordially.

Lord Sebastian choked.

"What is her name? Hermione?"

He goggled at her.

"I may have it wrong," added Ariel blithely. "You

know how it is with gossip; everything is twisted around."

"Gossip?" he cried. "You can't mean people are talking . . . no one could possibly know. Hardly knew myself till yesterday."

Ariel waved a hand. "It only requires the least hint. What *is* her name?"

Lord Sebastian sighed. "Georgina," he replied. "Lady Georgina Stane."

"Much nicer than Hermione," commented Ariel. "When shall I wish you happy?"

He sighed again. "Never."

"Really? Is there some obstacle?" Ariel saw that Hannah was watching her very closely. There might have been a twinkle in the older woman's eyes, or it might have been a trick of the light.

Lord Sebastian hesitated. The struggle between discretion and a strong desire to pour out his woes was evident on his face. The latter finally won out. "She don't care a snap of her fingers for me," he complained. "I have to fight my way through a battalion of fops and fortune hunters just to speak to her, and then, likely as not, she flits off just as I open my mouth. It ain't what I'm used to," he muttered darkly. "I don't wish to brag, but the ladies are generally dashed glad to talk to me."

Ariel remembered that Lord Sebastian had quite a reputation among a certain set of ladies. "It sounds just like *The Rake Reformed*," she offered.

"Eh?" He eyed her as if she'd spoken in a foreign language.

"That is a play my mother once acted in," she added. "The situation is very similar."

He simply stared.

"You see," she explained kindly, "young ladies are sometimes instructed not to take anything seriously from a . . . a certain sort of man. They are told that he doesn't mean what he says and that he is simply amusing himself at their expense."

"That's an outrage," complained their visitor, who had been guilty of precisely this fault on many occasions.

"The stratagem that the hero used in *The Rake Reformed* might be just the thing for you," she said.

"Stratagem?" She had his full attention now.

"Yes, it was rather clever. But, well, you have to really mean to marry the lady." She had no intention of helping him deceive a fellow female.

"I do," vowed Lord Sebastian.

She decided to probe a bit further. "Because you want her money?" she asked.

He nodded. "Couldn't marry without it," he claimed. "But it ain't just her money, though. Met a score of girls with money since I joined up. But Georgina . . ." He trailed off thoughtfully.

"What is it that you like about her?" Ariel asked.

The large cavalryman looked surprised, as if it had never occurred to him to think about this. His brow furrowed. "Dashed if I know," he concluded at last. "Odd, ain't it? There's just something about her. Can't get her out of my mind. Likely to make an ass of myself when I see her. Don't make sense, but there it is." He spread his big hands.

"I'll help you," Ariel resolved. "The best thing would be for me to meet her, or at least observe her. Why don't you take me along the next time you're likely to encounter her?"

"I can't just show up at a *ton* party with you on my arm," protested Lord Sebastian, aghast. "It's not the thing. People know who you are, and besides—"

"They won't notice me," put in Ariel, who had already thought of this obstacle and formed a plan to overcome it. "But I see what you mean. We need someone else, someone to give us the proper appearance." She frowned. "An older woman, very respectable-looking but not too striking—"

"This ain't a good idea," said Lord Sebastian loudly.

Ariel's eyes had drifted to the right. "Hannah," she said.

Lord Sebastian's eyes seemed to bulge.

"I could get her a perfect gown from the theater," Ariel continued. "If you got us in the door, we could—"

"You're mad," cried the visitor. "But it don't matter, because Hannah ain't. She'll never go along with this scheme, will you, Hannah?"

Both of them turned to look at the older woman.

She gazed back at them imperturbably. "What would I do?" she asked.

"Hannah!" sputtered Lord Sebastian.

"No one will notice us," promised Ariel. "Or if they do, they will dismiss us as unfashionable nonentities."

"Can you be certain of that?" asked Hannah.

"It don't matter, because I won't do it," said Lord Sebastian, looking stubborn.

"Do you know how the hero won his bride in *The Rake Reformed*?" insinuated Ariel.

"I don't know, and I don't care. Life isn't some dam . . . dashed play."

"It was exceedingly clever."

He stuck out his jaw. "Why don't you just tell me about it then, and I'll see if I want to give it a try."

Ariel shook her head. "I must observe Lady Georgina first, to make certain."

"Blast it!" He frowned again. "You think you can get her to take some notice of me?"

"I believe so."

He glowered over this for a bit longer, then made a gesture as if throwing something away. "Very well. I suppose I shall be very sorry for this, but let's give it a go."

Ariel smiled up at him. "If there is the least problem, we will abandon the scheme at once," she promised.

"Umm." He considered. "The Coningsby ball is to-morrow. Hundreds invited. Be a good place to escape notice."

Although she sincerely hoped to help Lord Sebastian in his courtship, Ariel saw no reason why she could not use the occasion to gather information about her mother. The ball would likely offer less scope than gatherings at Carlton House, but one could pick up a great deal simply by being alert.

"Perfect," said Ariel. "We'll be ready."

"Maybe you will," he muttered. "But will I?"

Ariel stood back from the long mirror and made a critical survey of her appearance. She wore the gown that had been her old schoolmistress Miss Ames's favorite. It was made of pale blue muslin with long sleeves and a high neck with a small frill encircling it. The bodice was other-wise unornamented and slightly loose on her; the skirt fell in heavy plain folds to her feet. All in all, the dress looked as if it had been sewn for a somewhat larger, heavier woman. Ariel looked childlike in it, her curves obscured.

She had bundled her glossy brown locks into a knot at the back of her head, without so much as a curl at the temples. And she had dusted her face with some of her mother's powder, dimming her glowing complexion to a pale shadow of itself. She looked countrified, short of money, and unimportant, she thought with satisfaction. Any member of the *ton* who did happen to glance her way would dismiss her instantly as unworthy of close scrutiny, and she was certain that no one who had seen her at Carlton House would recognize her tonight.

She moved in the mirror. She could almost hear her mother saying it—mannerisms were as critical as costume to a character. She bent her head and lowered her eyelids, slumping her shoulders just a little, as if conscious of her own insignificance. She took a tentative step, like someone who asks permission to exist. The transformation was complete.

Turning, she went downstairs to the front parlor where Hannah was waiting for her. The older woman wore a dress of rich materials but little style with a matching turban that announced her position as chaperone. "What do you think?" asked Ariel, walking across the room in her beaten-down gait.

A laugh burst from Hannah, quickly stifled. "No one would take you for the girl who left here to go to Carlton House," she admitted.

Ariel straightened and grinned. "I told you."

"So you did, miss."

The street before the Coningsby town house was choked with carriages letting off elegantly dressed passengers and moving on. It took a full twenty minutes for them to reach the entry and be ushered into the towering front hall. Attendants took their wraps and then they climbed the curving staircase along with a throng of others to where their hostess and the daughter she was presenting this year waited to greet them. Lord Sebastian had timed it so that they arrived at the peak hour, when most of the invited guests would also be filing past. No one could keep track of all the names at such a time, he assured them. And besides Lady Coningsby was a bit of a lightweight in the brains department.

Consequently, they were able to move by her with a muttering of names and a bare minimum of courtesies. "Slipped us in ahead of a countess," Lord Sebastian murmured as they continued on. "Knew she'd be champing at the bit to speak to her."

The ballroom was already crowded. As he had been instructed, Lord Sebastian found them a pair of gilt chairs against the wall and settled them there. Then he went off to find his Georgina and signal Ariel.

Ariel sat primly in the straight chair observing from under lowered eyelids. She had decided that it would be best to stay on the sidelines at first, until the dancing was well under way. She would drift through the crowd later and pick up what she could.

For the next half hour, Ariel secretly watched Lord Sebastian's chosen. Lady Georgina Stane had golden hair and pale skin. She was slender and willowy. Her face was piquant rather than beautiful, with large expressive eyes, a straight nose, and a pointed chin. At the end of the half hour, during which Georgina talked and danced and stood silent by the long windows on the far wall, Ariel made up her mind. Georgina appeared to be a woman of some intelligence, and impatience. She gave short shrift to the more fatuous-looking of her admirers and appeared to brush aside fulsome compliments. She obviously enjoyed the ball, but not all of the attentions her large fortune attracted. She was just the sort of person on which the strategems Ariel had been concocting would work.

This established, Ariel rose and suggested to Hannah that they take a turn about the room as a change from sitting. Hannah agreed, and they began to walk, Ariel keeping to her shy shuffle and subdued manner. They skirted the edges of the large room, forced to move very slowly by the press of people. Ariel listened to every scrap of conversation, prepared to linger if she heard anything of interest. But they made the circuit of the room without happening upon any mention of Bess Harding's death, which had apparently already faded from the consciousness of the *ton*. This wouldn't do, thought Ariel. She had to have a way to bring up the subject, but it would be quite out of the question for the character she was portraying tonight.

"Good God," said a male voice nearby. Footsteps rang

on the parquet floor, and then a large figure loomed. "What the deuce are you doing here?" it said.

Ariel looked up to confront Lord Alan Gresham in evening dress.

Before she could reply, he said, "Hannah!" in a shocked tone.

"Not so loud," urged Ariel. At least one person had turned to look, she saw.

He stared at her. "What are you up to? If you have—"

"We'd best go somewhere more private," interrupted Hannah.

"Yes," agreed Ariel fervently. She took Hannah's arm and hurried toward the exit, trusting that Lord Alan would follow them, and forgetting for the moment that she was supposed to shuffle modestly along the floor.

They moved down the hallway outside the ballroom, glancing into the open rooms they passed. All held groups of older guests drinking and talking or playing cards. But at last, near the end, they came upon a small parlor that was empty. Ariel ducked in, pulling Hannah after her. Lord Alan was hard on their heels, and he closed the door behind him.

"What the devil are you doing?" he demanded. "I called at the house, and I was told by the maid that you had gone out to a ball." He looked her up and down. "Why are you dressed as a schoolgirl?"

"I didn't wish to be recognized."

"Recognized," he echoed. He looked at Hannah as if for a more sensible answer, then winced at the sight of her turban.

"By anyone who saw me at Carlton House," she explained.

The thought of what some of those who had seen her at Carlton House might do if they encountered her alone and unprotected—and in this ridiculous disguise—made Alan's jaw clench. She really had no idea of the sort of libertines and roués who had marked her appearances

there, or of their ideas of amusement. "You are here without an escort and without an invitation?" he asked.

"We have a perfectly good escort," Ariel informed
him.

"Who?" he demanded. He was upon her in two steps,
grasping her upper arms. "Who?" he repeated, conscious
of the flare of jealousy her admission had roused in him.

"Enough of this, now," said Hannah sharply.

Two heads turned to look at her.

"We came with Lord Sebastian," the older woman
continued. "To see this girl he wants to marry. There's no
need to fuss so."

"Sebastian?" echoed Alan. "Marry?"

Hannah smiled a little. "It is a surprise, isn't it, my
lord? But he does seem to mean it." Her eyes shifted to
Ariel. "She seemed an acceptable young lady."

Ariel nodded, then wriggled. "*Will* you let me go?"

Alan dropped his hands and stepped back. "I don't
understand," he said. "How did you come to know anything about Sebastian's affairs?"

Ariel rubbed her upper arms. They didn't actually
hurt, but his touch left behind a kind of tingle that was
deeply unsettling. "There's no mystery about it," she
said. "He came to my house to talk to—"

"Me?" Here, finally, was something that made sense,
Alan thought. For some years now, his brothers had been
turning up pretty regularly to ask his advice. They
seemed to imagine that his studies gave him knowledge
about quite unrelated topics—like investments and
chances of preferment in the royal navy and the sound-
ness of the latest agricultural theories. Apparently it was
to be marriage next. The whole thing was a bit of a burden.

"No, he—" began Ariel.

"Why didn't he just come to Carlton House? It is
rather difficult to call there, I suppose." *He* wouldn't
want to, Alan thought.

"Actually, he was looking for—"

"What does he need?" he asked with a hint of resignation.

"Nothing now."

"What do you mean, now?" He examined her dowdy gown once again, and noticed that she looked pale. If Sebastian had involved her in one of his endless romantic tangles, he thought, he'd wring his neck.

"Matters are well in hand."

"What matters?"

"Matters of the heart," replied Ariel loftily.

"What?" She never behaved predictably, Alan thought. He was almost convinced she did it on purpose, to keep him off balance.

"I mean to offer him some advice," she said.

"You? What sort of advice?"

"About how to win the lady."

"Nonsense," Alan declared. "Sebastian needs no help on that score."

"This young lady does not seem—" began Hannah.

"Why are you really here?" he added.

"I told you."

"You're using my brother as a way to continue your investigations," he said, not even hearing her.

"I am *not*," Ariel said hotly. "I came here to help him."

"What exactly do you intend to do? Play the innocent schoolgirl and recommend him to the lady as a sterling character? You'll be caught out at that."

"You wouldn't understand."

"My understanding has been judged well above the average," he answered.

"Not about this sort of thing," she responded.

"What sort of thing?"

"Matters of the heart," Ariel told him again.

"We are speaking of Sebastian?" He let some of his

annoyance come out in sarcasm. She seemed to think he didn't know his own family.

She merely nodded. "He has fallen in love," she declared.

"Don't be ridiculous."

"He has."

"He told you this?" Alan was incredulous, both at the idea of Sebastian in love and at the notion that he had told Ariel Harding about it.

"Well, I'm not sure he is entirely aware of the fact as yet," Ariel conceded.

"Ah." He nodded in comprehension. "You have made up some kind of fairy story about—"

"It is not made up! And anyway, how would you know? You think there is no such thing as love."

"There isn't, particularly if you are talking of Sebastian."

She pressed her lips together and looked away.

She was infuriatingly beautiful, Alan thought, even in that silly dowdy gown. And for exactly that reason, she had to be made to understand that she couldn't wander about London pursuing any scheme that occurred to her. "You must stop this," he said.

"You haven't any heart," she answered, a slight tremor in her voice.

"My heart is in perfect order. It is an admirably efficient pump."

"Pump?" she repeated.

"See William Harvey's treatise on the circulation of the blood," he suggested.

"No, thank you," was the stiff reply.

He dismissed this with a gesture. "You must take more care—" he began, but just then the door handle rattled, and it opened on the buzz of noise outside.

"There you are," said Sebastian, peering through the opening before coming in. "I've been looking everywhere. Hullo, Alan. You here?"

"As you see," answered Alan sardonically.

Sebastian threw him a glance. "Anything wrong?" he wondered.

"Nothing at all," answered Ariel. "Everything is perfect."

Sebastian drew back a bit at her tone. There was a short silence. Hannah looked from one of them to the other with an interested expression.

"Came to see if you were ready to go. You did say eleven," Sebastian added finally.

"Quite ready," was the crisp reply.

"I'll escort you home," declared Alan.

"We don't require an escort, do we, Hannah?"

This appeal to a higher authority appeared to unsettle both the Gresham brothers. Hannah gazed at them for a moment longer. She might have been amused, or merely thoughtful. It was impossible to say. "I don't believe we do," she answered finally.

"Of course not!" Ariel swept out of the room, her schoolgirl pose forgotten, and Hannah followed.

"What set her back up?" wondered Sebastian.

"I haven't the faintest idea," replied his usually omniscient brother.

Chapter Ten

———— ❖ ————

Ellen offered to help Ariel get ready for the Carlton House masquerade, and she showed an unexpected talent for dressing hair. "I was studying with Harriet—her grace's dresser," she said when Ariel complimented her skill. "She's teaching me how to be a lady's maid."

"I'm sure you will be a very good one," replied Ariel warmly.

Ellen flushed with pleasure as she went to test the curling irons she was heating. Satisfied, she carefully picked one up and brought it over to begin transforming Ariel's glossy brown locks into the wild corkscrew curls of a Gypsy girl. She bit her lower lip in concentration as she wrapped strands of hair around the hot iron and twisted them for just the right amount of time—enough to curl but not to scorch. When she finally stepped back to assess her work, she grinned. "You look quite . . . different, miss," she said.

Ariel consulted the mirror. Her hair was a cloud of brown above the multicolored Gypsy gown. Her hazel eyes peered out of it brightly, like those of a small animal.

The glow of her cheeks and lips completed the illusion. She did look like someone else entirely.

Ellen began to pin the spangled scarf, with its dangling bits of gold, onto the top of Ariel's head. This tamed her hair slightly, though it still curled about her face. She slipped the gold hoops into her ears and checked the mirror again. It was a wonderful costume, she thought. She couldn't imagine anyone having a better one.

Ellen cocked her head and went to peer out the front window. "A carriage is here, miss," she said. "I'll see to the door."

Standing, Ariel shook out her voluminous skirts and tried tossing her head. She had seen lots of plays with Gypsies as a child, she recalled. It was easy to remember the way the actresses walked and turned and threw flashing glances. She wheeled before the mirror, raising one shoulder and looking back over it, then giggled at the effect. Picking up a black half mask from her dressing table, she headed downstairs.

Ariel was a bit surprised to see Hannah come out of the front parlor and cross the entryway as she came down. Lord Alan was standing in the center of the parlor when she went in. It would have been very interesting, Ariel thought, to have heard what Hannah had said to him.

"Do you like my costume?" she said in greeting. She lifted her arms and whirled about, drawing the bodice of her Gypsy gown tight across her breasts and making the ruffled skirts flare out. She moved her hips as she remembered seeing the actresses playing Gypsies do onstage.

"You didn't tell me you were wearing fancy dress," he pointed out. A flush mottled his high cheekbones.

"It's a masquerade."

"I'm well aware of that fact. But that dress . . ." He gestured in her direction as if he couldn't find words.

"Isn't it gorgeous? I found it among Bess's things. She was very extravagant about clothes, I'm afraid."

"It makes you look . . ." His flush deepened. His
eyes were hot. He looked as if he might explode.

Very flattered by his reaction, Ariel decided to go to
his rescue. "It makes me look exactly right for a masquerade. Many people will be wearing quite similar ensembles." She knew this was true from her mother's long-ago
descriptions.

She then surveyed his conventional evening dress.
"But I see you haven't troubled yourself."

"I have been occupied with arranging for more guards
and trying to secure every opening in the building. We
won't be able to identify any of the guests for certain. A
dozen 'ghosts' could make their way in."

"Oh." She should have realized, Ariel thought. The
progress of his investigation was all that was important to
him.

"However," Lord Alan added, "our haunters may
have other difficulties." He appeared grimly pleased with
this idea.

"What?"

"I have set a watch on the actors from the theater that
they will not be able to evade, as several of them have
before this. If they are behind these tricks, they will be
caught tonight. And that will be the end of it."

"You expect it to be them."

"I do. In fact, I expect this whole irritating farce to be
finished tonight." He took a breath as if this notion
cheered him considerably.

"Congratulations," she said, wondering why she
found the idea so depressing. A pall seemed to have fallen
over the entire occasion, which she had anticipated so
eagerly.

"Shall we go?" he asked.

Silently, she followed him out to the carriage.

• • •

Carlton House was lit from top to bottom for the evening, and streams of costumed and merely fashionable people were already passing through the door. "Just what do you intend to do tonight?" Lord Alan asked as he handed Ariel down to the pavement.

"Take advantage of whatever opportunities come along," she replied.

"What do you mean by 'opportunities'?"

"I won't know until they appear," she answered, and moved away before he could say more.

As always at the prince regent's festivities, the reception rooms glittered, the talk rose to a roar, and the champagne flowed inexhaustibly. Also, as always, it was stiflingly hot, and no unattached woman was safe from ogling glances and brazen approaches of the aging gallants who surrounded the sovereign—not to mention the sovereign himself. The addition of masks and supposed disguises merely intensified this atmosphere. The prince seemed to take it as license to be even more outrageous than usual, even though his portly figure was quite identifiable in the trappings of a Persian autocrat.

"You are not to wander off on your own," Lord Alan instructed.

"I have no intention of doing so," Ariel informed him. Indeed, she was quite grateful for his escort, considering some of the things that were going on in the room.

"I'm certain you have some plan for the evening," said Lord Alan. "Do you intend to communicate it to me?"

"I shall be a silly, empty-headed young girl who is fascinated with the idea of Bess Harding's ghost," she told him. "I shall ask everyone I encounter if they saw it, and then if they knew Bess, and then if they don't think it is terrible what happened to her. It will be much easier with people masked. They will say more than they would otherwise. And we shall see what sort of answers they give and where the conversation goes."

"And from this you expect . . . ?"

"To gather bits of information that can be pieced together to reveal something," she retorted. "Isn't that the nature of investigation?"

Lord Alan said nothing.

"Why are you looking at me that way?" asked Ariel. He was staring down at her as if she had said something extraordinary, or as if she were a house cat who had suddenly spoken to him. When he didn't reply, she raised one shoulder and turned to examine the crowd. "Do you know Lord Royalton?" she added. "I have heard that he and my mother quarreled over something. We should be sure to speak to him. Do you think he will be here tonight?"

"I have no idea. I am not acquainted with the gentleman."

"We must find out," urged Ariel.

"Must we?"

She threw him a look.

"Oh, very well. My father will know. I'll ask him."

With a satisfied nod, Ariel took his arm. "Shall we begin?"

"Do I have any say in the matter?"

Throwing him a reproachful glance from behind her mask, she tugged on his arm and led him into the chattering crowd. "There is no need to be sarcastic." Ariel surveyed the people before them. "There's Lady Feverel. She was well acquainted with my mother. I meant to talk with her, though I doubt she will remember me."

She was mistaken, however. As soon as Lady Feverel noticed them, she dismissed the small man she had been talking to and beckoned imperiously. "Bess's daughter, isn't it?" She peered through a glass mounted on a long, much-tasseled ivory handle, seeming to look right through Ariel's mask. "Yes, I'm sure it is." She turned. "And one of Langford's sons. The prince has you staying here, does he not?"

Lord Alan merely bowed in acknowledgment.

Large and stately as a frigate, and well draped in yellow satin, Lady Feverel turned again. "Forgotten your name," she stated. "My memory's shockingly bad. Something unusual, wasn't it?"

"Ariel."

"Yes. Out of a play, I believe. Bess was such an original."

Her wide-eyed innocent role would not be of any use here, Ariel thought. She nodded soberly. "I am trying to find out what happened to her," she said.

"Surely that's . . . er . . . clear," answered Lady Feverel.

"Not why it happened."

"Ah." The older woman paused, seeming to consider this. She blinked her small eyes at the chattering crowd like a sleepy bear.

"Did you see the ghost?" wondered Ariel.

"On several occasions. Once fairly close. It wasn't Bess, of course."

Ariel moved involuntarily.

"My dear, surely you didn't think it was?"

"No. No, of course not." She hadn't, thought Ariel. Naturally she knew better.

"Much younger woman," Lady Feverel was saying. "Not nearly so beautiful, under all the makeup." She shot a glance at Lord Alan. "Caught her yet?"

"Possibly," he said.

She gave a nod like a thoroughbred horse throwing up its head.

"Did you notice anything . . . odd before she died?" asked Ariel. "Was she different in any way? Did she say anything to you about . . . oh, I don't know?"

"Bess was the same as ever," said Lady Feverel. "Running about a bit more, perhaps—always in motion. But she had her moods."

Ariel nodded.

"She liked to laugh," said the older woman quietly. "Never wanted to hear unpleasantness. I miss her."

Ariel's eyes filmed with tears.

"I must go," added Lady Feverel. "My husband will tolerate only so much of these affairs, and then he begins to offend people out of irritation." She gazed at Ariel through her glass once again. "Take care, my dear." She moved off like a ship under full sail.

Ariel swallowed, then took a breath. "This is harder than I expected," she murmured. She felt a hand on her arm. Lord Alan was looking down at her with an odd expression on his handsome face. It might have been sympathy; Ariel wasn't sure. But something about it made breathing a bit difficult. She had to turn away and look for someone else to accost.

"Did you know Bess Harding when she was alive?" Ariel asked an aged roué some time later. He had come dressed in the powder and paint of his early youth and looked rather like a spectral figure from the past himself.

"Knew her intimately," he leered, his grin revealing a row of blackening teeth.

What a blatant lie, Ariel thought. Her fastidious mother wouldn't have come within five feet of such a man. "It was so shocking, what happened to her," she breathed. "You must have been deeply affected by it."

"Eh? Oh. Of course, of course. Shocking." The man's rheumy eyes were fixed on Ariel as if she were edible.

"Why do you think she did it?" she asked, trying to look even more innocent and gullible.

"What?" He looked surprised by the question, and completely uninterested in the topic.

"Killed herself," answered Ariel in a quietly relentless tone.

"No idea," was the reply. "Very foolish of her. Never the answer to anything, eh?" He leered at Ariel again, trying to look dangerously attractive, she thought. "Shall we stroll in the garden?" He crooked his arm and offered it. "Or take our leave? Even better, eh?"

Ariel let her eyes widen even farther, as if she couldn't imagine what he was talking about.

"I could show you a thing or two." He leered more markedly. "Experience beats out the young men every time."

"I couldn't leave the prince's entertainment," answered Ariel. She took a step back and, as she had counted on, bumped into Lord Alan close behind her. "I'm here with friends."

"Eh?" The old libertine's eyes traveled upward, and upward, taking in the tall figure of her escort. Then he blew out his lips in disgust and stumped away in search of other prey.

"Enjoying yourself?" asked Lord Alan, sounding amused.

"We are eliminating possibilities," replied Ariel. But she was less certain than she had been earlier in the evening. No one had told her anything interesting. All she had accomplished so far, she thought, was giving everyone the impression that she was a silly, naive chatterbox as well as Lord Alan's mistress. "Is Lord Royalton here?" she asked.

Lord Alan shrugged. "There is my father. I'll go and ask him."

Ariel made ready to follow him across the room. But she saw him make a small quick movement with his hand, and in the next instant his brother Robert materialized from the crowd at their back and made a mock salute. "At your service," he said.

Lord Alan merely gave him an admonitory look. "I'll be right back," he said, and strode off toward the duke.

"What was that about?" wondered Ariel.

Lord Robert raised his eyebrows as if he didn't know what she was referring to and said, "Would you like a glass of champagne? Or lemonade perhaps?"

"No, thank you. He gave you some sort of signal. I saw it."

"Dashed hot, ain't it? But then Prinny's evenings always are. You'd think he could do something about it."

Perhaps he hadn't wanted her to encounter his father, Ariel thought. Perhaps she wasn't of sufficient quality to converse with a duke. "Keeping me out of the way, are you?" she asked Lord Robert bitterly.

He goggled at her.

"Making sure I don't push in where I'm not wanted?"

"Eh?"

"You needn't worry," she continued icily. "I haven't the slightest interest in forcing an acquaintance with your family."

"No question of that," he stammered.

"There certainly isn't!" She clenched a fist on her fan. "As if I would ever do such a thing."

"No, I mean . . . nothing like that. Standing guard."

"What?"

"Me. I'm standing guard."

"Over me?"

Lord Robert met her masked eyes fleetingly. He seemed to grope for a suitable reply, and not find one.

"Lord Alan asked you to watch over me?" she repeated.

He looked hunted. "Told me to come along and lend a hand," he said finally. "Supposed to keep mum about it, though."

Ariel blinked. The idea that Lord Alan had planned carefully for her welfare, and asked the help of his family to ensure it, made her feel odd. It *was* arrogant interference in her life, like arranging for servants without telling her first. But it also meant that he was thinking of her, wishing her . . . well. She looked across the room to where he was in earnest conversation with his father. The duke glanced at her. Ariel couldn't tell if he was puzzled or irritated or just impatient. He turned back to his son and appeared to ask him a question.

Lord Robert cleared his throat.

Ariel returned her attention to him.

"Rather you wouldn't mention that I told you," he said.

"Lord Alan does not want me to know that he asked you to help him?"

This seemed a bit too complicated for her companion. "Asked me to keep mum about the matter," he said again.

"I won't mention it," Ariel assured him.

Lord Robert looked considerably relieved. He let go a deep breath. His habitual pleasant, somewhat vacant expression descended upon his handsome features once again. He wore a black domino over his evening dress, but this was the only concession he had made to the occasion.

"Do you often come to Carlton House?" asked Ariel.

He shook his head. "Not my sort of company. Too old, you know. I look in on the great fetes, but otherwise . . ." He shrugged, then made an infinitesimal adjustment to the intricate folds of his neckcloth.

"It was very kind of you to come tonight, then," she said.

"Alan asked me," Lord Robert replied, as if his compliance was a given.

"And you do whatever he asks?"

Lord Robert pondered a moment. "Yes," he concluded.

"You're very fond of him," suggested Ariel. This was how a family worked, she thought.

"Ye-es. Well, he's my brother." A tiny bit of feather floated off the intricate headdress of a passing matron and landed on his sleeve. He brushed at it. "The thing is," he continued as if it had just worked itself out in his mind, "Alan never asks anything. Always kept to himself a good deal, even when we were small. Always had some scheme of his own going, and never seemed to think any of us could be of the least use. So when he asked . . ."

Ariel, who was extremely interested in this, nodded encouragingly.

Lord Robert shrugged, as if the answer was self-evident.

"What sort of schemes did he have as a child?" she asked, wanting to hear much more of this.

Her companion made a vague gesture. "Examining things," he replied. "Puzzling out how they worked. I remember when we were still in the nursery, the servants were constantly finding a clock or some bit of machinery all in pieces in a corner. Alan was seven or eight when he got the knack of putting them together again."

Ariel made an encouraging noise to keep him talking.

"We all wandered about in the woods down in Kent, collecting things," Lord Robert mused, "but it went further with Alan. He was always reading some dashed treatise and trying to experiment." He grinned. "I remember once he got it into his head to stick things in the oven."

Ariel raised her eyebrows.

"To see how they responded to heat," Lord Robert explained. "Our mother's favorite vase exploded. Sounded like a cannon shot." He shook his head. "She shouted at him. She hardly ever did that."

A sudden vivid impression of a household including six young boys rose in Ariel's mind. Her respect for the duchess of Langford increased abruptly. Hannah, too, she thought.

"He had to play for her six nights running to get back in her good graces," Lord Robert added.

"Play?" echoed Ariel.

"The pianoforte." He shook his head again. "He's deucedly good. Teachers used to rave about it."

"He plays the pianoforte?"

Lord Robert looked self-conscious. "Ain't usual, I know. But then nothing about Alan is usual."

"No." Nothing at all, thought Ariel, assimilating this surprising new bit of information.

"And now he's not even acting like himself," he complained. "Hanging about London, going to evening parties. Not like him at all."

"The prince summoned him," Ariel pointed out.

"Yes, but my mother says . . ." He stopped, seeming to recall the identity of his listener. "Er . . ." He looked around the room. "Ah, here's Alan back," he finished with obvious relief.

Lord Alan joined them, to Ariel's regret. She was certain she could have gotten a great deal more interesting information out of his brother given a little time.

"Royalton is here, somewhere," Lord Alan said.

"We should find him," said Ariel, and received a grimace in response.

"Excuse me," said Lord Robert. "Have to speak to someone." He melted into the crowd.

"Your brother is very kind," ventured Ariel. She was becoming curious about all of the Gresham family.

"He's not a bad sort," acknowledged Lord Alan. "If he would find some useful occupation for himself, he might do very well."

"Work like yours, you mean?"

He smiled. "He wouldn't care much for that. It would have to be something that interested him. But Robert appears to care only for the latest fashion in dress and the gossip of the *ton*. He and Sebastian fritter away their days at the tailor or on the promenade. It would drive me mad to live as they do."

"Do they feel the same way?"

"What?"

"Would it drive them mad to live as you do?"

He stared down at her. "I suppose it might," he admitted.

"What about your other brothers?"

"James is the captain of a navy ship. Randolph is rector of a parish in the north. Nathaniel, the eldest, works with my father in managing the family properties."

"There are so many of you," Ariel murmured.

"A few too many, perhaps."

"You don't mean that."

Lord Alan shrugged. "I just hate waste, and it seems to me that Robert and Sebastian waste most of their time."

"Are all your brothers afraid of you?" wondered Ariel, half teasing.

"Afraid? Of course not. What a ridiculous idea." He looked down at her as if he couldn't imagine what she meant.

"Not afraid," she conceded. Belatedly, she remembered that she had promised Lord Robert not to mention his assigned role here tonight. So she had no excuse for asking if they all agreed to any request he made. "Shall we look for Lord Royalton?" she said instead.

"No," he replied. "I draw the line at Royalton. From what my father tells me, his reputation is . . . black."

"What is he? A libertine? A drunkard? Does he cheat at cards?"

He said nothing.

"If he is so bad, he is exactly the sort of man I wish to speak to," she announced. "Perhaps he threatened my mother!"

Lord Alan shook his head. "I will speak to Royalton myself, but—"

"Gresham. Ho there, Gresham," came an odd furtive cry. They turned to find the prince regent bearing down on them, his Persian costume billowing and glittering in the light of innumerable candles. Resignedly, Alan watched him approach. A trickle of sweat was running down the prince's neck from under his bulbous, bejeweled turban. His robe, though expensively tailored, still resembled nothing more than a spangled circus tent.

His pudgy face was red and his pale eyes bulged with some strong emotion. It was hardly the picture of a great monarch, Alan thought.

The prince stopped before them and looked stealthily to the left and right to see if anyone was listening, effectively drawing the attention of everyone nearby by his odd behavior. Then he leaned closer to Alan and hissed, "She's here! Bess is here!"

"What?" Alan was startled, and sharply disappointed. He had been certain that tonight he would trap the haunters and end this hoax.

"I saw her by the stairs," panted the prince. "She was . . ." His mouth dropped open. "No, by God, she's over there in the corner. How did she get . . . ? It's uncanny!"

Alan had already given a sign to one of the men posted about the room. "Stay here," he said to Ariel, and started toward the figure in the yellow gown.

The prince came panting along at his heels. "I left her by the stairs, I tell you. She couldn't have gotten all the way down the room by any ordinary means. If she's taken to hopping about the place like some sort of—"

"People are listening, sir," Alan pointed out. Ariel was right behind the prince, he noticed with annoyance.

Two of the guards converged on the suspected woman as they did, and took up positions on either side of her. The creature's face was powdered dead white, Alan observed, and her long hair was red. The yellow dress seemed the same. A half mask hid the upper part of her face. But instead of emitting frightening noises or calling for justice, this female offered a simpering smile and a curtsy. "Your Majesty," she said, as if delighted to see them all.

"Eh?" exclaimed the prince, shying like a spooked horse. "Bess?"

The woman tittered.

Ariel started to step forward, and Alan blocked her. "I

am afraid we must ask you to remove your mask," he said. "What is your name?"

The woman didn't hesitate or object. Pulling off the mask, she revealed a beaming face. "It's Nellie Jenkins," she said. "Surely Your Majesty hasn't forgotten the opera house, and the time we—"

"Oh, er . . ." sputtered the prince.

The woman batted her eyes at him. Brown eyes, Alan noticed. "Your costume?" he said, to verify a sinking feeling.

She tittered again. "I've come as the ghost," she told them. "Dora and I thought it was the best joke, didn't we, Dora?" She beckoned to another woman who hovered nearby, obviously longing to be presented to the prince.

The latter groaned.

"There's another one coming down the stairs," said one of the men Alan had summoned.

"There's one at the buffet as well," observed the other man.

Alan felt like groaning himself. He extricated the prince from the two fawning women and led him away. "Apparently, the ghost is a popular costume this evening," he said. "We will question all of them, but I think we will find that none of them is involved in the earlier incidents."

"I've become a laughingstock," moaned the prince, leaning heavily on Alan's arm as they walked across the room.

Alan met Ariel's eyes and saw his own response so clearly mirrored there that he had to press his lips together to restrain a smile.

"Champagne," said the prince then. "I must have champagne."

They reached the buffet where he downed one glass immediately and took up another. "It's like a nightmare," he said, emptying that glass as well. "Only I'm not asleep, you see."

"No, sir," replied Alan, keeping himself sternly in check.

"You said it would be all over tonight," he accused. The monarch drank off half of a third glass of champagne.

"If people consider it a joke to wear ghost costumes, then it has become a kind of fad," put in Ariel. "They'll forget all about it in a week."

"Eh?" The prince looked up as if he hadn't noticed her before. "Who's this? Oh, yes, the girl from the cupboard." His gaze sharpened, taking in her charming costume and the glow of her eyes and skin. "That's a dashed fetching rig," he commented.

"Thank you, Your Majesty."

"Gypsy, ain't you?"

Ariel nodded.

"Dancer, eh? Can you . . . ?" He gestured with his hands and waggled his broad hips. Ariel shook her head, smiling.

"Oh, come. Give it a try." The prince swayed again, his faux Persian robe fluttering. His eyes were devouring every detail of Ariel's person, and he seemed to have forgotten all about the uproar of a moment past.

"I have no talent as a dancer," responded Ariel evenly.

"Too hard on yourself," insisted the sovereign. "Nothing to it." Wriggling, he turned in a circle, drawing a host of amused glances and hidden smiles.

"You are very good, Your Majesty," said Ariel. "Perhaps you should have come to the masquerade as a Gypsy."

Alan choked and threw her a warning look, which she ignored.

"Oh, I did so, my dear, in my younger days," was the reply. "I could teach you a thing or two about . . . dancing." He leered down at her.

Ariel laced her hands around Alan's arm and leaned against him, causing him to forget everything in the room but the feel of her along his side. "You're very kind," she told the prince. "But my time is fully . . . occupied."

"Eh?" He looked from her to Alan and back again. "Ah." Conflicting emotions passed across his florid face. "Mustn't poach," he murmured halfheartedly. He glanced at Alan as if he expected him to hand Ariel over like a gift.

Ariel pressed closer. Her beast was molded against his arm, and Alan was washed by a wave of heat. She rested her head on his shoulder, providing the crowd with the very picture of an acknowledged mistress. He wanted to shake her. He wanted to make love to her.

The prince gave a disappointed grunt. "You told me the ghost would be finished tonight," he complained, his frustration clear in his tone.

"So I believe," replied Alan tightly.

"It'd better be," was the petulant response. "I didn't bring you down to London to spend your time dallying with the ladies. Eh?"

Blood pounded in Alan's temples, but all he could say was, "No, sir."

"Gypsy," muttered the prince, turning away toward the champagne. "Gypsy's supposed to dance."

As soon as he was well away Alan grasped Ariel's arm and hurried her along the polished floor and out into an anteroom. When a knot of revelers passed through this smaller room, he pulled her farther, into an ornate parlor that was at least temporarily vacant. There, he finally released her. Ariel gazed up at him. "You must stop pretending to be my mistress," he said in a low voice. "You have no conception of what such a game could mean, of the possible consequences."

"I have told you that I don't care about gossip or—"

"What about men calling at your house, perhaps forcing their way in? What about being accosted at any event you choose to attend—the theater, for example?"

"What do you mean?"

Alan could feel the blood surging in his veins. "Everyone now believes you to be the sort of woman who . . . You will not be given the opportunity to refuse."

She looked shaken, and he hated that. The last thing he had wanted was to increase her vulnerability. "You wouldn't listen to me," he said. "You flail about, rushing from one thing to another, with no system or method, never taking the time to carry through on an idea, leaping on to the next."

"You . . . you care for nothing but systems," she responded. "You think you have to prove what is completely obvious."

"You rely on whims and guesses," he countered. "There is no solid basis for your thinking. It is an illusion of intellect."

"You are shackled by rules," she cried. "They blind you to all the important things."

"What utter nonsense!"

"You are closed-minded," she said.

Goaded beyond his limit, Alan took hold of her upper arms. "I am not closed-minded," he replied through clenched teeth. "I am a man of science. Above all else, I maintain an open mind."

Ariel put her hands against his chest and pushed. Something about the gesture destroyed the final rags of his control, and he crushed her against the whole length of him and caught her lips in an unrelenting kiss.

He had been wanting to do this for so long. His pulse leaped, and every muscle tensed. She was softness and shadow and fire. The taste of her was far more heady than the prince's champagne. The scent of her excited him beyond bearing.

Alan left rational thought behind. He knew only wanting her, and making her want him just as urgently.

He softened the kiss and moved his lips on hers. Feeling her body relax somewhat in his grasp, he slid his hands over her curves and molded her even closer to him. He coaxed and gentled, and when her lips softened and parted he felt a surge of triumph greater than any in his life so far.

He lifted his head briefly to look at her. She was so beautiful—all glossy tones of brown and peach and cream—so delicately made and exquisitely finished. Gazing at her redoubled his hunger.

Ariel opened her eyes, which had been languorously closed. They sparkled with hazel lights. "Alan," she whispered, echoes of surrender in her voice.

He kissed her again, the pressure of his desire pushing her backward until she reached the wall of the room. He pressed her against it with his whole body in a kiss that seared through him, setting fire along his bones. One of his thighs parted her knees, and she made no move to resist. Instead, she clung, as if she wanted more of him.

Alan heard himself groan. He was burning up. He was relentless and exultant and half-mad. His hands ran along Ariel's thighs, pulling up her many-layered skirts in a froth of glittering material.

"Back here?" inquired an intrusive male voice. "I don't see . . ."

Jerking as if he had been shocked, Alan tore away from Ariel, leaving her limp against the wall. He turned to meet the intruders on their privacy, a man and a woman in fancy dress who were obviously looking for the same. His face taut, he more or less snarled at them. After one startled look, they ducked back the way they had come.

But they had broken the spell. Appalled, Alan faced the fact that he had been on the verge of taking her right here in Carlton House. "God," he muttered, rubbing a hand over his face.

"Alan?" murmured Ariel softly.

He couldn't look at her. He couldn't speak to her. If he did, all would be lost once again. Before she could say more, he turned his back and strode out of the room.

Ariel leaned on the plaster, trying to get her breath back. She was still dizzy with the feel of hard muscles and the fresh masculine scent of him. The compelling rhythm of his heartbeat still beat in her, and memories of auburn hair curling on his neck and mesmerizing blue eyes blurred her vision.

Ariel felt as if prickles were running along every inch of her skin. This was what her mother had continually warned against, said some part of her brain. But she didn't care. She took one deep breath, then another.

Where had Alan gone? she wondered. He could not have left her here. He would not have abandoned her in this house. In a moment he would reappear, and they would talk.

She concentrated on recovering her breath, on slowing the hammering of her heart. Moments passed before her legs felt wholly steady again. She straightened and moved away from the wall. Surely it was time for him to come back?

She heard footsteps approaching. Tidying her costume, which was rather crushed in the front, she prepared to face him.

"Hullo?" Lord Robert Gresham appeared in the doorway, peering in as if he half expected to find a wild animal awaiting him. "There you are," he added. "Alan asked me to escort you home."

"He what?"

"Wanted me to see you home," he repeated.

"Where is he?" replied Ariel in a dangerous voice.

"Had to go." Lord Robert spread his hands. "Pressing engagement. Very sorry and all that."

"How dare he!" burst from Ariel.

Lord Robert started back.

"Of all the . . . the wretched, cowardly . . ."

"Alan ain't a coward," interrupted his brother. "In fact . . ." He moved farther into the room and assumed a wise expression. "Not a good idea to make him angry. You wouldn't know it, but underneath, he's got a rather hot temper. I remember one time when we were out on the river—"

"*He* has a temper!" exclaimed Ariel. "*He?*"

Lord Robert was nodding. "You don't notice right away, but . . ." He stopped abruptly as Ariel's teeth showed in what was distinctly not a smile.

"I'll show him temper," she muttered. "Not a good idea to make *him* angry?" She blew out a breath. "I'll show him what is not a good idea!"

Lord Robert made a small sound, rather like a bleat. Ariel turned on him. "What?"

He made the sound again. "Ready to go?" he answered in a higher-than-normal voice.

"Quite ready," she informed him, and swept out of the room leaving him in her wake.

Chapter Eleven

— ❖ —

On her way downstairs the next morning, Ariel walked past the open door of her mother's former bedchamber. A flicker of movement caught her eye, and she stepped inside, puzzled. Prospero lounged magnificently on the coverlet of the huge four-poster bed. "You shouldn't be in here," Ariel said. "Come down to the kitchen. We'll get you something to eat." Prospero had charmed Ellen and Hannah from the day of their arrival, and there was no problem finding tidbits.

The cat ignored her. He stretched himself out at full length, extending his front claws luxuriously, and yawned.

"You'll leave fur all over that silk," said Ariel, reaching for him.

Rolling quickly over, he slipped from her grasp. Finding himself at the front corner of the great bed, he fixed his attention on one of its posts. This massive carved timber, six inches square, rose to the low ceiling. Bess had wanted a bed to match her old house, and she had convinced one of her noble friends to part with this relic of an earlier age.

Rising up on his hind legs, Prospero sank his front claws into the thickest part of the post, which was carved into small panels with a rosette in the middle of each side, and began to sharpen them on the iron-hard old wood.

"Don't do that!" cried Ariel. She grabbed for him again.

Prospero evaded her fingers, gazed at her with his great golden eyes, and enthusiastically returned to the post. Ariel heard the click of his claws on the wood.

"What's the matter with you?" she said. "Come here." She took him firmly around the middle to pick him up, but at that moment, one of the cat's claws caught in a crack. He tugged to free it, and one side of the bedpost opened like a tiny door, revealing a hidden cavity stuffed with papers. Prospero mewed in surprise and sprang to the floor. Ariel stood staring at her mother's secret hiding place. "The bed," she murmured. "I should have thought of that."

Ariel had always believed that her mother had some cache in the house where she hid papers and valuables. It was the sort of thing Bess would do. She had delighted in secrets, and she had never trusted banks or any other institutions. But search as she might, Ariel hadn't been able to find the hiding place. She'd been over the house from top to bottom. She had gone through every box and drawer. She had emptied each wardrobe in the attic and the wine bin in the cellar. She had even tapped on the paneled walls and floors looking for concealed hollows. She had tried to follow her mother's likely thought processes, and deduce the place from there. But although she felt certain the cache was in Bess's bedchamber somewhere, it continued to elude her, and she had more or less given up hunting. Now here it was, open before her.

She reached up and pulled one sheaf of papers from the cavity, and then another. The hollow was surprisingly large, extending up into the post for a foot or more. By the time she had emptied it, a small pile of rolled and folded paper lay on the bed, some of it looking years old. After pushing her arm into the bedpost and feeling around to make sure nothing else was there, Ariel pushed the tiny door almost closed, and then sat on the bed to look through what she had found.

She started with the largest bundle, tied with red ribbon. This turned out to be documents associated with the house, some of which Bess's man of business had been asking for; Ariel was pleased and relieved to find them. Setting these aside, she unfolded a larger parchment. It was a legal document recording a loan of three thousand pounds that Bess had made to a woman named Flora Jennings. In the top left-hand corner, Bess had written "sold ruby."

Ariel stared at it in amazement. This was a huge sum of money, given to someone she had never once heard her mother mention. Bess had been generous with small sums, even careless sometimes, but she did not part with amounts like this. Ariel examined the document more closely. The address listed for Flora Jennings was in a very poor part of town—an area where three thousand pounds would be a fortune. It wouldn't be sneezed at anywhere in London, Ariel thought, frowning at the page. Why would Bess have lent this much?

Setting the parchment aside, she opened another. This one was the deed to a house in the same area as the Jennings address. It also had the notation "sold ruby" written in the corner. Why would Bess have parted with this fabulous jewel for such purposes? Ariel wondered. Why would she have wished to own a house in a back slum?

Utterly bewildered, she put the deed with the loan document and continued her examination. Many of the other papers were letters. Scanning them quickly, Ariel grew embarrassed. Her mother had kept expressions of affection from many of the noblemen with whom she had formed connections over the years, revealing a sentimental streak that seemed at odds with Ariel's memories. Or had she kept them as a kind of insurance? Ariel was certain Bess would never have stooped to blackmail, but she would not have hesitated to expose secrets in order to protect herself.

Stacking the letters in a single pile, she put them back inside the bedpost, gathering the remaining documents to take to her own room. When she had set them on her desk and was sorting those to go to the solicitor from the others, she stopped suddenly and closed her fists, overcome by a sadness so deep it was frightening. Was she really never to see her mother again? Was Bess to disappear forever in a fog of mysteries and secrets?

Moments passed in a dark blankness. Ariel groped in it, trying to find her way. She couldn't just stay in the house, she thought finally. The walls were beginning to close in on her. She was starting to feel helpless. She needed to *do* something. Her eyes fell on the documents before her on the desk. She would visit this Flora Jennings, she decided, and ask her point-blank why Bess had lent her such a huge amount of money.

This resolve made her feel better, but only for a moment. She couldn't go into that part of town alone. And she couldn't ask Lord Alan Gresham, who had been her escort on other perilous forays, to accompany her. She couldn't even think of him, in fact, without becoming furious and confused. On the one hand, he insisted that there was no such thing as love and that he had no interest in romantic encounters. On the other, he kissed her until she could barely stand. He helped her and abandoned her, encouraged and criticized her, leaving her totally uncertain what would happen from one moment to the next. He was intolerable!

But who would take his place? No one could, an inner voice insisted. Ariel dropped the papers onto her writing desk, and stood looking at the floor. She would go mad if she did nothing.

And then she remembered that Lord Sebastian Gresham owed her some service. She had given him a splendid plan for winning his Lady Georgina. She would send a note round asking him to escort her.

The note was duly written and dispatched, and it received a prompt reply. But instead of Lord Sebastian, it fetched his brother Robert. "Sebastian had duty this afternoon," Ariel was told. "He couldn't get away, so he sent me." Lord Robert looked extremely curious. "What's this about a plan of campaign for winning the Stane girl?"

"Did you come in a carriage?" Ariel asked.

"Rode over," he replied.

"Then we will need a hack." She began to tie the strings of her bonnet under her chin.

"Where are we going?"

Ariel eyed him. "There is a call I must make," she answered. "And it is not in the . . . best part of town."

"Down in the City?" he wondered. "Solicitor or something like that?"

"Not exactly."

"Where then?" Lord Robert inquired.

Reluctantly, she told him.

"That can't be right. That's in a back slum, ain't it?"

"It isn't the best of neighborhoods," Ariel temporized. "But I must go there."

"I don't know . . ."

"I'll tell you all about the plan of campaign I suggested to Lord Sebastian," she offered.

"Well, but . . ."

"It is imperative that I visit that address," she declared. "That is why I asked for your escort."

Lord Robert looked torn between doubt, gratification, and reluctance. "Why ain't Alan taking you?" he asked, then frowned. "Has he forbidden you to go? Because if he has, I won't have anything to—"

"He has not," declared Ariel. "Will you come, or shall I go without you?"

"Where is he then?" responded Lord Robert stubbornly.

"Busy with his own affairs, I suppose." Inspired, she added, "He always has a great deal to do."

"That's true." He considered. "You'll tell the whole story—about Sebastian—if I escort you?"

Ariel nodded.

"Well . . . all right. Is it true he really means to tie the knot this time?"

She nodded again.

"So what did you tell him?" he prompted.

"To ask her questions," she responded.

"Questions?" he echoed, puzzled.

"To seek her opinion on various matters, to ask her advice," she elaborated.

Lord Robert looked bewildered.

"It all comes from *The Rake Reformed*," she went on. "In that play there is a young woman who is courted by all sorts of gentlemen. All of them tell her how lovely she is and how she has captured their hearts, but none of them cares a whit what she thinks, or what she wants in a . . . a larger sense, beyond a glass of lemonade between sets at a ball."

"Larger sense," he repeated, as if he had never heard the two words put together before.

"She has been constantly treated as an empty-headed doll, you see. But the hero of the play truly wishes to know more about her. That is the key, as I told Lord Sebastian. He must be *truly* interested."

He looked at her. "You think some scheme from a play will impress an heiress who's been brought up in the midst of the *haut ton*?" He shook his head. "It ain't going to work."

She smiled. "Let us discuss the matter again in two weeks' time," she said. "And then we will see."

"Huh. I'd give you ten to one odds it don't work."

"Five pounds," Ariel answered. "I'll bet you five pounds it does work."

"Females don't place wagers," he said, scandalized.

"Are you afraid you'll lose to a woman?" she wondered.

"I won't lose."

"Then we shall consider it settled. Now, can we be on our way?"

Lord Robert shifted from one foot to the other. "I don't know . . ."

"You are not going to cry off on me now!"

"No, but . . . Here now, stop that!" He suddenly jumped on one foot, shaking the other in the air.

Startled, Ariel looked down to find that Prospero had materialized in the room and had apparently applied his claws to the shining surface of Lord Robert's Hessian boots. "No," she said. "Leave them alone."

"That animal hates me," declared her visitor. "Whenever I come here he goes for my boots."

"Perhaps there is something in the polish used on them that attracts him," suggested Ariel.

Lord Robert looked dumbfounded. He seemed to be completely at a loss for something to say, and when a knocking sounded from the entryway, he responded, "Someone at the door," with visible relief.

Ellen was already opening the door, and in a moment Lord Alan Gresham was striding into the front parlor, looking surprised to find one of his brothers there. "Good day," he said.

As if nothing had happened between them, Ariel thought, her anger flaring up once again. What was it about him that made the room suddenly feel too small, and changed the atmosphere so that it was difficult to catch a breath?

"I need to speak to Miss Harding privately," he informed Lord Robert.

"Of course." The latter started toward the door with some eagerness.

"You promised to escort me on my visit," Ariel reminded him sharply.

"What visit?" asked Lord Alan.

"That doesn't matter. You must wait for me," she told Lord Robert. "I'll only be a moment."

Lord Robert shuffled his feet. "Er, I . . ."

"Why don't you go and speak to Hannah," Ariel finished.

He brightened slightly at this and hurried from the room.

"What visit?" repeated Lord Alan. "And what is Robert doing here? Was he looking for me? I don't understand why—"

"You wished to speak to me?" interrupted Ariel icily.

"Ah." His expression shifted. "Yes. I thought . . . it seemed to me important that we discuss last night."

"Really?" Ariel put all the sarcasm she could into the word.

He nodded. "The, er, incident went quite against our agreement, and was . . . unacceptable."

"Is that what you would call it?"

"You have my apologies, of course."

"Do I?" She was something more than angry by this time, Ariel thought, though she wasn't entirely sure what the muddle of feelings included. She did know that they made her hands tremble.

"Most certainly. My behavior was beyond the line, and completely out of character as well."

He seemed remarkably undisturbed by the idea, Ariel thought. Indeed, he talked about kissing her until she was limp as if it were some abstract event that had little to do with either of them.

"That is why I have devoted a good deal of time since then to analyzing the occurrence."

"Analyzing," echoed Ariel.

"In an attempt to explain it," he added. "And you will be happy to know that I have found the answer."

"Have you indeed?" He looked very pleased with himself, she thought, and not the least bit self-conscious in her presence. She, on the other hand, was not only trembling, but felt as if she might shriek or cry at the least provocation.

"Yes. I have concluded that Carlton House is the problem."

She stared at him. "The house?"

He made a dismissive gesture. "Not the building itself, of course, but the pernicious atmosphere there. Everything about the place works to disturb the balance of the bodily humors, perhaps the very balance of one's mind. And then one ends up doing things that would be unthinkable anywhere else."

"So you are saying that you kissed me because of Carlton House?" Ariel felt foolish repeating what he'd said, but she couldn't quite believe that was what he meant.

"Under the influence of the atmosphere I mentioned," he agreed. "However, I have solved that problem. I am moving out within the week." He gazed at her as if he expected congratulations.

Ariel returned his gaze. He was the most intelligent man she had ever encountered, she thought, and he was an idiot. Did he truly believe that this nonsense explained his behavior? And if he did, why did he wish to? She swallowed, suddenly finding the answer to this question all too clear. He didn't want to take any responsibility or face any consequences. She was forced to swallow again. Her mother had been right after all, Ariel thought. Men wanted to enjoy their pleasures and then go their way. The kisses that had devastated her meant nothing to him—except perhaps the threat of recriminations. And worse still, he refused to admit his own nature—that he was just like other men, after all. This hypocrisy was more despicable than crass seduction.

Ariel took a shaky breath. The realization hurt. It was a sad, sour pain worse than any snub or mockery she had ever endured before. The tightness of her throat increased, bitter with unshed tears.

"So, you see, I have found a solution," Lord Alan added encouragingly. "I came to tell you that you need have no concern for the future."

In other words, she was not to expect anything from him, Ariel thought. She was not to think she could make demands or assume any privileged position. She was to keep quiet and go along with his fabrications. Her chin came up. They would see about that. But she certainly wasn't going to whimper and cling. She wasn't going to protest that he had made her feel as if her heart had gone empty and vacant. She would make him believe it didn't matter. "What about the ghost?" she managed. "I thought the prince wanted you on the scene to stop it."

"Ah. I have good news on that score as well. Michael Heany and two of the other actors from the theater were apprehended last night as they tried to leave for Carlton House. The young woman was already made up as the 'ghost' and they had chains and other things with them that proved they had been behind the haunting."

Ariel drew in a slow breath, making a heroic effort to control her emotions. "So, it's over then."

"A very successful investigation," he agreed.

"And you . . . I suppose you'll be going back to Oxford, and your work." She wasn't going to see him again, Ariel realized.

For the first time in the visit, Lord Alan looked slightly uncertain. "Well, as to that, I thought I would have my things taken to Langford House."

She tried to read his expression.

"I need to make certain . . . to tie up any loose ends. And, of course, I have said I would be of assistance to you."

"You are going to keep helping me?" wondered Ariel.

"I gave my word," he replied, as if that settled the matter.

She scanned his face, but could find nothing in it. He had always said he wanted nothing more than to go home to Oxford. If he stayed now, when his task was accomplished . . . She didn't allow herself to think what that might mean. She couldn't afford hope. "I have found some papers of my mother's," she said a little breathlessly.

"Really?"

"Yes. Or rather, Prospero found them."

"Prospero?" He gave her a quizzical look.

"My cat."

He frowned.

"You've seen him about."

"Never."

"But you must have. He's gray, with golden eyes." Ariel looked around the room, but Prospero had gone.

"I would know if I had seen a cat," he said. "But the animal's existence, and indeed why you call him Prospero and how he was able to discover these papers, are all secondary. Did they contain any valuable information?"

"Well, I'm not sure. The most curious thing was that my mother loaned a very large sum of money to a woman I've never heard of, who lives in Whitechapel."

Lord Alan raised his auburn brows.

"I am going to see her and find out about it. I asked Lord Robert to escort me."

"I'll take you," he answered.

Ariel started to agree, then hesitated. He had had everything his own way. He was far too used to giving commands and seeing them obeyed. "You can come along with us, if you like," she responded coolly.

He looked distinctly taken aback.

"Lord Robert and I have it all arranged," she lied.

"You prefer the escort of a . . . a dandified . . ."

"You are very hard on your brothers," she declared, pleased with the reaction she'd elicited. Before he could reply, she went out and called down the kitchen stairs to Lord Robert. "I'm ready to go now."

After a short interval, he emerged, looking apprehensive.

"Lord Alan is coming with us," Ariel told him brightly. "Perhaps he will find us a hack?" She looked over her shoulder at Lord Alan. He said nothing, merely gave her a little bow and went out.

"If Alan's going, you don't need me," Lord Robert pointed out hopefully.

"Yes, I do."

"But why?"

"I just do." Ariel herded him before her out the door and along the pavement toward the hack that his brother now had waiting.

"But—"

"Get in," said Ariel, giving him a tiny push. Defeated, Lord Robert did so, and she climbed after him, leaving Alan to come last.

It was a silent drive. Lord Robert sulked. Ariel brooded. And Lord Alan gazed out the window of the vehicle as if he hadn't a concern in the world. His expression did change, however, when the character of the neighborhoods they passed through began to deteriorate. And by the time the hack pulled up at their destination, he was frowning. "You will wait for us as long as necessary," he told the driver when they had gotten out.

"I don't know, guv. It's a bad part of town."

"There's a guinea in it if you do," he added.

"A guinea! Yes, sir. Happy to be of service."

Ariel looked around the narrow street in which they stood. The broken stones of the pavement were gray; the ramshackle houses that leaned against one another on either side had only the smallest vestiges of paint and their wood was cracked and gray; only grayness was visible through most of the windows, and a gray sky arched over all.

The houses were large, however. Clearly, in some earlier century, this had been a better neighborhood. And the one they had stopped before showed more signs of care than any of the others. It was not painted, but its front steps were swept, and bright curtains could be seen. An oversized lantern hung beside the front door; when lit at night it would obviously provide a beacon in the darkness. On the other side of the entry was a signboard, rather like that at an inn, but smaller. It showed the house number and a picture of a child being admitted through a lighted doorway.

"What the deuce are we doing here?" said Lord Robert.

Still eyeing the sign curiously, Ariel started up the steps.

"Hold on," said Lord Alan. He moved in front of her and lifted his hand to knock.

There was no response at first, then they heard a clattering sound as the locks on the door were released from inside. It opened to reveal a slender boy of about thirteen dressed in a shirt and breeches of good cloth but no pretensions to fashion. He looked friendly but cautious.

"I would like to see Flora Jennings," said Ariel.

The boy's head dipped slightly. "Who'll I say?" he responded.

"Ariel Harding. Bess Harding's daughter."

His lips moved as he repeated this to himself. "Awright," he said, and started to push the door shut again. "I'm not allowed to let anyone in till I asks," he explained apologetically, and closed it.

Lord Robert muttered something unintelligible. He was looking up and down the street and fingering his watch chain as if he expected a pickpocket to emerge from the cobblestones and snatch it. "I don't like this," he said.

"That boy looked quite harmless," pointed out Ariel.

"But who's he fetching?"

The door rattled again. It was opened this time by a woman, who said, "Please, come in," and stood back to let them pass.

Ariel stepped forward. But Lord Alan was ahead of her, and thus the first to enter a narrow, rather shabby front hall.

Following him Ariel discovered a tall young woman, with black hair and pale skin. She held herself very straight and moved gracefully. Her plain gown of cornflower blue was very well made, fastened at the neck with an antique cameo, and her eyes were the same intense blue as her dress. She did not look at all like a denizen of this poor neighborhood.

"I am Flora Jennings," she said in a cultivated voice, looking at each of them in turn.

Ariel stepped forward. "Ariel Harding," she said again. "Bess's daughter."

The other woman's dark brows arched.

"And these are Lord Alan and Lord Robert Gresham."

This elicited a frown.

"May we speak to you?" continued Ariel.

Miss Jennings hesitated, then gave a little shrug and led them into a parlor to the right of the front door.

Ariel sank onto a worn velvet sofa. The furnishings of the room looked like castoffs from the town houses of the *ton*—fine pieces past their first prime but still sturdy and serviceable. "What is this place?" she asked.

Flora Jennings had settled opposite, her fine hands crossed in her lap. "It is a refuge for the children of the London streets," she answered calmly.

Ariel had to let this sink in for a few moments. "The

children . . ." she began, remembering her mother's story of her own origins.

"The children society has discarded like so much refuse," said Flora Jennings, and with her words, it became obvious that a fiery spirit burned behind her serene facade. Her blue eyes glowed with it. "The children who are allowed to freeze and starve and be preyed upon by any villain who wishes to exploit them."

"You give them a home here?" said Ariel.

The other woman looked regretful. "Some live here," she acknowledged. "But mostly we provide a meal or two, a bed for a night, a place to recover. We do not have room to house them all." Her tone made it clear that this fact galled her immeasurably.

"My mother was helping you," Ariel said. Her throat tightened suddenly with the full realization.

Flora Jennings smiled, and her rather austere face lit like stained glass when the sun comes from behind a bank of clouds. "She was a great benefactress. She helped me purchase this house. And she bought another nearby where we make homes for some of the older girls who would otherwise have no option but to . . ." She raised her chin. "But to sell themselves on the streets," she finished, looking as if she dared them to be shocked.

"That's wonderful," said Ariel. "Why didn't she ever tell me? I don't understand."

Her reaction softened their hostess even further. She relaxed slightly in her chair. "Bess liked secrets, I think. She seemed to delight in the idea that she was doing this and no one knew."

"She once told me that she grew up on the streets herself," Ariel confided.

"I know. There was so much she understood. And she was so good talking with the children."

This opened a whole new vista in her mother's character, Ariel thought. It made her proud, and yet also roused an ache in her chest. How she would have liked to have known before it was too late to express her admiration.

Lord Alan, who had been silently observing the scene, suddenly said, "You are a connection of my mother's."

Their hostess seemed to freeze in her chair. Her delicately sculpted mouth turned down.

"Second cousin, isn't it? You used to come to Langford House for the holidays years ago."

With patent reluctance, Flora Jennings nodded.

"Eh?" said Lord Robert, who had been standing like a statue in the corner, keeping one eye on their hackney through the window. "Jennings? You don't mean that absolutely terrifying female who used to visit us—Aunt Agatha, wasn't it?" He nodded, pleased with himself for remembering. "That's it. She was a tartar. Sebastian used to claim she had the evil eye. Say . . ." Knowledge appeared to dawn as he examined their hostess closely for the first time. "You ain't her daughter? Wasn't it you pushed Teddy Raines in the pond when he was bullying one of my brothers? James, I think it was. Do you remember, Alan?"

His brother shook his head.

"What the deuce are you doing in a place like this?" Lord Robert finished.

Miss Jennings's eyes flamed again. "I am doing something you wouldn't comprehend," she snapped. "I am doing good."

"Well, but—"

"I have rejected the parasitical life you refer to," she went on. "It is shameful—the waste, the heedlessness—when there are so many in need."

"I don't think—"

"Of course you don't. So-called fashionable society is nothing but a set of brainless idiots," she declared. "They are like thoroughbred horses—handsome and fast but utterly useless for any practical purposes."

"Here now." Lord Robert looked as if something had

struck him a sharp blow between the eyes. Ariel heard a snort of laughter from Lord Alan.

"Do you know how many children starve to death in London each year?" Flora continued relentlessly. "Do you know how many are brutalized or killed? Do you have any conception of the hopelessness, the despair?"

"Yes, but . . . street urchins," Lord Robert choked out. "They're filthy, and they steal."

The contempt in her face intensified. "I wonder how clean you would be if you were forced to live on the streets," she responded. "They don't have valets to run their baths, you know."

Lord Robert was beginning to look angry. "Of course, but—"

"And as for stealing—when your only other choice is to starve, the morality becomes a bit less clear-cut."

"There are almshouses, charity schools," he objected.

"Which aid a tiny part of those in need," Flora countered.

"Dash it, I've seen these children you talk about running in packs like wild animals. They rip the purses out of old women's hands and beat them senseless into the bargain," he said hotly.

The fire in Flora's eyes faded to sadness. After a moment, she nodded. "Yes, some of them do that."

"So they aren't such little angels," Lord Robert concluded with satisfaction.

"I never said they were. They are human beings, Lord Robert. And they deserve to be treated accordingly."

"You do remember us." He seemed rather pleased at the notion.

"Yes," she admitted.

"We ain't so useless, you know," he added. "Randolph is a preacher up north. James is captain of a navy ship. Nathaniel's always going on about building a new set of cottages for the tenants at Langford. Alan . . ." He paused for a moment, perplexed. "Unlocking the secrets of science, and, er, that sort of thing," he finished, gesturing at his brother.

Lord Alan raised one brow at this tribute.

"And you?" she asked.

"Eh? Oh, well . . ."

Flora Jennings waited a moment, then turned back to Ariel. Lord Robert eyed her back with startled indignation.

"You must have known Bess Harding rather well," commented Lord Alan.

Ariel threw him a glance. She had been about to say exactly the same thing.

"We worked together here," answered Flora Jennings cautiously.

Ariel leaned forward. "I want to know why my mother died," she said. "Is there anything that you noticed, or that she told you, that might help me?"

The other woman frowned. She didn't answer at once but appeared to give the question serious consideration. "We talked mainly of the work here," she said slowly. "She didn't tell me of the rest of her life." She paused. "She would get very, very angry at the plight of some of the children we took in. She could be almost . . . not frightening . . . but intimidating at times."

Ariel nodded in understanding.

"She would pace back and forth in this room and call down vengeance on the people who hurt or exploited the children." Their hostess smiled slightly. "It was terribly dramatic. I remember one little girl told me Bess was as good as a play."

Meeting her gaze, Ariel smiled back. It all sounded so much like her mother.

"And then at other times, she would fall into the dismals and insist that nothing would ever change, that our efforts were futile." Flora folded her hands rather tightly together. "That was far worse."

"Had she been despondent recently?" asked Lord Alan.

Miss Jennings looked at him. She seemed a bit puzzled by this caller, not entirely sure what to think of him. "Bess was always . . . volatile," she replied. "One thing one moment, and something else the next. I didn't notice anything particular. If I had, you may be sure I would have . . ." She stopped and clenched her jaw for a moment. "I would have done something," she finished finally. "I would not have sat back and allowed her to . . ."

The room was silent.

"I'm sorry," added their hostess after a time. "I would like to help you. But I don't know any more."

Ariel nodded. It was the same story she heard from everyone. "I would like to be of help in your work as well," Ariel replied.

"You won't recall the loan then?" was the relieved reply. "I was afraid you might have to."

Ariel shook her head.

"What backing do you have?" asked Lord Alan.

Both women turned to look at him.

"Support from those who could raise money or use influence in your favor," he explained.

Flora Jennings grimaced. "I don't have the time, or the stomach, to fawn and beg help from people who don't care," she declared.

"There are others in the world who care," he answered quietly.

Their hostess started to answer, then flushed slightly and said nothing.

"My mother would be most interested in what you are doing," he added.

"The duchess?" was the startled reply.

"She spends half her time on schemes for educating girls with no money," Lord Robert informed her with a mixture of triumph and defiance.

Surprised by his vehemence, Ariel looked at him, and encountered a smoldering glance.

"She does?"

"I'll mention your efforts to her," offered Lord Alan.

Miss Jennings looked torn between gratification and reluctance.

"Or perhaps you don't want any help," sneered Lord Robert. "That would prove you were wrong about us."

Their hostess glared at him. "Not about you," she snapped.

This was really rather interesting, thought Ariel. They both looked hot-eyed and resentful and very self-conscious. There were things going on under the surface in this room.

"We should be going," said Lord Alan.

Ariel wanted to protest, but she couldn't think of a good reason. "I'm sure we will see each other again soon," she said as she rose.

"I hope so," replied Flora Jennings much more warmly. When she escorted them to the door, she didn't look at Lord Robert even once, Ariel noted. He, on the other hand, threw her a number of defiant glances.

"She has a nerve," he burst out when they were seated in their cab once more. "She as much as called me a brainless ass!"

"A perceptive woman," commented Lord Alan.

Ariel threw him a repressive glance. "I believe she was speaking in general terms," she soothed.

"Do you? You didn't see the way she looked at me when she said it, then. When I think that a chit of"—he paused to calculate, ending up counting on his fingers—"no more than two and twenty would dare to speak to me in that way. It's beyond anything!"

"She is very committed to her cause."

"Committed!" He snorted. "Fanatical is more like it. And she seems to think nobody else knows anything. I've half a mind to show her that she's mightily mistaken on that score."

"Do you?" wondered Ariel. She was fascinated by the effect this woman had had on the usually blasé Lord Robert.

"Yes, I do," he declared. He straightened in the seat. "In fact, I shall."

"How?" asked his brother.

This stopped him. "Er . . . I don't know, but I shall think of a way."

"Go and see Aunt Agatha," Lord Alan suggested jokingly.

"Eh?" He pulled back as if he had threatened him with a weapon.

"Start with first causes," was the reply. "She has all the background."

It wasn't a bad idea at all, thought Ariel. She might have thought of it herself, in another moment.

"I wouldn't go near her for any money," said Lord Robert. "She's dashed terrifying." He frowned. "Anyway, what good would it do?"

"She would know Miss Jennings's reasons for doing what she is doing, the basis of her character, how one might, er, impress her," replied Ariel.

Lord Alan threw her a sidelong glance, then turned back to his brother. He was watching him as if he were an interesting specimen in his laboratory, Ariel noticed. "Of course, older relatives can be difficult," she added, blithely ignoring her complete lack of experience in this area.

"Difficult!" Lord Robert snorted at the inadequacy of the word.

"I suppose Miss Jennings knows you won't have the, er, inclination to look into the matter deeply," she added.

"You're saying she won't believe I have the courage to visit Aunt Agatha?"

Ariel wasn't sure how he had drawn this conclusion from her remarks, but she didn't contradict him.

His jaw hardened. "Well, she'll find she's mistaken there." He faltered slightly. "You wouldn't want to come along, would you?"

Ariel was just nodding when Lord Alan put in, "I would."

Both Ariel and his brother turned to stare at him. He met their gazes blandly.

Lord Robert let out a breath. "She'll see she was mistaken in me," he declared, though with a slight catch in his voice.

Chapter Twelve

During the remainder of the drive back to Ariel's house, Alan left the conversation to the others, fully absorbed in his own thoughts. It had been an extremely odd call, he thought. And the oddness had nothing to do with the neighborhood or the unusual household they found there. Why had he suggested that Robert visit Aunt Agatha, he wondered, or offered to bring together Flora Jennings and his mother, for that matter?

For years, Alan had kept to himself, remaining carefully free of the day-to-day entanglements of family life. He had needed to be unencumbered for his work, he thought. He had no time for trivialities. So why then had he put his oar in with Robert? He didn't really care, did he, whether Robert visited their crusty relative or managed to impress the eccentric Miss Jennings?

And yet, even as he assured himself of this, a spark of curiosity and amusement resurfaced. There was something irresistible about the situation. He had seen that in Ariel's sharp glances from Robert to Miss Jennings and back again, in her obvious fascination with their reactions. Ariel's presence changed something.

She was so interested, he thought. She appeared to think these small daily things were important—not trivial at all. She absorbed them with such zest and animation that he was forced to take another look, to reevaluate his long-held stance. Had he missed something? he wondered now.

He glanced at his brother, chatting amiably with Ariel about a horse he was thinking of buying, and shook his head. It seemed unlikely. And yet . . .

When they returned to Ariel's house, they found Sebastian waiting there, resplendent in uniform, his auburn whiskers gleaming. "There you are," he said when they came in, surging forward before they were even through the door. "I must have more questions. I've run out."

His eyes looked a bit wild, Alan thought, as they did when he was in some sort of scrape and needed to be helped out of it. He was only too familiar with the expression. "What sort of questions?" he replied, assuming that his brother spoke to him.

"For Georgina," answered Sebastian distractedly. "There's a ball tonight," he added, "and I've run out."

"Who is Georgina?" wondered Alan. "And why must she be questioned?"

"Lady Georgina Stane," said Sebastian, as if it were an explanation. "You have to help me."

"Before I can do so, you must tell me—"

"We agreed that you would begin to think of your own questions," Ariel said.

Alan turned to her in surprise.

"I know," replied Sebastian, running one hand through his hair. "But it's dashed difficult. And when she's talking, I forget that I'm supposed to be thinking of new ones. I just want to go on listening to her forever."

"You *have* been listening then?" inquired Ariel rather severely.

Alan looked from her to Sebastian, mystified.

Sebastian nodded. "She's got some dashed interesting ideas. You know, she said that those idiots smashing power looms in the Midlands are just terrified they're losing their livelihoods. She thinks they ought to be trained to use the new looms and promised work doing it."

"What do you know about the weavers' riots?" Alan asked in astonishment.

"Didn't know anything until a few days ago," Sebastian admitted. "But Lady Georgina did." He took a breath. "She and my mother are going to get along like a house afire," he told Ariel.

"I will give you one more list of questions," Ariel conceded. "After that, you have to find your own."

He nodded eagerly. "Could I have them now?" he asked. "I'd like to get in a good—"

"What the deuce are you talking about?" interrupted Alan, beginning to be annoyed by this incomprehensible conversation, and by the apparent understanding that had been established between Ariel and Sebastian without his knowledge.

Sebastian gazed at him, but he didn't seem to really see him. "Questions," he said, then turned to look hopefully at Ariel.

"I'll write some out for you," she responded.

"I don't understand," commented Lord Robert.

Alan nodded agreement. Someone, at least, was talking rationally, he thought.

"How are a lot of questions going to get Lady Georgina to marry Sebastian?" Lord Robert grimaced. "If he really wants her to," he added.

"Is this the girl you were talking about at the Coningsby ball?" put in Alan, memory returning. "Are you really serious about marrying, Sebastian?"

"I explained it all to you," Ariel pointed out to Lord Robert.

"I know you did, but it didn't make any sense."

"What do questions have to do with it?" wondered Alan.

"Why don't you just go and write a note to your Aunt Agatha?" Ariel suggested kindly to Lord Robert. "You could set an appointment to call on her tomorrow afternoon."

He went pale. "Too soon," he replied in a strangled voice.

"Aunt Agatha?" echoed Sebastian. "You don't mean that dragon of a female who used to visit Langford House years ago? About seven feet tall, with six or seven rows of teeth?"

Looking grim, Robert nodded.

"Haven't seen her in years." Sebastian shuddered slightly. "Do you remember the time she caught us on her window ledge? She has a voice like a steam whistle. I thought she was going to throw us off. And we weren't even going to *her* room."

Robert was looking even paler. "I'm sure she will be very different now," remarked Ariel sweetly. "That was a long time ago."

Alan was suffering an odd dizzying sensation. It was rather like being trapped in a coach with a runaway team and no driver, he thought. Events seemed to be speeding past far too rapidly. "Will someone kindly tell me what is going on?" he said.

Three pairs of eyes turned to look at him, and then three voices spoke at once.

"Complicated," said Robert.

"It's all very simple," said Ariel.

"I've got to have the questions first," said Sebastian. "Have to memorize them," he added when Alan looked at him. "Takes a devil of a time."

"I'll go and write them out for you," said Ariel, untying the strings of her bonnet as she headed for the stairs. "You can explain everything to Lord Alan while I do so."

She went out, leaving the three brothers staring at one another.

There was a short silence. Sebastian looked burdened.

He wasn't very good at explanations, Alan thought. He tended to duck out, leaving them to other people.

But his brother surprised him. "Decided to marry," he began.

"You astonish me."

"Astonish myself," agreed Sebastian. "But there's something about this girl."

"Just that she won't look at you," put in Robert. "If you want my opinion, that's the only reason you're after her."

"Well, I don't want your opinion," replied Sebastian, "because you're dead wrong. I ain't that pigheaded."

Alan refrained from expressing his doubt of this statement. "And what has this to do with Miss Harding?" he prompted.

"She's been giving me a few hints."

"Hints," repeated Alan.

Sebastian nodded. "Thought it was daft to begin with, but the thing of it is—it's working. I swear Lady Georgina had an eye out for me at the Simpsons' rout, and she gave me a smile the other day that . . ." His voice trailed off as he lost himself in the memory of it.

"Good God," declared Robert in disgusted tones.

Alan surveyed his two brothers. "No doubt your fabled charm would have won her over in any case," he said to Sebastian.

"Well, I don't think it would have," Sebastian replied. "Lady Georgina's deuced sharp on the subject of compliments and pretty speeches." When Alan raised a brow, he added, "She don't like 'em. Says that's all hypocrisy and, er, vacuity, I think it was. Ariel's put me on the right track, for certain."

"Ariel?" echoed Alan, startled at this familiar form of address.

"No joke?" asked Robert, and, when Sebastian shook his head most earnestly, added, "There goes fifty pounds."

His brothers looked at him, but Lord Robert had become lost in thought. "Say," he continued then, "I wonder if we ought to present Ariel to Nat?"

"What?" said Alan.

Sebastian looked puzzled, then a dawning comprehension lit his face. "Good notion," he agreed. "I've been wondering whether he and Violet were . . ." He gestured, indicating ambiguity.

"That's it," said Robert. He looked very pleased with himself.

"Were what?" said Alan.

He was treated to another wave of Sebastian's fingers.

"They are to be married in a month," Alan verified.

Robert nodded, at the same time giving a little shrug.

"I received an invitation to the wedding," said Alan.

"Oh, aye," said Sebastian. "It's likely to make Waterloo look like a Sunday picnic, from what I hear. Twice the planning involved."

"Perhaps that's it, then," offered Robert. "Violet's taken up with that."

"Perhaps," replied Sebastian doubtfully. "Still, did you see them at Almack's last week?"

Robert nodded solemnly. "Bit peaked," he admitted.

"Blue-deviled," corrected Sebastian.

Alan was transfixed by these observations, and by the resolution evident in the faces of his brothers. He had never known them to take an interest in how other people were feeling, and still less to want to do anything about it.

"I could bring Nat round tomorrow," suggested Robert. "See what she says."

"She?" responded Alan. He looked from one face to another. He seemed to have strayed into a realm where the most outrageous things were taken as commonplace, and where the brothers he knew himself to possess had become completely different individuals.

"Ariel," replied Robert. "She'll have some notion of what to do."

"About what?"

"Never seen a gel with so many notions," agreed Sebastian. "Can't think where she gets them all."

"Plays," said Robert helpfully.

The other nodded. "You know, I don't think I've ever properly appreciated the theater."

In the following silence, Robert nodded a measured agreement. Alan examined his brothers again, feeling a growing fascination. Had Ariel Harding somehow changed them? he wondered. Did her influence extend further than he'd realized? But how? And what would be the result of this revolution? "What time will you bring Nat?" he heard himself asking.

"Oh, twoish," Robert replied. "He's probably squiring Violet and her sisters to some ball or other till all hours tonight."

"Two," repeated Alan. "Very well."

"You coming?" asked Robert, surprised.

"I believe I am," was the bemused reply.

The three Gresham brothers arrived on Ariel's doorstep promptly at the appointed hour, and she greeted them with cordial curiosity. Lord Robert looked dapper and bright-eyed. Lord Alan, plainly dressed as usual, hung back and watched like a spectator at a play. And their eldest brother, Nathaniel, Viscount Highgrove, looked somewhat sleepy and completely mystified, thought Ariel as she acknowledged her introduction to him. Like all the brothers, he had blue eyes and auburn hair—in his case a darker hue nearer to brown. He was not as tall as Alan, or as smartly dressed as Robert. At first glance, in fact, an observer might have set him down as a nonentity. But there was a subtle confidence in his bearing, and a hint of strong character in his face. He looked like a man who was constantly conscious of his responsibilities, and striving to fulfill them to the utmost.

"I had to roust Nat out of bed," Lord Robert said cheerily.

"I was up until four," responded Lord Highgrove in his own defense.

"Escorting Violet and listening to her endless pack of relatives prosing on about virtue and duty," expanded Lord Robert. "Violet is Nat's intended," he told Ariel, ignoring his eldest brother's pained and somewhat scandalized expression. "Lady Violet Devere, earl of Moreley's daughter."

Ariel nodded and smiled, wondering whether she should have agreed to this visit. Lord Highgrove looked extremely uncomfortable.

"They've known each other since they were children," Lord Robert continued, oblivious. "Always understood they were to make a match of it. The thing was announced last spring, and they're to be married in a month."

"I am sure Miss Harding is not interested in—" began Lord Highgrove.

"She's the one got Georgina Stane living in Sebastian's pocket," Lord Robert informed him. "That's what made us think of getting her advice for you."

"I cannot imagine what you are talking about," replied his elder brother coldly.

"Oh, come. Everyone's gossiping about the way you and Violet sit like statues hardly looking at each other. Couple of cold fish, the gossips have it; frosted up to the eyebrows. Only I know you ain't. And if I remember Violet—"

"Robert!" exclaimed Lord Highgrove.

A choking sound emerged from the corner, where Lord Alan had taken his seat. He was finding this quite funny, Ariel thought, meeting his sparkling blue gaze. And he apparently had no intention of helping her with the awkward situation. It was just like him. He was probably viewing them all as some sort of experiment—incompatible chemicals put in a container together and allowed to froth and bubble. "There is no reason why I should be involved in Lord Highgrove's affairs," she said with determination. "We are not at all acquainted. And while I am most happy to have met him, of course, I wish you will not—"

"No, no, you don't understand," declared Lord Robert. "She can set it to rights between you and Violet," he told his brother. "She knows just what to do."

The viscount's face was scarlet. His mouth was a tight line. Ariel cast her eyes around the room in search of help. Lord Robert gestured at her, urging her on as if she were a pet reluctant to do its tricks. Lord Alan simply clamped his jaw, very likely suppressing a grin, she thought impatiently. "Really, Lord Robert—" she began.

"You didn't see them when they were younger," he interrupted. "Nat and Violet, well, there was never any question that the match was ideal. We used to tease him about it, didn't we, Alan?"

"Alan!" admonished Lord Highgrove.

Now he was caught, Ariel thought with satisfaction. Both his brothers were looking to him for support, and he couldn't pretend any longer that he was just a disinterested spectator, watching her flounder. He couldn't maintain that maddening distance.

Suddenly her interest sharpened to an almost painful point. What would he do, she wondered, when it was his family turning to him for help? Would he make excuses, find reasons to evade their appeals, tell them their difficulties were all due to the pernicious atmosphere of the *haut ton* or their own intellectual inadequacies? She examined his handsome face, searching for an answer.

"We did tease him," Lord Alan acknowledged quietly.

"And Nat endured it with his customary grace and magnanimity."

He wasn't laughing now, Ariel thought. There was real emotion in his expression. She felt a wave of inexpressible, and inexplicable, relief.

"But now it's all gone wrong somehow," Lord Robert continued relentlessly. "And it's a dam . . . deuced shame." He gazed at her like Miss Ames at a school recitation, silently encouraging her.

Embarrassed for herself, and much more so for the poor viscount, Ariel met the latter's eyes. They did indeed show humiliation. But there was something else in those blue depths as well, a hint of bewildered desperation, an uncomprehending pain. Ariel couldn't turn away from it. And yet, what was she to do in this really impossible situation? She glanced at Lord Alan again. But the concern was gone from his eyes, replaced by a challenge, as if he understood her predicament exactly and was daring her to escape it. Ariel cleared her throat. "Uh . . ." A solution occurred to her. "You may not know that an old friend of yours, Hannah Enderby, is living here with me."

"Hannah?" he replied in a somewhat strangled voice. He looked bewildered. "Is she indeed?"

"If you should ever wish to visit her, you would be most welcome." If he came, Ariel thought, it would give them an opportunity to talk. If not, then the matter was closed. Let him choose if that was what he wanted.

He blinked. "Visit."

"For a quiet chat," added Ariel significantly.

Lord Highgrove appeared to consider this. It took him quite a while. "Ah," he replied at last. "Perhaps I'll come by some afternoon and see her."

"Splendid," said Ariel.

"But you should explain—" attempted Lord Robert.

"I believe we have an appointment," Lord Alan interrupted. "We should be on our way."

Ariel gave him a grateful look. In return, he smiled at her in a way that made her pulse accelerate alarmingly. He looked approving and impresed, she thought. She had to remind herself that she was very angry with him.

"We don't want to keep Aunt Agatha waiting," he added.

"Aunt Agatha!" exclaimed Lord Highgrove.

Lord Robert blanched.

"Yes indeed." Lord Alan strolled forward with a wicked glint in his eyes. "We mustn't keep her waiting. As I recall, Aunt Agatha values punctuality very highly. Do you remember the time Sebastian was late for Christmas dinner and she—"

"Get your bonnet," urged Lord Robert in a strangled voice. "Why the deuce did I ever begin this?"

"I am extremely curious about that myself," responded Lord Alan. "Why did you?"

Lord Robert's reply was a harassed growl.

"Care to come with us?" Ariel heard Lord Alan saying as she left to get her things.

Lord Highgrove's resounding "no" followed her up the stairs.

Agatha Jennings lived in a part of town that was not particularly fashionable, though eminently respectable. Her husband, now deceased, had been a well-known scholar, Lord Robert told them during the drive, and he had insisted upon living near the British Museum despite the benighted nature of the neighborhood.

"What did he study?" wondered Ariel.

"Akkadian," was the prompt reply. "I've been doing some research of my own," Robert added in response to Alan's surprised glance.

"And what the deuce is Akkadian?" Alan said.

"Ah, well as to that, I believe it's some sort of old language, rather like Greek, you know."

"No," responded his brother, "I don't." His family had provided him with more surprises in the last few days than he could remember in the whole of his life before this, Alan thought. He had been startled to find that Nathaniel and Violet were experiencing some sort of difficulties. Like the others, he had thought them perfectly matched. But even more astonishing was the idea that Robert had made some sort of study of the Jennings family in advance of their visit. Robert was not known for planning ahead.

To add to his bewilderment, there was his brothers' apparent conviction that Ariel Harding could solve their problems. He had already been surprised by Ariel a number of times, but he had not understood the extent of her acquaintance with his family, or the schemes they had been hatching together.

And what about Robert's inexplicable insistence upon visiting Aunt Agatha? he asked himself. This mystery, at least, he was determined to solve today. "I am still curious," he said in conversational tones, "as to why we are paying a visit to Aunt Agatha."

Silence met his question. Alan kept his eyes on Robert.

"I don't know what I'm doing here," replied Robert distractedly. "Why I let Ariel talk me into making this visit."

"I?"

"Of all the harebrained, ridiculous starts," Robert muttered, "this beats them all."

Ariel was getting angry, Alan observed. He had never seen her angry when he wasn't in something of a temper himself. It was a riveting sight. Her hazel eyes positively crackled with energy. The warm peach tone of her skin deepened entrancingly. Her full lips pressed together in a way that made a man ache to . . . He shook his head to clear it.

"All of this was arranged for your benefit," Ariel was saying to Robert. "And at your request, I may add. If you don't like it, then tell the driver to turn around and go home again."

For a moment he looked hopeful. Then his face fell. "Wretchedly impolite," he concluded.

"What does it matter?" snapped Ariel. "You haven't seen the woman in years, and it seems unlikely that you will see her. She doesn't appear to move in society."

Robert brightened again. "That's true."

"And I don't care a snap of my fingers what Flora Jennings thinks of you," Ariel finished.

This stopped him. Robert sat back in the corner of the carriage chewing on his lower lip.

Alan gazed at his brother, who flushed.

"Shall I tell the driver to turn back?" wondered Ariel.

Robert had turned to gaze out the window. Resentment and resolution showed in the set of his shoulders. "No," he said.

"But if it is such a bad idea," she began.

"Oh, let me be," he replied.

At his tone, she subsided. Alan watched her as the anger faded from her features, to be replaced with a touch of embarrassment and some doubt. She had become totally involved in helping Robert, he saw. She certainly didn't do anything by halves, he thought somewhat wryly. The astonishing thing was that she had convinced his brothers that she really could aid them. "What's all this about Sebastian?" he asked her quietly.

"What do you mean?"

"Why was he asking you for questions?"

Ariel visibly hesitated. "I expect you should ask him about that," she answered finally.

"I am asking you."

"Yes, but it is a rather . . . confidential matter."

The reply that came to Alan's lips was forestalled by their arrival. The footman had jumped down and was opening the carriage door. Ariel started to climb down.

"Wait," exclaimed Robert.

She stopped and looked back over her shoulder.

Robert swallowed, gazing at the large red brick house before them. "Oh, very well," he said at last. "She can't eat me."

Ariel stepped down. Alan followed, and then his brother. The footman rang the bell, and the door was opened by a stately butler, who welcomed them in solemn, measured accents and led them upstairs.

"What's that?" exclaimed Robert.

Alan, who had been observing the furnishings and finding nothing out of the ordinary among them, looked. On the wall at the head of the staircase hung a flat slab of stone. On it was carved an unusual figure with the head of a man and the body of a lion. Crowned and bearded, it contemplated them with a stony stare.

"The master brought that back from his travels years ago," commented the butler with a hint of pride. "He was an authority on the Assyrians, you know."

"I thought it was Akkadian," said Robert a bit desperately.

"I believe that was their language, sir," was the reply. "But you must ask Mrs. Jennings. She will know for certain."

A rather unusual butler, Alan was thinking as they entered the drawing room and encountered their hostess.

The woman who rose to greet them was not at all as he remembered, Alan saw. His early impressions of Aunt Agatha tended toward the intimidating. He had expected that she would be about six feet tall and stout, with a prow like an armored battleship and a hatchet face. But their hostess was merely tall for a woman and sturdily built. She was definitely stately, Alan thought, and her nose did tend to the aquiline, but she was far from frightening. In fact, he realized, she bore something of a resemblance to his mother. Wondering if Robert was having the same reaction, he glanced at him. His brother looked like a stuffed owl. Ariel, on the other hand, was examining

Aunt Agatha with interest and what appeared to be amusement. When she caught his eye, she raised her eyebrows as if to say, "This is the ogre?"

"How do you do?" said Alan, when it became obvious that no one else was going to speak. "It has been too long since we met."

"Around fifteen years," answered Aunt Agatha with perfect composure. "I confess that I am rather curious about this sudden visit."

Forthright, thought Alan, and felt one corner of his mouth curve upward.

"I thought just one of you was coming," the older woman continued. "Which of you . . . ?" She examined them. "You're Lord Robert," she decided, guessing correctly.

Robert simply nodded.

"And you . . . ?"

"Alan, ma'am."

"Ah."

"And may I present Miss Ariel Harding?"

To his surprise, Ariel dropped a tiny curtsy. "I so admire what your daughter is doing for the street children, Mrs. Jennings," she said. "My mother was helping her, and when I found out about it, I wanted to meet you as well."

She was the very picture of demure admiration, Alan thought, startled. But the story was thin. He didn't think a woman whose gaze was as sharp as Aunt Agatha's would swallow it.

She had been diverted by the name, however. "Harding?" she repeated. "Bess Harding's daughter?"

Ariel nodded.

Their hostess swept them all with a probing stare. "You may as well sit down," she said, and did so herself.

Ariel sank gracefully onto the sofa opposite, maneuvering Robert onto the cushions at her side with a glance. Alan took an armchair a little apart from the others.

"How did Miss Jennings get started with her work in London?" Ariel asked.

"Why not ask her?" responded the older woman.

That was a facer, Alan thought, watching Ariel to see how she would parry it. She looked embarrassed, and at first he thought that Aunt Agatha had bested her. But then she said, "It is rather a delicate matter." She cast her eyes down, as if she didn't know exactly how to proceed. "You see, my mother lent Miss Jennings a large sum of money," she added finally. "And I did not want your daughter to feel that I was some sort of creditor, come to examine the books." She raised her lovely hazel eyes. "I am so interested in what she is doing, and I should like to help myself. But I wanted to know a bit more first."

Alan gazed at her, transfixed. She really was extraordinary, he thought. She was honest, wholly trustworthy, but still she was like quicksilver, slipping from one incarnation to another before your eyes. Was she the shy eager girl fresh from the schoolroom, or the undaunted seeker of justice who would not be diverted from her quest, or the gorgeous sophisticate who frequented Carlton House receptions? She was all of them, and more, in one unfathomable package. He felt something twist in his chest, a sensation between pain and exaltation. He wanted to protect her. He wanted to ravish her. He wanted to oversee her every move so that she didn't get herself into trouble. And he wanted to stand back and be surprised over and over by the new facets and abilities she continually revealed. The contradictory convolutions of it were dizzying.

"You might have said all that to Flora," declared their hostess, startling Alan out of his daze. "She would have understood perfectly."

"Do you think so?" asked Ariel, leaning a little forward. "I wasn't sure. And I did *not* wish to offend her."

Aunt Agatha did not look completely convinced, Alan thought. But her skepticism was definitely shaken. She pursed her lips. "Flora has always been passionate about causes," she said at last. "It seems to be her nature." A small smile softened her austere features. "She began writing letters to our member of Parliament when she was eleven, if I recall correctly. We had a hard winter that year, horridly cold, and she noticed that the children in the streets were freezing." The smile grew. "We must have bought fifty pairs of warm gloves in those months. Every time Flora went out, she came back with bare hands, having given hers away."

Alan took in the reminiscent glow in the older woman's eyes. How had he ever thought she was frightening? he wondered.

"She went away to school, and I thought she'd forgotten all about that sort of thing. But when she finished and came back to London, her one thought was to create a place where such children could find refuge." Their hostess's mouth turned down. "Of course I am not overly pleased to have her frequenting a back slum. And some of the people she deals with are . . ." She let out a breath. "But it is . . . difficult to argue with Flora. She has great force of character." The smile reappeared. "Her father was just the same."

"Akkadian," Robert blurted out.

Agatha Jennings's eyes lit. Her head came up. "You know my husband's work?" she asked, as if she couldn't believe it.

"The Assyrians," responded Robert, looking as he had the first time he put his pony to a fence. Alan had to swallow a laugh.

"Henry was one of the foremost experts on cuneiform," agreed Agatha enthusiastically.

Robert goggled at her, obviously past the limits of his knowledge.

"I'm afraid I don't know that word," said Ariel, coming to his rescue.

"The Akkadian language is written in cuneiform," Agatha informed her. "They are symbols—rather like our alphabet letters—made of combinations of wedge shapes and connecting lines. Cuneiform letters were inscribed on clay tablets while the clay was wet. The scribes used reeds as writing instruments—thus the wedges, you see—and when the clay dried, the tablets became a lasting record. Much sturdier than paper." She looked at Robert as if for confirmation, and he nodded somewhat desperately.

"How interesting," said Ariel politely.

"Have you read Henry's articles?" Agatha asked Robert, suddenly completely focused on him. "I had no idea that anyone in the family cared about his ideas."

"I . . . er . . ." Robert flushed a dull red.

"I believe what Lord Robert is trying to say," interposed Ariel sweetly, "is that his knowledge cannot compare with your husband's, Mrs. Jennings. He doesn't want to embarrass himself in front of you."

That, at least, was quite true, thought Alan, struggling to control his expression.

"You mustn't be embarrassed," Agatha urged in response. "Henry spent his entire life on his studies. Everyone must begin somewhere. The critical thing is the desire to learn."

"Lord Robert is terribly keen on learning," said Ariel.

Robert rolled his eyes in her direction. He was incapable of speech, Alan decided.

"If you would care to look over some of Henry's papers," suggested Agatha. "He left a great mass of notes, which Flora and I have been slowly putting in order."

"What an opportunity for you," exclaimed Ariel, giving Robert a significant look and receiving a glazed stare in return. "To work alongside Mrs. Jennings and her daughter," she elucidated. "And to learn from the work of a master."

"If you are truly interested," said their hostess, looking suddenly doubtful. "I know that my enthusiasm—"

"Lord Robert has told me of his intense desire to *show*

that he is a serious person," said Ariel. "Have you not, Lord Robert?"

He was gazing at her as if she were a stage magician who had pulled a poisonous snake instead of a rabbit out of her hat, Alan thought. In a moment he would break and run. But once again, Alan was surprised.

Robert nodded. "Have to start pretty much at the beginning," he managed.

Agatha Jennings smiled at him in a way that transfigured her dignified features. "That is where we all start," she replied.

Robert tightened his jaw. "Won't be like your husband," he warned.

"No one could be." The older woman looked around their group. "This is astonishing," she added. "I never thought to see . . ." She hesitated. "It was always so awkward visiting Langford House, you know. Because although your mother was very kind, I believed that everyone saw Henry as a hopeless eccentric and mocked him behind our backs. If I had realized that one of you boys . . . well . . ." She spread her hands, seemingly unable to say more.

"I don't recall anyone mocking him," said Robert.

Alan shook his head.

"Too busy being terrified of—" Robert bit off his words and gulped. He coughed. "Forgot what I was going to say."

A sputter of laughter forced its way past Alan's defenses. He turned it into a cough as well.

"Is it close in here?" wondered Agatha. "Shall I have a window opened?"

"It was so kind of you to see us," said Ariel, starting to rise. "I must go, but I thank you for telling me something of your daughter's work." She turned to Robert with a brilliant smile. "Perhaps you wish to stay a bit longer and look at some of the papers Mrs. Jennings mentioned."

"Eh? Oh, er, that is . . . don't wish to impose," fumbled Robert, turning to give her a horrified glare.

"Not at all," said Agatha behind him. "On the contrary, it would be a great pleasure to show you some of Henry's writings. We have a collection of clay tablets as well," she added, as if offering a special inducement.

"Tablets," Robert echoed, directing a final searing glance at Ariel before turning. "Splendid."

Chapter Thirteen

"I had no idea you were so cruel," said Alan as he handed Ariel into the carriage for the drive home.

She had miscalculated, Ariel thought. She had become so engrossed in Lord Robert's curious behavior that she had maneuvered herself into a journey alone with his brother, the last thing she wanted. And now he was joking as if nothing had passed between them but common civilities.

"You more or less forced my poor brother into learning Assyrian," he continued.

"Akkadian," corrected Ariel. "And I did not force him. He might have refused at any moment."

"Why didn't he?" asked Alan as the coach started up. He sounded genuinely interested.

"I believe he wishes to impress Miss Flora Jennings."

"Because she insulted him?"

"Possibly," replied Ariel.

"What might his other reasons be?"

"She is very pretty," Ariel explained. "I think he was rather taken with her."

"Indeed?"

Ariel wished he would stop looking at her.

"You know, you are not obliged to become embroiled in my brothers' affairs," he said.

She risked a glance. He was sitting back in the corner of the carriage, quite at his ease, achingly handsome and assured and apparently quite unaffected by her proximity.

"They will take all your time if you allow it," he went on. "I know from long experience. You mustn't let them be a bother."

"They aren't any bother," she replied.

"They will become one," he assured her. "They have no notion of when to leave off, or that others might have more important things to do than listen to their chatter. If their visits are burdensome, tell them outright."

Ariel couldn't understand what he was talking about. She delighted in having his brothers in her house, almost like a real family. She couldn't imagine wishing them gone, and going back to the emptiness she'd faced when she first came home. Was he really saying that he didn't want her getting too close to *his* family, and thus, perhaps, to him? He couldn't stop her from seeing them if they wished it, she thought defiantly. "They are not at all burdensome," she declared. "I am very happy to give them whatever advice I can."

Lord Alan smiled. "And just how did you become so expert in matters of the heart?" he asked.

His smile made Ariel's breath catch. It was so confiding, so inviting. He was reminding her of a lion again, a very large lion, lazing in the sun, deceptively innocuous. Did lions toy with their prey as Prospero did? she wondered. Was he mocking her? "It is all from plays," she answered breathlessly.

"Plays?"

"Lord Robert's situation reminded me at once of *The Bluestocking*, where the hero wins his lady by taking an interest in her studies," she answered, speaking a little too quickly, she realized.

"Her studies?"

"Natural philosophy," Ariel stammered. He *was* mocking her, she thought. Only it didn't seem exactly that. But he was watching her so steadily, letting his gaze move over her so warmly. He must know that he was making her skin feel hot and her pulse accelerate.

"You have an uncommon memory for plays," he said into the charged silence.

"I was known for it at the theater, when I was a child."

"Were you?"

He had to be aware of her state, Ariel thought. He was enjoying it, reveling in his power to unsettle her, while he sat back, cool and amused. She gathered her resolve. She refused to give him the satisfaction. She could match his detachment, she thought. If he wished to talk about plays, then she would talk about plays. "A really good villain makes a drama," she informed him.

"Yes?" he said.

Ariel nodded, not looking at him. "Well, a tragedy, anyway. The most successful ones have several. Think of *The Duchess of Malfi*. Both the duchess's brothers want to take her lands away. And there is the evil servant who tortures and murders the duchess and her children. And then, of course, nearly everyone kills each other in the end. They always do."

"Do they indeed?"

"In a tragedy," she said severely.

"Of course."

"In *The White Devil*, Flamineo murders Vittoria's husband and her other brother, as well as Brachiano's wife, so that they may marry."

"Who?" asked Alan, sounding lost.

"Vittoria and Brachiano. And then their mother goes mad with grief and dies. And then Vittoria is tried and put in prison, but she escapes and marries, and then avengers come and kill all three of them."

The carriage lurched at a break in the cobbles, and their shoulders brushed. Ariel swallowed and rushed on.

"Did you know that *The Spanish Tragedy* is one of the most popular plays there ever was? That is where the hero, Andrea, is Belimperia's lover, and he is killed by Balthazar. Then Balthazar is captured and delivered to Belimperia's brother Lorenzo, and he wants them to marry for political reasons. But Belimperia loves Horatio. So Horatio is murdered, and Belimperia is kidnapped. The murderers are killed, too, to keep the secret. But Belimperia is able to send a message, written in her own blood, to Horatio's father, and then he—"

"Ariel," said Lord Alan.

She met his eyes. His were fathomless wells of blue, lit by a sparkle like sun on water. She seemed to tumble into them, floating in a wordless space where time stretched out endlessly before them.

The carriage pulled up. "Here we are," said Ariel breathlessly. But she couldn't move.

Alan climbed down and offered her a hand out of the hack. She felt an electric tingle when she took it and stepped to the pavement. Then he was following her into the house, and they were standing awkwardly in the entryway, not looking at each other. "Ariel," said Lord Alan again.

She was afraid to look up.

"I—"

Ellen the housemaid appeared from the kitchen stairs. "This came for you, miss," she said, handing Ariel a small package wrapped in brown paper.

Ariel took it, and took a deep breath. "Thank you," she murmured. She was both glad and very sorry for the interruption. Something had been about to happen, she thought. But more than likely, it would have been just more of his explanations and analyses of how there was nothing going on. She took another breath and focused her attention on the package. "It's from Miss Ames, at school," she remarked. She tore off the outer wrappings, only to reveal another layer of brown paper. "No," she added. "It was sent to me at school from London. It's . . . it's from my mother." She handled the small box, perplexed and upset.

"They must have delayed sending it on to you," said Lord Alan. "The mail wouldn't have taken so long."

"Miss Ames was going away when I left," replied Ariel distractedly. "They must have put it aside for her to deal with." She stared at the package, feeling almost afraid of it. "What can it be?"

"You'll have to open it to see."

"Yes."

"Perhaps I should leave you alone."

She was afraid of it, Ariel thought. "Please don't."

He hesitated, then bowed his head in acknowledgment of the plea in her voice. "Shall we go into the parlor?" He led her there and seated her on the sofa.

Ariel fumbled with the brown paper that enclosed the package. Her hands were trembling. Finally, she tore it off, revealing a small pasteboard box. After a brief hesitation, she opened the lid—and gasped.

"What?" asked Alan.

Slowly, moving her hand as if she were afraid of being bitten, Ariel picked up the object. "It's my mother's ring," she whispered, letting the box fall to the floor. "I couldn't find it anywhere. She sent it to me."

Alan came closer and saw a delicate ring of dark green agate and silver. The design was a sinuous filigree; the large green stone was immaculate. It looked very old— Celtic work perhaps. His shoulder brushed Ariel's, as it had in the carriage, and once again a pulse of desire surged through him. He ought to go, he thought.

"My father gave it to her," Ariel murmured. "It's the

only thing I know that came from him. She always wore it."

She touched it with the tips of her fingers as if she had not examined it a thousand times. "You've never told me who he was," he said.

"I don't know." She clenched her fists at the difficulty of this admission. "Bess used to make up stories about him. But she never told me the truth."

"Stories?"

Ariel swallowed. "I'd ask her to tell me about my father. And she'd say, oh, that he was a great soldier, who died a hero in the fighting against Napoleon, or a Russian diplomat, or an adventurer from America." Her voice wavered. "But she never would tell me which story was true, who he was, really. She'd say, 'You have no father. You don't need one; you have me.'" Ariel glanced up, then down again. "It was a game we played," she finished, her voice breaking on the last word.

"Game," he repeated in astonishment. "It sounds like a remarkable piece of cruelty to me."

She looked at him as if she didn't know what he meant. "She ought to have told me before she . . ." She broke off with a helpless gesture.

A flash of anger at Bess Harding ran through him. How had she dared treat Ariel this way? Clearly, she hadn't deserved such a daughter. To keep from saying so, he bent and picked up the small box Ariel had dropped. "There are some papers here," he said, pulling them out. He unfolded the top one. It was small, torn from a larger sheet, and stained with water. "This looks like part of a parish register." He frowned at the faded writing. "It says that Bess Harding married one Daniel Bolton on April the eighth, 1799."

"What?" Ariel snatched the page and stared at the loops and whorls of ink. "1799," she murmured after a while. "Bess would have been . . . sixteen. She told me . . . or she always let me think that she had gone from the streets onto the stage."

She looked up at Alan, her lips parted, her hazel eyes intent.

"How could she not tell me? What became of this Daniel Bolton? Why didn't . . . ?" She stopped, her eyes widening in astonishment.

"What is it?" asked Alan.

"I was born in 1799," she said slowly. "In September." She gazed at him again. "He must be my father." She turned to look at the wall. "Daniel Bolton," she repeated, as if trying to accustom herself to the name, and to a whole new view of the world. She turned the paper over in her hands. "Where is he? How can I find him?"

"Unfortunately, this does not show which parish it came from. It might be in London, or anywhere in the country."

"But I have to find him!" she exclaimed.

"It may be possible, with some research."

Ariel rose and paced the room, looking excited and uncertain and upset. "What if Bess had some good reason for never speaking of him?" she murmured.

"The search should be discreet," Alan agreed.

"I don't care," said Ariel, answering her own question. "I want to know. I must know." She turned to him. "How do I begin to look?"

"I can set some of the prince's men to the task," he offered.

"Would you?" She gave him a tremulous smile that reached into his chest and twisted. "Thank you." She paced the length of the room again. "Daniel Bolton," she repeated. "Does this mean that I am really Ariel Bolton?" She shivered. "It's like finding out that you are another person entirely."

Alan didn't care for the concept. And he found that he was disturbed by the strength of her reaction to this news. "There is another piece of paper here," he said, noticing it wedged in the bottom of the box. He unfolded it and scanned it quickly, without really reading. "It is a note to you from your mother."

Ariel gave a poignant cry and grabbed it from his hand. As she devoured the words, her eyes brimmed with tears, which soon were spilling over her cheeks. After a few moments, she cast the paper aside and covered her face with her hands.

Unable to resist, Alan picked it up. The note was a muddle of slanting lines and unfinished thoughts, written in a hand that revealed a greatly disordered mind, he thought. The first few fragments read:

the play wears thin
the voice within
clamors
night and day

Then there was a space, and

the soul killed so young
can never revive
the woman—never child—
is not really alive

He frowned disapprovingly, then went on to read the rest. It was a bit more coherent, saying:

I've done my best to love you, and to make certain you don't follow me down into the black. I'm taking the coward's way. I know. You'll never understand how sorry . . .

Under this was a great scrawled signature—Bess—and a string of ink blots that suggested she had dropped the pen. Alan's frown deepened. It was appalling to think that Ariel had been left entirely alone in the world on the strength of this. He was glad he had never met Bess Harding, he decided. He didn't think he would have cared for her at all.

Ariel was struggling to control her tears. "The black," she muttered. "That's what she called it sometimes when she was blue-deviled."

Alan bit back a sharp response.

"If I'd only been here . . ." she began.

"You would have been able to do nothing," he said.

"You don't know. I might have—"

"You might have witnessed her disintegration more intimately," he cut in again. "You could not have stopped it. And it would have been the worse for you. She saw that much at least." It was the only thing he could commend in her mother, he thought, that she had kept her young daughter safely away.

"She did love me," said Ariel, catching her breath on a sob. "She did finally tell me about my father. She sent me to him."

Alan refrained from pointing out that if she had wanted to do that, she might have indicated where he was now. Ariel had started crying harder than before, and he couldn't bear the lost, forlorn sound of it. He went and folded her in his arms.

At first, this seemed to heighten her grief. She gave herself up to tears; they shuddered through her with a violence and abandon that he found rather alarming. But after a time, he felt her relax a little. She rested her head on his shoulder. Her breathing steadied somewhat. Her hands, which had been clenched into fists, uncurled and lay gently on his lapels.

Alan's body began to react to the feel of her breasts pressing against his ribs, the curve of her waist under his hand, the heady scent of her perfume in his nostrils. He drew back a bit. "I should call someone for you," he said. "Perhaps Hannah . . ."

"Don't leave me," she murmured. With a sigh, she let

herself rest fully against him. Her hip fitted into the hollow of his. Tendrils of her hair brushed his neck like gossamer fire. He couldn't do this. Grasping her waist with both hands, he pushed her gently away. "I must go," he said hoarsely.

Ariel stumbled and swayed. He had to catch hold of her again to keep her from falling. "Don't leave me," she whispered again. "I can't bear to be left again."

She wanted comfort and reassurance, he thought, and he was nearly out of his mind with wanting her. "I can't," he said through clenched teeth.

Tears gathered in her eyes. Her lips parted as if to speak, but she didn't.

"Ariel," he murmured helplessly.

Looking utterly desolate, she turned away. She began walking toward the door of the room, but her steps were uncertain and erratic. She moved like someone who had taken a stunning blow, he thought.

"I'll get Hannah—" he attempted again.

"No!" she said fiercely. "Nor Ellen. They'll just tell your mother and all your family. I can't bear that."

She continued into the hall. He followed and watched anxiously as she began to stumble up the stairs.

He couldn't leave her, he thought. But he couldn't stay.

Ariel tripped on a stair tread and caught the banister to keep from going down.

Alan tightened his jaw. He was a man of science, he thought. He was capable of remaining in control no matter what the circumstances. "You should lie down," he said firmly, and went to support her up the steps.

The first room they reached on the upper floor was Bess Harding's former bedroom, with its gigantic four-poster bed. Ariel turned that way, and he guided her through the door. "You should rest," he told her.

She raised her head to look at him, her face like a flower. Almost too soft to hear, she murmured his name.

Alan gritted his teeth. He was going to have to lift her onto the bed, he realized. The image was so vivid, and so enflaming, that he couldn't move.

Ariel turned a little. She was looking at him as if he were some answer to her grief, some compensation for all that she had lost. Alan's heart was pounding heavily, his breath had shortened. If only she wouldn't look at him like that.

She put her hands on his chest, then slid them up around his neck. The look in her eyes was less tragic now. Her full lips were parted and expectant. She leaned against him, feeding the fire burning through his veins.

Alan's resistance wavered—and broke. His arms came around her, pressing her tight against him. He captured her mouth and kissed her hard. She melted against him with no hesitation whatever, and the kiss went on and on until any hope of restraint was scattered to the winds.

Finally, after an eternity, Alan raised his head to look down at her. Ariel's eyes were closed, her mouth a little open. She was heartrendingly beautiful. Moving fast, he went to shut and latch the chamber door, then he came back and pulled her close again, trailing his lips lightly, slowly, across her mouth, feeling his whole body prickle with the thrill of it. He moved down her neck with quick, featherlight kisses, to her shoulder and then to the swell of breast above the neck of her gown. His hands roamed over her body, savoring it, smoothing her hair, caressing her back, cupping her waist. Ariel arched up against him, wanting more, and any remaining control he might have had went up in flames.

He took her lips again, increasing the urgency of the kiss, feeling her fingers tighten in his hair. He slid his hands down to her buttocks and pressed her hard against him. Ariel made a small, tremulous sound.

Alan buried one hand in the coils of her shining brown hair, reveling in the silken feel of it. He scattered the pins so that it came tumbling down around her shoulders, as he had so often imagined. He pushed the sleeves of her gown off her shoulders, exposing the rosy tips of her breasts, tight and erect. He showered more quick kisses on the soft mounds, then took one of the buds in his mouth and teased it with his tongue, exulting at Ariel's gasp of surprise and pleasure.

His lips found hers again, and he tempted the tip of her tongue with his. Her wholehearted response sent a galvanizing pulse of desire through him. All the hounds of hell couldn't have stopped him now.

Finding the fastenings of her dress, Alan undid them. As its folds pooled on the floor, he shed his own coat and shirt. Bending, he caught the hem of her shift and pulled it upward in one long gesture. Ariel raised her arms to let him cast the garment aside, her eyes wide and dark on his. When he pulled her to him again, the intimate sensation of his skin on hers enflamed him even further. She put her arms around him and ran her hands over the muscles of his back.

He pushed her back onto the wide four-poster bed. In the fading light, her hair gleamed and her skin was cream and roses. He reveled in the beauty of her nakedness, the sweet curves and enflaming secret places. "Alan," she murmured in a voice that struck deep inside him, and he knew all was lost. Joining her on the bed, he slid his thigh between her knees as he pressed her to the coverlet, his lips covering hers.

Ariel's hair had spread in a silken fan across the pillows. Alan breathed in its sweet scent as he kissed her neck and fragile collarbones. His lips roamed over her, eliciting gasps of pleasure as they fluttered on her pink nipples, whispered over the enticing softness of her stomach and hip.

He trailed his fingers like a feather along her inner thigh, up and down, up and down. Ariel shivered and moved so that the next time his fingers encountered the taut flesh between her legs. Then, she cried out at his touch and said his name in a way that drove him nearly mad.

Alan heard his own breath rasping in the quiet of the room. Jerking at the fastenings of his breeches, he rose above her, crushing her lips in a last tormenting kiss. Then, at last, he entered her—and came up against resistance. Like a man stumbling, he tried to catch himself, but in the next instant, the force of his longing had broken through. He hesitated.

"Please," Ariel whispered, clasping his waist, kissing his arm and shoulder and neck.

He began to move slowly. She matched him. Together, their tantalizing rhythm quickened. Then Alan had to go faster, and she clung to him with surprising strength as he guided them both through a flood of sensation that rose and rose until it flowered into ecstasy. Waves of pleasure shuddered through him, and he heard himself groan her name before he collapsed and lay still.

Chapter Fourteen

Ariel woke alone, in dimness. She lay still for a moment, disoriented. She was not in her own room. The early evening light from the window was in the wrong place, and this bed was too high. She had an instant's fright, and then memory returned. She was on the four-poster bed in her mother's old room—naked with a corner of the coverlet thrown over her—and Alan was somewhere nearby. She reached out across the broad expanse of the bed. It was empty. Perhaps he had stepped out for a moment.

Drawing her arm back, Ariel hugged herself under the silken folds. She could still feel his hands on her skin, his lips on hers. Her senses were filled with the power of him and the amazing responses he had drawn from her body.

Minutes passed, and there was no sound. Where could Alan be? Ariel wondered. Sitting up, she crawled across the huge bed to the opposite side where there was a small table holding candles and a tinder box. After a few fumbles, she got a candle lit and held it up to survey the room. It was empty but for her. Her clothes had been picked up from the floor where they had scattered and hung over the back of a straight chair. Of Alan's clothes, there was no sign whatsoever.

Ariel ran her eyes over the room again. But there was nothing more to see. He had dressed, and he was gone.

She put the candlestick down, sitting with her legs dangling over the side of the bed. He couldn't be gone. He couldn't have left her. She bit one knuckle, thinking, and noticed her mother's agate ring, which had somehow found its way to her own finger. She had begged him not to leave her alone, Ariel thought. He must be here somewhere.

Slipping from the high bed, Ariel dressed quickly. Taking the candlestick, she moved quietly to the door and opened it a crack. The hall was empty. It was very quiet. Standing still, she strained her ears, listening. Nothing. She crept down the stairs, drawing only a few creaks from the old boards, and paused in the entryway. The place might have been completely empty, she thought, as empty as she felt at this moment.

Then she caught a murmur of sound, a suggestion of life. Moving toward the back of the house, she lost and found the thread more than once before she realized that it was coming from the kitchen in the basement.

Had Alan gone down to visit Hannah? she wondered incredulously. The idea was ludicrous, yet when she stood at the top of the kitchen stairs, she could definitely hear a male voice coming from there. Militant, she marched down, pushed open the door, and confronted the pair sitting at the kitchen table—Hannah and Nathaniel Gresham.

For a moment, they all stared at each other. The candlestick wavered in Ariel's hand, sending shadows jumping on the wooden floor and walls.

"I . . . I was looking for Lord Alan," she managed at last. And then wished she hadn't said it.

"Don't believe he's here," replied the viscount. He looked at Hannah, who shook her head.

"Oh. I thought he . . . was."

"He left hours ago," responded Hannah, without any special emphasis. Ariel wondered whether she was glad or sorry that no one had noticed the length of his stay earlier. Or perhaps she was going mad, she thought, putting a hand to her head. Perhaps none of it had happened at all. But her own body told her differently.

"Is anything wrong?" wondered Hannah.

"No." She shook her head to reinforce the lie. "No." He had left her. Not only that, he had sneaked out, as if he were ashamed of what they had done.

Lord Highgrove cleared his throat. "I . . . er . . . I decided to take you up on your offer," he ventured.

Ariel stared at him.

"Came to visit Hannah," he pointed out.

She mustn't give anything away, Ariel thought. It would be too humiliating if they realized how she felt just now. She let out a long breath. "How . . . how nice," she said. "Are you having tea? I should like some."

Hannah rose to find another cup.

"You said I should come," added Lord Highgrove.

Ariel tried to smile pleasantly at him. "Yes, it's very . . ." Then she finally remembered their earlier conversation. "Oh, yes," she went on in a different tone. "Of course." She made a massive effort to gather her wits.

Hannah put a tin of chocolate biscuits on the table along with Ariel's tea. All of them sat down. Lord Highgrove's hands opened and closed nervously on the tabletop. "If Violet's grandmother could see this . . ." he muttered.

"She wouldn't approve?" asked Ariel, conscious of Hannah's suddenly alert expression.

"She doesn't approve of anything."

"She must approve of you," Ariel insisted.

He gave a mirthless laugh. "Me least of all. And if she knew what I was doing here, she'd . . ."

"What?"

He blinked at her.

"What would she do?" asked Ariel. "Call off her granddaughter's marriage to the eldest son of a duke, who's rich besides?"

"She would make my life a living hell," he burst out, then flushed, looking from her to Hannah. "I beg your pardon."

"And how would she do that, precisely?" Ariel asked, ignoring his apology for his language.

"By continually mentioning my lapses," he answered. "By pointing out my deficiencies and implying that I am not a paragon of perfection in absolutely every area of life. By dropping hints to Violet that she really ought to bring me to heel, and making her feel as if getting married is a dead bore—no, worse, a positive penance!"

"Why do you allow it?" asked Ariel.

"What?" he said a bit wildly.

The eldest Gresham son seemed to be an admirable fellow, she thought. If she were less agitated over her own dilemmas, she might go more slowly with him. But tonight all her patience was gone. And Hannah watching her like a hawk didn't help her temper. "I don't wish to embarrass you," she said to him, "but you must be an extraordinarily good catch. There can't be a great many wealthy dukes' heirs available."

A hint of amusement had entered his expression. "I believe we are rather thin on the ground," he acknowledged.

She nodded. "So Violet's family must consider itself fortunate. And I'm certain that if you hinted to one of them—you will know which would be best—that Violet's grandmother is giving you a distaste for the whole venture, someone would tell her to keep her opinions to herself. You might even imply that you are thinking of crying off."

"I could never do that," he responded, shocked. "Violet would be terribly upset at the idea."

"Tell her what you are going to do. I assume she does not agree with her grandmother."

"No. That is, I don't think she does."

"You don't know?"

He shook his head despondently.

"Don't you talk to each other? I thought you had been acquainted practically all your lives."

"We used to talk. There never seemed to be enough time to say everything we had to say. But lately . . . all the wedding preparations and . . . and so on have kept her so occupied. And her grandmother . . . does not approve of giving engaged couples a great deal of time together."

"Why don't you both tell her to go to blazes?" Ariel suggested.

"You don't understand."

Ariel opened the tin of biscuits, offered it to him and to Hannah, then took one herself and bit into it. "Explain it to me," she said.

He turned the confection over in his hands. "Violet and I have a great responsibility, you see. We will be—years and years from now, of course—the duke and duchess of Langford. We will represent the name, and a long proud tradition. It sounds a bit wet, I suppose, but we are both very conscious of that. We don't wish to do anything that would . . . well, put a bad light on the family. We have to be completely correct." He put the biscuit down as if it were heavy, and sighed.

"Just like your father was," said Ariel, taking a chance. "And your grandfather."

There was a small, unidentifiable sound from Hannah.

The viscount looked surprised. "Oh, well, as to that . . ."

Ariel gazed at him with wide, innocent eyes.

"My father kicked up a bit of a dust when he was young," he said slowly. "Always said I wasn't to follow his example."

"Did he? But your grandfather was a model of virtue, I suppose?"

A light blossomed in Lord Highgrove's blue eyes. His lips curved ever so slightly upward. "He was a dreadful old rip," he said. "I remember he always smelled of brandy. They say he fought more than a dozen duels, and nearly had to flee the country twice."

"Indeed. What a trial he must have been to your grandmother."

The viscount actually smiled. "I'm not sure she noticed. They do say that two of my great-aunts were most likely fathered by . . ." He stopped short, flushed, and cleared his throat again. "That is, she wasn't exactly a stay-at-home."

"Really?"

He laughed aloud.

"You know, I understood it was quite customary to allow engaged couples some time to themselves," mused Ariel.

"By Jove, it is," he agreed.

"You and Violet probably have many matters to discuss," she suggested.

"I shan't waste the time *discussing* anything," he declared. "That is . . ." He flushed again.

"These biscuits are quite good," said Ariel, taking another. "Where did you find them, Hannah? Won't you try one?"

Lord Highgrove took up his again. "Thank you," he answered in heartfelt tones and bit into it with enthusiasm.

Ariel sipped her tea, and saw over the rim of the cup that Hannah was watching her. She tensed slightly, but the older woman merely raised her own cup and gave her a small salute.

Full night had fallen by the time Lord Highgrove departed. Ariel went up and straightened her mother's bedroom before going to her own. She didn't want to have to make explanations to Hannah. But once this was done and she had gone to her own bedchamber, she was left with nothing to distract her from the fact that Alan had left her without a word or a sign.

How could he do this? she wondered. It was devastating, infuriating, insulting. Surely he must have known that it would be.

A sudden thought chilled her. Would he disappear now that he had conquered her? That was what Bess would have predicted, and she had no strong arguments to counter that inner voice that told her she was ruined. Not her reputation, she thought despairingly, but her heart, her very soul.

Suddenly, the words of her mother's note came back to her in a rush, and along with them a feeling of such desolation and loneliness that she wrapped her arms around herself, shivering. She wanted Alan so much that she didn't think she could stand it. If he were here, the emptiness would go away, the grief and pain would be manageable. She drew her arms tighter, wishing for him with all her might, praying that he would somehow hear her and return.

The house remained dark and silent. Even outside, there was no sound. And then a piece of the shadows detached itself and jumped onto her bed, resolving into a feline shape, which butted its head against her elbow.

"Prospero," Ariel said shakily. She reached out to scratch one of his ears, and he gave a low rumble of approval. "I am not feeling too . . . well," she told the animal.

He gazed at her, his eyes seeming to shine with their own light in the dim room, and that steady gaze brought Ariel crashing back to reality. What had she been thinking? she wondered. Lord Alan Gresham was not going to come and comfort her. Her connection with him rested on the haunting of Carlton House, which was now over. He would be returning to Oxford, and the work he loved. There was no place for her in his life, and indeed he had never hinted that there could be. It was foolish . . . insane to fall in love with him.

Ariel's breath caught in a gasp. She was insane, she understood, because she had fallen hopelessly, helplessly in love with him—the son of a duke, the man of science who spurned the whole concept of love. She had gotten what she had told her mother she wanted more than ten years ago—love. And it appeared that Bess had been right about this, at least. It hurt like the very devil.

Alan looked over the pages that he had filled with columns of figures and calculations, then put down the pen and rubbed his eyes. He had a raging headache, and his mouth felt as if it were coated with blotting paper. It was difficult to focus on what he had written, and even harder to think. In fact, he felt wretched. And this oppressive, unfamiliar condition was entirely the fault of his host, the prince regent, who had refused to accept any of the numerous excuses Alan had made not to join the sovereign and his cronies in a drinking party last night. They had to celebrate the exposure of the ghost, the prince had insisted, as well as see Alan on his way, since he was moving out very soon.

It had been the last thing he wanted to do, with his senses still full of Ariel and his emotions unsteady. The prince had not allowed him to merely sit at the table either; he had practically forced him to match the others drink for drink. How did people live this way, Alan wondered, looking around the overly ornate Carlton House bedchamber, which he had grown to hate. Sitting in a flimsy, ridiculously curlicued and gilded chair before a desk decorated with medallions of simpering shepherd-esses, he rested his forehead on his hand.

He was a man of science, he insisted silently, then rubbed his hand across his face. He could overcome this physical discomfort and think rationally and incisively. He looked down at the columns of figures once again. With some care, it ought to be possible for him to support a wife and the establishment such a change in his status would require. He had added up the expense of a house in Oxford rather than the college chambers he had been inhabiting. And it appeared he could manage it without asking his family to enlarge his income, which he did not wish to do. They were, after all, unlikely to approve the match he was about to make.

Frowning, he anticipated the likely reactions to his marriage. His parents would object. But great families had weathered worse, and he did, after all, have five brothers who seemed quite likely to marry suitably. No doubt society would have a field day over the duke's son and the nobody, as they would see it. However, he didn't care a snap of his fingers for society.

It wouldn't help his status at the university to marry the daughter of a notorious actress, he admitted. But his credit could withstand it. If the truth be told, he knew he had rather a privileged position at Oxford as an aristocrat with an income of his own. He had always been careful not to trade on this advantage, but if necessary he would do so now. Leaving his work and colleagues was unthinkable.

These rational considerations comforted him a good deal. He liked having the matter settled and a clear plan in place. He had not meant to marry just now, of course. Actually, he had been uncertain whether he would ever marry. His work was so much more important to him than any personal connections. Or, it had been, Alan thought. It still was, really. He was eager to return to his laboratory; he missed his intellectual pursuits damnably. It was just that Ariel . . . Somehow when he was with Ariel he lost touch with the cool observant persona that he had relied on for a decade. He became someone he didn't even know when he had her softness beneath his hands, her lips responding to his slightest signal, her . . .

Alan made an involuntary sound and banished this line of thought. There were advantages to being married to her, he thought. When they were settled down together, these unacceptable disruptions would cease. He would resume his work, and return home to her each evening, in an orderly way. There would be none of this turmoil. He would not have to sneak out of houses like a thief to make certain that no one knew he had been there alone with her and utterly destroyed her reputation. His life would be as calm and productive as it had been six months ago. He took a deep satisfied breath at the idea.

She was intelligent, he told himself. She had a lively interest in ideas. She might well win over his Oxford friends. And of course, he would have her in his bed every night. Heat flushed Alan at the thought. He remembered the silk of her skin, the slender suppleness of her body as it responded to his touch. His pulse quickened as he recalled the way her breath had caught when he introduced her to a particularly intimate caress and the heady mixture of innocence and roused passion that had enflamed him. His own body grew hard at the memories.

Alan rose abruptly. Catching a glimpse of himself in the overlarge mirror above the mantel shelf, he saw an unfamiliar figure with ruddy skin and a wild glitter about the eyes. He blinked, and so did this unacceptably flamboyant man. He raised a hand, and saw the gesture echoed in the glass.

Forcing a deep breath, Alan straightened his cravat.

His hair was mussed, he thought coldly. He looked like someone who had not slept well and had thrown on his clothes haphazardly in the morning. This wouldn't do. He rang for a servant and began to make ready for a formal call.

Chapter Fifteen

——— ❖ ———

Throughout a restless morning, Ariel wrestled with the overwhelming desire to smash something. Repeatedly, she consigned Lord Alan Gresham to perdition, and then had to fight a fierce battle with herself to keep from bursting into tears.

It was nearly two o'clock when she heard the sounds of arrival below. Though she tried, Ariel couldn't resist going to the stairwell and listening as Hannah opened the door. She heard the older woman greet Lord Alan and heard him ask for her. Relief and a certain excitement warred with anger in her breast as Hannah started up the steps. She hurried back into her room and was sitting at the writing desk by the time Hannah knocked and announced their visitor. "Oh?" she said. "Very well. I'll be down in a few minutes."

When Hannah was gone, she jumped up and surveyed herself in the long mirror hung on the wardrobe door. Her gown was all right. Its tawny silk brought a glow to her skin and hair. Or possibly it was emotion that was making her cheeks so red and her hazel eyes so bright, Ariel thought.

Catching up a gauzy scarf and draping it over her shoulders, Ariel checked the mirror once more. Lady Macbeth, she thought to herself; Cordelia, the queen of Persia. Her spine straightened and her chin came up; a regal hauteur entered her gaze and her full lips turned sternly down. She moved a hand, and the gesture was both languid and imperious. Satisfied, she raised her eyebrows slightly, and then walked from the room.

Lord Alan was alone in the front parlor when she reached it. He turned from the fire, checked slightly at the sight of her, then said, "Good day. You know why I am here, I imagine."

She allowed her brows to rise a little higher.

"I thought we would marry next week," he went on. "I have inquired about a special license, and it seems easy enough to procure. Under the circumstances, I don't think banns are really—"

"Marry?" said Ariel.

He nodded. "I have written to Oxford about houses that may be available. It will take a little time, of course, to find just the right—"

"Circumstances," Ariel echoed, still trying to take in his first statement.

"We can stay here for that time," he went on as if he hadn't heard. "And I know you will have things to clear up. Don't think I've forgotten that." He gave her a benevolent smile.

"You are asking me to marry you?" Ariel felt as if she had stepped out of her familiar front door and found nothing at all that she recognized.

He looked surprised. "Naturally."

"Because . . . because of yesterday?"

"Of course."

He was looking at her as if she were a half-wit, Ariel thought. "Because you think you must?" she elaborated.

"Of course," he said again. "I am not the sort of man who—"

"You feel there is no other course of action open to you?" she interrupted.

"There is not," he replied impatiently.

"Yes, there is." Ariel swallowed the anger she had been feeling earlier, mixed with a disappointment so sharp she could hardly stand it. He had said nothing about what he wanted to do, she thought. He had not mentioned love, or anything ridiculous like that. Here was a man of honor, Ariel told herself, the creature her mother had assured her did not exist. It was a surprisingly disappointing species. "I refuse," she said.

"I beg your pardon?"

He meant to do his duty, Ariel thought. No other course of action had even occurred to him. What did he think she was—a lapse, a mistake that he must remedy, a female ruled by her impulses who had trapped him into marriage? She dug her nails into her palms. "I won't marry you," she said.

He looked stunned.

"So you need not worry about the matter," she heard herself adding. "Let us forget it ever happened."

"It?" he repeated incredulously.

"I . . . I was overset by the arrival of my mother's note," she stammered. "I wasn't . . . I didn't know what I was doing. But one unfortunate lapse needn't spoil our whole lives."

His head jerked very slightly, as if he had taken a blow. Ariel couldn't interpret the look in his blue eyes.

"No one knows about it," she said.

"No," he agreed in an odd voice.

Was there something she hadn't understood? Ariel wondered. "Surely we can *both* rise above it," she attempted. She would show him that she was not some sort of manipulative female at the mercy of her emotions.

"If that is what you wish, I certainly can," he replied curtly. The lines around his mouth were harsh.

"Splendid," answered Ariel, and thought what a very stupid and unpleasant word that was.

She looked up at him, and their eyes locked. He seemed absolutely furious, but about what? Ariel found it difficult to get a breath. She was almost dizzy with conflicting feelings. If only he had said that he felt something—anything—for her, she thought.

The fire crackled in the grate; in the entryway, the front door opened and closed. But the two in the parlor noticed nothing until Lord Robert Gresham and his eldest brother strolled into the room. Sebastian was close behind them.

Lord Highgrove took a step toward Ariel. "I wanted to tell you, I had a word with Violet's Uncle Philip," he said. "Just as you suggested."

"Yes?" Ariel struggled to remember what in the world he was talking about. All she could see was Alan's face, stony and unreadable.

"Dropped a word in his ear about Violet's grandmother," the newcomer prompted.

"Umm." Their earlier conversation came back to her. "Oh. What did he say?"

"He went a bit white around the gills," was the pleased reply. "Told me I'd misunderstood her grandmother's comments, she admired me no end, that sort of thing. But he went haring out of the club five minutes later, calling for his horse." The viscount grinned. "I gave him an hour, then went to call on Violet. The upshot is, I'm driving her out to Kew Gardens tomorrow, just the two of us." He had a reminiscent smile. "She seemed quite taken with the idea."

"Good for you," applauded Lord Robert. "Violet's old harpy of a grandmother deserves a taste of her own medicine." He turned to Ariel. "She once told me I hadn't the wits of a grasshopper."

"Harpy," said the viscount meditatively. "I believe I like that even better than harridan." He grinned again.

"Has everyone lost their wits?" Lord Alan said, seeming to speak to the air above the others' heads. He stared at Ariel, strain evident now in his expression. "Am I the only rational person present?"

"It was quite a rational plan actually," answered Lord Highgrove, taking the remark as addressed to him. "I wonder I didn't think of—"

"Schemes taken from plays," Lord Alan continued, ignoring his brother. "Questions. Akkadian. And now . . ." He made a throwaway gesture. Ariel took it as a reference to her refusal. "She's driven the whole family mad," he concluded wonderingly. He put a hand to his head, then let it drop.

"Who, Ariel?" said Lord Sebastian. "Hasn't driven me mad." He frowned. "Don't think she has, anyway. It's true I've never talked so much to a female in my life," he added with a touch of mystification.

Lord Robert was nodding. "It's dashed peculiar," he agreed. "You can flirt with a girl for an entire season and never know a thing about her. But if you once begin to talk on a serious subject . . ." He shook his head as if the result were an unfathomable mystery.

"Akkadian?" repeated Lord Alan incredulously.

"I ain't the dunce some people think me," was the oddly dignified reply. "I took a Latin prize at Harrow, you know."

"By Jove, I'd forgotten that," replied Lord Sebastian. "Papa—"

"Nearly dropped his teeth," finished Lord Robert. "I remember. Everyone thought Alan had all the brains in the family, but he don't."

"Brains!" exploded Lord Alan. His features had reddened.

All of his brothers turned to look at him. "You ill?" wondered Lord Robert. "Not looking quite the thing."

"No, I am not ill," replied the other through clenched teeth.

"Alan's never ill," commented Lord Sebastian.

"Flushed," Lord Robert pointed out. "Not hot in here."

All three brothers peered at him. "You haven't taken a fever at Carlton . . ." began Lord Highgrove.

With a sound very like a snarl, Lord Alan pushed past them and strode from the room. In a moment they heard the front door slam behind him. Ariel jerked a little at the angry, final noise the panels made.

There was a brief silence.

"What the deuce is eating him?" said Lord Robert then.

The three looked at Ariel.

"I haven't the least idea," she lied.

"Sick of London, I wager," said Lord Sebastian. "Alan's always hated it here. When Mother made him do the Season, he moped and fidgeted the whole time."

"I remember," agreed Lord Robert feelingly. "Talk of your ill humors."

"He'll be going back to Oxford any day," said Lord Highgrove. "That'll restore his spirits."

No doubt, thought Ariel, and a forlorn vacancy descended over her, leaving her suddenly exhausted. "I'm a bit tired . . ." she began.

Lord Highgrove responded immediately. "Of course. I must go. I only dropped by to, er, give you the news."

"Dancing attendance on Violet's family again tonight?" asked Lord Robert, who seemed oblivious to her hint.

"I said I would see them at Almack's," he acknowledged. "I must go home and change."

"Don't go," suggested Lord Sebastian. "You want to throw a scare into them, don't turn up."

The viscount frowned, and looked tempted. "I don't wish to upset Violet," he objected.

"Send a note round to her." Lord Sebastian grinned. "Tell her you'll see her tomorrow."

"Have 'em slip it to her on the sly," added Lord Robert, getting into the spirit of the thing. "Let the rest of them wonder what's become of you."

"We'll have a hand of cards, make a night of it," said Sebastian. "That is, if it's all right with Ariel?"

All three of them turned to look at her. They were handsome men, she thought, with their auburn hair and blue eyes and fine figures. But none of them could compare to Alan. Stricken by a rush of despair, she made an uncaring gesture.

Lord Highgrove considered. "I'll do it."

Lord Robert gave a cheer. "I'll send my groom for some claret," he said. "Perhaps Hannah will make us some of that toasted cheese she used to do on the hearth."

His oldest brother looked surprised. "I remember that," he said. "Lord, it's been a long time." He looked around the room. "How long has it been since we spent an evening together?"

There was a short silence.

"Since we were boys, you mean?" said Lord Sebastian.

Lord Highgrove nodded, and another short silence fell.

"Have we ever?" wondered Lord Robert.

Another silence fell.

"Well, then, it's high time we did," exclaimed Lord Sebastian heartily. "What do you say to piquet?"

Feeling immeasurably weary, Ariel turned and left them. The murmur of conversation followed her past the first landing and faded only when she reached the second floor. She continued on to her own room and sat down there in the darkness without lighting a candle.

·   ·   ·

It was the first instant she had had to think, to try to sort out the welter of emotion she had been experiencing. Lord Alan's offer of marriage had been completely unexpected. Because of what her mother had taught her, she hadn't even imagined such a thing. In her worst moments, she had been afraid he would reject her, or despise her for giving in to him, or triumph at her surrender and try to take some advantage of it. At other times, she had been certain he would apologize and withdraw. And then there had been the secret, dangerous flashes of hope that he might care for her, that the gentle urgency of his touch had meant something more than desire.

There had been no sign of that in his proposal, she thought sadly. Bess *had* been wrong; all men were not users and seducers. But duty and respect were not the same as . . . love. Ariel acknowledged the word with a kind of breathless pain. In all these days they had spent together, in the searching and analyzing they had shared, she had come to love him so deeply, and now she had just refused to marry him. Something between a sob and a laugh choked her. She had refused the son of a duke. No one would ever believe it. Indeed, one part of her own mind was having trouble comprehending it. Why not have married him? that inner voice was saying. She would at least have been with him then. And who knows what the future might bring?

Ariel shook her head in the dimness. Impossible, she thought. She couldn't have endured the continual hope, and continual disappointment. He didn't even believe in love, she reminded herself. He rejected the very concept. He set such store in rationality, in being a man of science. He would scorn her for wanting such a will-o'-the-wisp. And that would be a pain worse than this.

Her breath caught shakily. She wouldn't see him anymore, she thought. A man who had been refused did not continue to call. Alone, safely hidden by darkness, Ariel allowed the tears to overflow onto her cheeks. She wanted nothing more than to marry him, she realized, if only it could be more than an obligation he felt bound to fulfill.

A day passed, and another, and as Ariel had expected, there was no sign of Lord Alan. What she had not predicted was that she would have to hear *of* him constantly. His brothers were in and out of the house, and they discussed him without any sign of self-consciousness. There was no chance to forget him, even for a minute. She had to speak of him as if nothing had happened, and keep up a facade of contentment. It was excruciating. And yet, it was disturbingly satisfying as well. She was hungry for news of him, for the sound of his name, for any scrap of information that might reveal what he thought, how he felt, whether the things that had passed between them had had an effect.

"Alan's moved out of Carlton House," Lord Sebastian informed her one afternoon.

"He has gone back to Oxford?" she said, and held her breath waiting for the answer.

"Moved into Langford House," was the puzzled reply. "M'mother's pleased, of course, but it's deuced odd. Can't think why he's staying. Usually he can't wait to get away."

"What does he say, when you ask him?" dared Ariel.

"Ask? Oh, well, I don't believe anyone's asked."

She tried to look innocently inquiring.

"One doesn't, with Alan. Particularly lately."

"Why particularly?" she wondered, trying to remember to breathe normally.

"He's in a foul mood," Lord Sebastian explained, seeming to see nothing out of the way in confiding this to her. "As likely to snap your head off as say good morning. Told Robert one of his waistcoats was a—what was it?—a shameful waste of the light needed to illuminate it."

A spurt of laughter escaped Ariel.

"No one's asking him anything," Lord Sebastian concluded.

She pondered this information for an evening, turning it this way and that to see what it might mean. She had come to no conclusion the next day, when she found Lord Robert in the kitchen telling Hannah, "He plays half the night. Thinks no one notices, but of course we all do."

"Notices what?" asked Ariel.

"Alan playing the pianoforte. In the dark."

"How strange." Her tone must have been strange as well, Ariel realized, catching a sharp look from Hannah.

"It's dashed peculiar," said Lord Robert. "He don't even like people to know he can play. And now there he is, pounding away loud as you please, as if all that fuss had never happened."

"What fuss?" Ariel sat down at the kitchen table and forced herself to look only mildly curious.

"My mother used to brag about him, when we were small," answered Lord Robert distractedly. "Told all her friends he was some kind of prodigy. Then they all started wanting to hear, and having him called down to the drawing room to play for them during morning calls." He shook his head. "Alan despised it. You remember, Hannah?"

The older woman nodded feelingly.

"My mother was sorry by then, but the cat was out of the bag, so to speak. Until Alan figured it out."

"What?" asked Ariel, strongly moved by the picture of the talented little boy on exhibit to the gossips of the *ton*.

Lord Robert laughed. "He started playing like a normal seven-year-old," he said. "Penance for the ears. After a while, everyone put down my mother as a doting parent with a tin ear, and the command performances stopped. I don't think he ever played for anyone outside the family after that," he added meditatively. "Keeps it dead quiet." He looked self-conscious suddenly. "You won't mention that I . . ."

"Of course not," Ariel assured him. She was afire by this time with the desire to hear Alan play. It was a moment before she remembered that she would probably never speak to him again, let alone be admitted to the select ranks of those who had heard him.

It was the fourth day by the time she saw Lord Highgrove again, and it appeared that he had come expressly to speak to her. "I thought this business with the 'ghost' at Carlton House was settled," he asked without preamble.

Ariel nodded. "Some actors were behind it. They've been stopped."

"Then what's Alan doing with the prince's men?"

She gazed back at him blankly.

"Spends half the day conferring with them, or sending them here or there. My mother is . . ." He hesitated, smiling slightly. "Curious," he finished. "Is there something else the matter with the prince?"

Ariel couldn't resist raising her eyebrows.

"Beyond the obvious," added Lord Highgrove dryly. "Something Alan's involved with."

"I have no idea."

"But I thought you and he were . . ." He broke off, and Ariel waited with a good deal of interest and trepidation to see how he would end the sentence. "I thought you were working together on the investigation," he said finally.

Ariel let out her breath in a sigh. "No longer," she answered.

"Oh. Er . . ."

Lord Highgrove didn't stay long after that. She had

made him uncomfortable, Ariel thought. But she didn't know what else she could have said.

By the fifth day, she decided she had to get out. This waiting about as if something was going to happen was unendurable. And the continual flow of secondhand information about Lord Alan was becoming frustrating and painful.

She had been wanting to ask Flora Jennings a few more questions, she thought. She had the sense that the woman knew more about her mother than she had revealed. She would go and see her. She had put on her bonnet, gotten her gloves and reticule, and marched downstairs to the front door when Lord Sebastian Gresham appeared from the basement stairs. "Hullo," he said amiably.

"Good," replied Ariel. "You can come with me."

"Where to?"

"I'm going to call on Flora Jennings." And she didn't really want to visit that neighborhood alone, Ariel thought.

Lord Sebastian expressed enthusiasm about making the acquaintance of the girl who had Robert studying dead languages. Outside, he flagged down a cab, and they clattered over the cobblestones in silence for a time, then her companion ventured, "Alan hasn't been much in evidence lately."

Ariel said nothing.

"Used to be in and out of the house like a regular jack-in-the-box," Lord Sebastian mused.

She felt his scrutiny, and kept her chin high.

"You two haven't quarreled, have you?"

"Quarreled?" repeated Ariel, as if the mere thought was ridiculous. "What would we have to quarrel about?"

He didn't answer, and when Ariel gave him a sidelong glance under her lashes, she saw that he looked uncharacteristically thoughtful. Let him think what he liked, she told herself defiantly.

Flora Jennings was at the house, and she welcomed Ariel with calm cordiality. To Lord Sebastian, she was merely polite, and she seemed completely impervious to the famous charm of his smile.

"I understand you have caught the ghost," she said coolly when they had all sat down.

"Yes," acknowledged Ariel. "Some of the younger actors at the theater were behind the hoax."

"Out of friendship for Bess?"

"The leader, Michael Heany, said they thought something more should be done about her death."

"And so it should," replied Flora Jennings intensely. "But Prinny has gotten his way, as usual. He can go back to thinking only of his own pleasures and ignoring the misery of his subjects."

"I don't know what he could have done for my mother," said Ariel, forced to be honest.

The other woman turned her bright blue gaze on her, staring as if she were trying to look right through her. "You are wearing Bess's ring," she said.

Ariel looked down at her right hand. "Yes. You remember it? She sent it to me, only the package went astray, so I just received it." She hesitated. "There was a note, too."

Flora leaned forward. "What did she say?"

"It wasn't very . . . informative. Mainly it showed that she was distressed and . . . despairing." Whenever she focused on that note, Ariel began to feel surges of grief.

Their hostess's gaze was unwavering. "What are you going to do?" she asked.

"I don't know what else to do," Ariel admitted. "I have spoken to everyone I can think of, and no one seems to have noticed anything out of the way. I suppose I will never really know the reason why she . . . did it."

"So you are giving up?" was the fierce reply.

Stung, Ariel said, "What do you suggest? I came here

today because it seemed to me that you must have known my mother rather well, through your work together. And yet you have told me very little."

Some of Flora's intensity faded. Now, she looked doubtful and sad. "If I knew the answer . . ." she began, then fell silent.

"If there is an answer," said Ariel.

The other woman's fists clenched and unclenched in her lap. "I cannot get over the injustice and unfairness of it. We seem to be surrounded by injustice and unfairness. Is there nothing to be done?"

"You are doing something," Ariel pointed out.

Flora made a throwaway gesture. "So little. Bess had grand ideas. We were going to raise larger sums through her acquaintances and find a house in the country where the children could . . ." She repeated the gesture. "That is all at an end now."

"Perhaps not."

"It can't be done without Bess," declared Flora very positively. After a pause, she added, "So, she's simply gone, then. Gone."

Ariel shivered as the tide of emptiness and loss swept over her again. She couldn't speak.

"That's the way it is," continued the other woman, in a bitter tone that said she had heard these words many times. She rose. "I must get back to my work."

"But couldn't we—" began Ariel.

"You must excuse me," Flora interrupted. "I really have no time for idle conversation."

A bit offended, Ariel stood. Lord Sebastian, who had been studiously silent, joined her with alacrity. They were seen to the door with what Ariel thought was a little too much eagerness, and in another moment they were in the street climbing into their waiting cab.

"Robert has lost his mind," exclaimed Lord Sebastian when they started moving. "That girl is exactly like Aunt Agatha."

Chapter Sixteen

———— ❖ ————

Early the following week, Alan stood stiffly in Ariel Harding's front parlor waiting for her to appear and wondering what he was doing there. He had been wondering what he was doing for several days, and disliking the sensation intensely. Yet he couldn't seem to stop. His state of mind had been disordered since Ariel had refused him.

At first he had been simply incredulous. He had made careful plans, gone through intense deliberations; he had overcome his reluctance to wed, set aside his disinclination to do so. And she had refused him! It hadn't even occurred to him to consider this contingency. And this simple fact had forced him to recognize that he had not escaped all the prejudices of his class. He had believed that he thought of himself as a simple scholar. But with Ariel's rejection of his proposal, the duke's son had emerged in outrage, asking how she dared?

She was the daughter of a common actress, this part of himself had pointed out with sardonic clarity, an actress whose personal life had been notoriously disreputable.

She ought to have gone down on her knees in gratitude for an offer from him, this drawling inner voice had continued. She ought to have been overcome with the magnitude of such an honor. She must be a trollop like her mother.

He hadn't liked this voice, had despised it, in fact. But it was true that in the world's terms, Ariel's refusal was astonishing. He was a better match than she could ever have hoped for. And setting this aside, he knew her to be a fastidious and honorable creature. It seemed logical that she would wish to marry to salvage her reputation. And yet, she didn't. There was nothing logical about this situation at all.

She simply didn't wish to marry him, Alan thought, with a mixture of disbelief, anger, and pique that he still had not sorted out. Not even for significant material advantages, not to regularize a slip that would ruin her if it became known. She had said that it would spoil her life to be married to him.

The worst of it was, Ariel Harding haunted him far more effectively than Prinny's ghost had ever managed at Carlton House. He had not been able to dismiss her from his mind like a failed hypothesis and go on to something more productive. He dreamed of her; he seemed to catch her flowery scent as he walked in the street. Sometimes, he felt as if he were going mad.

The only thing that had allowed him some respite from this storm of emotion was working to fathom the mystery of the documents she had found. Telling himself it was the intellectual challenge that drew him, he spent every waking hour in investigation. And now, at last, he had results to report. He would show her, he thought, though precisely what he meant to show remained unclear.

There was a sound from the entry, and then Ariel appeared in the doorway. She wore a simple gown of green muslin, and she looked heartbreakingly beautiful. Alan found himself unable to speak for a moment. She was looking at him as if she couldn't imagine what he was doing in her parlor. "I've found Daniel Bolton," he managed finally.

Ariel stood very still, her hazel eyes widening. "My father?" she asked.

He did not point out that this remained to be proved.

She was still and silent for another brief period, then she said, "Where?"

"He lives at Ivydene Manor in Somerset."

"Somerset?" she repeated, as if he had said China or Borneo. "In the country?" she added incredulously.

He nodded.

"But my mother hated the country."

For the first time, she met his eyes. She had forgotten everything else in this revelation about her supposed father, Alan saw. She wasn't thinking of him, or of their last awkward time together, or of whether she had been wrong to refuse him. He felt a spark of irritation.

"Are you sure it's the right man?" she asked.

"It is not an uncommon name," he admitted in rather clipped tones. "However, the evidence appears reliable."

"What evidence?"

"He was married on the day listed in the document you gave me," said Alan. "He is of the right age; he had been in London."

"But . . ." Ariel rubbed her forehead, then began to pace the length of the room. "What else? What is he like? Does he—?"

"We have not found out a great deal more about him as yet."

She was turned away from him, walking down the room. "It is rather unsettling," she admitted.

He acknowledged this with a noncommittal sound.

"You know nothing more about him at all?"

"Not as yet," Alan repeated. He intended to find out

everything there was to know about this Bolton, he thought with unexpected vehemence.

Ariel had resumed pacing, her expression miles away. He might not even have been in the room, Alan thought. She was totally engrossed in this unknown man, who might or might not be her father.

"I must go down to Somerset at once to meet him," she said. She clasped her hands before her as if to keep them from trembling.

Alan watched her.

"I must know what he's like," said Ariel. "For so many years I've wondered."

"It would be better to wait and let us investigate further," he replied, even though he could see it was useless.

"I can't. Now that I know my father is—"

"It is far from certain that he is your father," Alan couldn't help saying sharply.

"He must be." Ariel gripped her hands tighter. He could see the knuckles whiten with the pressure she exerted. "He has to be."

"It would be wise to proceed carefully," he began.

"I can't," she cried. "You don't understand. I have to know."

Although he had expected this reaction, he hadn't realized that it would annoy him so deeply to have Ariel completely focused on another man. She would go to Somerset, he thought, meet some stranger and designate him her father on irrational, emotional grounds, and never come back. He couldn't stop her. "I will escort you there," he said.

"You?" She looked startled.

Did she finally remember his presence? Alan wondered savagely. "Hannah will accompany us on the road," he added.

Ariel's expression could only be described as peculiar. He would have given a large sum to know what was behind it. "Hannah could come with me," she said. "You needn't accompany us."

Now that she had what she wanted, he was superfluous, he thought.

"We could hire outriders," she added. "I wouldn't wish to trouble you."

She was watching him as if his answer was very important. Alan wondered if there was something he had missed. But with her wide hazel eyes steadily on him, he couldn't seem to think clearly. "I intend to see this investigation through to the end," he said.

Ariel frowned. "I am very grateful for your help," she said, seeming to speak carefully. "And especially for finding my father, but I don't require your assistance any longer. You may go back to Oxford, as you have always wished to do."

And be damned to you, Alan thought, his annoyance becoming something stronger. "I cannot abandon my responsibilities until we are certain of Daniel Bolton's identity," he replied. "Once that is confirmed, I will be happy to leave you in his care."

A spark ignited in her changeable eyes. "Like some sort of annoying parcel?"

"That is not what I—"

"I don't require anyone's care. I am quite capable of taking care of myself!"

"That's not what you said when you received your mother's ring," he snapped.

She gasped.

Alan cursed inwardly. He hadn't meant to refer to that afternoon, and only partly out of consideration for her. The memories that flooded back were searing. She had been eager in his arms, he thought. She had seemed to want him as much as he wanted her.

"Why do you want to come?" Ariel said.

"To make certain this Daniel Bolton is . . . acceptable," he answered.

"So that I will have someone to take care of me?" she added, gazing at him intensely once again.

Somewhat mystified by her tone, he nodded. It was as good an explanation as any.

"Your responsibilities will be discharged. And then you will be free to go back to your work at Oxford?" she finished.

He supposed he would be. And she would stay in Somerset, miles away from him. His pulse was pounding in his temples. He longed to crush her in his arms, to command her to obey him. But he had no right. She had refused him. "Yes," he said baldly.

Ariel turned away toward the window and looked out at the street. He couldn't see her face. Her slender form was very straight. "Shall I order a post chaise for tomorrow?" he asked, controlling his voice as if it were a matter of indifference to him.

"Very well," she said quietly.

She sounded resigned. But in the elation of knowing that he would be spending the next several days in her company, Alan found he didn't care.

Summer was bursting over the countryside, and they drove through fields heavy with green. The air was soft, scented with flowers, and birds and squirrels were busy in the branches. When they set off on the second morning, mist rose from the grass and the sky was awash with pink and pearl.

Hannah and Ariel rode together in the hired post chaise. Alan ranged ahead of and behind the carriage on his great black horse, looking at things and breathing in great gulps of the sweet air. Occasionally, he would come up beside them and speak to Hannah. "Listen, there's a thrush," he told her. Or, "See that hawthorn? Remember the hedge in Kent?" When the carriage plunged into a ford, and Ariel hung on as water splashed up the sides, he set his mount cantering through the stream and laughed at the glitter of spray fanning out from its hooves on the wind.

"He seems to like the country," Ariel commented to Hannah. Indeed, Alan seemed like a different person from the man who had been trapped at Carlton House for the last few weeks.

"He always has," was the calm reply. Hannah apparently had not noticed that her two traveling companions rarely spoke to each other directly, but rather addressed her instead. At any rate, she pretended not to notice.

They spent that night at an inn in Bath, and the following morning turned south. The weather remained warm, but rain began around eleven and settled in. The road, which was worse than the London-Bath route to begin with, became a mire. They pushed on through mud up to the axles that day and the next, when the rain finally ended. But they did not reach Wells, with its great cathedral, until very late.

Fortunately, the inn there was a good one. In half an hour, they were settled before a warm fire and dining on roast chicken and fresh-baked bread. Ariel had a glass of wine and watched Lord Alan covertly from under lowered lashes. Was he really only here because of his sense of responsibility? she wondered. Was it really vital to his sense of honor to place her in her father's care? The man she had first met in a cupboard at Carlton House would not have thought so, she thought. He had been wildly impatient to get back to his work, and not particularly interested in anyone else's concerns.

And then they had worked together, and she had thought they had become friends. But even that wasn't enough to explain the change. No, it was the time they had been together in her mother's room that had altered everything. Ariel's cheeks reddened slightly as she recalled each detail of that afternoon, and she looked down into her wineglass, hoping no one would notice.

He believed he had ruined her, she thought, and that he had to make amends. But since he had come to call and had told her the news about Daniel Bolton, she had been considering this question more deeply. He was the son of a duke, and she was the daughter of no one in the opinion of the world. An offer of marriage had *not* been required of him. The most honorable nobleman of the *haut ton*, under these circumstances, would have offered money, perhaps support for her household and a position as his mistress—but never marriage. That she would have thrown the money back in his face was irrelevant.

And then there was the fact that when she had refused his astonishing offer, he had stayed in town, even though he hated it, and searched for her father. The more she examined the situation, the odder it appeared. She almost began to hope that responsibility was the least of it. She almost dared to believe that some stronger emotion was involved.

The landlady came to remove the dishes. A small yapping dog hurtled after her into the room, its fur like a bundle of rags, its bark like a series of hiccups. "Quiet, Lovie," commanded the woman. "Get out, then." Quickly putting plates and cutlery on a tray, she shooed the little dog with her foot. "Sorry, sir, madam. Lovie, get out!"

Lovie had other ideas. He trotted over to Alan and made as if to attach himself to his lower leg.

Alan made a sound like a growling wolf.

Looking startled, the little dog sat back on his haunches and stared upward. The landlady regarded Alan with an almost identical expression of amazement.

Lovie made a tentative move forward. Alan growled again and froze him in his tracks.

The landlady picked up the loaded tray, looking as if she wasn't sure whether to be offended. "Come, Lovie," she said as she walked out. The dog hesitated, then started backing away from Alan. Finally, he turned and trotted out as if this had been his idea from the beginning.

"What was that?" Ariel couldn't refrain from saying.

"Dogs are pack animals," Alan told her, "with a very strong sense of hierarchy. 'Lovie' responded to a signal of superiority."

"I'd hate to see a pack of creatures like that," commented Hannah, who had taken out her perpetual knitting.

"A dreadful prospect," Lord Alan agreed.

"My mother purchased a lapdog once," Ariel remembered.

"You surprise me."

She acknowledged the unlikeliness of it with a look. "She thought she might like having it about, but of course she didn't. It was a disgusting little creature. Bess was bored in a week, and Puff was left to the servants to care for."

"Puff?" echoed Alan with distaste.

"Well, that was how our cook felt, too. She and that dog hated each other on sight. Cook used to insist that Puff gorged himself on purpose, just so he could be sick on her bed."

"Ugh," said Hannah. "Why didn't she give the beast away?"

"Bess tried. But he bit, you see. Which tended to put people off."

"Understandable," said Lord Alan. "I suppose she didn't wish to have him put down?"

"She couldn't quite bring herself to that." A reminiscent smile curved Ariel's lips. "Finally, Cook could bear it no longer," she continued. "She went out into the streets and found a tomcat." She glanced at her audience; Lord Alan and Hannah looked back at her with a gratifying air of expectation.

"The largest, meanest tomcat in the neighborhood," Ariel explained. "A huge brindled creature with torn ears from all his fights. She lured him home with bits of beef. Then, she shut him in the dining room with Puff for an entire morning."

"Did they kill each other?" Lord Alan inquired.

"Oh, no. Puff was a complete coward. He wouldn't fight. He cowered in a corner while the tomcat strutted about before him and yowled, until Cook came back and freed the cat. After that, she kept a cloth with the cat's scent on it, and whenever Puff thought to misbehave, she pushed his nose in it."

Alan burst out laughing.

"He never bit anyone again," Ariel finished.

Their eyes met and held. Behind its screen, the fire hissed and muttered as it died to coals and ash. Hannah's knitting needles made steady muted clicks. Outdoors, the grass, dew-silvered, rustled with creatures on nighttime errands. The road was empty, the sky spangled with a million stars. After what seemed like an eternity, the gaze broke. Alan turned away.

Ariel looked down at her hands. She was trembling. She had forgotten to breathe. She drew in a deep breath, struggling to quiet the hammer of her pulse and the disorienting flutter in her throat. She felt as if she had run until she could run no longer, as if she had come within an inch of falling over a cliff.

It had definitely not been mere responsibility she saw in the depths of Alan's eyes, she thought. It had not been the resigned steadiness of a man fulfilling some obligation. She had glimpsed something far more complex than that. She wasn't sure precisely what he felt toward her, but she was certain that it wasn't cool and orderly. The man of science had given way to . . . someone else.

Hope caught at her, tremulous and exulting, almost too much to bear. She knew that if she stayed in this room, she wouldn't be able to hide it much longer. Rising, she quickly excused herself to go to bed.

Hannah folded up her knitting and made ready to follow. As she was leaving the inn parlor, she threw Lord Alan a sharp glance. But he was leaning on the mantel staring into the fire and did not notice.

Ariel had trouble sleeping that night, and she woke when the sky was barely washed with light. She had dreamed of Alan, but the dreams had been shifting and confused, a flurry of scenes where nothing could be pinned down or clearly understood. All she could recall once awake was a series of images of his face running the gamut of emotions from anger to tenderness and seeming very close, as if they were trying urgently to communicate with her.

She sat up in bed. A bird trilled outside the small mullioned window of the inn. Raising her head, Ariel saw the little creature silhouetted against a brightening sky. It was nearly dawn, dawn of the day when they would reach Ivydene Manor, and she would meet her father. Ariel wrapped her arms around her raised knees and shivered with mingled excitement and apprehension. What if he didn't want to see her? He had made no attempt to do so in twenty years. Perhaps he would turn her away at his gate. What if she didn't like him? There must have been some reason Bess had left him. Was he unpleasant, even monstrous?

She was very glad she had not made this journey alone, Ariel thought. Too restless to sleep anymore, she rose and dressed, being very quiet so as not to wake Hannah, then slipped downstairs. The inn was just stirring. She heard a mutter of voices from the kitchen at the back, but there was no one in the entry hall or the taproom. She slipped the bolt on the front door and stepped out into the rose light of sunrise. The air was damp and cool and filled with birdsong. Dew glistened on the spears of lavender planted along the front of the inn, and its fresh scent surrounded her.

She walked down the path to the street and turned to look at the great cathedral of Wells, rearing like a mountain against the sky. Pink light washed over the amazing west front, with its tier after tier of carved statues rising into the heavens. Ariel stood transfixed as the light grew, overwhelmed by the power of the place.

"It's very beautiful, isn't it?" said a male voice behind her.

Ariel started violently and whirled around, her heart pounding. "You startled me!"

"I beg your pardon," Lord Alan answered.

He looked as if he had been up for a while, Ariel thought. His auburn hair was neat; his coat and breeches gave no sign that he had spent days traveling. His mere presence created an atmosphere of confidence and optimism, she thought. It was impossible to imagine anything he couldn't do, if he set his mind to it. "It is beautiful," she replied belatedly.

"They spent decades building it, then carving and painting and setting glass."

"And all to make a prayer."

He looked quizzical. "What?"

"That's what a cathedral is, isn't it? A gigantic prayer?"

"I . . . suppose." He gazed up at the intricacies of the monument. "That is one thing it is, anyway."

"It's amazing," said Ariel.

"What?" he repeated.

She gestured toward the great building. "It's so huge, and so lovely. They spent all those years and all that effort to show how very much they wanted something."

"Wanted?" he echoed in an odd tone.

"No one does that sort of thing now."

"Yes, they do," he said.

"Build great cathedrals?"

Lord Alan shook his head. "That time is past, it's true. But there are still people who spend years and years searching for truth and constructing works to commemorate and . . . and honor it."

"Who?" asked Ariel.

"Scientists," he answered.

She smiled, wondering if he was joking. "It's not the same at all," she said.

"Why not?"

"Well, scientists don't make beautiful things like this." She indicated the cathedral again.

"I find a new piece of knowledge beautiful."

She looked up at him, impressed by the conviction in his voice.

"And of course it can be far more useful to the human race than a building," he added.

"Useful, practical, sensible," Ariel said. "I know science is all those things. You have explained to me that it is vital to be rational and orderly and logical."

"It is vital," he said forcefully.

"But artists made this cathedral," she continued. "They had the intensity, the passion to make their wanting real. Scientists don't have that."

He took a step toward her. His blue eyes were burning, Ariel saw. His mouth was a tight line. At first she thought she had made him angry. But he didn't argue or rail at her. His hands were trembling slightly, she noticed, as if he labored under some great emotion. Abruptly her chest tightened and her breath grew short. He was looking at her as he had last night.

"You're wrong," he said.

She swallowed.

"A man who spends endless hours alone in a laboratory, repeating an experiment again and again, has as much passion as a stone carver," he declared. "The desire for knowledge burns in the veins just as intensely as the desire to create. It *is* a desire to create."

Ariel stared at him. He looked as surprised as she was by his own words.

"If you think that because a man is a scientist, he does not want . . ."

His fists had clenched. Ariel held her breath.

"You're wrong," he said again.

His gaze transfixed her. He was breathing hard. Ariel had to struggle to produce a response, even though she wanted more than anything to speak. "Does he want only science?" she murmured at last.

"Only . . . ?"

Did he also want love, with the same sort of ferocity? Ariel longed to add. But she couldn't quite say it. She didn't want him to tell her again that love didn't exist. Or that she had misinterpreted the emotion she thought she saw in his expression. She couldn't bear the idea that she might be wrong.

"My lord," someone called from the direction of the inn.

It was a member of their escort, Ariel saw.

"The horses will be harnessed in half an hour," the man said.

The spell broke. Lord Alan stood straighter, drew in a deep breath. The pink dawn light was gone, Ariel saw, and more prosaic daylight picked out every detail of the scene.

"We'd best find some breakfast," Lord Alan said. He indicated that Ariel should walk ahead of him, and she had no choice but to do so. "Did you ask directions?" he said when they reached the outrider.

"Yes, my lord. The innkeeper knew the place."

They began to discuss travel plans. Lord Alan seemed his practical self again, Ariel thought as she made her way toward the inn. There was no sign of the very different man she had seen a few minutes ago. But she knew now that he was there. She knew that hope wasn't entirely foolish. Hugging that knowledge to her and suppressing the shiver of excitement it brought, she vowed to search for other opportunities to lure him into the open.

Chapter Seventeen

The innkeeper gave their driver exact directions to Ivydene. By midmorning they were well away from the town, traveling along a narrow, twisting lane. Unable to sit still, Ariel leaned out the coach window, breathing the summer air and watching for the last turn. The high silhouette of Glastonbury Tor rose in the distance like a monitor from ancient times. The leaves rustled in a stiff breeze. And then, they were there. An ancient moss-covered boulder stood beside the turnoff, "Ivydene" deeply carved into its surface. Ariel experienced another tremor of doubt. If she said she wished to turn back, to go all the way home to London, no one would object. Now that the moment was here, she wondered whether she actually wanted to meet her father.

She took a breath. She wanted to know, she thought. If she didn't like what she found, then she would leave.

The coach moved forward. The drive, which was somewhat overgrown, wound through thickets and groves of small trees. Though she leaned out again, Ariel could see nothing but the next curve and more trees.

Then, they emerged at the top of a small hill, and the prospect opened up. Below was a little valley. Beside a rocky stream, nestled into a fold of the land, sat a stone house that looked as if it had been there forever. It wasn't large, but the mellow stone, almost completely overgrown with ivy, and the arched, diamond-paned windows made it beautiful. Sheep dotted the park, keeping the grass cropped between clumps of oak. An apple orchard covered the opposite side of the valley. There was no one in sight, but a wisp of smoke floated from one chimney.

The driver flicked the reins, and they started down. Ariel took a deep breath and sat very straight, hanging on to the strap and rehearsing the words she had planned to say to whoever opened the door.

In the end, it was simple. The old woman servant made no protest when they asked to see Daniel Bolton, but merely took them through a great hall to a door at the back. Knocking, she opened it without waiting for a reply and said, "Someone here to see you," before tramping off. Trembling, Ariel stepped into an odd room, which seemed at first to be empty.

Shelves along the whole length of two inner walls held bits of stone and broken pottery, along with piles of manuscript and bundles and jars of dried plants. There were instruments she could not identify and, incongruously, a pickax and shovel leaning in the corner. The trestle table before the two wide windows was strewn with drawings that seemed to be architectural; ink from the quill pen had smeared one. There was a small movement, and Ariel realized that a cat sat on the window ledge—the largest cat she had ever seen. Its gray fur blended into the stone lintel, but its eyes, whose blinking had finally attracted her attention, were bright gold.

It looked astonishingly like Prospero, she thought, and for one wild moment wondered whether he had somehow preceded her here. The cat stared at her as if it knew her thoughts, then rose and wove its way along the ledge to a great carved chair that faced away from the door. It leaped onto the arm, and a man's voice said, "Eh? What? What is it, Ptolemy?"

An arm appeared, and then a head, peering around the tall chairback. Ariel had a moment of sheer panic as the man hidden in the chair rose and stood facing her.

It was like looking in a magic mirror that showed her as a fifty-year-old man, she thought. Like her, Daniel Bolton had glossy brown hair and sparkling hazel eyes. His skin was ruddy, his face rather round. Also like her, he was not overly tall, though he was stocky and strongly built instead of slender. His nose was straight and his lips full. No one could have doubted that they were members of the same family.

"It's Ariel, isn't it?" he said.

Surprised by this immediate recognition, Ariel couldn't speak.

"Little Ariel. I always hoped you'd visit me one day."

This wasn't right, she thought. He wasn't supposed to know her, to speak as if she had neglected him. Nor was the man himself what she had expected. In her childhood fantasies, he had been a duke, a hero, a diplomat—wondrously handsome, rich, and well bred. When she had learned his identity, she had feared to find a crude country squire, drinking and hunting and falling asleep before the fire with a belch. "You know who I am?" was all she could manage to say.

"How could I help it? You've been the image of me since you were born." He was examining her, too, and he looked as if he was pleased with what he found.

"Since I was . . . you knew?" Ariel felt as if she might fly to pieces from conflicting feelings. "Why didn't you ever visit me?" she cried.

Bolton's jaw hardened. "Bess didn't want me to interfere," he replied crisply.

"Interfere?" echoed Ariel, disoriented. All this time,

he had been a few days' journey away, and neither of her parents had seen fit to let her know that.

"When she left, she said she didn't wish to hear from me again. I take it she has changed her mind?" Though he spoke coolly, Ariel heard the eager undertone.

"Bess Harding is dead," said Lord Alan flatly.

Their host swung around to stare at him as if he hadn't even noticed him until now. "Dead? Bess?"

"She killed herself," Lord Alan added, looking as if he rather enjoyed the harshness of the words.

Bolton turned white. He put a hand on the trestle table and supported himself. "When?"

"Two months ago."

The older man rubbed his free hand across his face. "This is dreadful news. Dreadful," he muttered.

Ariel felt a pang for the way he had been told.

"I have thought of her as alive," he added dazedly. "I didn't feel it. I didn't know." He groped his way back to his chair. His eye lit upon an abandoned tankard of ale sitting among his papers, and he picked it up and drained it. "I always thought that, one day, she would regret leaving," he said. "I knew it was foolish, but I kept believing that she would come back." He shook his head. "Not really believing, I suppose. More of a daydream." He shook his head again, as if he couldn't quite assimilate this new knowledge. "Little Bess," he murmured.

"When did you see her last?" asked Lord Alan. He sounded almost suspicious.

"See her?" Daniel Bolton looked sad. "It's been nearly twenty years since I saw Bess." He sighed. "Twenty years. How can it be possible?" Making a visible effort, he pulled himself together. "So. Bess is gone, and . . . and you have come to me," he said. He focused on Ariel once again.

She didn't know how to react. Was he going to try to pretend this was a simple family visit?

"We tracked you down," Lord Alan corrected.

"Tracked?" He looked from one to the other.

"I never knew who my father was, or where you were," Ariel accused. "After Bess . . . was gone, I found a scrap of paper with a record of her marriage. I never even knew she was married!"

He looked stricken. "She never told you? Nothing about me at all?"

"She made up stories," replied Ariel bitterly. In her secret heart, she had thought that her mother needed the stories as a defense, that perhaps the truth wasn't something to acknowledge. She had tried to spare Bess's feelings, she thought angrily. No one seemed to have considered hers.

"Stories," Bolton repeated, bewildered. "Bess liked stories."

"And she had no reason for them at all?" asked Lord Alan harshly.

The other man's eyes sharpened. "What do you mean by that?"

"She must have had some reason for concealing your existence."

"Reason?" Bolton gave a mirthless laugh. "Bess always had her reasons, but I could never fathom any of them."

"But not to tell her daughter . . . ?"

"What are you trying to say?" demanded their host. "Do you imagine I beat her or degraded her in some way? I didn't!"

The two men stared at one another in tense silence. A bird called outside.

"Don't," said Ariel.

As if to second her request, the huge cat jumped down to the floor and began twining around Bolton's ankles. The latter took a deep breath and relaxed slightly.

To ease things further, Ariel formally introduced Lord Alan and Hannah. The older man nodded to them. "You have thought all your life that I abandoned you," he said heavily then.

Ariel nodded.

Bolton rubbed his face again. "What a tangle."

"Perhaps you'd like a bit more ale, sir," suggested Hannah.

He looked startled, then rueful. "You must excuse me. I have not been a very gracious host. Let us all have some refreshment. I'll go and ask Gladys to bring you some of our cider. It's very fine."

"I'll go," said Hannah. And before he could respond, she had slipped out the door. In a few minutes, she returned with the old servant woman, who carried a tray filled with small tankards of cider. Bolton grasped one and lifted it. "A toast to our reunion," he said, and drank. After a brief hesitation, the others joined him.

"I hope you will stay awhile," he added. "I should like a chance to . . . explain."

After a moment Ariel nodded. She very much wanted to hear an explanation.

"Gladys will find you rooms. Ask her for anything you need." He hesitated, then added, "I'm very pleased you have come, Ariel."

Dinner that evening was plagued with silences. When the dishes had been cleared away, Bolton suggested they sit for a while in his study. "It is the most comfortable room in the house," he told Ariel. "Some say it is the only comfortable room."

When they were settled before the hearth there, he spoke again. "Perhaps you would listen to my story?" His face and tone were deeply earnest. "I would count it a great favor if you would."

Alan watched Ariel nod, clearly increasingly drawn to this man. He knew she was intensely curious about the past and the secrets her mother had kept, but it seemed to him that she was going beyond mere curiosity. He wanted to warn her not to trust too far, but he had had no opportunity. And perhaps he hadn't the right, either, he thought bitterly.

Bolton folded his hands before him and gazed at the chimneypiece as if staring into the past. "I want you to understand," he began. "I have made mistakes, I know. But if I explain, perhaps you . . ." He made a dismissive gesture. "Never mind. Let me simply tell it." He appeared to gather his thoughts. "I have always been of a scholarly bent," he said then, "and in my youth I went to study at Oxford."

Alan started slightly. This explained the specimens on the shelves and the masses of papers. Logically, this would seem to form a link between them. But he found he didn't like the idea of Bolton as a scholar at all.

"I was extremely happy there," the other continued. "Learning has been a passion since I was a child. Indeed, my fellow students at Oxford used to mock my diligence and devotion to my work." Bolton looked at Ariel briefly as if he was a bit reluctant to continue. "It was because of their jokes that I agreed to attend a drinking party one evening, when I was visiting in London. I thought to show them that I was not too wrapped up in my studies to be convivial." He paused. "So, on that night I was part of a noisy crowd at an inn in the city. I was returning from the . . . er . . . the privy when a young girl stopped me in the yard behind the alehouse."

He paused again, his eyes eons distant, his face sad. "She was the loveliest thing I'd ever seen. Hair the color of sunset, face like an elfin princess. I thought at first she was something the drink had conjured in my brain. Then she said, 'You're one of them students?' and I noticed her poor clothes and her accent and knew she was real. When I admitted I was a student, she came closer and said that she wanted to learn to read and asked if I would teach her."

Ariel blinked. She let out the breath she had been holding. She was enthralled, Alan thought. Moment by moment, this stranger was drawing her under his spell, and away from her former friends and life. He noticed that his fists were clenched.

Bolton turned his head away. Alan thought his cheeks reddened slightly. "I wasn't used to drinking so much, and I was still smarting from my fellow students' mockery, so I played the arrogant young sprig and asked her what she'd give me for the teaching. She said, 'Anything' and took my arm in a way I thought was practiced. I abandoned my friends and hurried her back to my lodgings and . . . into my bed. By the time I realized that she was, er . . . untouched . . . and frightened, and younger than I'd taken her for, it was too late."

He stopped then, definitely flushed with embarrassment. After a few moments, he swallowed, and sighed. "What fools we are when we're young."

A nicely abstract excuse, Alan thought sardonically.

"I was appalled at what I'd done," he went on. "But Bess merely got angry and said I'd promised to teach her and when could we begin?" He shook his head. "She was such an odd combination of cynicism and innocence. How many men would have kept such a bargain?"

Ariel looked touched, Alan thought. And by what? A tale of common seduction. He gazed at Bolton with dislike.

"Or maybe any man would have done anything to keep her," their host continued. "In any case, I took her back to Oxford with me. I got new lodgings outside the town. And I taught her. How I taught her." He clamped his lips tight for a moment. "She learned as a starving person eats," he went on. "I had to make her sleep, some nights, or she would have worn herself out. She wanted to know how to speak properly. And stories—always she wanted more stories."

He paused, his flush deepening. "Then, she found she was with child."

"Me," said Ariel.

He nodded. "By this time, I loved her as I'd never loved before."

Alan felt his lip curl. That word—"love"—used by so many to excuse so much dishonorable behavior.

"We were married that very week," Bolton said, "and I brought Bess back to Somerset as my wife. A few months later, you were born."

"Here?"

"Indeed."

"But . . . I don't understand." Ariel gazed around the room. "What happened? Why did she leave?"

Raising his eyebrows slightly, Alan waited for the answer to this important question.

Bolton frowned. "Bess didn't care for Ivydene—not the place itself, but being so isolated. She missed the bustle of a town, all the people around her there. I claimed that a husband and child should be enough for her. And when she raged at that, I retreated further into my work, which only made her angrier. It was a wretched time." He sighed.

Ariel's eyes were fixed on his face as if he were the answer to all her prayers. Alan's mouth fell into a grim line.

Bolton shook his head. "She came to me one day and said that she was leaving for London and that she didn't want me to come. I argued, but I was a stiff-necked young fool, and after a while I told her to go and be damned to her. I didn't think she really would. But she took you and went."

There was a silence.

"I wonder she didn't leave me here," said Ariel. "It must have been much harder for her, having a baby to care for."

Her father shook his head. "Bess would never have left

you. You haven't understood her if you think so. You were *hers*. From the moment you were born, she held on to you like a tigress. No one could interfere. Once, when we were arguing about going to London, I threatened to keep you." He laughed without humor. "I thought she would kill me."

Again, they sat in silence for a time. Ariel looked like she was fighting tears, Alan thought.

Bolton rose and stood at the window, half turned away from them. "Soon after she left, I became very ill. It was weeks before I threw off the fever. And then I had word that Bess had made a great success in the theater. It . . . it made me angry." He looked a bit ashamed. "I'd hoped she would find she couldn't get along in London and come back to me, you see. But it seemed she was happy?"

"She loved the playhouse," Ariel replied, "the cheers, the drama, the comradeship."

Bess Harding had apparently loved the gowns and jewels and male attention, too, Alan thought, but no one mentioned that.

"And the chance to have a hundred lives, in the characters she played," added her father, surprising Ariel with his insight. "Bess wanted everything. Every taste, every experience she could cram into a day."

The silence that followed was laden with the unspoken. Alan wished they had never come.

The next day, Ariel's father showed her the house and grounds, explaining something of his life as he did so. "I'm interested in the properties of herbs," he said as he took her around a large garden full of plants she didn't recognize. "There's an old woman in Glastonbury who is extremely knowledgeable and has shared her wisdom with me. Do you know that there are herbs to cool fever and banish backache, to soothe the stomach and bring sleep? It is one of Nature's great bounties."

"My mother always used to laugh about my love for books," said Ariel. "I never understood why until now. I must have gotten it from you." It was odd, suddenly having a heritage that went beyond her mother, she thought.

The look he gave her was unsettling.

Ariel still didn't know how she felt about all this. She was strongly drawn to this man who was her father. He seemed intelligent and kind and eager to form a bond with her now that they had met. But all the years when he had made no attempt to see her or contact her stood between them. The fact that Bess hadn't wanted him to come wasn't enough of an explanation. How could he be so glad to see her now, and yet never have tried to do so in twenty years?

The contradictions made her uneasy, and she did not feel the least at home in Ivydene so far. And to add to her discomfort, Lord Alan seemed to have withdrawn from her again, after those hopeful moments on the road. He had hardly spoken to her since they arrived, and his expression remained coldly noncommittal. Perhaps he *was* just waiting for an opportunity to go and leave her in the care of Daniel Bolton, Ariel thought nervously. Her father's name didn't even sound familiar yet.

Well, she wasn't going to be left, or kept, or anything but what she decided to do, she told herself fiercely. But it was growing harder and harder to maintain a pleasant, interested facade with all this happening around her.

"I explore the past," her father said later as they sat in his workroom watching the sun sink behind the orchard. "Glastonbury is an ancient place. There was an abbey here seven hundred years ago, and our family has lived here as long."

"Family." Ariel had never heard the word used in reference to herself.

He smiled. "Your ancestors came over with the Normans. And one of those adventurers married the Saxon mistress of Ivydene, so the bloodline goes back even farther. Some member of the family has always occupied the place."

"Seven hundred years," Ariel marveled. She couldn't comprehend it. In the blink of an eye, she had changed from being a woman with no heritage to one with a vast line of ancestors behind her. It made her giddy, as if she had spun too fast in a circle and upset her sense of balance.

In the stableyard outside, Alan was speaking to one of the men who had come with them, and who had been surveying the house and grounds. "A prosperous country estate," he was told. "I didn't see anything out of the ordinary. Could be a bit better kept up. There are very few servants. Stableman says the man's some kind of scholar. Hasn't traveled for years."

"Umm," said Alan.

"None of the horses here would get him anywhere," the man added. "Two spavined nags and a lame hunter."

To himself, Alan acknowledged that this was probably a waste of time. Daniel Bolton was no doubt just what he appeared to be—a slightly eccentric country landholder immersed in his studies. By rights, he should have admired such a man, Alan thought. So few of his class cared anything for books or ideas. He should welcome him as a comrade in the pursuit of knowledge. But for some reason, he felt only resentment and restlessness.

He would have rather enjoyed discovering something disreputable about Bolton, Alan realized. Ariel seemed to be accepting anything he said at face value and hanging on his every word. She might have shown a bit more wariness, he thought resentfully. The man was a total stranger, no matter how much he resembled her.

Alan's mouth set in a hard line. It didn't matter, he concluded. He intended to be careful and wary enough for all of them.

On her second afternoon in Somerset, Ariel and her father walked in the soft sunshine up the small rise at the end of the garden, past the flowers near the house and the ranks of fragrant herbs. A path led into the trees and they followed it upward.

It was a rare, golden summer day, brilliantly warm. The hum of bees and birdsong surrounded them, and the air was heavy with the scent of growing things. "It's so beautiful here," said Ariel.

"I'm glad you think so," he replied.

The path kept on rising up the wooded hillside, and they walked in the shadows of leaves. It finally ended at a clearing—a semicircle of trees that overlooked the entire valley. Within it were scattered piles of stones, the remains of a building.

"What was it?" Ariel asked.

"It used to be a small chapel. It's left from the times before King Henry VIII abolished the great abbey at Glastonbury and all its satellites," her father told her. "The countryside hereabouts is dotted with such remains."

Ariel went to examine the half walls of stone and the remnants of the slate floor. "Oh, look," she said, pointing to a great hawk circling above the hill. Its wings were spread wide to catch the mild breeze. Its beak and feathers gleamed in the sunlight. Despite the distance, she thought she could see its fierce yellow eye intent on its prey.

"Hunting," said her father. "She'll be after mice or small birds for her hatchlings. Feeding a nest full of half-grown hawks is quite a labor."

Like taking care of a child, Ariel thought. "Why did

you never write me, or try to see me?" she couldn't help
but ask. "No matter what Bess said, weren't you . . .
even . . . curious?"

He turned to look down at her, his face partly shaded
by the trees. "I was more than curious," he answered.
"But you see, I didn't realize that Bess had told you
nothing about me. It simply didn't occur to me that she
would cut us off so completely, or that she would allow
the world to believe she had a . . . a fatherless child. I
suppose I didn't understand her very well."

Ariel wondered if anyone had.

"I thought you knew who I was and where I lived," he
added. "Indeed, I wondered, as time passed, why you did
not write to me."

"I was a child," she protested.

He nodded. "I know. You're right. It was my place,
and my responsibility to contact you. It should have been
my great pleasure to do so." He shook his head, and the
patches of light and darkness shifted across his face. "I
held on to my resentments long past the time when I
should have let them go," he continued sadly. "I let my
disappointments and anger at Bess live far beyond their
time. And as a result, I lost you. I deserved that punish-
ment, but you most certainly did not. I can only hope
that you will let me make it up to you now, and in the
future."

Ariel didn't know what to say. She wanted to agree,
but it wasn't simple or easy to forget years of absence. "I
hope we can," she said, not knowing herself exactly what
she referred to.

Her father smiled. "Hope is as much as we can manage
just now," he replied. "But it is a very . . . hopeful
thing, isn't it?"

Ariel returned his smile, relieved that he asked no
more from her so soon.

"With that settled, may I ask you a father's question,
even though I have no real right?" he went on.

"What?" she wondered.

Daniel Bolton eyed this daughter who looked so like him, and yet was a complete mystery. Fortunately, he enjoyed mysteries. "I do not understand why you are traveling the countryside with a nobleman who is not related to you," he said, and noticed that her smile faded at the words. "Perhaps he was a friend of Bess's?" The idea was unpleasant. He had never faced the near certainty that Bess had enjoyed male company during her life in London. The relief he felt when Ariel shook her head surprised him.

"He didn't know her," she said. "We met because of her ghost."

"Her . . . ?"

She told him the story of the haunting of Carlton House, and how she and Lord Alan had met in pursuit of the supposed phantom of her mother. "I helped him with the actors at the theater," she finished, "and so he has helped me search for . . . my history."

"Very charitable of him," murmured Bolton. "Ariel, I know I have not been any kind of father to you, but—"

"Oh, you needn't worry," she interrupted. "I am a sort of responsibility, you see, and his sense of duty is very strong. He hopes, you should know, to leave me here in your 'care.' "

Bolton was taken aback by the emotion in her tone. He examined his newfound daughter closely, making good use of his talent for observation, honed to brilliant keenness by years of study. "You would be most welcome to stay here," he ventured. "I would be delighted to give you a home after my years of neglect."

He watched as she blinked furiously, and then bit her lower lip. She seemed touched by his offer, and yet far from satisfied with it.

"You should get acquainted with the neighborhood," he tried, "since Ivydene will be yours one day."

This shocked her out of whatever feeling had been plaguing her. "Mine?"

"Of course. You are my only child."

Ariel looked out over the broad valley that stretched below the chapel ruins, at the rows of apple trees on the other side. Daniel Bolton knew it was a gorgeous sight. But it did not seem to ease the tension he had noted in Ariel. "You need not be dependent on Lord Alan, or anyone," he added, probing for what was distressing her.

"I can take care of myself!"

Her father felt an overwhelming impulse to make things right for her. It was a new feeling for him, and he wasn't sure at first whether he liked it. He was not an interfering man—quite the opposite. He was barely acquainted with his neighbors. He did not inquire into the lives of his servants or tenants. He gave everyone leave to live as they chose, and took the same privilege for himself.

But this was different somehow. Not only was Ariel his child, but he owed her an extra measure of concern because of the years when he had selfishly left her to fend for herself. He couldn't presume to dictate. But surely the gifts he had might be of some use.

First, however, he had to discover what was wrong. "It is gratifying to meet a young man who takes responsibility so seriously," he ventured, feeling much as he did when he was extracting a delicate tincture from a combination of the herbs in his garden. One false move and . . .

"I am *not* his responsibility!" responded Ariel.

"Ah. But you are . . . friends, perhaps? When people work together toward a goal, they often become friends."

"Yes," she agreed baldly.

"It's not as if you knew his family, of course," her father probed, exploring the limits of the relationship Lord Alan Gresham had offered her.

"Oh, I am well acquainted with his brothers," she told

him. "And Hannah is their former nanny, so she is a kind of family, I suppose."

"His brothers?" he echoed.

"Yes. I have been advising them."

Bolton blinked. This mystery was more intriguing than he had imagined. "Advising them about what?" he asked.

"Well, I showed Lord Sebastian how to catch the attention of an heiress he wishes to marry. And I explained to Lord Highgrove how to manage his fiancée's family." She smiled slightly. "I'm not sure what I have done for Lord Robert, but he is certainly having some interesting experiences."

"You must be very resourceful," commented her father, bemused.

"It isn't I," she assured him. "It all comes from plays. I learned a great many plays, you know, growing up with Bess."

"And so you tell them the story of a play, and they . . ."

"Do the same," she finished. "It has worked quite well."

"Amazing. And so life follows art. Are you advising Lord Alan as well?"

Ariel's expression shifted at once. "No," she said.

"He does not require any help in his romantic adventures?" he probed, testing the hypothesis that was forming in his mind.

"I have no idea," she answered rather curtly.

"Ah," he said again. "Well, as I told you, you are very welcome to remain here. If you like, I will tell Lord Alan he is free of his responsibility and may go."

His daughter looked at him rather wildly.

"And I would be happy to escort you back to London myself, should you decide to go," he added.

"We . . . we just arrived," stammered Ariel.

"Of course." He felt a little guilty enjoyment in the

rapid play of expression over her face. He did like teasing out information, he thought, and confirming his theories.

"I . . . don't . . . I shouldn't wish Lord Alan to think that I did not appreciate the help he has given me," she stammered.

She cared about this young man a great deal, Bolton thought. It was obvious in her eyes and expression, in her distress at the idea of his leaving. What were Gresham's sentiments in this matter? he wondered. He found that a father's protective instincts came very naturally despite his long separation from his daughter. "Well, well," he said. "You must decide. I stand ready to help you in any way I can."

She frowned, and bit her lower lip.

"Shall we go back?" he suggested, and saw that she was grateful to agree.

They had reached the low stone wall around the herb garden behind the house when they heard the music. It floated on the soft air like a fairy melody, fading in and out with the vagrant breeze.

"Someone is playing the pianoforte," said Bolton, surprised. "My mother used to play. She loved the instrument so that I have kept it in tune for her sake. But who . . . ?" Glancing at Ariel, he saw that she was frozen in place, her full lips slightly parted, her eyes wide. "Shall we go and see?" he asked.

"No! I mean . . ."

He watched her struggle for words. Another piece of the puzzle emerging, he thought, but an obscure one.

"We . . . we shouldn't disturb . . . them," she said. "I believe . . . I believe it is very annoying to be interrupted when you are playing."

She didn't want him going to see who was playing his pianoforte, he thought. And she was fairly certain who it was. That meant it had to be the glowering young lord she had brought with her. Fascinating. "We wouldn't have to disturb them," he couldn't resist replying. "We might just look in."

"No. I . . . I don't think we should."

She looked a bit frantic, and Bolton took pity on her, shrugging agreement. "I have some papers to look over," he suggested experimentally.

The relief in her face was so obvious he almost laughed a little. He must stop teasing her, he thought. "I'll be quite all right on my own," she said. "I don't wish to take you from your work."

He let her go. But he would have been happy to give stiff odds that she was heading straight for the front parlor and the pianoforte.

He would have won those bets. Two minutes later, Ariel was standing outside that room, all her attention focused on the music that was pouring out of it.

It was beautiful. And it seemed to her full of passionate emotion, driven by will and need and desire. She could have listened for hours. But even more, she wanted to see the player. What did he look like when he produced this melody? What was in his face; how did he move? Yet if she opened the door, he would stop. She was certain of that. He must think they were still out walking. Soon, he would decide his time was up.

Silently, she slipped away from the door and out of the house into the garden once more. Following the wall around the corner, she counted two windows for the dining room. The next should be it. Ariel eased her way up to the next tall window and peered around the side. Yes; she could see the pianoforte across the room and Lord Alan leaning over the keys. Unfortunately, what she could see was his back.

She moved quietly around the corner of the house to the front wall, where another window gave the opposite view. This one was very close to him, though. Ariel crouched beneath the sill, and then cautiously raised her head to look over it.

She was barely three feet from Lord Alan, gazing upward into his face as his fingers moved over the keys. The golden afternoon light slanted across him, illuminating his entire figure. She could see every nuance of expression, every shift in those handsome features. He looked at once abstracted and intent—almost exalted. You might have called his face immobile, Ariel thought, if you didn't notice the eyes. They burned with a controlled fire, a wild serenity, that was like nothing she had ever seen before. This was the sort of passion he had been talking about in front of Wells Cathedral, she thought. It burned in him, the force that guided his life. He was no cold, rational machine. His logic and systems served something far grander.

But was it reserved for science and music? she wondered, her hands gripping the windowsill. Were people excluded from that warmth? He had rejected the whole concept of love. Watching him, listening, she wished with all her heart that he was wrong about himself.

Abruptly Lord Alan's head jerked, as if he had heard some sound from the rest of the house. At once, his hands lifted from the keys and the music stopped. Ariel dared to watch a moment longer as he gathered himself, his customary cool expression returning to his face. But when he started to rise, she ducked out of sight, not wanting to be caught. She sat there under the window, behind the shrubbery, for some time before making her way up to her room.

Chapter Eighteen

———— ❖ ————

Daniel Bolton sought out Lord Alan in the early evening, when Ariel had gone upstairs to change for dinner. "I wanted to thank you for making such efforts on my daughter's behalf," he said.

Lord Alan bristled as if he had insulted him.

"You are very tenacious in this matter."

"What I do is no concern of yours," he snapped.

Their eyes locked. For a long moment, the air sang with tension. This was a formidable man, Bolton thought. But he had a strong will himself. "True," he said. "But it is surprising, really, that you would spend so much time on Ariel's affairs. I suppose you have little else to do."

The younger man's eyes flared. "I hold a fellowship at Oxford," he snapped. "I am engaged in important scientific researches there."

"Are you?" Impressed and interested despite himself, Bolton added, "What sort?"

"I am studying the nature of light," came the curt reply.

"Really? After Goethe? Or perhaps Young?"

"You know Thomas Young's work?" said Lord Alan, looking surprised.

"I was extremely interested in his theory of color vision."

The younger man looked impressed. "I am continuing his experiments with refraction and dispersion," he said, "but I intend to demonstrate definitively that light is by nature a wave, rather than a corpuscle."

"Fascinating. You are working with the principle of interference?"

Lord Alan nodded. "I have just set up an experiment to test it under rigidly defined conditions. Or I had, before all this began." He looked rueful.

This made Bolton recall his original purpose. "I am surprised you can bear to be away from your work for so long," he said.

"It is difficult," the younger man answered.

"Why are you doing it then?" he asked bluntly.

"That is . . . somewhat complicated."

Bolton waited.

"I was called to London by the regent."

"Ariel told me about the supposed ghost."

"Did she?"

Lord Alan had grown suddenly uncomfortable, Bolton thought. The resolution and authority with which he had begun this conversation were gone.

"I gave my word that I would help her look into her mother's death," he said.

"And you traveled down from London with her on this errand?"

"Of course."

He left a short silence once again. "A father might be concerned about your intentions toward her," he said then. "It is a rather unconventional association."

To his surprise, his assured, aristocratic visitor flushed like an awkward schoolboy. At once, he looked angry at his own reaction. "I have no intentions toward her!"

"Ah." Bolton raised his eyebrows in what he was sure was a very annoying way.

"I mean, it is not a question of . . . my sentiments toward Miss Harding . . . I would never harm her!"

"I see."

"You don't see anything," was the heated reply. "You know nothing about her. You met her only two days ago."

Jealousy, thought Daniel Bolton. That was very interesting. "True," he conceded. "And yet I find I am all the more concerned because of my previous neglect."

"Well, you haven't any right to be," Lord Alan snapped. "I can take very good care of . . " He stopped, clenching his fists and looking utterly frustrated. It took him a moment to regain control of himself. When he had managed it, he said, "You must excuse me. There is something I must see to." His tone was icy, and he did not wait for an answer before turning and leaving the room.

Extremely interesting, thought Bolton. He would have to observe these two more closely, though he had little doubt that he was right about the state of their feelings.

A sudden impulse made him raise his head and sit very still, then grin like the precocious boy he had once been. It was an outrageous idea, and yet . . . irresistible. Rising, he went to his writing table and penned a note to his friend the bishop at the great cathedral in Wells. He would have it delivered in the morning. And in the meantime, he would see what else he could stir up in the volatile situation he had uncovered. Having a daughter was really quite intriguing, he thought. He'd been a fool not to try it sooner.

The following afternoon Alan found Ivydene Manor curiously empty. Hannah had gone out somewhere with the housekeeper, Gladys, with whom she had struck up a friendship. There was no sign of Ariel's father. In the stables, the men they had brought with them from London were accompanied only by a stableboy. "Where is Bolton?" Lord Alan asked them when he went out to inquire.

"He walked out this morning with a large basket," said one of their men.

"He'll be collecting plants then," explained the stableboy. "He's always goin' into the fields and the woods lookin' for new 'ens."

"Without telling anyone?" demanded Alan.

The stableboy looked startled. "I reckon he tells Mrs. Moore."

"The housekeeper is not here either," Alan informed him.

The boy shrugged his ignorance.

Returning to the house, Alan saw Ariel walking through the garden toward the back gate, and he walked faster to catch up with her. "Where are you going?"

"Up the hill," she replied a bit stiffly. "My father showed me a ruined chapel that I—"

"You shouldn't go alone."

She bridled at his tone.

"Why is there no one here?" he added before she could speak. "I find it extremely odd that Hannah, the housekeeper, and Bolton have all gone out without telling us."

"Do you imagine that Hannah has joined some sort of conspiracy against us?" she said as she turned away.

"Of course not. But . . ."

Ariel opened the garden gate and stepped through.

"It's just deuced odd," he grumbled, following her onto the path that led uphill.

"Why do you dislike my father so?" demanded Ariel.

"I don't dislike him," he answered stiffly. "I scarcely know him."

"Anyone can see his good qualities. He is so kind, and intelligent, and sympathetic."

"Perhaps he exhibits these more to you than to others," replied Alan dryly.

This silenced her.

"You're happy, aren't you?" he added then. "It means a great deal to you, finding your father."

"Of course."

"It changes things for you."

"I like knowing I have a family. A place."

"It makes other parts of your life less important," he concluded, and felt a heaviness descend over him like a stifling winter cloak.

"I don't know about that," objected Ariel.

"Perhaps it becomes the most important."

She cocked her head to consider this. "It changes everything," she agreed finally. "I don't have to wonder anymore. And I'm no longer a . . . a nobody." She hesitated, then said, "My father has told me that Ivydene will be mine one day."

"So your future is settled," he said bitterly.

Ariel frowned at his tone, as if she found something insulting in it. "Well, I am no longer an actress's bastard child," she answered.

"That is not what I—"

"You can be as haughty and distant as you wish. You are a duke's son."

"I have not been—"

"My father is a respectable man who seems to care about me despite our long separation," she added. "Of course that means a great deal."

"I understand that. I simply think that you should go slowly and—"

"Oh, how could you understand anything about how I feel?" Ariel cried. "You have always known your status and been respected and admired. You have always had family around you. You can't imagine what it's like, making up stories about your father and enduring the petty gossip and malicious speculation of schoolgirls. You have no notion . . ." She broke off and started walking rapidly again.

Alan followed in silence. She was right, he thought. He never would really know what she had endured in this instance, or in many others. "I hope I have never appeared to feel any difference in our stations," he said. "Because I do not."

Ariel glanced at him, then looked at the ground. "No," she said. "No, you didn't. I beg your pardon. I did not mean—"

"No one in my family was ever allowed to become snobbish," he added. "My mother despises that sort of thing."

"They have been very kind to me," acknowledged Ariel formally.

A silence fell. They walked along the wooded path side by side, sunlight slanting over them through the branches.

"What will you do now?" Alan asked at last.

"What do you mean?"

"Will you stay here?"

She threw him another quick glance. "As you wanted me to?"

"I?"

"You said that you would leave me here, if Daniel Bolton turned out to be my father."

Something in the way she said the words "leave me" shook him. He tried to read her expression, but she continued to gaze at the ground.

"My father has offered me a home," she said then. "So, you see, you don't have any responsibility to me any longer. You may cast off that burden with good conscience."

"Burden," he repeated, trying to work out what she really meant.

"Well, duty, or at any rate a promise you wish you hadn't made. You can be free of it now."

"You want me to go?" he asked.

She didn't reply at once. He very much wanted to see her face, but she continued to hide it from him.

"You can do as you like!" Ariel said at last, and turned to start down the path. "I don't want to see the chapel after all. Let us return to the house."

But Alan caught her arm and held her back, forcing her to look up at him. "I regret no promises I made," he said.

Ariel looked pale and strained. "You are a man of your word," she said, tugging at her arm to free it from his grasp.

He let her go. "Yes," he acknowledged.

"It is very important to you."

"Performing what I have said I will do? Yes." He couldn't understand why she harped on this point.

She gazed at him. They were very close together. "Or what others say you should do," she added.

Alan shook his head. "I am not bound by—"

"Such as when you offered for me," she interrupted.

She stood stock-still, gazing up at him with those mysterious dark eyes. What were they asking him? Alan wondered. He could not bear to hear her refuse him again. "I had taken unforgivable liberties," he hazarded. "I am not the sort of man who—"

She stepped away from him. "I was there," she said. "If they had been unforgivable, I would have mentioned the matter!" Turning, she started down the hill away from him.

He was right behind her. "I wanted to show you that I am not like the men you had been warned about," he protested.

She stopped so suddenly that he nearly careened into her. Hands on hips, she said, "You think I am unable to tell the difference? Of course, a feeble intellect such as mine would not be capable of much discrimination, would it? Well, you have made your point. I am completely convinced that you are a man of honor, who does his duty no matter how difficult or distasteful it may be."

"You are distorting what I—"

"I beg your pardon. Have I misunderstood again? It is so difficult for a mere female to comprehend your great mind."

"Stop it!" He took hold of her shoulders and shook her slightly.

She glared up at him.

The small sounds of the forest faded from his consciousness. He could see nothing but her lovely face. Alan couldn't stop himself. He pulled her hard against him and kissed her as if their lives depended on it.

Her lips were as sweet as he remembered. The contours of her body were as soft and arousing. There was nothing in the world that he wanted more, and when she relaxed in his embrace and opened her mouth to his, he pulled her even closer, exultation hot in his veins. He would never let her go again, he thought.

But this certainty was broken by the sound of someone clearing his throat, and then a polite, "Pardon me?"

Alan released Ariel, who swayed a little on her feet, and turned to find Daniel Bolton standing among the trees beside the path. The basket on his arm was overflowing with leaves and flowers. "I was on my way back to the house," he said as Alan silently consigned him to perdition.

Alan and Ariel moved a step apart.

Bolton cleared his throat again. "I feel I must ask, er, what's all this then?"

"I intend to marry your daughter," declared Alan.

He said it like a knight throwing down a gauntlet, Daniel Bolton thought. But the way he glanced toward Ariel made it difficult to tell whom he was challenging. "Do you?" It was really quite gratifying, he thought, to have one's conclusions so clearly confirmed. Time to test the rest of it. "And is she in agreement with this plan?"

Both men turned to Ariel. Bolton watched emotions shift across his daughter's lovely face. "I must say, speaking as a father, that it appears to me—"

"You have no say in this," declared Alan. "You have barely met. You have no right to interfere."

"Still, I am her father," was the calm objection.

"Whom she hasn't seen in twenty years."

"Nineteen."

"Be quiet," said Ariel.

Looking surprised, the two men obeyed.

Ariel thought of the man she had glimpsed outside the cathedral at Wells, of the passion she had seen in his eyes as he played the pianoforte. But even more she considered the way he had just kissed her. She should have been relying on her own perceptions since the day he first touched her, she thought, and not on what he chose to say. She had had ample evidence that on matters of the heart he often didn't know what he was talking about. Of course, he thought that he did. It might be quite difficult to convince him otherwise.

Her newfound father turned to her. "If you are going to be kissing young men in the forest—" Bolton began, but then stopped.

Birds twittered unconcernedly in the ensuing silence.

Ariel took a deep breath. With the sense of taking a long step into the unknown, she answered, "Then I had best marry . . . him."

"Ah." Her father looked oddly satisfied. "That's settled then?" He looked at Lord Alan.

The latter nodded strongly.

Bolton rubbed his hands together like a man who has finished some ticklish task. "You will be married from Ivydene."

"I'll ride up to Wells and get a special license," Alan declared.

Daniel Bolton's hazel eyes glinted. "Fortunately," he replied with what was obviously a great deal of enjoyment, "I have already requested one from my old friend the bishop. It will arrive tomorrow."

The two young people stared at him.

"You will allow me the great joy of standing up with you, I hope?" he said happily to Ariel.

The wedding of Ariel Bolton of Ivydene Manor, a woman who hadn't existed a week ago, to Lord Alan Gresham, sixth son of the duke of Langford, was a small affair, attended only by the bride's father and a few servants.

It did not lack excitement, however. For just as the vows had been spoken and the clergyman had given them his final blessing, a commotion outside the windows drew most of those present to look out.

In the stableyard, a man in livery was climbing down from a lathered, exhausted horse. The rider looked worn out himself, but extremely determined.

"Isn't that a royal courier?" wondered Daniel Bolton. "What can he be doing here?"

A muffled curse escaped Alan.

"What can he want?" wondered Ariel.

Without answering, Alan strode out of the room. In a moment he reappeared outside and approached the courier. The sun drew bright copper tints from his hair and glinted on the buttons of his blue coat. His movements had such ease and strength, Ariel thought. She watched him speak briefly with the messenger, and then the man handed over a sealed envelope before heading for the kitchen and some refreshment.

Alan returned to the house. Ariel waited for him to come back to the parlor, and when he didn't appear, she and her father went in search of him. They discovered him finally in the study, frowning over an unfolded sheet of paper.

"What is it?" said Ariel, fearing some catastrophe.

"Nothing wrong in your family, I hope," added Daniel Bolton.

Alan raised his eyes from the page. "The ghost is back at Carlton House," he informed them with obvious irritation, "and the prince is . . . agitated." He took another sheet of paper from the envelope that lay before him on the table and scanned it quickly. "The man I left in charge there says it cannot be the actors. They have been under close watch." His frown deepened as he read on.

"What is it?" said Ariel.

"The incidents are growing more serious," he replied. "A footman was pushed down the stairs by a 'ghostly' hand and broke his leg. And there have been other things as well." Putting down the page, he sighed. "I am commanded to leave at once and deal with this matter."

"I'll go and pack," said Ariel, starting to turn.

"There's no need," Alan told her. "I shall have to ride. The coach will be too slow. You can stay here, if you like, and visit with your father until I can settle this."

"Of course I am coming with you," she protested.

"I shall ride with the courier," he pointed out. "You couldn't keep the pace even if we had a mount for you."

Knowing this was true, Ariel bit her lower lip. "Hannah and I will follow in the carriage then," she declared.

"I would rather you stayed here," said Alan. "These recent incidents sound . . . disturbing."

"Do you intend to leave me practically at the altar?" Daniel Bolton looked from his daughter to her new husband, hesitated, then silently slipped from the room.

"I believe that expression refers to those who do not show up for a wedding," Alan replied dryly.

"You know what I mean. How can you think of leaving me?"

"It is for your own safety and—"

Ariel turned toward the door once again. "Hannah and I will set out as soon as we are packed," she said.

"I see." He let out a breath. "There is nothing more to be said in that case. And I have no time for arguments. I must be on the road." Brushing past her, he left the room. Moments later she heard his voice in the stableyard calling for his horse to be saddled.

Was this what it meant to be married to him? Ariel's fists clenched tighter. Had she made a terrible mistake?

She unclenched her fists. She had known this marriage was going to be a challenge, she reminded herself. She couldn't abandon hope so soon. Straightening her shoulders, she went to find her husband.

He had already packed a small kit, she found. And his horse stood saddled and ready. The royal courier had reappeared and was telling the stableboy that he would pick up a fresh mount in Wells. Most of the household stood about as if watching a performance.

"There you are," said Alan.

Where else would she be, Ariel felt like saying, but she didn't. At least it seemed he hadn't been planning to go without saying good-bye.

"I'm sorry for this," he added.

"So am I."

The courier swung up onto his horse.

Ignoring the circle of curious eyes, Ariel went over and put her arms around Alan's neck. She had an instant's anxiety when he seemed to hesitate, but then he pulled her tight against him, every line of his body pressing into hers. "Damn the regent," he whispered.

She raised her head to look at him, and he kissed her— a public kiss, not one of those that made her think her knees would give way and she would never catch her breath again. When he drew back, he looked distracted, already elsewhere.

"I must go," he said.

Reluctantly, she let go and stepped back to allow him to mount. "We will be in London by the end of the week," she told him.

He merely nodded and, with a small salute to the others, wheeled his horse toward the gates. The courier followed, and soon the sound of hooves was fading on the lane beyond.

It was three hours later that Ariel sought out her father to tell him good-bye. She found him in his gardens, standing very still amid the fragrant herbs.

The traveling carriage stood in the stableyard at the side of the house, the team of horses tossing their heads and stamping.

"It's time to go," said Ariel. "And there are so many things we haven't had the chance to talk about."

"You will come back and visit, I hope." He took her hand. "I don't intend to lose you again."

"Of course I will."

"If there is anything I can do to help you, you need only ask," he added.

"Thank you." She looked around the fragrant garden regretfully, and then they turned to walk together to the carriage. Hannah was already inside, and Ariel climbed up to join her.

"Little Ariel," said Daniel Bolton, retaining possession of her hand for a long moment. Finally, he stepped back, and the driver gave the team the signal. They leaned into the harness, and the coach moved across the cobbles and through the gates. Ariel hung out the window to wave until Ivydene disappeared among the trees.

Chapter Nineteen

The coach clattered through the cobblestone streets of London and pulled up before the high old house that Ariel had inherited from her mother. "There are lights in the parlor," Ariel told Hannah. Alan, she thought, her pulse speeding up despite the fatigue of the journey.

But when they went inside, they found not Alan, but the other three Gresham brothers who were resident in London. They came surging into the entryway when the front door opened and set up a glad cry of welcome. "I told you it would be tonight," said Lord Sebastian. "Pay up, Robert, you owe me a guinea."

Ariel looked past them for Alan, but he wasn't there.

"Open the champagne," Sebastian added, ushering them into the parlor where an array of bottles had been set out, and obviously sampled rather freely already.

"Stand back," said Nathaniel. "Give Ariel the armchair."

"A toast," cried Sebastian, filling a tray of glasses. "To our new sister—our first sister, as a matter of fact."

The brothers jostled for position but finally all raised glasses together and saluted her.

"Alan told you?" she said.

"He did," replied Nathaniel.

"About time, I thought," said Robert.

"And I should like to say that we are all very glad," added Nathaniel with a certain solemnity.

"I hear you can trace your ancestors back further than ours," teased Robert.

"Good thing," murmured Sebastian.

"You are glad that I have family credentials?" wondered Ariel, a bit offended at this exhibition of snobbery.

"It doesn't matter a whit to us," said Nathaniel quickly. "But it will to a great many people. And so, it makes things . . . simpler."

"What things?"

"Social things," continued Nathaniel. "People's opinions."

"Nat should know," commented Robert. "He's become a positive paterfamilias. You'll be happy to hear, Ariel, that he's now the terror of Violet's entire family. He's got them bowing and scraping and tripping over themselves to grant his smallest wish."

"Robert," objected his oldest brother. "You exaggerate things out of all proportion." But there was a gleam of satisfaction in his blue eyes.

"Ariel," put in Sebastian. "I am an engaged man. Lady Georgina has accepted me."

"And twenty disappointed suitors want his head," added Robert. "Stedding's trying to find an excuse to call him out, and Sinjin Lawrence is threatening to put a period to his own existence if she don't reconsider." Suddenly he jumped. "Here, where did you come from?"

Prospero, who had materialized near one of his shining Hessian boots, now wound around his leg. "He's looking for scraps," said Ariel.

"He's looking for my boots," complained Lord Robert, moving away from the cat. "I swear that animal is uncanny. You arrive, and here it is. And we thought it had run off or been killed. It was as if he knew you were gone and wasn't coming round till you returned."

"My father has a cat that looks just like him," said Ariel, staring at Prospero. He raised one paw and set it on her shoe, as if to remind her that she had not offered him a single tidbit. "Ptolemy?" said Ariel experimentally, even though she knew it was foolish. Prospero simply looked at her with his fathomless golden eyes.

"We're to be married down at her family's place in September," commented Sebastian, sticking to his point.

"I'm so glad," answered Ariel.

"We can get in some hunting while we're there, eh?" said Robert. He poked his brother in the ribs. "That way it won't be a complete waste of time."

"If you're invited," retorted Sebastian.

For a moment Robert looked disconcerted.

"Oh, I won't stand up without all my brothers," Sebastian assured him. He grinned. "We'll even make James set foot on land for a few days. And I'll order starched collars for the lot of you." Sebastian lifted his glass. "To all of us settled men," he said. "And to Robert, who's next."

"Bite your tongue," commanded Robert. "You won't get me to the altar for twenty years yet."

"Says the man who spends three afternoons a week studying Akkadian," teased Sebastian.

"I've found I'm rather interested in the subject."

Nathaniel raised an eyebrow. Sebastian jeered openly.

"Where is Alan?" Ariel managed to interject.

Robert waved a hand. "Camped out at Carlton House looking for this ghost. It's turned nasty, you know. Prinny's having an apoplexy. We told Alan we'd keep an eye out for you in the meantime."

"Did you?" replied Ariel, in a voice that made Nathaniel's head jerk up. "And what did he say to that?"

"Doesn't say much of anything these days," was the unsatisfactory reply. "And if he does, he's liable to bite your head off."

"Really?" Ariel set her jaw. "We'll see about that when he gets home."

"Won't be coming home," Robert informed her. "Said he'd be at the regent's for the duration."

"What?"

"Has to finish this thing," continued Robert. "It's a dashed nuisance, you know."

"Oh, yes," said Ariel. "I know."

Robert caught the nuances of her tone at last, and became suddenly aware of the looks passing between his brothers and the uneasiness of the atmosphere. "What?" he said.

"Alan always did become completely engrossed in any task he began," offered Nathaniel.

"Single-minded," agreed Sebastian. "Devilishly hard to get his attention sometimes."

"Really?" responded Ariel again with a glitter in her hazel eyes that made all three brothers sit back.

Night had fallen by the time the Gresham brothers could be persuaded to end the celebration and take their leave. Ariel went up to her room, but she made no move to change out of her traveling dress. Instead, she went through her luggage, picking out a few things and putting them in a small cloth bag. Then she redonned her bonnet and, taking the bag, went down to the entryway. At the front door, she hesitated. She had to tell Hannah she was going. There would be an embarrassing uproar if she just disappeared. But she was not going to tolerate any arguments, Ariel determined, holding her head high as she went to knock on the door of Hannah's bedchamber.

The older woman was just beginning to prepare for

bed. "I am going out," Ariel told her firmly. "I do not know when I will be back, but you needn't worry."

"At this time of night?" wondered Hannah, taken by surprise.

"Yes." Ariel tried to escape, but Hannah followed.

"Where are you going?" she asked.

Biting her bottom lip, Ariel debated about her response. "Carlton House," she said finally, deciding on the truth.

"Ah." They had reached the entryway of the house by this time, and Hannah's shrewd gaze took in the small bag sitting beside the door. "How are you going to get in?"

"What?" Ariel had expected objections about the lateness of the hour or her destination, but not this.

"You can't just walk up to the front door and knock," said Hannah. "It would cause a fuss."

Ariel closed her eyes on a vivid image of this scene.

"And don't they have guards about?"

Probably more than ever, Ariel acknowledged silently. She remembered the way Alan had stationed men about the place when they were hunting the ghost earlier. "I have to go," she insisted.

Hannah looked at her, then frowned. "I know the prince's butler," she said. "We're from the same village."

Ariel's spirits revived. "Would you . . . would you write him a note?"

Hannah shook her head. "That's no good. They might refuse to give it to him." She paused again, seeming to consider the situation from all angles. "I'll go with you," she said at last. "If I ask for him, they'll fetch him." She turned back toward her room, moving quickly now. "We'd best hurry, though. The prince most often keeps his staff up late, but we can't be sure."

"Hannah," said Ariel.

The older woman stopped and turned.

"Thank you."

The answering smile was surprisingly impish. "Do him good," she said, and was gone before Ariel could respond.

They approached Carlton House from the back, going up the path to the servants' entrance. They were stopped twice by men watching the place, but Hannah got them through each time, partly by her manner and partly by her appearance, which seemed to remind both guards of some formidable female relative.

As promised, when she inquired for the butler they were admitted and taken to the huge kitchen, which was far from empty despite the hour. "Wait here," Hannah said, indicating a shadowed corner, and she stepped forward alone to meet a tall imposing figure in black.

After a cordial greeting, the two conferred inaudibly. Ariel saw the man glance at her more than once, and his face showed a variety of reactions—from disapproval to surprise to what seemed to be ironic appreciation, though of what she didn't know. In the end, Hannah returned to say that all was settled. "He'll send someone to show you the way," she told her.

"Thank you," said Ariel again. Even if she had managed to sneak in, she realized, she never would have found her way to Alan through the maze of Carlton House. "You have been very kind to me," she added, referring to far more than tonight.

"He never was like the other boys," was the oblique response. "I could see from the time he was a baby that he'd have a different sort of life, and would need something different to be happy."

On impulse, Ariel hugged her. "I'm going to see that he gets both," she said.

The twinkle that she had seen before appeared in Hannah's eyes. "Will he, nil he," she replied. "Go along now. I'm ready for my bed."

• • •

Five minutes later Ariel stood before a paneled door in a dim corridor. As requested, her guide had left her there, and now she listened for sounds inside the room she faced. There were none. The silence was deep and impenetrable. What should she do? she wondered. Knock?

Now that she was actually here, Ariel was assailed by doubts about her plan. She had intended to confront Alan and tell him very forcefully that this was not her idea of a marriage. But as she stood in this huge silent house, the task seemed somehow larger.

Putting out her hand, she gently tried the door handle. It yielded easily. She opened the door, giving thanks for well-oiled hinges, and peered in. The chamber was dark, but enough light filtered in from the corridor to show her it was empty. Noting the location of a candlestick on a side table, she slipped in, shutting the door behind her, and went to light it.

That done, she heaved a sigh of relief and put her bag on a chair. She took off her hat and smoothed her hair, then turned to examine the place where Alan had been staying.

There was little sign of him in the large ornate room—a few personal possessions scattered over the flat surfaces. Mainly it looked like an anonymous chamber in a grand house where the owner's taste ran to the florid and overblown.

Ariel took another deep breath. It was good he wasn't here, she thought. She could get her bearings and be exactly positioned when he did arrive. She looked around. There was an inlaid writing desk on one wall, with a carved chair that didn't look very comfortable. There was a wardrobe in the far corner, between two windows over which the curtains had already been drawn. And directly opposite her, there was a large canopied bed.

Ariel swallowed. It was not as large as her mother's

bed, she thought, and then flushed at the associations that idea brought.

Turning, she opened her bag and pulled out a bundle of creamy silk, which she shook out and held up before her. It was a nightgown, the one she had planned to wear on her wedding night.

Moving quickly now, not wanting to be caught, she undressed and put on the gown. Then she loosened the pins in her hair and let it fall about her shoulders. Trying the wardrobe, she found that there was a mirror inside the door, and she examined herself critically in it. The folds of silk fell onto the floor around her bare feet. The scooped neckline of the nightgown showed off the curve of her breasts. Her skin glowed against the pale material, and her hair floated around her face. It was an image to entice a man, she told herself. She had not spent years with Bess Harding for nothing. But as Ariel climbed into the large bed, she noticed that she was trembling. She settled against a pile of pillows, pulling the coverlet over her feet, and set herself to wait.

The candle burned down. The night deepened. Despite all her resolutions, Ariel grew drowsy. She had been traveling for days, and fatigue was taking its toll.

She didn't want to be asleep, and shook her head to clear it. She wanted to be awake and ready when he walked in. But as the minutes ticked past, it got harder and harder to keep her eyes open and to resist the impulse to slide completely under the covers and give in to oblivion.

At last, just when she thought she would have to surrender, she heard a soft click. The door opened a crack. Ariel sat straighter watching the small opening. No one appeared. There was an ominous pause, long enough for her to begin to worry, then the door crashed back against the wall, making every nerve in her body jump, and Alan appeared in the doorway holding a pistol. "Who's there?" he demanded. "Show yourself!" He moved the pistol back and forth, covering the entire room. His eyes were darting from one corner to the other, taking in the lighted candle and the clothing laid over a chair.

"Alan?" said Ariel in a voice that quavered from reaction.

His implacable gaze came to rest on her where she lay in the shadows. His grim expression shifted slowly to astonishment. "What the devil are you doing here?" he said.

This was not the greeting she had imagined.

"How did you get in?"

Worse yet, she thought.

"Have you lost your mind?"

"I didn't think so," Ariel muttered, taking a deep breath to counter the reaction his entrance had caused.

Alan came into the room and put the pistol on the writing table. Then he took a key from his pocket and locked the door. "How did you get in?" he repeated. "I thought I had this place completely secure."

"Hannah knows the butler," answered Ariel, and was displeased to find that her voice sounded rather small.

"Hannah . . . ?" He shook his head, then ran a hand wearily over his face. "I don't understand what has come over Hannah lately."

"I thought you would be glad to see me."

"I am always glad to see you," he replied. "However—"

"You certainly didn't act as if you were glad just now."

"You don't understand. This—"

"No, I don't. If this is what you think marriage—"

"This house has become a dangerous place to be," he continued, cutting her off. "A number of the servants have been hurt, and it seems to be getting worse."

"I thought you might be thinking a little of me, instead of how to help the prince regent," she said. She had been thinking constantly of him. And now she was terribly afraid that she had given her heart to a man who would never know the meaning of love.

"I have thought of you," he retorted. "Why do you think I am bending all my efforts to get this matter finished? I want to take you up to Oxford and find a house and begin our life together."

"Oh."

"We need a settled life," he added distractedly.

"Settled," echoed Ariel, not entirely satisfied.

"I have calculated that we—"

"Calculated! Is that all you think of? Calculations and analyses and plans. What about how I feel?"

He didn't seem to know what she meant.

Ariel started to tell him that all she wanted was a husband who loved her. But she couldn't quite manage to say it. She didn't want to hear that it was impossible. "I come home to find you not even there," she said instead.

"I knew my brothers would tell you where I was."

"The brothers that you sent to welcome me home in your place?" she responded sarcastically.

"They seemed eager for the task. I thought they'd do it well." He sounded a bit accusing.

"They did, complete with champagne."

"Have you been drinking? Is that why you played the trick of sneaking in here?"

Ariel just looked at him.

"I should go and speak to the butler," Alan added. "He knows he is not to let anyone in."

He was going to go, Ariel thought. He was going to leave her sitting in his bed, in the middle of the night, as if she were some annoying visitor. She had a vision of spending her life trying to divert his attention from the tasks he had set himself—and failing. She swallowed and fiercely repressed threatening tears. She couldn't have spoken even if she had known what to say.

Silence fell over the room. The candle sputtered, and the scent of wax floated through the room. The tension that had been buzzing between them as they flung words back and forth receded, but in its place came not peace but a thickening of the air, a hyperawareness. Looking up, Ariel saw that Alan was staring at her as if he had just noticed where she sat and what she wore. The intensity of his gaze was almost too much. She shifted on the pillows, and one strap of her nightgown slipped off her shoulder like a glancing caress. She shivered.

"Ariel," said Alan.

She crossed her arms over the folds of her silk nightdress. His auburn hair was gleaming in the golden candlelight. He looked very large, and very serious. Another shiver ran through her.

Alan moved. Slowly, like a man moving through water—or a dream—he came toward the bed. He was still staring at her, and Ariel flushed, suddenly far more conscious of her hair tumbled around her shoulders, and her nakedness under the thin silk.

He loomed over her. The light was behind him now, leaving his face in shadow. She wanted more than anything to read his expression, to try to understand what he was feeling, but his broad shoulders cut off the glow of the candle and made him a dark outline haloed in gold. She waited for him to speak, or give some sign, but he simply put a hand on either side of her on the bed and bent to take her lips with his.

His mouth was warm and confiding. It seemed to offer all the reassurance she had been hoping for, the certainty that his feelings were as deep as hers. She let herself relax a little, following the enticing lead of his mouth on hers.

His kiss grew stronger; it coaxed and insisted, pleaded and demanded. Ariel's flush deepened with a different kind of heat. She put her arms around his neck and clung as he pressed her back against the head of the bed, filling all her senses.

When she felt as if she were drowning, his hands moved. She felt them first on her hips, warmly caressing.

Then they moved up to her waist and along her ribs, his touch sure and very intimate. When he cupped her breasts and let his thumbs rove over them, she had to gasp. This was much more deliberate than the first time they had been together—slower, more tantalizing. Her whole body was trembling.

He kissed her throat and her shoulder and then took her lips again as his hands slid down under the coverlet, pushing it aside, to find the hem of her nightdress. His fingers heated every inch of her as he very, very slowly eased the garment up over her knees and thighs and higher, slipping it from under her and then suddenly up and off as Ariel raised her arms to let it go.

He was looking at her again, with that devouring inexorable gaze. But she didn't mind it now. She even arched her back, wanting him to go on touching her.

"You are so beautiful," he whispered, encircling her waist with his hands and kissing her again.

Then he stepped back and stripped off his coat and shirt. Ariel reached for him, and ran her fingertips along the muscles of his back. With a low sound, he drew a little away again to shed the rest of his clothes, and she saw him before her in the candlelight—the sculpted strength of his arms, the russet hair sprinkled across his chest, and more. "Oh," she said, fascinated at her first sight of a man. Irresistibly drawn, she reached out and touched his tautly aroused manhood.

Alan groaned, and she pulled her hand quickly back. "Isn't that right?" she said.

"Very right," he answered. Pushing her gently backward, he joined her on the bed, capturing her lips again and parting her knees with one of his. Ariel forgot her questions in his kiss and his hands running over her. She needed his touch now, and as if he knew, his fingers moved to the center of the ache and made her cry out with pleasure. She murmured his name as his lips moved to her shoulder, her breasts, and then her mouth again.

He was taking her out of herself, as he had that other day when she had clung to him and begged him not to leave her. He wouldn't leave her now, Ariel thought. He was her husband.

Then she couldn't think anymore. The sensations were too amazing, his lips and hands too distracting. She was gripped by a delicious tension that seemed likely to overwhelm her.

Alan drew a little away. She pulled him back, protesting softly.

"A moment," he murmured. And then she felt him enter her, and the pleasure mounted as he moved, rising unbearably until every muscle in her body was taut with it, and she clung to him as tight as she could as it went on, and on. And then it burst and spread through her whole body in wild, tempestuous waves. It was as if she were drowning indeed, but in pleasure instead of water.

Alan cried out softly and gripped her hard, making it impossible to breathe for a few moments. Then his arms slackened, and he rested against her, his breath hard and rapid.

She held him, their hearts pounding in unison, their breath ragged. He was closer to her than anyone else had ever been. "I love you," murmured Ariel, the words unstoppable, inevitable. She couldn't have decided not to say them. They were so much a part of everything else she had felt that she had no control over them. But as soon as the phrase was out, her mouth went dry.

Alan raised his head and looked down at her. "What?"

Had he not heard? She didn't know if she wished that or not. He looked startled, at a loss. "Nothing," whispered Ariel. "Nothing."

He hesitated, as if he might speak, but instead he dropped a gentle kiss on her lips, and then a whole series of quick kisses, like the caress of a butterfly's wing, like the embodiment of tenderness. Ariel trembled again under his touch—hopeful, uncertain—wondering whether this was enough of an answer.

Much later, Alan slipped back into his bedchamber after a quick tour of the perimeter of guards he had set about Carlton House. Ariel was still sleeping, he saw, going straight to her to make certain all was well. He had hated to leave her here alone, locked in, while he made his rounds, but the tenor of the haunting had become profoundly disturbing. He had even begun to worry that someone intended to assassinate the prince; the incidents had an almost murderous quality. He would get Ariel out of here at first light, and make her promise not to return.

Standing beside the bed, he watched her sleep. Her lashes made dark crescents on her glowing cheeks. Her tumbled curls smelled of flowers, and the rise and fall of her breasts was enthralling.

He had heard her say she loved him. It had roused a kind of triumph in his breast, which was silly because he didn't believe in what people called love. He had seen a score of friends succumb to it, and in nearly every case, it was a simple matter of attraction. A few of his acquaintances had been fortunate enough to be friends with the ladies of their choice, and this had made for more lasting bonds. He put himself in their ranks. But this supposed metaphysical ideal that poets praised and youngsters mooned over—it was a fantasy, he told himself as he gazed at her. It was a daze of chemical responses designed to encourage the propagation of the race.

And yet . . . Lately so many of his thoughts seemed to end in "and yet." When he looked at Ariel, when she turned unexpectedly and smiled at him, when he held her in his arms, he felt something that he had never felt for another human being. There was plenty of desire in it, along with protectiveness and pride and admiration.

The more he tried to analyze his state, the harder it

was to define. Probably it was the newness of the thing, he decided. And the fact that he wanted her so fiercely no doubt distorted his reasoning processes. After they had been married a few months, he would understand the connection in all respects, and find it had a much more rational basis than so-called "love."

Satisfied, he removed his shirt and breeches and slipped into bed again, reveling in the brush of Ariel's silken skin and her warmth. He tried to be sorry when she opened her eyes and murmured sleepily, but he wasn't. He gathered her to him and ran his hands down the delicious curve of her back.

"Where have you been?" she murmured.

"Did you hear me go? I tried to be quiet."

When she said nothing, he added, "I had to check on the house."

"Oh." She drew a little away from him. "Is all well?"

"Yes." He reached for her again, but she sat up.

"You should get the actors to help you. They must know all the ways in and out of Carlton House and the best hiding places."

He gazed at her, much struck. "That is a good idea. I should have thought of it."

"Astonishing."

"We suspect someone is hiding inside," he told her. "They might well be able to show us where. Excellent."

"You admit that I have had a good idea?" said Ariel.

"Of course."

"Even though I am a female?"

"What?"

"And females are unable to think rationally?"

"You are a unique female," Alan replied. "I acknowledged that long ago, as you know very well."

"I do?"

"Don't be ridiculous. Didn't I admit your contributions to our investigation?"

"No."

"Of course I did. And I have certainly mentioned the revolution you seem to have initiated in my family."

"Would you call it a—"

"I believe I have given you full credit for your unusual abilities almost from the beginning."

Ariel gave him a glinting look. "Do you indeed?"

"Why else would I have married you?"

She gave a little gasp. "I am not unique, you know," she said. "There are a great many females who could have done the same."

"Nonsense."

"Flora Jennings, for example. Look what she has accomplished with the poor children. And you have told me that your mother's educational schemes are—"

"These are exceptions that prove the rule," insisted Alan.

"Or one of those rules that has more exceptions than examples," Ariel muttered.

"What?"

She merely looked down at him. He didn't understand what they were talking about, or why they were bothering to discuss it just now. "I have an idea," he said.

"Oh?"

Reaching out, he pulled her down onto the pillows and then knelt above her, running his hands over her shoulders and breasts and down all the way to her knees before starting back up.

"Oh," said Ariel, looking up at him in the dimness and taking in his aroused state.

"A better idea," he said, and bent to the honey of her lips.

Chapter Twenty

———— ❖ ————

Alan and Ariel were wakened early the next morning by one of the prince's servants, agitated by some new outrage by the haunters in the kitchens. This limited their farewells to a disappointing few minutes, amid a flurry of dressing and preparing for the day. "Promise me that you will not come to Carlton House again until this invasion is stopped," Alan said when they were ready to go. "This house has become a dangerous place. I don't want you exposed."

She wanted to make him admit that last night had meant a great deal to him. But the concern in his face stopped her. "Very well. But it will be over soon, won't it?"

He nodded grimly. "If I have to take the place apart piece by piece."

He escorted her to the front door and squeezed her hand in a last good-bye before hurrying off to deal with the latest problem. Ariel sighed as he disappeared through a doorway, then turned to the footman stationed there. "Can you find me a hack?"

"Of course, my lady." With a small bow, he opened the door, and then took a surprised step backward. Lord Robert Gresham stood on the doorstep, his hand raised to knock. Behind him, one step down, was Flora Jennings.

The moment Miss Jennings spotted Ariel, she surged forward. "I must speak to you."

Ariel blinked at the urgency of her tone.

"We called at your house, and they said you were here."

She looked extremely agitated, Ariel thought—startlingly so for the composed Flora Jennings. "Shall we go back together?" she suggested.

"I can't wait any longer!"

"What the deuce is going on?" demanded Lord Robert.

"Please!" said Miss Jennings.

Responding to the strain in her manner, Ariel asked the footman, "Is there somewhere we could talk?"

The tall servant looked dubious. "I've been instructed not to admit callers," he said.

"This is not a morning call," she replied. "Perhaps in here?" She opened the door on the left, and was assailed by the most dreadful smell she had ever encountered. It made her eyes water and her nose sting and drove her back coughing and sputtering into the hall.

"Not there," exclaimed the footman, who had sprung after her too late. He slammed the door shut again, looking exceedingly harried.

"Good God," said Lord Robert.

"I am not supposed to—" began the servant.

Ariel was still coughing. "Find the lady a place to sit down," Lord Robert told him.

The man dithered for a moment, then turned and led them along one corridor and into another. Everyone they passed in the usually bustling Carlton House looked furtive and worried today. Finally, the footman opened a paneled door, rather gingerly, and peered inside, then indicated that they should enter. "This should be . . . suitable," he said, scanning the empty, inoffensive parlor with relief. "You'd best not . . . that is, I wouldn't wander about."

"We won't," Lord Robert assured him.

"Thank you, my lord," replied the man, bowing and shutting the door behind him.

Silence descended over the room. Although Flora Jennings had gotten what she wanted, she now looked hesitant. "Perhaps . . . perhaps you would wait outside, Lord Robert?" she said at last.

"Dashed if I will," he answered heatedly. "You roust me out of bed, drag me through London, force me to take you to Carlton House when Alan has forbidden all of us to enter, and now you think I'll cool my heels in the hall while you tell Ariel why?" He shook his head. "Not bl . . . not likely."

"Even if it's none of your affair?"

This stopped him for a moment, and Ariel looked back and forth from one to the other.

"Yes," said Lord Robert defiantly then.

"A gentleman would not—"

"Oh, now I'm to be a gentleman, am I? One of those disgusting, overbred gentlemen you're so ready to despise when you don't need one?"

"Lord Robert!"

Ariel watched them contend silently, through burning gazes, for a time. Then, finally, Robert gave in, though with no good grace. "I'll sit over there in the corner," he grumbled. "I ain't standing in the corridor."

Flora watched him stomp over to an armchair, turn it away from them, and sit, his arms crossed. After a further slight hesitation, she pulled Ariel as far from him as possible and said, "I must tell you something."

By this time, Ariel could hardly wait to hear what she would say.

"I should have told you some time ago, but I . . ."

What could it be? she wondered. Some scandalous secret, something about Bess?

Flora took a deep breath, as if bracing herself. "I am the one behind the haunting of Carlton House," she said in one swift rush.

Ariel stared, transfixed. Whatever she had expected, it had not been this.

"I was so . . . I was so *angry* when Bess died," the other woman continued. "I wanted it to be marked somehow. I wanted there to be some great upheaval. And also . . ." She stopped and swallowed. "I know Bess never told you this. She said she didn't want to burden you with her dark memories, that she was afraid they would blight your life as they did hers. But when she began visiting the children I care for, they started to come out, you see, and she had to speak to someone."

Ariel waited, utterly alert.

"When she was very young, Bess was taken from the streets by a nobleman who imprisoned her in a house he has and used her for his . . . pleasures."

"What?" Ariel sat bolt upright.

"She was kept there until she began to . . . mature, and then she was thrown out into the streets again, to make her way as best she could." Flora looked as if she had tasted something bitter. "Lord Royalton does not like women, only little girls—and boys."

"Lord Royalton!" Ariel's head was reeling. "They said Bess had quarreled with him."

Flora gave a thin smile. "It was far more than a quarrel. Bess was trying to have him exposed and prosecuted, but he has too many powerful friends, and he blocked her at every turn. It was like a kind of game to him, I think. All she accomplished was to make him more . . . discreet."

"But how is that possible? How can he . . . ?"

"No one listens to children from the gutter," was the

acid reply. "They can accuse, but if he denies . . ." She shrugged. "He is a peer of the realm, and a close friend of our glorious sovereign." The last two words dripped with sarcasm.

Ariel bent her head, trying to take all of this in. Each new vista that opened on her mother's life brought fresh pain. "Poor Bess," she murmured.

Some of the fierceness faded from Flora Jennings's eyes. "Poor Bess indeed," she repeated. "I wanted some revenge for her, so I suggested the haunting to the younger actors. They never knew who sent them the plans, but they didn't need much prodding. They were delighted with the idea."

"There's more to this," Ariel said. "They were caught."

Flora released another sigh. "That is why I'm here, and what I must tell you." She looked down at her hands. "I should have been content with the actors' tricks. The prince was humiliated; everyone was laughing at him. It was all I could expect. But I wanted . . . more." She looked as if she had bitten into something bitter.

"And . . . ?" prompted Ariel.

"I spoke with some of the young people Royalton had used and discarded. Bess had been searching them out and helping them as she could. I suggested that they might want to carry on with the pranks, and they jumped at the chance." She paused and put a hand to her mouth. "What I didn't understand was the depth of their anguish and their hatred," she went on. "How could I understand?" But she made a gesture to negate the protest. "I should have."

"And now they are going too far," Ariel added. "People are being hurt."

"It's worse than that," replied her guest. "They intend to kill Lord Royalton—tonight, I believe—and anyone who gets in their way . . ." She gestured again, as if throwing something away.

"Alan," exclaimed Ariel.

"And the servants," Flora agreed, "and guests, perhaps even the prince. Not that I care so much about him."

"We must go at once and warn him, tell him how to find them."

"Yes. That is, warn him, certainly. I don't know how to find them."

Ariel gazed at her.

"They don't trust me anymore. I tried to tell them that their plan was foolish, and that all they would accomplish was their own destruction." Her expression grew bleak. "They said they were already destroyed."

"We must go and find Alan at once."

Flora nodded. "Will . . . will you have to tell Lord Robert?" she asked. She flushed with embarrassment, either at the thought or the request, Ariel couldn't tell.

"I don't see why," she answered.

"I . . . should hate for him to think me a fool."

Even in her haste, Ariel had to suppress a smile at the idea. "I'm sure he never would," she said.

"No?" Flora looked hopeful and doubtful at the same time. Ariel merely nodded and turned toward the door.

Lord Robert rose at once. "What?" he said.

"We have to find Alan," Ariel told him.

"Why?" Lord Robert looked from her to Flora and back again.

Flora made a distressed sound, then seemed to gather resolution. "I have information vital to Lord Alan's task," she replied. "I must go and tell him. It is my duty."

"What sort of . . . ?"

She gave him a stern look, looking remarkably like Aunt Agatha, Ariel thought. "My duty," she said again.

Robert frowned. "Have you been filling her head with melodramas?" he asked Ariel. "This has the sound of one."

"Do you doubt my judgment?" snapped Flora. "I do not say a thing is important if it is not."

This silenced him. He frowned, started to speak, then changed his mind. "Let's go."

They moved together to the door. The corridor outside was empty, but the atmosphere of Carlton House had become distinctly unnerving, Ariel thought. There was a sense that traps lurked everywhere. Exchanging glances with the others, she saw that they felt it, too.

Side by side, they started down the hall, moving as silently as they could. At the first turn, they stopped and peered carefully around the corner. This passage, also, was just as usual, except for the fact that there was no one in it. "Where is everyone?" whispered Flora Jennings.

Somewhere nearby, a clock chimed, and Lord Robert jumped.

"This is silly," said Ariel, abandoning her furtive pose and striding along the carpet. "We will go back to the front door and ask . . ."

She turned another corner, and the world abruptly went black.

She had the worst headache of her life, Ariel thought. It pounded in her temples and behind her eyes and most particularly in a spot right above her left ear. She tried to raise a hand to the pain, and found she couldn't. She couldn't see, either, she realized. She was in a place without light, lying on some hard surface. She tried to move and discovered she was most efficiently bound; all she could manage was a wriggle, which only intensified the pounding in her head.

She groaned, and took in the fact that her mouth was free. "Hello?" she ventured. Her voice sounded curiously flat and muted. "Help!" she tried, louder.

There was no response.

Straining, she listened to the silence. Where was Flora? Where was Robert? "Help!" she cried again.

Again, nothing.

Despite the agony in her skull, she pushed with all her strength against her bonds. When they didn't yield she attempted to roll over, and found that she was imprisoned in a small space, perhaps a closet or storeroom, hardly bigger than a coffin.

Hastily she suppressed the comparison. What had happened? she wondered. They had been walking down the corridor, and . . . That was all she could remember. Flora's young friends must have attacked them, she decided, and put them out of the way so that they could carry out their plans. Someone would find her, eventually.

There was a soft scrabbling sound, and then utter silence again. Where was she? Ariel wondered a bit frantically. The cellars? Unbidden came images of rats and beetles. She struggled against her bonds again, but they were tight. She was alone, in the dark, apparently far from anyone who might hear her cries and come to the rescue. She had to get free! But though she squirmed and strained and twisted in the narrow space, Ariel made no progress whatsoever against the ropes.

"It would be far wiser, sir, to cancel this card party," Alan was saying to the prince regent. "We cannot guarantee that your guests—"

"A man has to have a little amusement," whined the monarch.

"Of course," answered Alan, controlling his temper with great difficulty. "If you would only go down to Brighton for a—"

"At this season? The place'll be empty as a tomb. Shocking unfashionable. What would people think?"

"If you prefer to put yourself at risk . . ."

"I can't understand Bess," complained the prince for the thousandth time. "Why would she do this to me?"

Alan had given up correcting his assumption that the dead woman was responsible for the invasion of Carlton House. All he cared about was getting rid of the invaders and taking his life back. His life, and his wife, he thought savagely, memories of the night with Ariel vivid in his mind. At such moments, he came perilously close to throttling the ruler of his country.

"Did they get that '96 claret?" asked the unwitting object of his wrath.

"I don't know, Your Majesty," said Alan stiffly. "You will have to ask the butler."

"Eh? Oh, right." The prince rubbed his hands together. "I'll do that. And you'll see that we have no unfortunate odors or visitations tonight. Just a few friends in for cards. A man must have a little amusement," he repeated plaintively as he waddled out.

Alan found he was grinding his teeth and stopped. How was he to guarantee a lack of visitations when this new "haunting" seemed to be managed by spirits indeed, he thought. Wires materialized across staircases; noxious smells wafted from corners; bloodcurdling shrieks plagued the night. The culprits were in the house, he had concluded. No one except trusted servants was getting in or out; he was sure of that. Yet they had searched the place from top to bottom and found nothing conclusive. They had exposed every hiding place the actors had used without result. It was frustrating, maddening.

At least Ariel was safely away from this now. She had sworn she wouldn't set foot in the place, and he could think of her sitting calmly in her own front parlor, out of danger, perhaps sewing. Alan grinned at his own imaginings. More likely she was pacing the floor and cursing. But she was safe. As always, when he thought of her, his pulse accelerated. It was damnable that he should spend the first days of his marriage trapped with Prinny in

Carlton House, but when he had mentioned this fact to the prince, the only response was, "Married? My dear boy, how could you make such a disastrous mistake? Marriage is pure hell."

The prince's might be, Alan thought grimly. But if he ever got the chance . . .

"My lord?"

He turned to find one of the guards under his unwanted command. "Just wanted to let you know," the man added. "It's probably nothing, but we seem to have a footman missing."

"Missing?"

"They're still looking. And he could have taken to his heels."

Several servants had simply fled in the last few days, unnerved by the barrage of malicious pranks. "Let me know," he said curtly.

The man nodded and went out. After a moment, Alan followed to check on his other arrangements.

The prince's cronies began arriving at seven. Watching them assemble in the room that had been set up for their card party—with enough bottles to stock a pub—Alan thought that if you removed the trappings surrounding these aging men, they would resemble nothing so much as the drunkards one saw lying in the gutters. The prince did have friends who were intelligent and more moderate in their habits, he acknowledged to himself—his own father insisted that the monarch was a fascinating conversationalist when he wished to be—but those friends were not here tonight. These were the gamesters, the libertines, and worse, who gave the prince's subjects such a distaste for him at times. And listening to the joke one of them was telling, Alan could only share that sentiment. His longing to return to his own life swept over him so strongly that he had to clench his fists.

The guests gradually settled in their chairs, and the cards were dealt. Servants were kept busy refilling glasses and fetching various small articles that were called for. The air grew smoky and close. Alan was fighting an uncomfortable combination of mind-numbing boredom and wild impatience when one of his men beckoned urgently from the far doorway. Instantly alert, he made his way around the perimeter of the room, praying for action and for a chance to end this cursed vigil once and for all.

In the next room he found several of his men standing in a loose circle around his brother Robert, who looked as if he had been crawling through a coal bin. This extreme departure from Robert's customary dapperness left him speechless for a moment.

"They've got Flora and Ariel," Robert said, moving toward him with a slight stagger. "We have to find them."

Alan felt apprehension shudder through him in a breath, as if a giant hand had grasped his heart and squeezed. "Who has her? Where?" he demanded.

"These villains. Here in Carlton House." He stumbled again. "The devil! They tied my legs so tight I can scarcely feel my feet."

Alan looked sharply at one of his men.

"We were patrolling the house," he reported, "and we heard noises from below. We found him in the coal cellar, trussed up like a Christmas goose."

Robert glared at him, and then seemed to notice the state of his clothes for the first time. He groaned aloud.

"No one else?" asked Alan.

The man shook his head. "A few footprints in the coal dust—smeared."

Alan turned back to his brother, who was holding his head as if it ached. "What the devil are you playing at?"

"Flora said we had to come," he answered. "Practically the crack of dawn . . ."

"To Carlton House?" Alan's voice was grim.

"To find Ariel. And then they said she was here. Told her we should wait till she returned, but Flora was . . ." He made a gesture. "Not like herself at all."

All of Alan's muscles had tightened. "Why?"

"I don't know!" protested Robert. "They wouldn't tell me, damn them."

Making a heroic effort, Alan managed to refrain from trying to shake sense into his brother. Pulling him to a chair, he sat down opposite and put his elbows on his knees to lean close. "Tell me exactly what happened," he ordered.

"Flora was dead set on visiting Ariel," he replied.

Alan nearly told him that he didn't care a whit about Flora, or what she wanted, but he held his tongue. All of his faculties were occupied in controlling the unfamiliar roil of emotion inside him. What if something had happened to Ariel? a frantic voice kept demanding. He wanted to race to her rescue, to annihilate her enemies, to howl like an animal.

"They had their heads together for half an hour or so," added his brother. "And then they said they had to find you. Matter of great urgency and all that, but they wouldn't say what," he complained.

Alan heard an odd sort of sound issue from his own throat.

"If you think I could have kept them from it, you're dead wrong," responded his brother.

"And so," prompted Alan, ignoring this.

"The footman didn't want to let us in," said Robert a bit disjointedly.

Alan looked up. "The missing footman?" he asked one of the men.

"Most likely, my lord."

"And you still haven't found him?"

The other shook his head.

Alan knew that he couldn't sit still much longer. "What then?" he asked Robert.

"We went looking for you, and when I came around a corner something hit me, and I woke up on a pile of coal." He flexed his legs and seemed to find them restored. "They must have served Flora and Ariel the same trick. We must find them."

Alan was already standing. "Get the men together," he told one of them.

"Even the ones who are . . . ?"

"All of them." Let the prince go hang, thought Alan.

The man left to do his bidding. Robert walked back and forth across the room, testing his balance. Alan beckoned to one of the other guards. "We have to comb every inch—" he was saying when there was a shout from the room behind him and the sound of breaking glass.

Cursing, Alan ran back to the prince's gathering. A chair had been overturned, and two of the players were standing. All of them were staring toward the far corner of the room, where a slender young man stood holding a pistol.

There was no way he could have gotten in, Alan thought. Yet there he was—a handsome lad of about sixteen in drab clothes, with eyes that burned like hot coals.

He moved slightly left, sighting the pistol as if he had found his target. Alan had a moment's fear that he was going to shoot the prince. And then he fired and put a bullet, and then another, into Lord Royalton's chest.

There was a frozen moment when blood spurted, men gasped or whimpered, and then everyone moved at once.

All of the card players except the regent fell to the floor. The guards came pouring through the rear doorway. Surprising Alan, the prince knelt next to Royalton and sought to assist him. Alan himself dived for the intruder. But the youth had already cast the pistol aside and lunged through the doorway at his back—where there ought to be a guard, Alan thought as he raced after him. No doubt he was sharing quarters with the lost footman. But he didn't care greatly about either of them. The only thing that mattered was catching this intruder who was his best hope of finding Ariel.

At last he could move, do something. Fear and fury pounded in him in equal parts as he ran. What if they had hurt her? kept beating in his brain as he went. These were murderers. What if she was . . . ? But he couldn't tolerate that thought. It made him want to rip the world apart and throw the fragments to the winds. He couldn't face life without her. The idea was irrational, insane, but he had never uncovered a fact more true.

The boy ran like a frightened deer. When a pair of servants appeared ahead of him, he ducked and wove from their reaching arms, startling them at the last moment with a shriek like a steam whistle. The prince's servants were jumpy at best, Alan thought, as the two hesitated and lost their chance to capture him. He pounded on, aware of steps behind him now but caring only for his quarry.

The boy knew the house intimately. He was taking a route that avoided the more populated areas and any dead ends. But he couldn't hope to escape, Alan thought. He must have known that wasn't possible when he took up the pistol.

He was gaining on him. Triumphant, Alan pushed harder. He told himself that he was running toward Ariel, and away from all that had bedeviled him at Carlton House for the past weeks. The need for her beat in him like a score of hammers. He would find her; she would be all right. And by God, he would never let her out of his sight again.

The boy came up to the turn of a corridor and skidded around it. But that slight slowing was enough for Alan, who lunged and caught hold of his arm, bringing him down with a crash and falling half on top of him.

Alan sat up at once, and was surrounded by a group of

his men, as well as Robert, he saw with some surprise. They all looked to the captive, who still lay on the floor struggling for breath. He had knocked the wind out of him, Alan saw, resisting the impulse to lift him bodily and try to throttle information out of him.

At last the youngster drew a shuddering breath. He jerked his arm, but did not get free.

"Where are the women you imprisoned?" demanded Alan.

"Go to hell," muttered the boy.

Alan grasped his other arm and jerked him up so that they faced each other. "Tell me, or I'll . . ." But the gaze he met was so blank, so filled with the expectation of pain and loss, that he couldn't finish the threat. "One of them is my wife," he said instead. "I am extremely . . . worried about her." As the boy's eyes showed a flicker, Alan marveled at the inadequacy of words. Of course he had been worried before in his life—"worried" was a good description of the moderate anxiety he had felt on occasion. It was ludicrous when applied to the emotion that pervaded his body and soul now.

"What have you done to Flora Jennings?" asked Robert, pushing forward. "If you have hurt her . . ."

"We wouldn't do nothing to her," the youngster mumbled. "If she hadn't come to blow the gaff on us, we wouldn't've had to tie her." He raised his head suddenly and sat straighter. "But I don't care about nothing now. You can do what you like to me. I killed him." He heaved a sigh, then as suddenly looked anxious. "I did kill him, din't I?"

Alan nodded.

"Huh." He looked satisfied and, oddly, vindicated.

"Show us where the women are," commanded Alan.

"Will you let me go if I do?" was the cunning reply.

"No."

The youngster glanced at Alan, then shrugged. "We

never meant nothing to happen to them," he repeated, and started to struggle to his feet.

He led them back toward the servants' wing, and then down into the basements. They passed well-stocked storerooms and a magnificent wine cellar and finally came up to a blank brick wall. "If you are playing some trick . . ." began Alan.

For the first time, the boy grinned. Stepping forward in the dim light of the lanterns they had been forced to light, he took hold of what appeared to be a piece of wall and opened it like a door. "It's fake, see?"

One of the men held up his lantern, illuminating a continuation of the cellars behind this panel.

"This is where you have been hiding, you and your friends?" said Alan.

He grinned again. "They're long gone. You'll never find them. We drew lots, and I won."

Or lost, thought Alan, for the boy would surely hang for Royalton's murder. "Show us," he said gruffly.

There were rats, Ariel thought nervously. She was sure she had felt one against her ankle, and though the sensation had stopped as soon as she wriggled, the idea filled her with revulsion. Her arms ached, too, nearly as fiercely as her head. She had steadfastly refused to give way to fear, but it was getting more and more difficult. What was happening upstairs? she wondered. Had the plot to kill Royalton succeeded? And far more important, had Alan gotten in the way? The possibility made her whole body shudder with fear and the need to do something to help.

She heard voices. A sliver of light showed, revealing the position of a narrow door to her prison. She debated whether to call out. Was this rescue, or merely her captors returned? And then the door creaked open and her eyes were dazzled by lantern light.

"Ariel!" exclaimed a hoarse voice.

"Alan," she cried. "Thank God you're all right."

"I?"

Her eyes adjusting, Ariel saw her husband gazing down at her. But it was not exactly her husband. The calm, rational man she knew so well was not there. Alan's teeth were bared; his blue eyes blazed. His coat was torn, and his hair disheveled. He looked like a completely different person.

A young man next to him suddenly jerked and pulled away. Alan reacted with lightning swiftness, catching his wrist.

Then Ariel heard Lord Robert's voice. "We ain't through with you yet. There's still Miss Jennings to be found."

A clatter of footsteps followed, and she was alone with Alan.

For a moment he stood like the personification of vengeful justice. Duty was making its undeniable demands on him, Ariel thought, recognizing the expression and the stance. His fists clenched at his sides, he looked wild and dangerous, driven and inexorable. Duty would draw him away from her again, Ariel thought.

Then he said, "Devil take it," and made a gesture as if throwing something away. He knelt on the stone floor, reaching for her bonds. His breath rasped as if he had run a long way. It was loud in the small space. "Are you all right?" he asked.

"Yes," she whispered.

"When I heard they had attacked you, I wanted to kill with my bare hands," he said.

Even his voice sounded different, Ariel thought. It vibrated with emotion.

"I was ready to tear the place apart bit by bit to find you," he said.

His knuckles were white, she noticed. The muscles in his neck were rigid.

"I would have done anything—anything."

He gazed at her. His eyes still burned, Ariel saw, but with something other than rage. He finished untying the ropes that bound her. They fell from her arms. "They didn't hurt you?" he asked again, touching her wrists and shoulders as if afraid.

She stretched her aching muscles. "Not really."

"Damn them to hell," he said.

She gazed at him. Alan's eyes were full of tears. She couldn't quite believe it, but then one spilled over and fell onto the lapel of his coat. She was afraid to speak.

He bent to tear the ropes from her ankles, throwing them aside so hard that they thumped against the wall in the corner.

Sitting up stiffly, Ariel put her hands on his broad shoulders.

Alan pulled her close, lifting her from the floor and then rising with her in his arms, carrying her out of the tiny chamber where she had been imprisoned and into the cellars. He was silent as he walked across the stone floor. There were sounds in the house about them, as if it were being cleared. Ariel heard a thump and a distant flurry of voices.

She stole another glance at Alan's face. It was hard and impassive as stone. But that one tear had been followed by another. They made two astonishing trails over his cheekbones and into the hollows under them.

Upstairs, they passed a few people in the corridors, but Alan paid no attention to any of them. He carried her to the bedchamber where they had spent the previous night—so long ago it seemed now, Ariel thought—and placed her on the small sofa in the corner, falling to his knees beside her. "Are you sure you're all right?" he said then.

She nodded.

He gazed at her, his burning blue eyes seeming to devour her face. "Is this love?" he said in a choked voice. 'This chaos, this terror?"

Ariel blinked.

"This is what they meant?" he went on. "All those friends I thought were idiots. This . . . dependence? When I thought I might have lost you, I didn't see how I could . . ."

Ariel saw his muscles tighten to an almost unbearable pitch. Then he bent and put his head in her lap.

She stroked his russet hair. "Love?" she whispered, hardly daring to believe he had used the word.

After another moment, he straightened and looked at her again. His handsome face was taut and strained. "Poets are fools," he said gratingly. "Flowers, vows— none of them write of feeling as if your heart were being torn out of you."

Ariel was not going to argue with him about literature.

"You said you loved me," he added. It was almost an accusation. "This is what you feel?"

She swallowed, remembering certain moments when she thought her heart was breaking. "I've felt it," she acknowledged.

He looked wild.

"But that's not all of it. Not even the main part."

"What is the main part?" he demanded.

Ariel let out her breath. He was asking the impossible. How could he expect her to define love? Did he think she could list its properties, categorize and analyze, and then understand? "The . . . the joys of being together," she tried. "The knowledge that someone cares for you."

His gaze was steady. He looked far from satisfied.

Ariel grimaced. "Love is wild and safe and frightening and comforting and . . . rapturous."

She glanced toward the bed opposite them, and he followed her gaze. When he looked back at her, there was a bit less confusion in his expression. "It seems very disorganized," he complained.

"Yes. Irrational, too," she couldn't resist adding.

He gave her a look. "I'm not used to this kind of"—he made a gesture—"turmoil."

He really meant it, Ariel saw. As she had hoped, and dreamed, she had broken through to the passionate, unfettered man at the core of this man of science. "I know," she replied. She felt a tremulous smile spreading over her face.

"Do you get used to it?"

"Not exactly."

He gave her a pained look.

"If you got used to it, it would be . . . habit, routine—even boring. That is one of the best things about love; it makes life thrilling."

"Thrilling," he repeated, as if he had an idea of what she meant, but wasn't sure he approved of it. "You have never bored me," he allowed.

A tremor went through Ariel. Partly, she wanted to laugh; partly, she was touched by the admission, an immense compliment, from him.

"This is all very . . . unsettling." His breathing had returned to normal, but his expression hadn't. "It ought to be studied, systematized. There ought to be some warning."

"That would be like trying to put light in a box to dissect it," Ariel responded.

He stared.

"Love is not an exact science," she said, slipping her arms around his neck.

"Obviously!"

"It is always surprising."

"I have never cared particularly for surprises," he protested, but his arms had encircled her waist.

"Perhaps you could learn," Ariel murmured, and kissed him softly.

His arms closed hard and demanding around her. "I have always had a passion for learning," he acknowledged, and took her lips for his own.

Epilogue

❖

"Y ou did not *rescue* me," said Flora Jennings in a tone that suggested she was repeating herself.

"I deuced well did," responded Lord Robert's equally determined voice. "Why you cannot simply admit that—"

"I had nearly gotten free of the ropes," she interrupted.

"Nearly? Only if you were counting on having a month or so to work on them."

"They were distinctly looser."

"You could scarcely wiggle a finger," Robert uncharitably pointed out. "What is the matter with you?"

There was a brief silence.

"Is it so intolerable to think that I might have done you a service?" he added in quite a different tone.

The silence was longer this time, and Flora's reply did not carry through the tall boxwood hedge that concealed Ariel from her houseguests.

That was just as well, Ariel thought as she moved away along the garden path. She hadn't meant to eavesdrop. She hadn't even known that Robert and Flora had come outdoors until she stopped to look at a rosebush and their conversation had come floating over the hedge.

What would become of that unconventional couple? she wondered. Were they even a couple at all? It hardly seemed so. And yet when she had asked Flora to come and stay in Oxford for a few days, Robert had immediately invited himself along. Perhaps he had no one to quarrel with in London, she thought with a smile. He seemed to have developed quite a taste for it.

Ariel stopped before a bed of tulips and daffodils, blossomless now in late summer and looking rather bedraggled. She wondered whether to have them cut down. The old gardener who had more or less come with their house here in Oxford would tell her. Indeed, he would be delighted to tell her; he had made it his special task to educate her about all things horticultural.

Ariel took a deep breath and let her eyes wander from the flowerbed to the high red brick garden wall to the mellow Georgian facade of the house that was now hers. Really hers. It had been quite empty when they took possession, and she had been slowly making it her own, room by room. It was such a pleasure. She had never had a place that was completely her own. Just as she had never had any family but her mother, and now she had a father and a whole network of kin by marriage.

"Ariel?" called a deep voice from the small terrace that lay between the house and the garden.

And a husband, Ariel added to her list. Most important of all, a husband. "Yes?" she answered, moving along the gravel path toward him.

"Ah. There you are."

Alan stood on the flagstones, his auburn hair gleaming in the morning sun, his tall figure very handsome in a blue coat and riding breeches. He held out a hand and Ariel took it, feeling a familiar tremor of love and amazement.

"I am going to the laboratory," he said. "But I'll be back early."

She nodded. "Nathaniel is bringing Violet to dinner," she reminded him, just in case he had forgotten.

"Dinner? All the way from London?"

"They're going to stay the night." Ariel refrained from adding that she had told him this twice already. There were certain things that men simply could not keep in their brains, she had found. They might be awesomely intelligent and conduct brilliant experiments on the nature of light, but they were utterly incapable of remembering where they had put their keys or the name of the new housemaid. It was rather endearing.

"Are they?" Alan's smile was slightly rueful. "I wonder what's come over Sebastian, then? I'm surprised he's missing such an occasion."

"He's on duty tonight," answered Ariel absently. Was that shouting from the back of the garden? she wondered. Lately, Robert and Flora had begun to rouse each other to shouting.

"Ah. And I suppose my mother has some social engagement that prevents her from attending."

"She's coming in October with Lord Randolph."

"Of course. Another brother."

"I'm looking forward to meeting him," she said. Flora and Robert *were* shouting, she decided. They would have to settle it between them, whatever it was.

"Perhaps I'd better write a letter of warning," replied Alan dryly.

Ariel looked up at him, her guests forgotten. "What?"

"Let him know what he's in for. Do you have someone in mind?"

"Someone?"

"For Randolph. There's our neighbor across the way, though she's a bit mature."

"Sixty at least," acknowledged Ariel.

"True. What about Wrenshaw's daughter? She seems a nice enough chit."

"And barely fifteen," answered Ariel, letting him enjoy his teasing.

"Really? That's rather young."

"Isn't it?" She smiled at him. "I have no intention of looking for a wife for Lord Randolph."

"No? I understand he wants one. Very isolated, that parish of his up north. What he needs is the daughter of a bishop or some such thing, to help him rise in the church."

"I'm sure he will find a proper—"

"Ah, but will he know what's proper?" Alan shook his head, his blue eyes twinkling. "No, I'm sure you'll be able to set him right, just as you have the rest of us."

"All I did was—"

"All you did was create a revolution. The Greshams will never be the same."

"Nathaniel and Sebastian chose their own wives," she protested. "And Robert . . ."

Alan raised one auburn brow.

Ariel spread her hands in helpless incomprehension.

"Robert, who never spent a single night in Oxford before you came. Sebastian, whose visits were even rarer. Nathaniel, who was always too busy to bother. Even my mother, who might have summoned me to London if Randolph was in town, but never would have brought him here. I haven't seen so much of my family since I was in short coats."

Suddenly anxious, Ariel examined his face for clues to what he really felt. "Have I invited them too often? It is just that I never had any family, and it is so pleasant to be able to . . ."

Alan took a step forward and put his hands on her shoulders. "I'm not sure I ever had a family either," he said, no longer teasing. "You showed me that."

Ariel wasn't entirely convinced. "You know you have only to say if you don't want them to come."

"Really?" His eyes glinted again. "You don't think Sebastian would ride up on his charger and storm the doors?"

"I mean it."

"And Nathaniel would come the older brother and send me a stiff note," he added as if the picture amused him. "Robert would—" He stopped suddenly, and his eyes lit with a positively unholy glee.

"What?" said Ariel.

"James," he replied.

"James?"

"The last of my brothers. He commands a navy ship in the South Seas."

"I remember who he is," she answered. "But what has he to do with . . . ?"

"We must get him home," said Alan, his expression still full of mischief. "He would offer you a real challenge." He grinned. "A wife for James—now there is a concept."

"I really have no intention—"

"Did my mother tell you about the gift he sent her from the islands?"

Ariel shook her head.

"Ah." He laughed. "You would have to see that first."

"Alan!" She raised her hands to his chest as he looked down at her. "Be serious."

One corner of his mouth curved upward. "I have spent most of my life being serious. I believe I'll give it up."

"But your family . . ."

His arms slid down to encircle her waist, and the merriment faded from his eyes. "You've given me the gift of my family, and for that, as for so many other things, I am deeply grateful."

Ariel held his gaze. She found she was holding her breath as well.

"A man never made a better bargain," he added, pulling her closer.

Ariel relaxed in his embrace. "I got the best of it," she replied.

"Do you think so?"

She nodded.

His smile broadened. "I intend to make sure you never change your mind about that," he said, and bent to kiss her.

Jane Ashford grew up in a small town in southwestern Ohio, where she discovered the romance of history at an early age in the public library. After extensive travel in Europe, she settled in Cambridge, Massachusetts. She has written novels of romantic suspense as well as numerous Regency romances. She has also taught literature and writing, and written speeches, book reviews, and newsletters.

For current information on Bantam's
women's fiction, visit our Web site
Isn't It Romantic
at the following address:

http://www.bdd.com/romance